SIX IDIOTS WITNESS A MURDER

Rob Hickman

Disclaimer

This is a work of fiction. Whilst all of the locations are real, all names, characters and incidents are fictional and any resemblance to actual persons, living or dead is purely coincidental. Although the part about the car purchase is based on a real event.

Dedications

For Erica Louise

Table of Contents

PART ONE

Chapter 1

Oh crap. Morning already.

Tom jolted up in bed at the sound of the alarm on his phone and rubbed his eyes. What time was it? More to the point, what day was it? Last night had been a late one where the beer had been flowing more freely than it should. Although it probably didn't matter too much because it was Sunday morning. Wasn't it?

Tom was about to turn back over in bed but suddenly realised last night was Sunday which meant today was more than likely to be Monday. He looked at his phone and saw that it was just before 8am - the time he would normally be getting into his car and beginning his regular 30-minute commute to work   Or the Dungeon of Despair as he and most of the other employees called it.

Suddenly Tom was in a panic and shot out of bed to begin his morning routine. Luckily, he had an en-suite bathroom and was able to stumble the eight steps from his bed to the shower in a few seconds. It seemed like it should be Sunday. Why wasn't it Sunday? After being on annual leave for ten days that included the Easter bank holidays at the beginning, Tom had got his days mixed up and was in a mild and slightly hungover panic as he stumbled into the bathroom. He showered, shaved and got dressed before grabbing his phone, running downstairs, picking up his laptop, wallet and keys from the table by the front door and heading out to his car.

The drive into Brighton took about 20 minutes and then he had a ten-minute walk from the parking space in the city centre that he rented from a rich person with a big driveway and no car of their own. It was a sensible and cost-effective arrangement and meant he didn't have to use public transport. Tom liked people - but not first thing in the morning before he'd had coffee.

It was 9:13am when he arrived at work and tried to sit at his desk without too many people noticing. As with most things Tom tried, it didn't go as well as he'd hoped and his manager was waiting for him.

"Good morning," said Katrina.

"Morning boss," replied Tom with as much nonchalance as he could muster (which was not very much). "How's everything going?"

"We've had a good morning so far. Which you might have been able to participate in had you been here on time."

"Yeah, sorry about that, Katrina," said Tom.

"Don't worry - but make the time up, okay?" said Katrina.

"I will," Tom promised, settling into his seat. He always did.

His immediate focus was on remembering his password, logging on the main system and reading the 287 emails that had no doubt arrived during his time off - most of which he'd assume were about things that had subsequently been resolved so he could delete. At some point one of these deleted emails was bound to come back and bite him but he could always ask the sender to resend it. That's what everyone else did.

As the Project Manager on the company's largest current IT project, Tom seemed to receive certain privileges that the other more lowly (in his opinion) employees did not enjoy. Either that or his line manager found him incredibly attractive and totally awesome in every way. That was probably more likely he thought as his screen flickered to life.

"How was your week off?" asked Sue, one of his colleagues who sat directly opposite him.

"Not bad, thanks. A few too many late nights though." Tom replied, noticing that Sue's halitosis still hadn't cleared up. He'd noticed it on the day he joined the company just over four years ago and, if anything, it had got worse over that time. Either that or someone had gradually moved their desks closer together so he could smell her breath more easily.

Tom went to make a coffee - the first of many if every other day was an indicator. Like so many people in offices around the world, Tom relied on coffee to help him get through the day. Coffee disagreed with his digestive system but he still needed at least eight cups to retain his focus while sitting at a desk. Sometimes he'd be offered an extra cup by HR if they called him up to respond to an accusation of inappropriate behaviour in the workplace. This happened quite often and as he went back to his desk and looked at his online calendar he saw an invite from HR for this morning. That's good, he thought. The coffee was so much better in HR than it was in the IT department.

Most of his colleagues would be mortified to be summoned to HR more than once or twice in their entire career but Tom saw it differently. Not only did he have his own seat in the HR waiting area (other employees would vacate the chair by the plant when they saw him arrive) but he liked the women in the HR department. Well, not so much liked them...he found most of them physically attractive and was sure the only reason they called him in as often as they did was because they thought the same way about him. They didn't, of course, but he didn't know that and just assumed they were being coy and mysterious.

"Hey mate! How are things?" Martin appeared in the kitchen area with an unfeasibly broad smile. Martin and Tom were childhood friends as well as work colleagues and Tom knew Martin well enough by now to realise he had some ridiculously trivial triumph from the weekend to gloat about. Martin and his wife Irma had so far produced two children - both boys - and Martin was forever sharing random and completely pointless things that one of these two nightmares had done.

"Hi Martin," said Tom with more enthusiasm than he thought he would be able to generate given his hangover and the fact that he didn't really care. "How are Irma and the boys?"

"Well mate, it's funny you should ask. Since Max turned three, he's become a lot boisterous and on Saturday he tried to set Ben on fire!"

"Wow!" said Tom with genuine enthusiasm for once. Finally, something truly interesting was happening rather than something that only Martin and Irma found interesting.

In a bid to retain his sanity and avoid the never-ending stream of pictures of the boys eating, running around and shitting (often at the same time) Tom had turned down repeated friend requests on Facebook from Martin and Irma. When Ben had been born just over a year ago, they'd even set up a 'cute' joint account called "BenMax" to showcase the more mundane aspects of the boys' lives. Although 'cute' wasn't the word Tom thought of when Martin told him about it for the first time - 'nauseating' was his choice, but Martin was unmoved and still thought it was cute.

"How did he set him on fire?" Tom asked.

"Well, we had the family round for Irma's birthday. Her sister left a lighter on the table and Max just picked it up and started playing with it next to Ben. The next thing we knew, Ben's trousers were smoking," replied Martin.

"Shit!" said Tom.

"Exactly. We stopped it before it did any lasting damage but that pair of trousers is ruined so now we have to throw them out. Although we obviously have to throw out Max's trousers too," said Martin.

"Why?"

"Well, Irma likes to dress the boys in the same clothes every day so we can spot them both when we're out. Unfortunately, if one of them ruins a t-shirt or some trousers we have to get rid of the other boy's t-shirt or trousers as well. Ben's blue trousers were ruined so Irma threw out Max's blue trousers too," explained Martin. "I just wish my kids would stop setting each other on fire. It's costing us a fortune in new clothes."

"That's a bit odd. So...if one of them broke a leg - just as an example - would you have to somehow injure the other one's leg so they both had matching plaster casts?" asked Tom, quite reasonably he thought.

"Of course not! We're not monsters for fuck's sake," said Martin and walked off.

"At least you'd be able to spot them when you were out," Tom called after him. Although it wasn't like they'd be running away if they had matching broken legs.

***

After pouring his coffee, Tom went back to his desk and decided to keep quiet for a while until Martin had calmed down. They had been best friends for many years since Tom's parents had moved into the street where Martin already lived. Tom had been 8 and Martin 6 when they first met and grew up together as part of a larger group of children of different ages.

The street where they had lived was a cul-de-sac and had a large green space in the middle, with houses placed around the side. Tom had once gone up in a light aircraft and flown over their houses and from the sky he could see the road surface looked like a question mark. The shape of the development as a whole (including the green space and the houses round the edge) looked like a mushroom. Or the head of a penis. Which may explain why Martin thought Tom was a dick.

After going their separate ways career-wise, the two had started working together in the IT department of a large British retailer almost a year ago when Martin joined and were gradually coming to terms with this new dynamic to their relationship. This was especially worrying for Martin as he had an unfortunate nickname growing up that he didn't want anyone at his new job to know about. Tom knew about it - mainly because he'd given it to him when they were teenagers - and it had sort of stuck. Even Martin's parents sometimes used it and Martin was dreading the day that it finally came out - which it surely would.

Martin had recently had his 30th birthday but still couldn't shake his nickname and, while he appreciated this new job that Tom had helped put a good word in for him to get, he still felt a sense of anxiety every time the office conversation turned towards certain subjects.

"You're clearly happy to be back at work after a week off," said Martin sarcastically.

"Not really," replied Tom. "To be honest, I'm not really feeling it today after a few late nights."

"You'll be fine once you've had a few more coffees," said Martin, turning back to his screen and getting his headphones out of his incredibly messy desk drawer.

Tom watched him put his headphones in to drown out the background office noise and thought about tidying up Martin's drawer just to mess with his system of organised chaos. It was taking Martin a long time to put his headphones in and select a playlist...surely he must be done by now.

"Dopey bastard," Tom whispered to himself.

"Hey! I haven't selected my playlist yet. At least wait until the sweet, melodious sounds of Taylor Swift are filling my ears before you insult me."

Tom apologised and Martin gave him a cheesy thumbs up signal that belonged back in the 80's before selecting what he proudly called his "Sexy Women of Country" playlist. Given that some of these 'sexy women' were long dead and most of the others were over 70, everyone on the team was worried about Martin's taste in women - especially those who'd met his wife Irma.

"What a dick," said Tom.

"I can still hear you," complained Martin with a pained expression that also contained a hint of a smile.

Tom turned back to his laptop wondering how long it took for somebody to select a playlist. It seemed to take Martin forever; sorting and shuffling his songs into the perfect order for the day ahead only to be called away for a meeting two minutes after he'd 'locked those babies in' as he was fond of saying. All it needed was another creepy thumbs up gesture and Tom would have strangled him right there and then with his headphone wire.

Also, who still uses wires? Weren't those wireless earbuds that looked suspiciously like miniature tampons the way forward? Tom suspected Martin still had a VCR at home while everyone else had moved over to video streaming services. Maybe he would send him a fax later and ask him.

Luckily for Martin, he turned back to his computer and got on with whatever it was he was paid a lot of money to do (and not very well, in Tom's opinion) and therefore avoided a Monday morning strangling. Which was a shame for everyone else because it would have brought some excitement to their day. Tom was never happy to be back at work after a week off so the team tried to keep out of his way for the first couple of hours.

As Tom grumbled his way through the start of his day, he started to think that mornings were stupid. Also, nobody liked Mondays - apart from old people - but even some of them never seemed to know what day it was judging by the number of pensioners in the supermarkets every Saturday and Sunday. He'd never understood why the people who'd had all week to themselves with very little to do other than drink tea, talk about the war and forget the names of their grandchildren waited until the weekend to do their food shopping. That was the only time that people who worked all week could go.

Tom decided that one day he'd take a Monday off work and go and stand in front of them at the post office - old people love the post office he reasoned, so that would be a great place to get back at them for clogging the shops up on the only days when he and his friends were able to stock up on avocado toast, falafel wraps and quinoa.

Chapter 2

The HR department was the heart of the company where Tom and Martin worked and was the only department that spanned both the UK operation in Brighton and the fledgling US operation in Atlanta, Georgia. The company sold traditional British clothing to high-end department stores and online - typically the kind of clothing that a country gentleman or lady might wear when enjoying a long weekend away fishing, hiking or whatever other outdoor pursuits interested the type of people who had more money than fashion sense and enjoyed being out in the rain all day.

Most of the clothing options were dark green or khaki and - being a British company that catered primarily for British outdoor pursuits - everything had to be made of waterproof materials. The UK enjoys 156 days of rain each year on average but whether the 38 million tourists that visit also enjoy it is not something that 'Visit Britain' (the snappy and rather dictatorial new name of the British Tourism Authority) seems to monitor or report.

Anybody visiting Britain - or indeed locals holidaying in the country - has to be mindful of the weather at all times of the year and this was something that Classic Country Clothing Ltd. had always been keen to capitalise on. The more rain there was, the more waterproof jackets, hats, gloves and boots they sold. For people who took their dogs out in the rain, they even sold an extensive range of obscenely-priced waterproof dog jackets.

The company had been founded in 1949 and was originally headquartered in a barn in the Sussex Downs, a beautifully scenic part of Southern England. Unfortunately, they had been forced to move to different premises in 1988 after an unfortunate incident with a flock of sheep, an office door that had been left open and a pile of sales orders for the coming season.

Having lost most of the sales orders for 1988, along with Margaret, a timid, softly-spoken sales manager who nobody remembered employing but had been there since day one, the company decided to move to a more urban setting where they were less likely to be bothered by sheep eating their paperwork.

Margaret had not been attacked or bothered by the sheep but did not make the move with the rest of the company due to an aversion to commuting to work. She had always walked to work and didn't see why she should ever have to change and gave this as the reason for her sudden retirement at the age of (what seemed to most people) 104 but was in reality only 63.

The move to new offices Brighton on the Sussex coast, the introduction of primitive computers and a large talent pool of eager employees allowed the company to grow exponentially over the next few years and it now employed more than 200 staff in the UK. It also owned two manufacturing companies in Vietnam where, in a bid to stimulate the local economy, it had offered low-skilled jobs to some of the very youngest members of Vietnamese society. This also helped to keep their costs lower than their more ethically-minded competitors.

As the business expanded, they had set up a Marketing department in 1990 whose first task was to design a new company logo. They had come up with a line art drawing of a hooded outdoor jacket beneath three capital 'C's taken from the company name. Unfortunately, the jacket looked like something a medieval executioner would wear and the arrangement of the three letters made them look like a badly made set of handcuffs designed for people with a particular sexual fetish. And an extra arm.

Just over a year ago, one of the new junior managers in the Marketing department had suggested the business adopt a 'new and hip brand identity' by changing their name to 'Klassic Kountry Klothing', which would both 'disrupt the market' and at the same time be more 'funky and edgy' for today's 'switched on, internet-savvy, cash-rich but time poor consumers.'

Initially this was not well-received by the directors as the company took great pride in being a 'traditional purveyor of clothing for the more discerning high-end customer' but the Marketing department pushed ahead regardless - with commendable enthusiasm but very little support from around the business.

A new logo was designed and subsequently revealed at a board meeting to what the marketing people expected would be a triumphant reception. The department had since re-invented themselves as 'Global Corporate Branding' but were still staffed by four hyperactive university graduates and overseen by two junior managers who looked as if they had to be up early for school tomorrow.

Unfortunately, the response to their creation was far less enthusiastic than the ponytailed hipsters in Global Corporate Branding had hoped for. All but one of the board members present were horrified by what they saw, with only the Global Production & Logistics Director (known to everyone in the company as Racist Roy) expressing any positive views. At this point the Marketing department accepted defeat when it was pointed out to them that a logo of 'KKK' and a hooded coat was less than ideal - especially given the company's plans to establish a new location in Atlanta, the birthplace of the American civil rights movement.

The heavily-pregnant HR Director was the first to express her concern by swooning face down at the table in the Company's boardroom, her head narrowly missing her responsibly-sourced coffee that she carried round in her environmentally-friendly coffee mug.

She had subsequently taken a leave of absence to recover from the trauma and then started her maternity leave without coming back to work. Having successfully negotiated her pregnancy and delivered a healthy baby boy, she had only just returned to work last Tuesday to pick up where she left off and was already regretting it.

Today was only her second week back at work but she had just received an extremely worrying email from the US operation in Atlanta and also, as she scanned her calendar for the day ahead, she noticed a familiar name in her list of appointments. She suddenly felt like she had never been away and called out to her assistant in the open-plan area just outside her office.

"Debbie? Can you come in here please?"

Debbie got up from her desk and walked the short distance into her director's office. "Hi Lisa, is there anything wrong?" she said.

"I'm looking at my list of appointments for today and I see Tom from the IT department is on it again."

"Yes," said Debbie. "You told me before you went off that you wanted any future transgressions of his to be dealt with at director level."

"I know," said Lisa. "Why on earth are we still employing him?"

"Well, he's by far the best Project Manager we've got," replied Debbie.

"Maybe. But before I went off on maternity leave he seemed to spend more time up here than he did in his own department. Are these things still happening?"

"On and off, yes. We still have a few inappropriate comments and he does make some of the staff uncomfortable," Debbie confirmed.

"The female staff have a right to be protected in the workplace," said Lisa. "This is the 21st century, not the dark days of the 1970s."

"Some of his male colleagues find him a bit much too," offered Debbie. "He's just incessantly cheerful and makes a lot of jokes. They don't tend to like that in IT."

"So, what's he done this time?" Lisa asked with a weary sigh.

"He made a few comments on our last charity dress down day just before Easter. We had to wait for him to come back from a week's leave before calling him in."

"Well whatever he said I'm pretty sure it was unacceptable," said Lisa. "I think I'll deal with him once and for all this time."

"Well, before you do that...it may have been partly our fault," said Debbie.

"Our fault? How could it possibly be our fault?!"

"On the Thursday before Easter, just before you returned to work, the 'Rocky Horror Picture Show' was in town at the Theatre Royal. Most of the staff had tickets for the show so we thought it would be an ideal costume theme for charity because they could then go straight from work. It was meant to be easier and more environmentally responsible than everybody leaving early, going home to change and then coming back again," said Debbie.

"The 'Rocky Horror Picture Show'? Is that the one where everyone dresses up in a burlesque style?"

"Yes," said Debbie.

"So...let me get this right," said Lisa. "We actively encouraged our female staff to come to work in basques, corsets and fishnet stockings for charity?"

"Yes," said Debbie, looking down at the floor. The HR department had realised their mistake within a few minutes of the office opening and the first staff arriving so Debbie had half-expected Lisa to also spot the issue when they told her.

"I bet the men had a great time ogling the women in basques and suspenders all day!"

"Yes, they did," admitted Debbie, growing more uncomfortable by the second.

Lisa rolled her eyes and then stared up at the ceiling for several seconds. She could not believe what she was hearing.

"Some of the men were also dressed up," said Debbie, more brightly than she should have and then immediately blushed.

"It just keeps getting better," said Lisa. "So, what is Tom accused of? Actually, don't worry about it, I'm sure we both know that whatever it was he definitely did it."

"Various inappropriate comments mainly," said Debbie.

"Anything else?" asked Lisa.

"Well, he dressed up too and his outfit upset two of the women on his team."

"How?" asked Lisa, dreading the answer.

"They said he looked better in a basque and suspenders than they did."

Lisa looked out of the window and tried to regain her composure. Her long blonde hair was in its customary ponytail and Debbie watched as she played with the hair band that was holding it together. She recognised this is a symptom of stress and had seen it many times before.

"I imagine that the whole day was total chaos then," said Lisa, turning back around and looking even more exasperated.

This was not what she had expected when she returned from maternity leave. Couldn't these people be left for five minutes to run things in her absence? For somebody only five feet tall, Lisa was fierce and didn't take any crap from anybody. She wasn't angry with Debbie, despite it being her who had overseen this travesty of an idea; she was angry with the laid-back attitude of the rest of the directors who only seemed to act on any staffing indiscretions when they threatened the company's existence.

"Well, not the whole day, fortunately. We heard reports that it was causing a few concerns so we sent everyone who had dressed up home at lunchtime to get changed into something more appropriate. Unfortunately, it was the start of the Easter weekend so the roads were busier than normal and none of them made it back into work by the end of the day."

"For fuck's sake! So, we lost most of the company for over half a day because of this??" Lisa was getting more and more agitated.

"Unfortunately, yes. But it gets worse."

"How the fuck could it get any worse?!" shouted Lisa.

"Well," began Debbie. "You know how we normally collect the money at 4pm for the charity?"

"Yes."

"Well, because nobody made it back in time..." Debbie began.

"...nobody was here to pay for the right to dress down so we didn't make any money at all for the charity."

"Yes."

"What a total fucking disaster!"

Lisa was now apoplectic. This was becoming the worst day she'd had at the company since she started ten years ago and it wasn't even 11am yet. At this rate she would be going to the pub at lunchtime and staying there all afternoon. She briefly looked back at her time on maternity leave where she'd spent much of her day sitting at home watching children's TV while covered in baby vomit. That life was becoming more appealing by the second and she thought about jumping on her husband when she got home so she could soon have another few months away from this circus of a company.

Lisa got up from her desk, walked over to the window and banged her fist on the windowsill before staring down at the street three floors below. Debbie could see that she was lost in thought and went to get up and leave but Lisa motioned for her to remain so she sat back down.

Lisa stayed motionless for well over a minute, far away in her thoughts until suddenly snapping back into the room.

"I have an idea that might solve two problems at once," she said. "Let me think about it."

Debbie left Lisa's office and returned to her own desk wondering what this potential miracle cure would be. She and Tom had always got on well because he wasn't like most of the other socially awkward people in the IT department. He was fun and a bit cheeky - although that might be why he was always up in HR explaining his actions while the rest of his department were always down in IT doing what they were paid to do and not causing any problems.

She hoped he wouldn't be fired but knew there was a strong possibility he would be. Whatever happened, he would at least be getting another warning.

Chapter 3

Monday morning at 11am meant that it was time for the weekly Project Team meeting. In the fast-moving world of IT these meetings were known as 'stand-ups' and allowed (or forced) everyone on the team to gather round one of the large screens in the office and take turns to update each other on the status of their work while the rest of the team tried to look interested but instead thought about what they wanted for lunch.

Time was also allowed at the end for a general discussion about the weekend and what people had been up to, although this attempt at forced personal interaction did not always work as well as intended. Normally Katrina would begin by telling people about her yoga and her disruptive teenage son before Colin took centre stage and updated everyone on one of his latest home improvement failures. These were often the source of great amusement - especially if he had fallen off something or broken something expensive - but lately they had become less exciting and amounted to little more than him arguing with his wife about paint colours for their spare bedroom.

Sue would then deliver a 5-minute soliloquy on her dogs and how much better they were than most humans and Tom would then regale them all with stories of his week-end or, in this case, his week off. Martin normally concluded the sessions by recounting in meticulous and painful detail every single inconsequential thing that each of his boys had said, done, eaten, drunk or shitted out of their bodies. Katrina purposefully made him go last so she could wrap things up if too many of the team started to glaze over.

Occasionally Martin would mention his love of photography as well, although there was nothing on that subject this week because he'd just bought himself a new camera and was still trying to work out how to use it. Martin was an enthusiast who had very little aptitude. The cameras he used were generally of the rangefinder type which meant when he was taking the picture he was not looking directly through the lens and had been known on many occasions to unknowingly take multiple pictures with the lens cap still on.

He would be immensely proud of what he'd shot on the day but then totally distraught when he got the photos back from the developer only to find most of them were com-pletely black and helped contribute to the longevity of his nickname. To save money and embarrassment he'd once built his own darkroom in the garage to develop the pictures himself, although Tom was always threatening to go round and open the door to let all the 'dark' out. Martin eventually moved over to cameras with SD cards which allowed him to delete any accidental close-ups of the lens cap; this also had the happy side-effect of annoying Tom by thwarting his plans to mess with Martin's darkroom.

"I'm so glad that's over for another week," said Martin to Tom as they returned to their desks via the kitchen.

"I think we all are," said Tom.

"I always wonder if people are a bit bored hearing about the boys all the time."

Tom remained silent as they made their coffee and headed back across the large, open-plan office to the corner where the rest of the team were already settling back into their work. When they got back to their desks, they were just in time for Colin to tell them something he had forgotten to share at the meeting. As it wasn't about home improvement (or home destruction in Colin's case) it was understandable he hadn't remembered.

"Guys, I forgot to tell you I bought a new car on Saturday. It's a few years old and nothing fancy but it's newer than my previous one."

"Cool," said Tom. "What is it?"

"A Seat. It's eleven years old but it's only got 60,000 miles on the clock," said Colin.

"What colour is it?" Sue asked.

"It's yellow," said Colin

"Why didn't you get a normal colour?" asked Tom.

"It is a normal colour. I think," Colin replied with slightly less enthusiasm for the car than he had before he'd mentioned it.

"It sounds great, Colin. Are you pleased with it so far?" asked Katrina.

"Yes I am, thanks."

"Except it's yellow," added Tom.

"Yes." said Colin.

Out of the corner of his eye, Tom could see Martin shifting uncomfortably in his chair. Tom knew exactly why this was and could be traced directly back to the start of Martin's unfortunate nickname. Every time the topic of cars was brought up in any work or social situation Martin's mind inevitably went back to the day that he bought his first car from his cousin Graham. It then moved forward to the day he first drove it.

When Martin was 18, he'd started taking driving lessons and his dad Brian had seen this as an ideal opportunity to also learn so they devised a family competition to see which of them would pass first. They both ultimately had their driving tests booked for the same week with Martin's scheduled for Tuesday afternoon and Brian's set for Thursday morning.

Martin failed his test on Tuesday and Brian then failed his test on Thursday.

Two months later, they were each ready for their second test and Brian (in a commendable show of consistency) managed to fail again. Martin passed, however, and immediately started to look for a car. As luck would have it, his cousin Graham had a car he was willing to sell and they arranged to meet the following weekend. On the day Graham came round with the car, Tom was waiting with Martin.

"How much does he want for it Martin?" asked Tom before Graham arrived.

"I don't know, but I've got £2,000 saved up so hopefully it won't be any more than that."

"Here he comes now," said Tom as a light blue car came wheezing up the cul-de-sac where they both lived and shuddered to a halt next to them.

Graham switched off the engine of the battered old Ford and got out. Martin immediately went to greet him and they spent a few minutes catching up on family news before Martin proceeded to walk round the car and kick each of the tyres in turn.

"Why are you kicking the tyres?" asked Graham.

"Because that's what you're supposed to do," said Martin.

"Are you?"

"Well, I've seen it done on television and my dad told me to."

"So, what have you learned from that?" asked Tom, looking at Graham with both young men now having smirks on their faces.

"I don't know," admitted Martin. "But my dad might be watching from the window and he'll shout at me if I don't kick the tyres."

"Don't kick them too hard or the car might fall apart!" said Tom, laughing at the percentage of rust compared to the amount of original metal.

"Oh, shut up. It's better than your car," said Martin as he got in and sat in the driver's seat.

Martin took the car for a short test drive leaving Graham and Tom to await his return. After about 20 minutes, the car came wheezing up the cul-de-sac again sounding like the last one standing in a demolition derby. Martin got out and asked Graham how much he wanted for it.

"I'm upgrading to a brand new one so I need £1,500 from this for the deposit."

"Oh, that's okay," said Martin. "I've got £2,000 saved up."

"That's fine," said Graham. "You've got yourself a new car. Let me have the two grand by the end of the week and I'll bring the car round on Saturday morning."

They shook hands and Martin went in to tell his dad that he'd bought the car. Graham drove off and Tom went back to his house wondering what he'd just witnessed.

"Did Martin buy that car?" asked Tom's mother when he walked in.

"Yes. Graham only wanted £1,500 for it but Martin offered him £2,000."

"What?"

"Graham accepted the £2,000."

"I bet he did!" said Tom's mother. "Martin's always been a bit dopey."

"He's getting worse."

A few days later Graham brought the car round and Martin was finally the proud owner of his first car - having managed to negotiate the price up by 33%. His first task was to drive his annoying 10 year-old sister Emily to the library, which proved to be the last time anyone would get in a car with him for a very long time.

Tom watched the two siblings drive off from his bedroom window. He couldn't hear the day's first crunch of metal against another hard, unyielding material but he certainly saw it and watched Martin scrape the right side of the car along the small wall that separated his parents' house from their neighbours. Undeterred, Martin began his journey and Tom saw the car swerving slowly down the street as Martin struggled to remember that turning the steering wheel left made the car go left while turning it right made the car go right.

When Martin returned, Tom went over to his house to see how he'd got on. As he walked up the path, he couldn't fail to notice that the car looked a lot different from the one he'd seen earlier.

"Why is the car so battered? I saw you scrape the wall but that doesn't explain the damage on the left side or the back," asked Tom. "Did you kick the tyres too hard?"

"Very funny. I was driving Emily to the library and another car was coming towards me. I moved over to the left a bit to let him pass but misjudged it and scraped the side of a parked car," said Martin sheepishly.

"Did you stop and leave a note or try to find the owner?"

"We were late and the library was closing for lunch so I was going to do it on the way back," said Martin.

"That sounds fair enough. What did the owner say?" asked Tom.

"I don't know. We came back on a different route so I forgot."

"What happened to the back?"

"When we got to the library, I was trying to park and reversed into a concrete post by mistake."

"Well, you wouldn't do it deliberately."

"No," said Martin. "So, Graham is coming round to help me tidy the bodywork up a bit."

"Is he going to charge you?" asked Tom.

"I don't know," said Martin.

"Well, if he does, make sure you don't offer to pay extra like you did when you bought it," laughed Tom. "You're so dopey sometimes Martin; you're like Captain Dumbfuck, leader of all the dopey bastards in the world."

"Captain Dumbfuck! Captain Dumbfuck!" sang Emily, as she walked into the room. "I'm telling everyone!" she squealed with the kind of glee that can only be mustered by siblings when their brother or sister does something stupid.

"Oh no," said Martin with a groan. "This is going to stick isn't it?"

"Probably," said Tom. "Can I go and kick the tyres now?"

"No."

"Have you taken any photos of your car yet?" asked Tom.

"Fuck off," said Martin.

"Mum!" shouted his 10 year-old sister excitedly. She loved seeing her brother get into trouble and if there was ever a chance she could help she would take it. "Martin said 'fuck'. Come and tell him off!"

Tom took the impending family argument as his cue to leave and go back to the relative calm and serenity of his own house. Growing up as an only child definitely had its advantages.

Chapter 4

Brighton, UK

"I see you've got a meeting with HR today, Tom," said Katrina, once the very small amount of fuss about Colin's new car had died down. Martin breathed a sigh of relief that Tom hadn't brought up the story of his first car purchase and his subsequent unwitting attempts to wreck it on the first day he drove it.

"Is it anything I should be worried about?" Katrina went on.

"Not really. I think they only invite me up there because they fancy me," said Tom. "I mean, who wouldn't?!"

Everyone on the team looked at Tom and started laughing. At 32, of average height, average build, average attractiveness and with slightly thinning brown hair he was not most women's first choice. Or second choice for that matter. His most recent girlfriend had said he was very nearly a solid five out of ten - although she had been drunk at the time so it wasn't clear whether she was overstating it or understating it - and a previous girlfriend had once referred to him as a 'placeholder' which he'd never been quite sure if that had been a compliment or not.

Either way, Tom was undaunted and had the philosophy that if Captain Dumbfuck could find a job, get married, have kids and have a happy life then anything in the universe was possible. Confidence was the key - even if in most cases it was badly misplaced.

"I'm sure they do," said Martin, laughing harder than everyone else, relieved that the subject had been changed away from cars and his secret had been preserved for another day.

"I think it's something to do with the last dress down day we had," said Tom.

"I missed that one," said Colin. "I heard it was quite a day."

"We're all trying very hard to forget it, Colin," said Katrina.

"Hopefully they'll be another one soon," said Tom. "Maybe we can have a toga party?"

"I'd need a big toga," said Martin.

Everyone started to lower their heads and soon became absorbed in their work again. Martin had always struggled with his weight but it had never bothered him and he often made jokes about it. Growing up in less sensitive times had exposed him to some unpleasant comments as a boy but he wasn't fazed by anything. He'd always enjoyed his food and had ultimately married a woman who'd trained as a chef and had a habit of trying out new recipes on him.

Martin was enjoying his life, had everything that he'd ever wanted and was one of the few people Tom knew who could genuinely say they were truly happy. The bastard. And he had thicker hair than Tom. Double bastard.

***

Tom looked back at his screen and saw an email arrive from Karen in the American office. He looked at the clock and saw that it was just after 12:30pm; it was only 7:30am over there so she was in a lot earlier than usual.

"Hi Tom, I hope you had a good break from work. We may have an issue with a data breach over here - I'm sure your people will share it with you sometime today but we could use your help later on. Warm regards, Karen."

Karen was the IT manager of the American division in Atlanta and had been recruited to run that department as the business started to sell its clothing in various high-end stores over there. The business had only been set up a few weeks when she joined so she was both the newest member of the company and, at 35, the youngest.

Classic Country Clothing (UK) Inc. had been formed so the company could reach a whole new market of American consumers who had the same surplus of money and shortage of fashion taste as their British counterparts. The location in Atlanta, Georgia had been chosen partly to limit the time differences that would have made dealing with a west coast site almost impossible but primarily because Atlanta was known as 'the city in a forest.' There was no faulting the logic behind the decision and the new office had currently been up and running for six months.

So far, the company had a Sales and Marketing department, a Customer Services department, a Shipping and Logistics department and an IT department. They also had various levels of management, with each one more incompetent and ineffective than the one below it. In the same way as the UK original, the US company sold its clothing to high-end stores and were now also selling items online through their website and a dedicated smartphone app.

Setting up an overseas company from the UK had not been easy and when the warehouse operation had experienced some teething problems they couldn't resolve locally, there was no alternative but to fly over the Global Production & Logistics Director to help with the warehousing and shipping issues.

Before the UK company had grown and new departments had been formed to segregate the increasing workloads, Roy White had been in charge of production, warehousing, logistics and IT and was just about the most knowledgeable person in the business. As time had passed, his internal empire had been reduced to just warehousing and logistics but his breadth of knowledge was unmatched by anybody else so he was the obvious (but rather unfortunate) choice to go to Atlanta.

Roy was nearing retirement and had spent his whole career upsetting people of various different backgrounds and beliefs. He was short-tempered, grumpy, narrow-minded and (not surprisingly) single. Change was not a welcome feature in his life. He hated large cities, meeting new people or trying new things. One of his favourite sayings was 'I don't know, I have no interest in knowing and I don't want to learn' which made teaching him anything new almost impossible.

The move to Brighton (the unofficial LGBTQ capital of the UK) had not sat well with Roy and many of the staff had guessed it would be a step too far for his outdated and unpleasant attitudes. He struggled with the bohemian atmosphere at first but then realised that given the choice between doing a job he liked in a company he was settled in was preferable to taking his chances at a company where he would almost certainly be required to learn new things and deal with new people. He therefore accepted his fate and decided to stay in his current role until he retired.

Everyone in the company knew Roy was just about the most intolerant human being since Genghis Khan and while at first they accepted it, as time went on and attitudes changed, more and more people found him offensive. Some people started to make fun of his prejudices, however, and every time somebody who didn't look or think like Roy started working there the rest of the staff would relish his growing discomfort.

When news came out that Roy was being sent to resolve the issues in the American warehouse it was greeted with a mixture of horror and delight. After just two days in Atlanta (a city of over 5.5 million people with a racial mix of 40% white and 60% black, Asian and other races) Roy was struggling. Combine this with the highest LGBT population per capita in the USA and a local populace who were friendly, polite and welcoming and Roy was so far outside his comfort zone that he paid for an early flight home.

When he returned to the office, he was challenged by the CEO. After keeping him waiting for a couple of hours, he went up and promptly resigned, citing a mystery incident in a local bar on the second night he was in Atlanta as the reason. He left the business immediately and had never been seen or heard of again.

Despite the loss of Roy's knowledge, the Atlanta warehouse was eventually set up; local staff were then recruited and a new security system was implemented. Unfortunately, because this had taken longer than expected, the first shipment of clothing arrived from the manufacturers in Vietnam before the security system had been fully implemented and - two days after the stock arrived - there was a break-in and some of it was stolen.

Nobody was sure why the thieves had not taken more of the clothes, although the staff assumed that because they didn't like the clothing, nobody else would either and it was clearly a 'niche' item. Or as Hank, the newly-appointed US Logistics Director had put it "this British stuff ain't worth shit - why would some dumbass want to steal any of it?"

***

Tom stared at the screen and read Karen's email again. It wasn't like her to be in work that early in the day and it wasn't like her to be so concise. Normally her emails were at least two pages long and - while any phone call with her would initially start on topic - it would soon go off on a tangent as she rambled on about some minor injustice or other that had affected her.

She always had a complaint about something. Sometimes it was quite reasonable like the weather or the traffic or the slow service at her local coffee shop but other times it was more specific like her mother calling her in the middle of her eating dinner, the neighbours having a baby or her sister Wendy working out the identity of the killer on a TV crime show before she did.

Unfortunately for Karen, her sister Wendy had recently moved in with her and brought along four cats and some unusually fussy dietary requirements. This change to her living arrangements had not improved Karen's already fraught temperament.

On the day after the break-in at the Atlanta warehouse, Karen's first complaint to Tom when she called him was that the thieves had not taken her co-worker's ugly, purple and mustard patterned jacket that had been on the coat rack in the office.

"They must have seen it!" she had said. "It's one hell of an ugly ass jacket. Maybe that's what scared them off?! They probably saw it and it gave them the creeps. I was so pissed when I came in and found it was still there. If I'd gotten in first, I would've just thrown it in the trash and told her the thieves took it."

"Maybe they only wanted the quality, waterproof garments we sell," said Tom.

"Oh man! I love your cuteness but the only quality of these garments is poor quality," laughed Karen.

Tom liked Karen; she was fun and loud and always made him laugh. Tom often wondered if she actually needed the phone as he was convinced she could just shout from the top of her building and he'd hear her just as well. Martin had spoken to her too, as had Katrina, and they both liked her as well. Everybody in the UK that had dealt with her liked her - in fact the only person that didn't was no longer with the company.

Racist Roy had taken an instant dislike to the confident, young, mixed-race woman in charge of IT when he'd visited - as well as almost everyone else in the company and across the city. He'd started by complaining about the local accents ("it was like being in an episode of The Dukes of Hazzard") before moving on to the food ("I couldn't get fish and chips anywhere"), the good manners ("why do they have to call everyone 'sir' all the time?") and finally ending up criticising the local sayings ("why does everyone I talk to say 'bless your heart' after everything I say?").

When he arrived at the building on the first day, Roy was immediately dismayed and said it was "too big - like everything else in America" and when he saw the ethnically-diverse group of staff ready to welcome him, he made up his tiny, uncultured mind that he didn't like anything or anyone the country had to offer.

Two days after arriving, he took a flight home at his own expense and by the end of the week he'd left the company completely. He'd quite liked that woman's purple and mustard patterned jacket though.

Chapter 5

Brighton, UK

Tom came back from lunch wondering what Karen was referring to in her email about the data breach and how serious it could be. He knew they were building up customer mailing lists and trying to get more retailers across the USA to stock the company's products but it didn't seem as if there could be much more to it than that. No doubt the team would be given more details later, but it was approaching two o'clock and he had to prepare for his meeting with HR.

"Good luck mate!" said Martin, as Tom returned to his desk and picked up his laptop.

"It was nice knowing you," said Colin cheerily.

"I wouldn't go that far," said Martin. "I've known him for 25 years and it's been average at best."

"Thanks Captain Dumbfuck," said Tom as he walked away from the team, out into the corridor and headed towards the stairs that led to HR.

Martin put his head down and hoped nobody had heard what Tom had said. Luckily they hadn't and his embarrassing nickname was safe for another day, although he was beginning to wonder if he should just let everyone know to save the embarrassment later. That would be a sensible approach - although if Tom got fired today Martin would be in the clear. He decided to cross his fingers and hope for the best - or the worst, depending on who you were.

The HR office was situated at the top of three flights of stairs and, as with many corporations, it was on the top floor of the building near the directors' offices. Whether this was meant to be intimidating to staff members who were called to HR was never quite explained but it did give them a degree of privacy that they wouldn't have otherwise had if they'd been downstairs with the plebs.

As Tom walked up the stairs, the warm spring sunshine was streaming through the windows and he could see the myriad particles of dust floating in the air. Living and working in a bustling seaside city in the south of England was a real bonus and he couldn't imagine living anywhere else - unless he got fired and had to move back in with his parents.

The HR office was an oasis of calm away from the often argumentative IT department where most of the staff considered themselves to be 'alpha males' - especially the women - and where heated debates over how best to implement a technology solution were often won by the person with the loudest voice and the longest staying power rather than by the person whose solution had the most merit or was the most cost-effective.

Meetings over which email program the company should use and how often the employees must change their passwords could take hours to resolve and usually became a war of attrition. They often went on late into the evening so managers had to have strong bladders, unwavering voices and no need for food or drink. If somebody stopped talking, suggested a coffee break or went to the toilet they were effectively 'out' and the debate raged on with one less competitor. This continued until all but one voice had been silenced and their idea was adopted while everyone else wearily made their way home broken, defeated and with suspicious wet stains on the front of their trousers.

Most people in the IT department liked the challenging environment they'd created because it brought the best out of everybody but Tom preferred to visit other areas of the company and get to know different people. One thing that had always struck him about HR was the overwhelming number of female staff working there compared to most other departments. It was definitely an area he would like to work in one day, although he knew the only way the HR Director would have him working there would be so she could keep a closer eye on him. He could accept that, in fact it seemed like a win-win situation.

Tom headed towards Debbie's desk and smiled at some of the women as he walked through the office. They all knew him and he enjoyed what he called 'celebrity status' in that department, even though most of them didn't return his smile and immediately turned back to their work with a shudder.

"Good afternoon Debbie, how are things with you today?" Tom asked brightly as he arrived at the HR waiting area.

The area contained a small round table with four chairs, a filtered water machine, a large potted plant and four other chairs against the wall where the employees waited to be called into Lisa's office to learn their fate. Debbie's desk was situated at the front of this area and the whole layout made her seem like a modern-day Cerberus, the mythological Greek gatekeeper of the underworld. Only without the three heads and the loud bark.

"Hi Tom. Did you have a good week off?" asked Debbie.

"Not bad thanks. I had a few late nights and had to visit my grandfather a couple of times too. He's taken a turn for the worse in the nursing home."

"Oh, I'm sorry to hear that," said Debbie. "What's his condition like these days?"

"Much the same, although dementia is beginning to kick in a bit now. He's stopped chasing the nurses around and making lewd comments to them so he's clearly not himself anymore."

"I'm sure they will look after him as well as they can. I guess that's where you get it from?"

"Haha! Maybe," said Tom. "I'm sure if granddad was working here, you'd be seeing him more often than me."

"I think you'd both be up here equally," said Debbie, breaking into a broad smile. "You'd be fighting over that seat by the plant," she laughed.

"Oh no...that would be his seat. He'd outrank me in that area. I'm a bit scared of him so I'd just let him sit where he wanted."

The two laughed as Tom took his customary seat by the potted plant and waited for Lisa. It seemed she was running late so Debbie offered him a coffee, which was willingly accepted.

"Thanks, Debbie. I only come up here for the coffee; it's much better than ours."

"I thought you came up because our department is full of young women?"

"That too, of course," said Tom. "The IT department is full of smelly middle-aged men who spend hours arguing which font we should all be using for our email signatures."

"I'm sure it isn't that bad down there," said Debbie, who was quite sure it was every bit as bad as that down there.

"As we get into the summer and the weather gets warmer some of the guys always seem to forget that they are allowed to use deodorant. Up here everything is far more fragrant - although I was expecting to see a lot more sundresses and summer clothes here today."

"I think they knew you were coming up so they dressed more conservatively," Debbie explained, only half-joking.

"That's not fair!" said Tom with mock indignation. "I'll just come up unannounced next time," he added, just as Lisa came out of her office, her high heels clicking on the wooden floor to announce her arrival.

"I think we see you far too often as it is without you coming up without an appointment," said Lisa. "Come into my office, we've got a lot to talk about," she said, before turning on her heel and heading back through the open door, her long blonde ponytail swinging behind her.

Tom picked up his coffee and laptop and followed Lisa into her office, looking back and nodding to Debbie as he went through the door. Debbie smiled back, hoping this wouldn't be the last time she saw him.

"Sit down," said Lisa. "We have a problem."

"Oh?" queried Tom, sitting in the chair that Lisa had indicated while she remained standing.

"Katrina tells me you are working on the main project for safeguarding the personal details of UK customers on our mailing lists. Is that right?"

"Yes, it's a significant upgrade to our data collection and storage processes to keep us compliant with the latest legislation," said Tom, slightly thrown off balance and wondering when he would be disciplined for the dress down charity day issues. No doubt Lisa was building up to this but he didn't want to rush her, just in case she forgot.

"You know that the team in Atlanta have been working on a similar thing for the US customer mailing lists I presume?" Lisa continued.

"Yes. Their rules are slightly different so I think there have been some complications with the secure storage and one or two issues with the data being collected. "

"Well..." Lisa paused and then sat down.

Lisa's face darkened and she exhaled loudly. Clearly there was something major happening over in the Atlanta office. Tom wondered if this was what Karen had alluded to in her email when she'd mentioned the data breach.

"We have a bit of a problem over there. There's been a data breach and we have lost some of our customer data," said Lisa, almost spitting the words from her mouth. "It came to light over the weekend and they're now looking to establish how the breach happened and what we can do about it."

"I understand," said Tom. "Do they need to use parts of our solution to improve theirs?"

"Possibly. But we have a much bigger problem," said Lisa, seemingly not wanting to get to the point in the vain hope that it wouldn't prove to be true if it wasn't spoken aloud.

"What else?" asked Tom. Maybe this was so big he wouldn't be getting disciplined at all. Surely she wouldn't be telling him all this if she was planning to fire him?

Lisa got up and walked to the window. Four hours ago, she was looking out of this same window wondering what to do about the employee who was now sitting in her office. Every muscle and bone in her body wanted to throw him out the window onto the hard, paved street below but she knew that the problem in the US could easily blow up and the company needed its best people on it to develop the solution.

Unfortunately, one of the company's best people was sitting in her office now, unaware of both the grisly fate she had originally imagined for him and the new fate that she would soon be handing out. She hoped Tom had a valid passport as she turned back to him.

"There have been some errors in the data collection processes. The software we originally used was bought from another company and came highly recommended by the former IT director there," explained Lisa. "He adapted it for us and it seemed to work well but then the supplier went into bankruptcy and because we weren't able to get any technical support we had to modify it ourselves."

"Was that Johnny Pervert, the guy that came over here a while back?" asked Tom. "He was a bit dodgy. But well-named."

"His surname was Perver," said Lisa. "But you're right in a way," continued Lisa.

"We all knew him as Johnny Pervert. What a name...and what a guy," said Tom, trying not to chuckle.

"Anyway, it seems that Mr. Perver's chief contribution to the business was to recommend this data collection software, make some changes to the settings and then leave without sharing his knowledge with anyone," said Lisa.

"Why did he leave? Were the rumours true?" asked Tom.

"They had to let him go because they found him in the office watching certain 'materials' on his computer," said Lisa.

"We heard rumours that he'd been masturbating to porn in the office and the cleaner caught him after everyone else had gone home," said Tom.

"Well - and this is strictly confidential - there might be some truth in that," said Lisa.

"Apparently she made him clean his own office that night."

"Whatever," said Lisa in disgust. She really didn't want to think about that at this time - or in fact at any time.

"We all knew he was dodgy. First the name, then the comments about British women when he visited and the fact that he wanted to spend every night of his visit in a strip club. Total legend, that guy," said Tom.

Lisa looked at him blankly. Why couldn't she just throw him out of the window, forget the data breach in Atlanta and just go home and drink as much gin as her body would take until she passed out?

"I mean legend in a bad way, of course," Tom added, noticing that Lisa did not appear to agree with him on Johnny Pervert's legendary status. Luckily she didn't seem interested in knowing who had taken him to the strip club every night - although if she had, she would have found the culprit sitting right in front of her. Good times, good name, dodgy individual. What more could you want from a night out with someone?

Lisa sat back down and put her head in her hands. She held in there for several seconds before looking straight at Tom, seemingly staring into his very soul. It creeped him out a bit. Well, quite a lot actually.

"The software that we installed on his recommendation worked with an app on the customer's smartphones to build up a picture of their habits and preferences. Every time they went out it would access their location, the local weather and whether there was a store locally that sold our clothing. It would then make recommendations and give them discount vouchers if they had spent more than a certain amount with us," explained Lisa.

"That's ahead of what the UK version does," said Tom. "It sounds perfect."

"It sounds perfect but it isn't," said a deep voice from Lisa's office door. "Sorry I'm late Lisa, but we're still trying to understand the damage here."

Tom recognised the voice as belonging to Keith, the IT Director. He was a tall, white-haired man in his late 50s with the deepest voice Tom had ever heard. Keith oversaw the whole of the IT department and was also Katrina's boss. He often sat in on meetings so he knew Tom, Martin and the rest of their team well and the whole department agreed that if he ever changed career, he would be an obvious choice to take over from the person who did the voice-overs for all of those Hollywood movie trailers.

"No problem," said Lisa. "Would you like to go over the technical issues for us?"

Chapter 6

Brighton, UK

The streets of Brighton were bustling with both tourists and locals enjoying the April sunshine, heading down to the beach or sitting in a bar or restaurant. Almost every establishment had tables and chairs outside it to entice weary shoppers and visitors to rest for a few minutes with a coffee and a panini, a cake or even a cocktail. On any given day you could throw a stone anywhere in the centre of Brighton and hit someone who was eating or drinking. It wasn't something the tourism department advised, but you could do it.

The vibrant south coast city attracts more than 11 million visitors each year, many of whom flock to the pebbled beach, the famous Victorian pier and the Royal Pavilion. On warm spring days there were few better places to be in Britain - unless you were sitting three floors above street level in the HR office of a company that had just found a major security breach that threatened its very existence.

Keith sat down next to Tom, nodded a greeting and continued where Lisa had left off.

"The app they developed was a giant technical leap forward in terms of the data it collected about people. It managed to bypass a lot of the controls and restrictions on people's phones and did things like checking the user's location at school pick-up times to work out if they had children or not so it could recommend kids clothing at the same time."

"Impressive," said Tom.

"In a technical way, yes. But it wasn't altogether legal. It also checked their Facebook accounts and stored details of all their contacts and cross-referenced them against any other contact information it had to work out the age and date of birth of everyone the user knew so it could recommend products as birthday presents," continued Keith.

"A lot of apps do stuff like that though," said Tom.

"Yes, they do, however this went further still. The app had screen-reading functionality too; if the user had a banking app on their phone whenever they opened it, the app would record the screen and use optical character recognition software to look at the figures and check the level of disposable income they had. It would then make recommendations for more or less expensive items according to how much money they had."

"That's cool. Scary, but cool," said Tom.

"Unfortunately, it gets worse. Far worse..." said Lisa, her voice tailing off to a whisper.

"How?" asked Tom, now on the edge of his seat learning about the capabilities of the American version of their shopping app which were equally awesome and terrifying. This was getting more exciting by the second and it seemed that Lisa had forgotten the main reason for his visit which was even better.

Lisa paused and looked at Keith.

"It reviewed their browser history," she said. "The software automatically recorded details of the customers' browser history and fed it into our main database," she went on.

"Browser history?! Oh no. That's not good," said Tom, with a slight smile.

"It's not amusing, Tom," Lisa admonished.

"No it's not," Keith agreed. "They sent us some examples. Not only do we know that Martha from Connecticut bought one of our 'Stay Warm and Toasty' range of jackets, but we also know she is single with no kids, has a brother in New York that she hasn't called or messaged for at least a year, likes hiking on three trails near her home and is behind on her mortgage payments."

"That's not so bad," said Tom.

"Agreed," said Keith. "We also know that Martha watches several hours of lesbian porn on her phone each week and has purchased three vibrators online in the last month."

"Well if she's behind on her mortgage, maybe she needs some relief," suggested Tom.

"It's not funny," said Lisa, privately admitting to herself that Tom could be quite funny sometimes.

"We also know that Bill in Tennessee is married, has been watching a lot of threesome sex videos online, spends a lot of time around schools despite not having any kids of his own and has recently bought some pills to make his penis bigger," Keith added.

"Do we know where he got the pills from?" Tom asked.

"What?"

"Asking for a friend," said Tom.

"Moving swiftly on, we know from the salary deposits into his bank account that Bill also works as a data security officer at one of the stores that sells our products," said Lisa.

"Which means he's the type of person that would be likely to request a copy of the data we hold on him," Keith explained.

"And if he does that and then goes to the media..." said Lisa, not needing to finish her sentence.

Lisa picked up a printout of an email received from Karen, the IT manager in Atlanta who was currently heading up the investigation while a new IT Director was being recruited.

"Keith and I received an email this morning giving a handful of examples like this but Karen says there could be many thousands of compromised accounts," said Lisa.

"We know the full browsing history, location information, family situation, sexual preferences and purchasing history of adult products for all our American customers?" asked Tom.

"Any products bought online are included," said Keith. "We know their tastes in books, films, games, music, clothing...everything our customers have bought online over the last 3 months has been captured by the app and stored in our database."

"That's not good," said Tom.

"The loss of this data has also highlighted security issues within the database and it seems that none of the data was encrypted or hidden from view. Anyone accessing our website on a computer could just add the words 'customer data' to the end of the URL and see everything."

"So, we use the app to steal their data and then publish it online?"

"Yes."

The room fell silent, with only the gentle hubbub of noise from the street below coming through the open window. All three of them looked at the printed email Lisa had since put back down on her desk, none of them knowing what to say next. Lisa broke the silence.

"There have been a lot of meetings here today about this. We have just set up a quarterly email of offers and discounts on all of our products - along with any related products from what used to be our carefully selected partners. Unfortunately, the software system has corrupted our smartphone app and decided that every business our customers have recently used or even browsed is now a carefully selected partner," she said.

"The emails are scheduled to go out at the end of next month but we can't send our customers a list of offers from inappropriate businesses," said Keith.

"We're worried that Martha will get one voucher for a 20% discount with us and another for a 15% discount off a vibrator or a lesbian couples weekend retreat? And Bill will get the same, only his email will include vouchers for kids clothing and penis enlargement pills? That's going to be difficult to explain to his wife," said Tom.

"Exactly," said Lisa.

"What's our plan of action?" asked Tom.

"Well, we have two issues," said Keith. "First, our data collection has been far too rigorous; we need to stop that and delete the data we've already collected before the email goes out offering discounts on inappropriate products. They would then question where we got our data from and that would cause us a major headache."

"That seems an obvious place to start," Tom agreed.

"We then need to re-write the code so it behaves properly in future," added Keith.

"So far, so good," said Tom.

"The other part is to focus on the data breach itself. We don't want thousands of our customers being contacted by third parties and blackmailed over their browsing history."

"Most people have a dodgy browsing history," said Tom.

"I'm sure they do; maybe some more than others," said Lisa, looking Tom straight in the eye and creeping him out for the second time. "But they certainly wouldn't want their families and friends finding out about it."

Tom accepted this and looked down at the floor, partly out of embarrassment at his own browser history and partly because he was worried that if Lisa stared at him a third time it might turn him to stone. And he certainly didn't want that - almost as much as their dodgy customers didn't want their families to know what shady stuff they looked at online.

"The Atlanta office doesn't have the IT skills to sort this out internally so we'll be sending a small team over there for a couple of weeks to find out what's gone wrong with the data collection and storage side. We need to set up new data collection rules for the future and also delete all of the unnecessary data we currently hold," said Keith.

"Would I be right in guessing that I'll be part of this team?" asked Tom.

"Yes. We need to fix this as soon as possible - and certainly before the promotional emails are sent out next month. I'm assuming you have a passport?" said Lisa.

"Yes of course. Although can't we just stop the emails from going out?"

"Sadly not," said Keith. "They're sent by a third party and our contract with them means we have to pay whether they go out or not. There is also a financial penalty if we delay them so we need to stick to the schedule."

"Also, the Global Corporate Branding department wants to send out details of the summer range before Memorial Day at the end of May. It's seen as the start of summer over there and they want to take advantage of that to boost sales," Lisa added.

"Are sales more important than the company's good reputation?" asked Tom, unable to hide his bemusement.

"No, but sales haven't been exactly brisk so far and we need them to pick up soon or the future of the American division will be in doubt. On a more personal level, the whole of the Global Corporate Branding team has been promised a weekend away if they hit their lead-generation targets over there."

"Where are they going?" asked Tom.

"Dresden in Germany," said Lisa.

"Dresden?! It's not exactly the tourism capital of Europe. Why don't they go somewhere good? What are they going to do in Dresden?"

"I have no idea, but they seem very keen to go. Which is why we need you to focus on fixing the data collection and storage issues before they start marketing to all these customers again and sending them vouchers for things they'd prefer we didn't know they were interested in."

"What about the data breach?" asked Tom.

"We're going to try and sort that from here. We've hired a specialist security firm to do that so your job will just be to focus on the data collection and storage problems," said Keith.

"You'll be the Project Manager but we haven't finalised who else is going yet. We'll let you know as soon as possible," added Lisa.

"This is awesome! When are we going?" asked Tom, failing to keep his excitement under wraps.

"Firstly, it's not awesome that we could be heavily fined for collecting highly sensitive and embarrassing data about our customers. It's also not awesome that we allowed our database to be hacked so that our customers' personal data is made available to people that may try to exploit is," said Lisa. "And we all know what a litigious bunch the Americans can be. If this gets out, we could be sued for millions and it could ruin the company."

"Those bits aren't quite as awesome," Tom agreed.

"You'll be going this Saturday. Tarquin's PA is booking the flights and hotels today. You'll get the weekend to relax and acclimatise and then you'll start work at 8am Monday morning. There will probably be four of you and Karen will be your contact over there," said Lisa.

"Okay, I'll speak to her later," said Tom, getting up and heading towards the door.

"Just one more thing," said Lisa. "Don't fuck this up. Don't do anything stupid and don't upset, embarrass or insult any of the female staff over there. If I hear of anything inappropriate you'll be fired immediately and I will personally re-book your flight ticket home so you have to go through Iran, Somalia and North Korea," said Lisa.

"I'll be on my best behaviour," said Tom.

"You'll need a visa for entry into the USA if you haven't got one. I think it's called an ESTA and you can apply online. We'll reimburse you for the cost of course."

"I've already got one. I was in Las Vegas over New Year so it should still be valid."

"I didn't know you went to Vegas," said Keith.

"Well, you know what they say - what happens in Vegas stays in Vegas," said Tom.

"I've heard that," chuckled Keith.

"Well in my case I brought it back with me. But a course of antibiotics and some cream from the doctor soon cleared it up."

Lisa grimaced and started to wonder if this was really the best option they had. Deep down she knew there was nothing else they could do and could only hope that Tom and the team they sent with him got it done without making things worse. She and Keith had scheduled a conference call with Karen later that day to discuss exactly what was needed and how to cover the resource requirements with as few people as possible but she couldn't help but worry.

This had all happened so suddenly that the company hadn't had a lot of time to react but she knew they needed their best Project Manager involved and Tom's name was at the top on the list. Not only did he have the skills they needed in that area but he also had experience in data analysis and getting to the root cause of problems quickly.

The added bonus was that sending Tom out of the country for a while gave the female staff in the UK office a bit of break from him - even if it was only for a couple of weeks. Also, she knew a lot of Americans carried guns so maybe he'd upset someone and they'd shoot him.

Chapter 7

Brighton, UK

Tom spoke briefly to Debbie after he left Lisa's office and told her of his upcoming trip. She wished him luck and was visibly pleased that he hadn't been fired. Tom said good-bye and made his way back downstairs where he saw Katrina walking towards him as he crossed the office.

"Hi Tom, I've had an email from HR telling me you'll be going to Atlanta next week. Are you okay with that?" she asked.

"I can't wait! It will be brilliant to meet Karen and the rest of the team over there. You know I love travelling so I'm really looking forward to it."

"That's good," said Katrina. "But if you change your mind let me know as soon as possible."

"Don't worry, Katrina. I'm really excited about going."

"I'm sure you're excited to fix the problem they have. We've just had an email from our CEO explaining what's happened. I suggest you read it before you speak to Karen."

"I will."

"Just remember it's not a holiday...you're going over to resolve a major issue."

"It's still exciting. I'd much rather be fixing an issue in sunny Atlanta than in a grim, featureless data centre on a grey industrial estate somewhere in Siberia," said Tom. "Or Wolverhampton."

Tom returned to his desk and noticed a buzz around the team; in fact, the whole office was full of excited chatter. He put his laptop back into the docking station on his desk and waited a few seconds for the screen to be displayed on his monitors before *opening the email from the CEO.*

"Dear colleagues,

It is with great regret that I must inform you of an incident that has occurred at our Atlanta office in the last few days which has come to light this morning.

As you will be aware, we operate in a highly-sophisticated digital world which - while delivering many advantages - also brings with it a number of risks. One of these risks is data loss and it appears that we have been the subject of an attack by a malicious third party. The result of this is that our customer data has been compromised and may now be available to criminals or other nefarious individuals seeking to profit from this information.

Whilst this is a serious enough issue in itself, we have also discovered that the customer data we were collecting and storing went far beyond what would reasonably be expected - or indeed allowed by law - and every aspect of our customers lives, including financial details, family details and even their internet browsing history has been captured in error.

It is this data that has been breached and we will now be working with the relevant authorities in both countries to mitigate the damage, correct our systems and implement new processes to ensure this does not happen again.

You are formally instructed to not discuss this with anyone outside our company; if you are contacted by any media outlets please refer them to our Communications department.

I will contact you all again when we know what the next steps are, but until then it is business as usual and you should go about your roles with the same passion and diligence as always.

Warm regards,

Tarquin Fotherington-Smythe

CEO

Classic Country Clothing Ltd."

Tom stared blankly at his screen for a minute. Reading about the problem in an email from the CEO had somehow made it more real. Upstairs in HR it had just seemed like a problem that had to be solved but after reading the email and hearing the nervous chatter from his colleagues it really brought home the fact that the company had a serious problem and he was charged with helping to fix it. No pressure then.

Suddenly his desk phone rang. He could see the international code 001 followed by the area code 470 and knew the call was coming from Atlanta. It must be Karen.

"Hello, Tom speaking," he answered.

"Hi y'all! How are you guys doing over there today?" came the cheery and surprisingly upbeat voice.

"Hi Karen, I'm good thanks. How are you?"

"Oh man, things ain't too good over here. We just got a copy of the email the CEO sent so I'm guessing you've been clued in on this situation too?" she said, sounding slightly less upbeat than she had done a moment ago.

"Yeah, I just read it," said Tom.

"Well, the way I hear it, some of y'all are coming over here to help us fix things up."

"That's right - I got Georgia on my mind!"

"No way man! For real? They're sending you?!"

Tom wasn't sure if this was being said in a welcoming way because they were finally getting to meet and it would be great to put a face to the voice or a slightly disappointed way because Karen wasn't totally convinced of his credentials to solve this particular crisis. Or to help. Or at least to not make things any worse than they currently were. He soon got his answer.

"Why the fuck are they sending your sorry ass over here?!" said Karen with a huge belly laugh. "I mean, don't they have anyone else? Like anyone AT ALL?!!"

The laughter went down Karen's phone line, travelled more than 4000 miles across the Atlantic Ocean, came up the phone line to the receiver by Tom's ear and out across the team. Sue and Martin sat closest to him and they both could hear Karen's booming laugh so they immediately started to laugh as well.

"It sounds like Karen's finding something funny," said Sue.

"Tom probably sent her a dick pic," said Martin, beginning to laugh harder.

"Ewww, that's gross," said Katrina. "Why would anyone ever send something like that? And why would she be laughing?"

"Maybe it wasn't very impressive?" Sue suggested as the whole team erupted into laughter.

Tom was getting laughed at on all sides as well as from the other end of the phone. This was some achievement - even for him - but he regained his composure and changed the subject.

"How was your weekend, Karen? Apart from letting everyone around the world know what kind of kinky stuff our customers are into."

"That wasn't me," Karen protested amidst more laughter. "And I can't control what these folks look at in their spare time."

"What exactly do they look at in their spare time?" asked Tom. "We were given a couple of examples but I bet there's a load more."

"Well, we got these big-ass spreadsheets here with all the data on by state. There must be more than 50,000 names on them all. You can filter the data columns and find out just about anything on anyone that has ever installed our app. Some people are into some freaky ass shit. It's the married ones that are the worst - especially the women."

"That's a surprise. I thought it would be lonely, single men that were the worst," said Tom.

"Like yourself you mean? I bet you're thinking yourself lucky that you didn't buy anything from us!" said Karen and sent yet more booming laughter down the phone line towards the UK office.

"He's obviously just sent her a picture of his balls as well," said Martin to renewed laughter on the team.

"Anyhow, yeah my weekend was good," said Karen. "Except for my dumbass sister moving in with me last week with all her damned cats. I think I already told you about that; we spent most of this weekend clearing away her shit but the place still looks like crap."

"Why has she moved in?" asked Tom

"She got fired from her job a couple of weeks ago for being a lazy ass bitch. I always worried that she'd lose her job someday and move in here if she couldn't afford to pay her rent."

"That's not good," said Tom. "Why did she get fired?"

"She was a receptionist at one of the museums here but she hates talking to strangers on the phone. She has a real phobia about it," Karen continued.

"Some people prefer to communicate by text," said Tom.

"I get that, but when you're the receptionist and you've got people calling you up for opening hours and shit you have to answer the damned phone. People don't send text messages for that stuff. It's just strangers though; she can talk to family and friends just fine."

"That's weird," said Tom.

41

"She's weird. Anyway, she told them she had a phobia of answering the phones so they fired her ass."

"Why did she take the job in the first place if she doesn't like talking on the phone?"

"She didn't take it. There used to be two of them working there - Wendy worked on the front desk and Edna answered the phones. Edna was 65 years old and liked to sit down all day while Wendy liked meeting people in the flesh so it worked out well."

"Presumably Edna retired?" asked Tom.

"No, she died in an armed robbery," said Karen.

"No way! That's so sad. Was it at the museum?"

"No, it was at a convenience store in Midtown."

"It's still sad to be caught up in something like that at her age," Tom said with genuine sympathy.

"Yeah, the cops took her out as she left the store - three bullets to the chest as she opened fire on them."

"What?!"

"Edna and her husband had knocked off a string of convenience stores to help prepare for their retirement but they got unlucky this time."

Tom was silenced for a moment. As Karen had been telling the story he'd had a vision of a sweet, white-haired old lady accidentally being in the wrong place at the wrong time, being caught up in a robbery and dying of a heart attack due to the stress of the situation. Instead she'd been one of the gun-toting perpetrators and had died in a hail of bullets like a geriatric Bonnie and Clyde.

"So, what happened to Wendy?" asked Tom.

"They told her to answer the phones while the security guard covered reception duties but she didn't want to so they fired her."

"That's a shame."

"Well it sure is a damned shame for me now I got her sorry ass and her four stupid cats living with me. I swear that girl went out and bought a load of extra crap before she moved in just to mess with me. My house looks like there's been an explosion in a factory that sells a whole bunch of useless shit."

"What has she got?" asked Tom, visualising a mad cat lady moving in with piles of clothes, shoes, ornaments and pictures.

"What ain't she got?" said Karen, becoming even less upbeat as the phone call went on. "A whole bunch of clothes, a ton of stuff for her cats and a lot of strange craft stuff. She thinks she can make a living as an artist selling crappy painted plates, knitted blankets in different colours, dreamcatchers and all sorts of crazy shit you'd normally just throw in the trash."

"It sounds like fun," Tom sympathised.

"Yeah...well it ain't. And don't go getting me started on her eating habits. Man, I knew she was weird but she's got this crazy diet thing going on and she just does not shut the hell up about it. I mean, ever."

"Is she a vegan?" asked Tom.

"Yes. That's it! How did you know?"

"Just a lucky guess."

"Well, she bored the britches off my neighbour Justine yesterday. She was talking about her food for nearly an hour in the heat. I felt so sorry for Justine. She looked like she'd aged 5 years by the time Wendy let her go. Justine's the type who would have told her husband everything just so he didn't miss out on all that misery either," Karen said.

Karen and Tom both broke into laughter and then said goodbye. It was almost home time in the UK while Karen was thinking about going out to get some lunch and as Tom put the phone down he began to reflect on the day and how it had delivered a trip to Atlanta, some important work that he'd presumably get a bonus for (assuming he and whoever he went with could fix the problems) and the knowledge that everyone on the team thought he had a small penis and routinely sent pictures of it to people.

This had become a far more interesting day than he'd been expecting when he first woke up this morning and had realised it was Monday rather than Sunday. He'd nearly called in sick but was glad he hadn't now because it had been quite a successful day - apart from the part about him having a small penis; he wasn't sure how they knew that. Surely Lisa and Keith hadn't said anything?

***

"So, you're off to Atlanta then mate?" said Martin as the team were all beginning to pack up for the day.

43

"Yes, it's going to be awesome. First class flights, 5-star accommodation, generous expense account and two weeks of that hot Georgia sunshine and fine Southern food," said Tom, trying to gloat as much as possible.

"Don't get carried away," said Katrina. "The company is quite tight when it comes to these things. Last year Roy went to Vietnam to check on the main factories there and he said it was a horrible experience."

"Yeah, but Racist Roy didn't like anywhere that was different," said Tom. "He didn't even like that company conference we had in Worthing and that was only 15 miles away."

"True," agreed Katrina. "Was that the one where they served pizza and pasta for lunch and he stormed off to get some fish and chips instead?"

"That was the one."

"Didn't he end up in a hotel that was full of Chinese back-packers in Vietnam?" asked Sue.

"Yes," said Katrina. "He hated it apparently. He complained about the food, the staff, the other guests, the weather, the time zone difference, the language and just about everything else too."

"It couldn't have happened to a nicer person," said Tom.

Murmurs of agreement came from everyone on the team. Roy had been universally disliked and everyone in the company was happy that he'd left. Sending him to Vietnam and the deep south of the USA were always going to challenge his long-held, unpleasant beliefs and his colleagues always assumed that he'd be murdered by somebody he offended one day; most of them had been disappointed that they wouldn't get to hear about it now.

"So, what are you doing this evening?" asked Martin, as he did every day when they were about to leave work.

"I was thinking of walking the dog," said Tom. "But I'm not sure now because I need to pack for my trip."

"I didn't know you had a dog!" said Sue excitedly. "What breed is it? Have you got any pictures? Is it a boy or a girl? How old is it?"

As the team's resident dog-lover, her eyes had lit up when she heard this and suddenly found Tom not quite so obnoxious as she normally did. Almost as obnoxious, but not quite.

"He doesn't have his own dog," Martin clarified. "He offers to walk his neighbour's dog a couple of nights each week to try to pick up women in the local park."

"That's terrible!" exclaimed Sue, her feelings about Tom returning to their normal level with this rather disheartening news.

"It's genius," said Colin. "It shows women he has a caring side and likes animals."

"But it's false!" moaned Sue. "What do they do when they find out he hasn't got a dog?!"

"Well, it hasn't worked yet so I think the local women are safe," said Martin with a grin.

"Can't you get your own dog, Tom?" Sue asked. "At least then you'll be genuine and dogs are such good company."

"I know, but I don't like the idea of picking up their shit and carrying it around in a plastic bag all afternoon," said Tom.

"What do you do when the dog you borrow has to do its business?" asked Sue.

"I just leave it there," said Tom.

"That's disgusting! No wonder you haven't met anybody," she said, totally horrified.

"I did meet somebody once," protested Tom. "A few weeks ago I met a nice girl called Jane - or was it Julie? I can't remember now."

"And what happened?" asked Sue.

"It didn't work out."

"You know why it didn't work out though, don't you?" said Martin.

"Maybe," said Tom.

"What happened?" asked Colin, as transfixed as everyone else on the team.

"Well...." Tom began.

"They got up from a bench they'd been sitting on together and she was about to give him her number when she stepped in a big pile of shit that the dog had just deposited," Martin told them.

"Yuk!" said Colin as everyone on the team stared open-mouthed.

"She was wearing sandals," said Tom sheepishly. "And the shit came up over the sides of her feet and went in between her toes. It was only on one foot to start with but there was quite a lot of it and it spilled over onto the other one. I couldn't believe it when he'd crapped it all out a few minutes earlier. He's not a big dog; how much shit can one little dog have inside it?"

"You didn't get her number then?" asked Sue.

"No, I have a feeling that might have put her off."

"The 'Shitgate' incident," said Colin.

The whole team began laughing. This was becoming a common theme today and Tom wasn't enjoying it. He much preferred it when they were laughing at somebody else on the team so he said goodnight and went home.

As he left, Tom heard Katrina calling Martin over to one of the meeting tables - presumably to tell the dopey bastard off about something - but he didn't stay to find out what. He had to get ready for his trip to Atlanta at the end of the week and needed to start organising things. Maybe he'd give the dog-walking a miss this evening.

Chapter 8

Brighton, UK

Tom arrived home, took out a frozen pizza and put it in the oven. While it was heating up, he got his suitcase out ready to pack for he was now calling his free holiday to Atlanta. Admittedly he'd have to do some work but he was confident that it could be knocked out in a few hours each day leaving him and the others (whoever they were) to enjoy their evenings. Hopefully they would do most of the work for him and he could just 'oversee' it.

He was especially looking forward to the first weekend where there would be no work expected from him at all; just him and some colleagues out on the town for a day and a half of drunken debauchery. He'd heard that American women loved a British accent so he was looking forward to sweeping some of them off their feet - and potentially into his hotel room. In reality, it had been a long while since he'd swept anyone anywhere and since that incident in the park with the dog most of the local women were keeping their distance.

Tom turned his attention back to the oven and got his pizza out. He'd also got himself a beer and had just cut the pizza into slices and sat down to eat it when his phone rang. He looked at the screen and saw the name 'Captain Dumbfuck' displayed above a picture of a potato. Tom's heart sank as Martin only normally called to tell him of something mind-numbingly mundane that one of his kids had done. Why couldn't this wait until tomorrow?

"Hi Martin. How's it going?" he said, shovelling the first piece of pizza into his mouth.

"Hi mate, it's going great thanks. In fact, it's going all the way to Atlanta!" said Martin, unable to contain the excitement in his voice.

Martin had been to Disney World in Florida a month ago with most of Irma's family and it was fair to say that it hadn't gone smoothly and their villa had soon been dubbed 'The Unhappiest Place on Earth.' The nightmare group of ten people included a family of four (Martin, Irma and their two boys), Irma's sister and her boyfriend (who she was about to dump because she had started to see his brother but didn't have the heart to end it with him just before a holiday that he'd paid for), their parents (who hated fun of any kind) and two of Irma's female friends who were last-minute additions and didn't know anyone else in the group.

The trip hadn't gone as well as they'd all hoped - especially as there were ten people sharing a villa that was only meant for eight. Several arguments had ensued over excessive bathroom usage and the lack of cleanliness and tidiness shown by almost everyone.

Not only were Martin and Irma very untidy but her family were the same way. Added to this was the fact that they were all incredibly lazy and not one of them had the slightest inclination to clean up after themselves. The two 'outsiders' were initially the only ones who wanted to keep the villa clean but they soon gave up in the face of the mounting arguments from the rest of the group who said they hadn't come away to spend their whole holiday being clean and tidy.

It seemed that everybody wanted the place to be kept clean and tidy but nobody wanted to do it themselves so eventually an uneasy truce was reached where nobody would do anything but they'd agree to a clean-up fee when they left. After three days, the villa resembled the aftermath of a teenager's first house party with their parents out of town, only without an uninvited stranger lying face down in the pool drunk (or dead).

When they returned, Martin said he'd never go away with Irma's family again and she agreed that it was a good idea. It wasn't clear whether she agreed that the four of them should not go away with the others again or if it was just Martin who wouldn't be going. He would doubtless discover which way she'd meant it the next time they went to book a holiday - but he did have a slight suspicion that he might be going somewhere alone.

"Cool! It'll be just like the old days," said Tom, immediately looking back to the times they went to Spain with 'the lads' when they were younger.

"Yeah - as long as I don't fall off a moped again," laughed Martin.

"Definitely! Or drop your camera in the sea," said Tom, joining in the laughter. This discussion wasn't going to end well for Martin.

"I was gutted about that," said Martin dejectedly. "That camera cost a lot of money."

"I know. Hopefully you won't lose your wallet either. Or get kicked up the arse by a horse. Or crack your head open on the swimming pool diving board," Tom added, warming to the theme of Martin's multiple mishaps.

"Yeah. I don't know why people call them the good old days. I spent most of my time in the local hospitals," said Martin. "I hope Atlanta is better."

"It will be," said Tom. "Going to Florida with Irma's family was alright, wasn't it? Once you were outside the villa."

"Mostly," said Martin. "Apart from when that roller-coaster broke down with Irma and me at the top."

"I'd forgotten about that," said Tom. "But they got you down eventually."

"It took an hour and a half," said Martin with a slight shudder.

"Well there you are. I bet the view was good from up there though," said Tom.

"It might have been...but we were upside-down the whole time," moaned Martin.

Tom continued to eat his pizza while Martin complained about the roller-coaster incident. It would be good to have Martin along - not only as a friend but also because Martin enjoyed doing all the methodical (and dull) data analysis work and that would save Tom doing it. He guessed that there would also be a programmer going over to fix any bugs in the data capturing software and re-program everything properly.

"Stuart and Bhavna are going too," said Martin as Tom began his second slice.

"That makes sense," he mumbled through a mouthful of dough.

"There will be four of us. Katrina wants me to review the data, you to design the approach to the fixes and the programmers to do the fixes. You, me and Karen will then test them once we're finished."

"Sounds good, Martin," said Tom. "What does Irma think?"

"She's got no idea. She can't even work her phone properly so she wouldn't be much help on something like this." said Martin.

"I mean about you going to Atlanta, not the data problem."

Tom sighed. Martin was not quite as dopey as he had been when they were kids but he still had his moments.

"Oh right. After the problems we had in Florida she's quite keen for me to go away on my own," said Martin.

"How do you feel about leaving the boys?"

"I'll miss them but I'm sure they won't change too much in a couple of weeks," said Martin. "I'll bring them something nice back. What is Atlanta famous for?"

"Infectious diseases and zombies I think," said Tom.

"What?"

"Well, that's where they have the CDC - the disease factory."

"I'm sure they don't manufacture diseases," said Martin. "Or do they?"

"Who knows?" said Tom. "I think they monitor diseases and try to find cures and stuff."

"But what if they can't? What happens to the people that are infected?" asked Martin, sounding less sure about the trip than he had done a few minutes ago.

"I think they probably shoot them," said Tom.

"Fair enough," said Martin. "What about the zombies?"

"They definitely shoot them," said Tom, beginning to see some of the 'old' Martin shining through.

"Will we need guns when we go over there?"

"To shoot the zombies? I think they may have specially-trained people to do that."

"I mean to protect ourselves," said Martin, knowing that Tom was just being difficult.

"It might be worth getting one," said Tom. "Although the security people might not let us take them on the plane."

"Good point. So, what should we do?"

"You could always go out for a walk once we've settled into the hotel. There must be a dodgy part of the city where some guy on a street corner will sell you one," suggested Tom

"Maybe," said Martin, sounding uncertain. "I'll speak to the hotel receptionists when we get there and see if they know anyone who can help us out."

"Good idea," said Tom. "See you tomorrow."

Tom finished his pizza wondering if Martin had regressed back to the time he'd bought his first car or had just been messing with him. Most of the time people thought Martin was messing with them because they didn't think anyone could be that dim but Tom had known him a long time and could confirm to anyone who asked that yes, he absolutely could be that dim.

After getting another beer from the kitchen Tom carried on with his evening. There was no dog-walking on the agenda tonight so he started sorting his clothes and toiletries out. Although he didn't really give a crap about anything or anyone outside his own sphere of influence, he prided himself on being well-prepared and wanted to impress the people in Atlanta - both at work and during his free time.

As a teenager, Tom had recognised that boyish good looks, a winning smile and a charming personality weren't going to get him very far in life - especially as he didn't have any of those things. Not only did he recognise the lack of these things in himself, his parents, teachers and friends had recognised the lack of them too and reminded him on a painfully regular basis.

Instead of breezing his way through life with a smile that unlocked doors, Tom realised that study, preparation and hard work were the only things that would help. He consequently spent a lot of time outside work researching different things - some related to work and some not - to give him an edge and help him keep up with the hand-shakers and the arse-lickers that seemed to blight large parts of the corporate world he'd chosen to make his living in.

Once he had an idea of what he needed to pack for his upcoming trip he settled in front of his laptop and researched the history and culture of Atlanta, the layout of the city, its districts, the tourist attractions (surely they wouldn't be working all the time) and - most importantly - the best restaurants and bars.

As he scoured the various travel resources available on the internet, Tom learned that the city had been founded in 1836 when the state of Georgia had decided to use Atlanta as the railway terminus for a line being built to the Midwest - wherever that was.

He looked at an online map and found it was located in what most normal countries would call the North Central, although closer inspection did highlight a few states that could (with some degree of poetic license) be said to be right in the middle of the country. Of these, only two of them could reasonably be considered part of the 'west' - if you were a blind man with a broken compass that had also had the letters 'N', 'S', 'E', and 'W' rubbed off.

Putting aside his own ideas of how the various geographical regions of the United States should be divided up and what they should be called, he delved into the history of the city and then the state of Georgia.

He was immediately surprised to learn it was the state capital - don't American states usually choose somewhere totally random to fool people competing in trivia quizzes?

He had lost count of the number of times people he knew had thought Los Angeles, Dallas, Miami, Chicago and Michigan were US state capitals. This had never made any sense to Tom or to anyone who had ever given one of those answers in a trivia quiz instead of Sacramento, Austin, Tallahassee, Springfield or Lansing. Although to be fair, the UK was much the same with its county towns.

Tom lived just outside Brighton, which was by far the largest and coolest city in East Sussex but not the county town. That honour belonged to Lewes, a small town situated a few miles to the north-east. In fact, Brighton had only been made a city in 2001 after many years of lobbying the Queen; and even then they had to form a tag team alliance with neighbouring Hove - or 'Hove, actually' as the locals called it whenever anyone asked them if they lived in Brighton.

Searching further on the internet, Tom discovered that Atlanta had been a major distribution hub for the 'South' in the American civil war, the birthplace of Dr Martin Luther King Jr. and the home of the civil rights movement. He also learned that it was the world headquarters of Coca-Cola and the Olympic Games had been held there in 1996. The city also counted CNN as one of its major corporations.

Finally, he found out that Atlanta was the home of the largest aquarium in the United States and while this was not perhaps the most earth-shattering fact he'd discovered, he was a big fan of aquariums so this was the cherry on the top as far as he was concerned. It sounded like a great city and Tom immediately knew it would be a place he'd enjoy visiting, providing they didn't want him to do too much actual work while he was there. That would be a downer.

Chapter 9

Karen looked at the clock and saw it was nearly 5pm which meant it was officially quitting time so she started to shut down her computer and think about heading home. She enjoyed her job but wasn't yet convinced that this random British company had what it took to survive in retail America.

The first worry she had was the quality of the garments they were selling. As far as she could tell, there were two factories - one in Ho Chi Minh City and one in Hanoi - with all garments for the US operation coming from the Hanoi factory while the UK received garments from both, although primarily the one in Ho Chi Minh City. This might explain why the UK office didn't get as many complaints as they did and why the Customer Services department in Atlanta was the fastest-growing part of the company.

When Karen had started at the company the conversion of the warehouse was being finished and the stock had just begun to arrive. Most of it was green and brown and everybody there had laughed at it so it wasn't a big surprise that even the thieves who had broken in had left far more than they'd stolen.

"Who the actual fuck is going to buy any of this shit," she'd said to her co-workers on her second day in the job and was greeted with murmurs of thoughtful agreement from the older staff and raucous laughter from the ones closer to her age.

"I'd rather get wet than wear any of this," said Delores, whose own lack of fashion taste was proven every day by the appearance of a purple and mustard patterned jacket wrapped around her as she walked through the office door.

Fortunately for Karen and her co-workers (although maybe not for the customers) the clothing did sell - and in sufficient numbers to keep them all employed. Returns had become a problem, however, and it seemed that a lot of people had rushed to buy them in the first three months but soon realised they weren't of good quality and returned them to get their money back.

I wish I could get my money back from doing this job every day, Karen thought as she packed her laptop into her bag. There was only one good thing about this job and that was that it paid the bills; well, it had so far but what would happen now her sister Wendy had moved her lazy ass in was anybody's guess. Although they hadn't made her move into Johnny Pervert's old office when he was fired so that was probably a positive thing too.

No-one had wanted his old office even though it had been cleaned - hopefully the new IT director would get it and nobody would tell him what had happened in there. Every-one knew Johnny had been a big fan of Louis Armstrong and Duke Ellington so it had now become known as The House of Jizz. It gave Karen the willies just thinking about it as she walked past.

***

Outside the building, she got into her car and began her 20-minute drive home north on the I-75 towards Cumberland where she had (until last week) enjoyed living alone. Her normally pristine house had been her sanctuary and her safe place until her sister moved in with her four stupid cats. Karen's small, three-bedroomed home was now a mess as the two of them had struggled to combine two lots of furniture into one space and she didn't even want to consider what state it would be in when she got home this evening. She thought about going for a drive just to delay getting home. Possibly to Mexico.

As Karen got closer to home, she began to think of the events of the last couple of days. First the data breach and then the knowledge that head office was sending a team of people over to fix it. She didn't really care about the breach because it wasn't her fault; all she wanted was for people to continue buying their clothing so she'd still be em-ployed and could pay her bills. It was none of her business if a single mother from Des Moines was buying a suspiciously high number of cucumbers. Although she'd rather not know what she did with them.

Karen was more focused on the impending visit from Tom and the others (whoever they were) at the end of the week. After spending several weeks talking and laughing they'd got on really well and Karen was excited to see what he and the rest of them were like. She wondered if he would be wearing a three-piece pinstripe with a bowler hat and carrying a briefcase and umbrella. He had to be better than the previous person they'd sent over who'd only lasted two days.

As Karen pulled up outside her house and got out of the car everything seemed normal. There were no obvious signs of damage and no flames coming from anywhere so she braced herself and went in.

"Hey sis!" said Wendy as she heard the door open. "Good day?"

"Hi Wendy. Not bad, thanks."

"Good. You'll be pleased to know that me and the girls have finally settled in and unpacked all of our stuff," said Wendy, walking over to give her older sister a hug.

"The girls?" asked Karen.

"My cats. I've always called them my girls," explained Wendy.

"But one of them is a boy," said Karen, looking at Wendy like a mother who had just been told her 15 year-old child had scored the lowest ever mark on a school test and was now being sent back a few years.

"Well, technically that may be true," Wendy laughed. "But I used to have three girl cats and I can't stop calling them my girls just because one of them is a boy."

"But they're not all girls," complained Karen. "You can't call them girls if they ain't all girls. That's just wrong."

"They're my cats - I'll call them whatever I want," said Wendy and went into the kitchen.

"Well you're my sister so that means I can call you a dumbass."

"I love you too sis!"

Karen stared at the space that Wendy had just vacated. This was going to be a long...she stopped herself. How long was Wendy planning on staying? She'd arrived less than a week ago and already the whole place was chaotic with four cats, noise (why couldn't she ever stop singing?!) and crap on just about every free surface in each room.

If things didn't improve Karen would soon be looking online for a solution. She wasn't sure if she should be looking for a rent-free apartment for Wendy, a pair of noise-cancelling headphones for herself or an unemployed former Mafia hitman to provide a more permanent solution. Each of these options had distinct benefits and she'd favoured each of them at different times over the last few days, although one of them was now in her head far more often than the other two.

Karen sighed as Wendy came back from the kitchen. Life wasn't like those movies from the 1940s where if you needed someone whacked you just went into a bar with an envelope of cash and found someone to do it. These days there were just far too many rules - not just against murdering someone which, to be fair, had always been frowned upon - but also the health and safety of any potential assassin she hired. The way the country was going with all of these new rules designed to protect employees she'd probably need to provide healthcare and dental coverage before anyone would even think about taking the job on. It was just too much hassle trying to get rid of Wendy so she wearily resigned herself to her current fate.

"I made you some coffee," said Wendy.

"Thanks," said Karen, taking a mug from Wendy that she didn't recognise. "Are these mugs new? What happened to my green ones?"

"Yes, I got them yesterday. I have a phobia about the colour green so I can't use your mugs. These are mine but you can use them while I'm here."

"You have a phobia about a colour?!"

"Sure. I got drunk one night a couple of months back and passed out in a park. When I woke up there was grass everywhere and I freaked out. I didn't know where I was and my therapist thinks that's where I got the phobia from. There was literally green everywhere."

"Your therapist must be a rich man by now," said Karen. "You spend more time on his couch than you do anywhere else."

"I can't help having a few phobias. I think I may have been dropped on my head as a baby."

"That would explain a lot of things, Wendy," laughed Karen, almost spilling her coffee as she went to put it down on the table beside her. "So how do you go out anywhere?"

"I don't have a problem with going out."

"But what about when there's trees and grass and shit? Doesn't that mess with your head?"

"I'm okay outside if the trees and grass stay away from me. It's just when there's something green right in my face that I have a problem."

"You're weird," said Karen.

"Thanks sis! Anyway, I heard there's a new phobia workshop starting up this week. They meet on Tuesdays and Fridays so I'm going to go along so I can talk about my shit with people that suffer with the same things; they'll probably be more sympathetic than some people I know," said Wendy, looking straight at her sister.

"Hopefully that will help. Which day are you going?"

"I'm going to go both days. I've got quite a lot of phobias so I don't think we'll have time to cover them all in just one session - especially if I have to sit and listen to everybody else's crap too."

"That's very public-spirited of you," said Karen. "Where is it?"

"Just round the corner near the Braves' stadium," said Wendy. "I'm super excited to meet up with some like-minded people for a change."

"You mean other weirdos like you?! laughed Karen.

"Exactly!" said Wendy triumphantly.

"It sounds good Wendy. When you've done that maybe you can start looking for a new job and a place to live too."

"I can only focus properly on one thing at a time," said Wendy. "You know I have a phobia of multi-tasking," she added as she left the room and went upstairs, leaving four pairs of hungry eyes looking at Karen from the sofa.

"Have you got a phobia about feeding your cats too?" Karen shouted up at Wendy but a sudden attack of selective hearing had kicked in so she couldn't hear her. Karen sighed and went into the kitchen to feed them - as she had every evening since Wendy had moved in.

Once Karen had fed all of Wendy's cats, she began fixing something for herself and Wendy, who was fast becoming the most difficult person to feed in the entire world. Karen had a very simple diet and generally ate fried chicken, gumbo, jambalaya, pizza, pasta, fish, Chinese food and burgers. Although she ate a lot of fruit and vegetables, she was basically a carnivore who also had a love of dairy products.

Karen had known about Wendy's veganism for a long time but until she moved in a few days ago had not really considered the details of it and just assumed that a selection of vegetables and fruit would be sufficient and that Wendy would cook for herself. For the first few days, Karen had been out with friends at meal times so tonight was the first time she was cooking for her sister and she chose a vegan-friendly meal with plenty of vegetables and a vegan-friendly spicy sauce. This would be simple enough, or so she'd assumed.

Wendy came into the kitchen, saw what Karen was cooking and stopped her in mid-flow.

"You do know I have a phobia of the colour green don't you?" Wendy said.

"What? I thought that was just coffee mugs. How the hell are you supposed to eat vegan food if you don't like anything green?"

"It's not easy," Wendy admitted.

"So, what do you eat?"

"Tomatoes, mostly. And corn."

"What about nuts?" asked Karen.

"I have a nut allergy so that rules them out."

Karen looked Wendy up and down. For the first time in a while they were in close proximity and Wendy was wearing one of her trademark baggy t-shirts and some skinny jeans. Karen noticed how thin she was and the baggy t-shirt didn't help.

"How do you eat and maintain your strength?" she asked.

"It's quite difficult, but it means I can get into the clothes I wore in high school, so there's that."

"But that shit went out of fashion ten years ago."

"Style is always in fashion, sis, and I'm the most stylish person I know," Wendy boasted.

"You clearly don't know that many stylish people then," laughed Karen as she opened the kitchen door to let one of Wendy's cats out.

Wendy went to close the door after the cat had left but as she did so a gust of wind blew in and knocked her off balance.

"Oh man! What's wrong with you Wendy?!" said Karen in a raised voice.

"It's this baggy t-shirt - it got caught in the wind and nearly knocked me over."

"Does this happen a lot?" asked Karen.

"More often than I'd like," said Wendy.

Karen turned back to where the food was being prepared and sighed. This was going to be an even longer week...month? year? than she'd first thought.

"Let me cook something tonight," Wendy said brightly. "I can show you how it's done so it'll be easier for you in the future."

"The future? Just how long are you planning to keep your lazy ass here?" asked Karen.

"Just until my business gets up and running," said Wendy. "I'm going to start selling craft items online. You know...blankets, hats, scarves, feather ear-rings and all of that cool stuff. There's a big market for it out there."

"From who?" asked Karen. Her face was frozen in a mixture of surprise, horror and fear. Was her airheaded sister really thinking she could sell craft stuff on the internet and make enough money to pay rent somewhere?

"There's loads of weirdos out there if you know where to find them," said Wendy.

"I bet there are. And you'd certainly be the one to know where to find them."

Wendy ignored her sister and began to cook. To break the silence, she asked Karen about her day at work.

"Well, we had a data breach over the weekend and they're sending some Brits over to fix it for us. They think we can't clear up our own shit," said Karen.

"Can you clear up your own shit?"

"Well, no, we can't - but that ain't the point."

"When are they coming over?" asked Wendy, chopping up a selection of non-green vegetables and putting them into a wok with some oil.

"They're coming on Saturday but they won't start work until Monday morning. They've asked me to babysit their asses."

"That sounds nasty," said Wendy. "Is your friend Tom coming with them?"

"He's not my friend!" said Karen, a little more firmly than she'd meant too. She also felt a hot flush on her cheeks.

"I swear you're blushing behind me sis!" laughed Wendy, turning round.

"Oh, shut your mouth and cook those stupid tomatoes and shit," said Karen and walked out of the room.

"How long are they here for?"

"About two weeks," shouted Karen from the living room.

"Are you going out with them in the evenings?"

"What the hell is this? Jeopardy? Leave me alone and just focus on that pan of hot rabbit food you're making."

"Well don't bring any of them home. I have a phobia of foreigners," said Wendy.

"A what? You seem to have a phobia of just about every damned thing on this planet. How do you manage to get through your day?"

"With more difficulty than you'd think."

Wendy turned round and went back to stirring her pan of tomatoes, corn and whatever that purple vegetable was. She knew it had a name that didn't suit it and had even used the emoji of it on her phone - although she'd only used the emoji when she wanted to signify a penis and was hoping that it wasn't actually a penis in real life. That wouldn't sit well with her veganism.

Chapter 10

Brighton, UK

Tom arrived at work on Tuesday morning with a spring in his step, knowing that after today he only had three more days before they left for Atlanta. Going with Martin would be good and he had worked with Stuart before and knew he was cool - although he did have an unruly beard that seemed to take over more and more of his face each week. As far as he was aware, Bhavna did not have a beard and wasn't planning to grow one. He'd never worked with her but had heard she could be a little pedantic at times.

As Tom sat down at his desk with his first coffee of the day, Martin was even more cheerful than usual. Clearly the idea of being away from his family for a couple of weeks wasn't troubling him as much as it would some people.

"So, you two are off on a jolly to Atlanta then," said Sue, trying - and failing - to hide the jealousy in her voice.

"Yep! We're flying out on Saturday, although we're so awesome we'll probably have this whole thing wrapped up in a couple of days," Tom answered. "It's the dream team on tour!"

"Please try to remember that you're supposed to be doing some work while you're over there," said Katrina.

"Yes boss," said Martin as he and Tom both mockingly saluted Katrina.

"I'm not sure they're taking it very seriously," said Colin.

"Well, they should," said Katrina. "The eyes of the business will be on them."

"How come they get to have all the fun?" moaned Sue.

"They don't. The rest of us have a special treat lined up," said Katrina, now standing up so she could be seen more clearly across the monitors and fans that cluttered everyone's desks.

"What are we going to be missing out on?" asked Tom.

"There is a team-building event next week across the IT department," said Katrina.

"Phew! I'm glad we're missing that," said Tom. "We've dodged a bullet there. Maybe a whole hail of bullets."

"Why?" asked Colin. "I always think they're good fun because you get to bond more closely with your colleagues in a different environment. What's not to like about that?"

"They're not fun at all," said Tom. "Everyone hates them because they're stupid and they force you do stupid things you don't want to do with people you can't stand. It just puts everyone in a bad mood and makes them want to kill each other."

"I still like them."

"That might just be me then," said Tom.

As the oldest member of the team - and some would say the laziest - Colin enjoyed meetings, workshops, team-building events and anything that got him away from his desk and prevented him from doing any actual work. He was counting down his last few years to retirement and was effectively working at 75% capacity (or less). Most of the team saw him as an 'uncle' figure, only without the lewd comments and inappropriate touching at parties.

"We were hoping that you'd be our official photographer, Martin, but now you're going to Atlanta we'll need to find someone else," said Katrina.

"That's a shame. I would have enjoyed that," said Martin.

"Have you thought about Alan from the network team?" suggested Tom. "He's always taking pictures of people."

"He's no longer with us," said Sue.

"He died?!" asked Colin.

"No, he got arrested."

"What for?"

"For taking pictures of people without their knowledge or consent," Sue explained. "You must have seen it on the news a couple of weeks ago?"

"Was that the guy they called 'Upskirt Alan'? I didn't realise he was our Alan," said Tom. "The company kept that quiet."

"Well they would, wouldn't they?" said Katrina. "It's not good for our reputation."

"I guess not," said Tom. "So, he's not available for the team-building event then?"

"No, he isn't. But I'm sure they'll find someone else."

"What's the event this year?" asked Colin.

"It's a surprise at the moment - you'll all be told on the day," said Katrina. "But I'm reliably informed that it will be less terrible than last year."

"What happened last year?" asked Martin. "That must have been before I started."

"The first exercise was for everyone to pick three people at random and tell them something we liked about them and something we thought they could improve upon. They called it 'Good News, Bad News' or something like that," Tom began.

"Oh...that sounds like something that could easily go a bit wrong," said Martin.

"It went very wrong," Tom continued, warming to his tale. "Not everyone was as tactful as they could have been and after a few minutes there were arguments and tears."

"And a fight," added Sue. "George in the facilities team told Upskirt Alan that while his ability to keep the network up and running during bad weather was excellent, he wasn't quite so keen on him taking pictures of his wife under her desk each time Alan went up to the Finance department to fix her computer."

"What happened next?" asked Martin expectantly.

"Alan pushed him backwards and then George kicked him in the balls."

"Ouch," said Martin.

"They ended up rolling around on the floor trying to grab each other. It wasn't like one of those fights you often see in the movies where good, clean punches are traded - it was more like two blind men trying to swat an invisible bee," said Tom.

"Would it matter that the bee was invisible if the two men were blind?" Sue queried.

"I guess not, but you know what I mean."

"Most of the staff were left in tears or in shock so the event was curtailed," said Katrina, trying to bring an air of calm to what had suddenly become a very animated discussion.

"I'm sorry I missed that," said Martin, clearly disappointed.

"You also missed the one before," said Tom.

"What happened at that one?" asked Martin, perking up at the thought of another office brawl.

63

"I don't think we need to go into that one," said Katrina.

"Maybe not - but it would serve as an important lesson for Martin in case he was ever asked to organise a team-building event of his own," said Tom.

"I'm sure Martin won't ever organise a team-building event, but you may as well carry on; I know you'll only tell him outside work anyway."

"One of the exercises was a trust test - like when someone falls backwards and you're supposed to catch them."

"What do you mean you're 'supposed' to catch them?!" said Sue. "Surely, you definitely have to catch them?"

"I expect it depends on whether you like them or not," said Colin.

"Anyway - getting back to the subject - this was a food tasting test where people were paired up and one was blindfolded while the other put different foods in their mouth; the 'eater' had to guess what each of the foods were."

"Did someone bite the other person's finger off?" asked Martin, looking quite worried. "I don't think I would trust anyone enough to put my finger in their mouth."

"Not quite. One of the guys fed the Marketing Director's PA a peanut. Nobody knew she was allergic and she had an anaphylactic shock," said Tom.

"Shit," said Martin. "What happened?"

"An ambulance was called but she sadly died on the way to the hospital," said Katrina.

"Shit," Martin said again.

"But the rest of the day went well," said Sue, brightly. "Apart from her team being one person short for the rest of the activities. That did unbalance the events a bit and I felt sorry for them being one person down - especially when we were all told to build human pyramids to climb over a wall."

"That was tough to watch," said Tom. "They weren't the tallest team to begin with and watching them struggling to reach the top of the wall with one person less meant they had no chance."

"Didn't one of the guys try leaping up from the top of the pyramid and grab onto the top of the wall?" asked Sue.

"He tried, yes. That was the guy that fell and broke his arm, remember?" said Colin.

"Oh yes," said Sue with a chuckle. "It's all coming back to me now. I know there was someone who broke their arm at one of these events but couldn't remember who."

"That wasn't him," said Tom. "He only broke his wrist; it was the guy that he landed on who got the broken arm."

"You're right," said Colin. "Good times."

The rest of the team started teasing Colin about his age and poor memory. As with most office teams, the oldest man is usually the butt of the jokes about age and forgetfulness (until one of the younger ones needs some practical advice about home improvement or car maintenance) while the oldest woman is normally the shoulder to cry on if anyone has any personal problems they need to talk about. She also tends to make most of the tea.

***

Tom and Martin went off to get another coffee and when they returned to their desks the team had already settled down into the seemingly endless cycle of reading emails, replying to emails and putting PowerPoint presentations together to show how much progress they were making on each project. As they both sat down, Tom's phone rang and the display showed a familiar international number.

"Good morning, Tom speaking."

"Hey Tom. How are y'all doing today?"

"Hi Karen, I'm good thanks. How are you?"

"It'll be a hot one over here today; we've got 75 degrees already," she laughed. "I hope you boys can cope with this heat. Those folks at the local weather channel reckon it'll be in the high 80s every day next week."

"Wow! What's that on the real temperature scale?" asked Tom.

"I have no idea but it's going to be too damned hot for you pale-skinned Brits. The trees over here are going to start bribing the dogs soon."

Karen's laugh once again came straight down the phone, went in Tom's left ear, reverberated around his skull for a few seconds and then went out through his right ear so the rest of the team could enjoy it too. He changed the subject before they all started laughing at him again like they had yesterday.

"How's it working out with your sister?"

65

"It's not good. She's so messy and those damned cats of hers are just getting every-where," said Karen, now with a serious tone.

"How long will she be there?" asked Tom.

"I have no idea. She wants to make hats and scarves and shit and sell them on the internet to folks with more money than sense. A bit like our customers. Hey, maybe we can give her the data about our customers who like that kind of shit?!"

"I'm not sure we're allowed to but if that would help her get a job and leave you in peace I'll email her a copy of it today."

"That would really be appreciated because I don't think she'll ever move out."

"That's bad news. Can't she get a proper job?"

"I don't know. She's got so many phobias - she's even afraid of foreigners now," laughed Karen,

"Wow! We'll have to meet her and freak her out," said Tom.

"Oh man! I would love that so much...scare her stupid ass into getting herself a job and moving into her own place!" roared Karen down the phone, the laughter echoing across Tom's open-plan office, through the open windows and out into the busy streets of Brighton.

"It's a deal then. I'll wear a t-shirt with a picture of the Queen on it. Martin went to France once so he can wear a beret."

"You guys do that! She won't know what hit her. How can anyone have a fear of for-eigners? It ain't like we're living in some kind of bubble over here. I'm sure she's just making most of these phobias up," said Karen.

The conversation then moved to work matters, IT reports and how they were going to approach the problem next week. Tom told Karen it had already been decided that Martin would analyse the data that had been collected, Stuart and Bhavna would look at where it was stored and he would oversee everything and discuss the solution with senior managers in both offices. Once it was agreed, Stuart and Bhavna would take care of the re-programming and then Tom, Martin and Karen would re-analyse the data and ensure it was no longer capturing every aspect of their customers' lives - especially the more sordid aspects.

"That seems like a good plan," said Karen. "Although I don't see too much work with your name against it."

"I've got to design the solution, discuss it with the directors, make sure everything works properly and then test it. That's a big responsibility."

"Hmmm," said Karen, not entirely convinced. "What about your day job over there? Who is going to cover that?"

"I don't do much over here so I'm sure it'll be fine," said Tom.

Katrina and Sue both looked up, which then made Colin look up too. Martin was lost in a world of musical love stories and women wondering whose bed the boots of their menfolk had been under so he was oblivious to Tom's admission and the furrowed brows it had caused across the rest of the team.

"What I mean to say, Karen, is that I do a lot of highly-skilled and valuable work here but I'm so good at it that I make it look effortless. Most normal people could be forgiven for thinking that I don't do much," Tom added loudly.

"The rest of your team are looking at you aren't they?!"

"Yes," said Tom as the human-sized meerkats across from him lowered their heads and went back to their work and Karen's laughter came gushing down the phone line once again.

"One good thing has come out of this though," Tom continued. "We don't have to go on a shitty corporate team-building event they've got planned while we're away."

"Oh man! You have those things there too? Those things are crazy bad!"

"I know! That's what I've been telling everyone here," agreed Tom.

"We had one at my old company once," said Karen. "We all had to go out in the woods in teams of ten with just a map, a compass and a few crappy flashlights. They took our cell-phones from us so we couldn't use GPS because they said it would be good for us to experience what things were like in the 'old days' before technology got to where it is now."

"Ouch," said Tom.

"I know, right? Each team was dropped off in a different spot and had to find their way back to a hunting lodge where we were staying overnight."

"That sounds both fun and terrifying," said Tom.

"It sure does. There were six teams and each team was abandoned five miles in a straight line away from the lodge. It was 2pm and they told us we should be back by 5pm at the latest."

"What happened?" asked Tom, knowing that Martin would love to hear this too.

"Well, the fools just left us to it and everyone in our team started arguing about which way we should go. One of the managers said he would take charge, took the map, picked a random direction and walked off."

"What did the rest of you do?" asked Tom.

"We couldn't do anything without a map so we just trudged along behind his dumb ass until we reached a small river that he couldn't find anywhere on the map."

"You'd gone off course?" Tom was loving this and couldn't wait to tell Martin and the rest of the team - especially Colin who really disliked the countryside. Hopefully the team-building event next week would be outdoors and Colin would hate it.

"Hell yeah; we ended up finding a road and walking along it until we eventually found a gas station and used their phone to call a bunch of taxis to take us back to the lodge."

"That sounds terrible," said Tom, not being able to disguise the excitement in his voice.

"I know, right!" Karen laughed. "We got back to the lodge well after five o'clock and most of the other teams were getting ready for dinner."

"Were you the last team back?"

"No we weren't. One of the teams came in about 8:30pm," said Karen. "The worst thing was there were only nine of them when they returned. They'd lost Gerry, one of their sales guys."

"They lost him?"

"Yeah. That's why they were so late back. They'd been wandering around the forest for hours and when they finally saw the lights of the lodge they did a group hug out of relief and noticed he wasn't with them. So, they re-traced their tracks a bit to look for him but it then started to rain and they were worried about getting lost again so they gave up."

"What did the organisers say?"

"Nothing. The group didn't tell them at first because they were cold and wet and just wanted to be somewhere dry with a beer and some food. Also, nobody really liked Gerry so they didn't want to have to go out looking for him in the dark."

"I guess they mentioned it eventually?" asked Tom.

"Yeah. When they got their participation trophies the Sales Director asked where Gerry was and it came out that he'd been lost for a few hours so they called the Forest Service to send some guys out to look for him."

"That's good news, at least. So how did Gerry take it all?"

"We don't know," said Karen. They never found him."

"Fuck! What did the company do?"

"They advertised his job the next day."

"Really?"

"Yeah, there was a big sales convention coming up the following week and they needed a full team."

"Poor Gerry," said Tom.

"Poor Sales," said Karen. "The guy they hired to replace him was a total loser and they had to fire him and hire someone else a few weeks later."

At the end of the call Tom put down the phone and looked across the desk at Katrina, Sue and Colin. They had all been following his half of the conversation with interest and were desperate to hear the other half so Tom told them and was met with three horrified faces. Martin was still listening to women singing about suds in buckets and promising to always love someone so Tom nudged him.

"What?" said Martin.

"I've just been talking to Karen about team-building events. You're going to love hearing about the one she went to. It's brilliant!" said Tom as he re-told Karen's story to them all.

"That's hilarious!" said Martin once Tom had finished.

"I think it's more tragic than hilarious, to be honest," added Katrina. "Don't forget that."

"Of course; it's definitely tragic. But it's hilarious too. Let's go on the pier and get some lunch," said Tom to Martin.

The two of them got up to go for lunch while the rest of the team carried on with their work.

"That was a tragic story," said Katrina.

"Very sad," said Sue. "Poor Gerry."

"Definitely," said Colin looking to his right where he could see both Katrina's and Sue's shoulders shaking as they tried to contain their laughter.

Chapter 11

Atlanta, USA

After chatting with Tom, Karen called her sister Wendy to check if she was still going to the new phobia workshop. Wendy had a habit of saying she would do something or go somewhere and then not following through so Karen took it upon herself to give her a kick sometimes.

"Hi sis! Are you checking up on me?" asked Wendy breezily.

"Hell yeah! I know what you're like for committing to stuff and not doing it."

"Don't worry, I'm just outside the building, although I'm worried I'll be the weirdest one there."

"Probably. Just don't let it bother you and you'll be fine. You could let the others speak up first and judge how weird your shit is compared to theirs and then just tell them the tame parts."

"Thanks Karen, I love how you're always looking out for me."

"Don't thank me. I know for sure you'll be the weirdest one there. I'm more worried about those other fools," Karen's laugh was equally loud when talking to family and friends as it was at work and Wendy had learned to hold the phone away from her ear whenever she sensed it coming.

"I'll talk to you later."

"Okay. Good luck," said Karen and ended the call.

As Wendy walked towards the building, she saw a young blonde woman standing in front of the door staring at it. She was about Wendy's age but a good few inches taller than her.

"Excuse me," said Wendy. "I need to get in there."

"Me too!" said the tall blonde. "I'm Sadie. I'm here for the phobia workshop."

"Hi Sadie, it's nice to meet you. I'm Wendy and I'm here for the workshop too. Why aren't you going in?

"I have a phobia of opening doors," said Sadie.

"Okay. Let me get that for you," said Wendy with a smile and opened the door to allow them both to enter the building.

Once inside the door the two of them approached the registration desk and a surly octogenarian looked at them before pointing at a dilapidated book and a pen with a chewed end and gesturing for them to sign in.

"He seems nice," said Sadie as they walked into the main hall.

"I might ask him for his number later," laughed Wendy, instantly liking Sadie.

"You'll have to fight me for it!" said Sadie.

As the two entered they were greeted with a warm smile by Lloyd, the workshop organiser. He was a tall, broad, immaculately-dressed African-American man in his mid-sixties and shook each of their hands in turn.

"Good morning," he said. "Welcome to the first of our bi-weekly phobia workshops. Please help yourselves to some coffee, tea or water from the table at the back and then if you'd like to take a seat, we'll introduce ourselves once everyone has arrived."

Wendy and Sadie greeted Lloyd and then went to get some coffee. She liked Sadie but there was something different about her that she couldn't quite grasp. Sadie was certainly a lot taller than her - maybe approaching six feet - but there was something else as well. Wendy poured her coffee and went to sit down, thinking nothing further of it.

"Good morning to you all," Lloyd began, now standing opposite a semicircle of chairs where a total of five eager participants had seated themselves. "Thank you all for attending. My name is Lloyd and I will be your guide as we talk about our phobias, try to understand where they came from and support one another on our respective journeys."

Wendy looked at Sadie and the others as Lloyd's voice boomed out across the room.

"Let us begin by introducing ourselves and telling the group a little about our background and our phobias," Lloyd went on. "Let's start with you and work our way along the line," he said, pointing to a young man at the opposite end of the row from where Wendy and Sadie were sitting.

"Hi everyone. My name is Lucas."

"Hi Lucas," said Lloyd and the rest of the group in unison.

"Hi. Again. Well I'm 21 and I live with my parents but I have a phobia of authority," said Lucas. "I can't ever get a job because I get violent when people tell me what to do."

"Come now," said Lloyd, smiling in encouragement. "I just asked you to introduce yourself and you did. That could be seen as a form of authority by some."

"I know. I'm thinking of punching you in the throat."

Lloyd was taken aback while the others looked shocked and Wendy spat some of her coffee out on the floor in front of her.

"So why didn't you act on your impulse, Lucas?" asked Lloyd, regaining his composure but taking a slight step backwards in case Lucas attacked him.

"Well, I'm afraid of physical contact too," added Lucas. "That's another reason why I can't ever get a job because if I went to an interview the hiring manager would want to shake hands with me and I wouldn't be able to do it."

"I see," said Lloyd, relieved that the threat of physical violence appeared to have now passed, although theoretically there was nothing to stop Lucas throwing a chair at him. Lloyd made a mental note to move back another few steps before he spoke to Lucas again and addressed the young woman sitting next to him.

"My name is Alisha and I have two phobias; one of them is clowns and the other is birthday parties where there may be clowns in attendance."

"Hi Alisha," said everybody.

"Welcome, Alisha. Are you sure that's not just one phobia?" asked Lloyd.

"No, it's definitely two. I fear clowns and I also fear parties that may have clowns there, like a children's birthday party. They always have clowns."

"What about parties where there are no clowns?" asked Lloyd.

"I don't know. I never go to any parties just in case there are clowns there."

Lloyd was struggling to fully see what Alisha meant but thanked her and moved along to the next member of the group.

"Hi everyone, I'm Dave and I have a phobia of water...as well as spiders, snakes, insects, fish, birds, wild animals, pets and zoos."

"Hi Dave," said the group.

"Welcome Dave. It seems that you are afraid of all animals, fish, birds, insects and reptiles," said Lloyd.

"No," said Dave. "I like dolphins."

"Anything else?" asked Lloyd.

"No. Just dolphins," said Dave.

"Thank you, Dave. Moving on to these two young ladies at the end," said Lloyd.

"I also have a fear of heights so I live in my parents' basement. They keep asking me to move into the main house but I prefer things on ground level or underground."

"Thank you again, Dave. Ladies, please would you now share your phobias with us."

Sadie was next to speak and from what Wendy had already heard she was hoping Sadie would have more than one phobia or she would be embarrassed when it came to her turn. Wendy had been worried about being the weirdest one there and so far, it was proving to be true. While the others were sharing just one or two phobias Wendy's mind was busy organising a whole list.

"Hi there everyone - I'm Sadie! It's great to know y'all," she began.

"Hi Sadie," said the group, growing less enthusiastic with each introduction.

"What can I tell you about myself?! I am 29 years old and I am currently couch-surfing at some of my friends' houses. I used to be Steve and drive a truck but then I had an operation and now I'm Sadie. I work as a hooker offering comfort and support to Atlanta's poor and homeless and I have a phobia of opening doors - you just never know what's on the other side. I also have a phobia of television and I don't like boats or handcuffs."

Lloyd looked aghast. They seemed to be getting worse as he moved from left to right along the line. He briefly looked at the other members of the group and they were all equally shocked, except for the mixed-race woman who had come in with Sadie. It was possible they were friends - although she seemed to look more relieved than anything else. Did that mean she was almost as bad? Lloyd hoped not.

"Welcome Sadie. You seem to have led a very interesting life," said Lloyd as diplomatically as he could.

"Thank you Lloyd! It's certainly been a fun ride and I'm not just talking about sitting on top of a homeless man behind a dumpster on a cold winter's night," she said, with a level of vitality and enthusiasm normally only found in the very young. Or the very stupid.

"I'm sure it has. May I just clarify something?"

"Sure thing Lloyd."

"Did you mention that you used to be called Steve?"

"Yes. Before I got the operation," said Sadie. "I was a trucker but I never felt comfortable as a man so they just snipped it right off and now here I am!"

"Thank you Sadie. And now for our final friend," Lloyd said as he turned to Wendy.

"Hi Lloyd and hi everybody. I'm Wendy and it's great to be here," said Wendy, finally having an answer to the query she had earlier had about Sadie.

"Hi Wendy," mumbled the group, still in shock over Sadie's introductory revelations.

"So, what phobia do you have Wendy?" asked Lloyd.

"Well, I have more than one," said Wendy. "I have a phobia of talking to strangers on the phone and I recently lost my job because of it."

"That seems a little unfair," said Lloyd.

"It was but I was a receptionist at a museum and they said it was the main part of my job so if I didn't do it they'd have to fire me."

"I see," said Lloyd. "Please continue."

"I also have a phobia of foreigners, the colour green and multi-tasking. That last one also helped me get fired because I can't do two things at once," said Wendy. "I'm a vegan as well so maybe I have a phobia of meat and dairy products."

"Maybe I'm a vegan too because I don't like animals," said Dave.

"Maybe," said Wendy.

"I couldn't go without meat," said Sadie. "That would be no fun at all."

"I'm sure," said Lloyd.

"I do love a good steak," said Dave. "Fried chicken as well."

"You're probably not a vegan then," said Wendy.

Lloyd rolled his eyes and began to question some of his life choices. What had he done to deserve this? A neighbour had recently told him to join the local church to help fill his time now that he had retired. He could run workshops that would help people in the local community, she said. It would be fun, she said. Today was the first of Lloyd's workshops and so far it had been anything but fun.

As Lloyd contemplated the best way to kill his neighbour for suggesting this and put together a shortlist of remote locations where he could hide her body, Wendy started talking about her phobias again.

"I also have a fear of the moon," she said and then hesitated. "And a fear of children."

"You have a fear of children?" asked Dave. "Why?"

"They're too short," said Wendy. "It freaks me out the way they run around being all short and full of noise. They make more noise per inch than any other creature on earth. I don't mind them once they've grown up - it's just the little short bastards that mess with my head."

"I hate them too," said Sadie. "Also, the parents who think they're so perfect and encourage them to do stuff make me want to puke."

"Like what?" asked Dave.

"Well, you know how every time little Jenny or Johnny draws or paints some lame picture and the parents immediately put it up on the front of their refrigerator like it's some important work of art? That shit sucks," said Sadie.

"It really does," agreed Wendy. "That's why you don't see any parents with young kids working as art gallery curators."

"Why is that?" asked Lucas from the far end of the row.

"People with kids don't know shit about art or they wouldn't put all those crappy pictures up on their refrigerators. If they were in charge of displaying pictures in an art gallery what do you think they'd put up? It wouldn't be the Mona Lisa; it would be a stupid finger painting of a dog with three legs or a family where the father is twice as tall as everyone else and both parents have a penis. No offence, Sadie."

"None taken," said Sadie.

"Why do they always draw huge dicks on their parents?!" Wendy asked rhetorically, throwing her hands up in the air.

"Maybe their parents ARE huge dicks," laughed Dave.

"If these parents think their kids' shitty paintings are art then they probably are," said Wendy.

Lloyd stood motionless, staring into space while the conversation meandered from children's paintings to veganism and touching on just about everything else in between. He snapped out of his trance-like state with the mention of the moon. As a keen astronomer he was interested in what they might have to say on this subject.

"Why don't you like the moon, Wendy?" Alisha asked Wendy after she'd sensed a gap during her rant about children's paintings.

"For one thing it's too big. Why does it need to be that big? I'm worried it might fall on me one night but then it disappears and hides for a couple of weeks each month. That's some spooky shit going on there."

"I know what you mean!" Sadie agreed. "Sometimes when I'm with one of my clients under the overpass downtown it's all nice and dark and romantic and stuff but then suddenly that bitch is up there shining her light down on everything and the cops see me."

"That might be the clouds moving across it," said Alisha.

"The moon should either be there all the time or not be there at all," said Sadie. "Sometimes I'm trying to find a good spot for my client and then the moon comes out and shows a dead body right behind us. It's just creepy."

"So how many dead bodies have you seen?" asked Dave.

"More than I want to," said Sadie. "Working in the seedier parts of the city means I get to see a whole bunch of stuff that most folks don't."

"Is it dangerous?" asked Wendy.

"It can be but I can look after myself - as you'd expect."

"I bet," said Wendy.

"Although it's not all fun," she continued. "I get arrested quite a lot so I think that might be where my fear of handcuffs comes from. Or maybe it was that time two guys handcuffed me to a boat in San Diego and ran away with my purse. I was there all night until the police saw me the following morning and arrested me."

"What did they do?" asked Dave.

"Well, they released me from the handcuffs on the boat."

"That's good," said Dave.

"But then they arrested me and put me straight in some more handcuffs."

As the other group members listened to Sadie with a mixture of awe and horror, Wendy felt a pang of admiration for her. Not only had she had the courage to have gender realignment surgery but she also did a 'job' that she enjoyed - if you could call it a job. She had no problem with Sadie's profession but she seemed to mainly work for free which wasn't very profitable. Her life might be a mixture of couch-surfing and having sex with homeless bums but she clearly enjoyed it.

***

Lloyd walked across to the other side of the room and found himself a chair. He brought it back to where the group were still in an animated discussion about handcuffs and tried to bring the workshop back to some semblance of order. He started by delving into each person's phobias more thoroughly, although without any of the enthusiasm that he'd opened the session with. He just wanted to go home, sit on his porch and ask his wife Millicent to bring him a glass of sweet iced tea. How many sessions had he signed up to run? So far, one was proving too many. He'd have to find a way of getting out of them but first he needed to bring this one to a close so he got up.

"Thank you so much for your contributions today, everyone. I think we can all agree it has been most illuminating," he said. "I hope to see you all back here next Tuesday morning at the same time although I, for my sins, am running a second workshop on Friday mornings as well."

"I might come along to that one," said Wendy. "I have a few more things I need to talk about."

"That sounds fun!" said Sadie. "I'll join you. Anyone else?"

Lucas and Alisha both looked at the floor in front of them and said nothing but Dave mumbled that he might come along. Lloyd looked up at the ceiling, as if imploring something or someone to strike him down with a bolt of lightning. Or possibly strike the others down. Maybe they could strike his neighbour down too for suggesting he took these sessions in the first place.

"Good," Lloyd managed to say, although he'd sorely wanted to say 'fuck' instead. "I will see some of you again on Friday and the rest of you next Tuesday. But please do not feel obligated to come to these sessions when they no longer serve your needs."

While a mentally-beaten Lloyd was vainly trying to sow the seeds of future non-attendance in their minds, everybody else got up and headed towards the door to leave. Sadie reached the door first and stopped in her tracks, causing everyone else to bump into the back of her.

"Sorry," she said. "It's the door phobia thing again."

Wendy reached forward and opened the door so they could all leave and while Lucas and Alisha nearly sprinted out of the open door, Dave hesitated.

"Hey Sadie, I'm sure I recognise you from somewhere," he began.

"That old line!" said Sadie. "It never worked for me as a man and it's never worked on me as a woman," she laughed.

"I've been arrested a few times too; I wonder if I've seen you at one of the local police stations," said Dave, undaunted.

"Maybe," said Sadie. "They usually take me to Zone 5 or CNN."

"I'm usually in Zone 5 or Fulton County. The guys at Zone 5 are pretty cool."

"Why do you get arrested?" asked Wendy. This was turning out to be a great day and she'd finally met some people who were weirder than her. Well, almost as weird as her.

"I get drunk a lot when I go out and me and my buddies can get a bit boisterous sometimes."

"Do you all get arrested?" asked Sadie.

"No, it's just me usually."

"Why?"

"Well they usually run off as soon as any trouble starts but I just carry on drinking so I'm the only one that gets caught. Also, they've all got responsible jobs so they can't get a police record or they'll get fired," said Dave.

"What do you do?" asked Wendy.

"Mainly odd jobs here and there. I just started as a swimming instructor."

"Didn't you say you had a phobia of water?" asked Sadie.

"Yeah...I can't swim either. So far I'm just winging it from the side of the pool."

"How's that working out?"

"It's going well so far. For the first three lessons I just put all the kids on chairs and made them wave their arms about a bit and shake their legs. It might get tougher when they want to get in the pool though."

"That doesn't sound like the best job you could do," said Wendy.

"No - but it pays ten bucks per kid and it's not the worst one I've had. Last year I tried out as a stuntman for a local production company who were producing a movie about zombies. It was a spin-off from that TV show they filmed here."

"What happened?" asked Sadie.

"Well, their office was in a glass-fronted building near Centennial Park and I had to walk down a bunch of steps to get to the entrance. I was rushing because I was late and I tripped on the top step and fell all the way down, crashed into some tables and chairs outside the main doors and then went straight through their plate glass window."

"Oh no!" said Wendy. "What happened?"

"They gave me the job," said Dave, proudly. "But I couldn't start work because of my injuries. It was a real bummer."

Sadie and Wendy looked at one another not knowing whether to laugh or not. Dave sensed their dilemma and started laughing himself as a prompt for them to join in. The two women duly obliged and as the three of them left the building they swapped phone numbers and arranged to see each other again on Friday at the next workshop.

Wendy got in her car and drove back to Karen's house. It had been quite a morning so far and she couldn't wait to tell her sister about it. Karen would love the stories she'd just heard, although she'd be judgemental, of course. What was it with older sisters that made them like that, Wendy asked herself. At least she was there for her - and Karen's house was in a far better location than her apartment had been so she couldn't complain. She certainly couldn't complain as much as Karen did.

As Wendy pulled up outside Karen's house she looked forward to a couple of hours of peace before her sister got home and started bitching about some trivial thing or an-other. Wendy often wondered if she'd been on a course called 'How to Complain' and imagined all the attendees being given name badges on their first day with spaces for 'stars' like employees in fast food restaurants.

Wendy sat for a few seconds staring down the street and imagined Karen earning three stars on the first morning and then being asked to run the course from the second day. She chuckled to herself before getting out of her car and going into the house to reunite herself with her cats, hoping they hadn't pooped anywhere they shouldn't have done.

Chapter 12

Atlanta, USA

Sitting at her desk, Karen was bored. There was a lot of work to do but the last week had seen her sister move in (temporarily, she hoped) and a major IT breach at the company where she was the IT manager. Some security experts in the UK were investigating what had happened while the mothership - as they all called the UK office - were sending a team over to help them clear up the mess they were in.

She began to wonder how life had suddenly got so crazy. Just over a week ago everything had been fine and everything was moving along at a nice relaxing pace but now it was total chaos. She needed to clear her head and do what she always did when faced with a crisis - get back to nature. She promised herself a trip to her favourite hiking trail at nearby Stone Mountain Park this weekend and maybe she'd invite those Brits that were coming over too - well, one of them at least.

As she started to lose herself in thoughts of cable cars, views stretching for up to 60 miles and some fresh Georgia air, her phone rang. She jumped out of her daydream and saw the caller was the person she was most likely to invite for a hike.

"Hi Karen. It's me again," said Tom.

"Hey! How are y'all doing?"

"I'm good thanks; the company is making arrangements for our flights and stuff. We'll be staying in the downtown area of the city at a place called the Ocean Hotel."

"The Ocean Hotel? Man, there ain't no ocean within 200 miles of here!" laughed Karen. "Are you sure they're sending you to Atlanta and not Atlantic City?"

"I didn't think the Ocean Hotel sounded very likely," agreed Tom. "But I checked and it's not named after the ocean, it's named after the owner. Anyway, how's your day going so far?"

"It's all good here. I haven't heard of that hotel though, maybe it's just an old one and it's got a new name?"

"Maybe. How's life with your sister?"

"Don't ask. She's got so many phobias and weird hang-ups I'm thinking of kicking her ass to the kerb," said Karen. "She's at some kind of phobia workshop for weirdos today and she's worried she'll be the weirdest one there."

"And will she be?" asked Tom, knowing exactly what was coming next and moving the phone away from his ear in preparation.

"Hell yeah!" followed by Karen's trademark laugh.

"She sounds like a bit of a character with all her phobias and dietary issues," said Tom.

"Ain't that the truth!" said Karen, still laughing.

"How is the food part of it going? Do you have to cook at different times?"

"I've told her she needs to cook for herself from now on because she says she can't be in the kitchen when I'm cooking a steak or some fried chicken. She's been on this vegan diet for the last two months."

"How is that going?" asked Tom.

"She's lost 14 pounds so far - although most of it was personality."

Tom moved the phone quickly away from his ear again as Karen's laugh got louder, prompting the rest of the team to look up at him.

"You two should get a room," said Martin, able to hear the laughter between the songs he was listening to.

He'd just heard about a boy being told to check yes or no on a note at school and was now about to listen to the tale of a gambler's final words on a late-night train but the pause between the two had allowed him the benefit of hearing Karen's laugh. Martin was starting to wonder what he was letting himself in for on the trip to Atlanta. He just wanted to go over there, get the job done as quickly as possible, take a few photos of the city and then get back home to his family without any incidents or excitement. Tom had told him there was an American football museum there and as a big fan of the sport that was the only attraction he wanted to see.

Martin didn't really like excitement. He'd never been full of confidence and often made mistakes that resulted in people laughing at him - like buying a car for £2,000 when his cousin had only wanted £1,500 for it - so he kept to a small circle of friends and family. He liked his job, his family and his photography and that was about it; he'd never understood people who enjoyed jetting off all over the world visiting new places and trying new things. Martin preferred routine and liked his family to be around him whenever he went anywhere new - although after a few up and down weeks at home with

Irma he was now quite excited to get away. He was also glad he'd have his best friend with him.

***

Tom and Karen ended their conversation and the UK project team then went into another of their weekly meetings. Karen put the phone down to get on with her day but first decided to call her sister to find out how the workshop had been. Hopefully she would have met a millionaire who'd instantly fallen totally in love with her and invited her to move in with him that day, although knowing Wendy it was more likely she'd meet a couple of unhinged drifters and bring them back home with her. The drifters would probably both have cats as well.

"Hey sis!" said Wendy as she answered her phone.

"Hi Wendy, how did your meeting go?" asked Karen.

"It was great," said Wendy. "I met some interesting people there and I wasn't the weirdest one."

"Really?"

"Well I'm sure I have the most phobias..."

"I knew it!"

"...but there were a couple of people there who are both as quirky as me so that was pretty cool," said Wendy.

"That is cool," echoed Karen, somewhat dubious. "Are you sure they're as messed up as you?"

"I prefer the term 'quirky' but yes - although in different ways. One guy keeps getting arrested for being drunk and boisterous and is literally afraid of every animal, bird and fish in the world apart from dolphins. He's quite cute actually."

"He's afraid of every living thing on this planet apart from people?"

"Pretty much. He's also afraid of water."

"Does he ever take a bath?" asked Karen.

"I don't know. I haven't got close enough to smell him yet," said Wendy.

"Yet? Are you fixing to make a move on a guy who always gets arrested and never showers?"

"We'll see how it goes," said Wendy with a smile that Karen could almost hear over the phone.

"But he won't like your cats."

"That could be a problem, although we also met a hooker called Sadie who used to be a man called Steve. She keeps getting arrested as well and she's hilarious."

"I see what you mean about them all being as messed up as you."

"I'll tell you more when I get home - I have to go and do some stuff now," said Wendy. "I won't be back until late tonight - I'm going to see some friends."

"Okay, I'll catch you when I see you; I got some stuff to do here too."

"They want you to actually do some work?" asked Wendy.

"Yeah. If I didn't do it this whole damned place would fall apart," laughed Karen as she said goodbye and returned to her work, happy that Wendy was making some new friends who would embrace her weirdness.

The rest of the day dragged by and Karen had very little motivation to do any work. All of the excitement and stress of the week so far had started to take its toll and she was now feeling both mentally and physically tired. Having Wendy and her four dumb cats in the house didn't help either so she decided to leave work early today, go home, take a long hot bath and go to bed early with her favourite book and a large whiskey. She might even take the bottle up with her.

***

A few miles from where Karen worked, down in the Midtown part of Atlanta a man was enjoying his afternoon walk around Piedmont Park. He was comfortable in the heat and loved to be outside seeing people enjoy themselves in the afternoon sun. On one memorable occasion last week he'd stumbled across a young couple enjoying themselves (and one another) in some bushes near the tennis courts; they hadn't seen him but he'd certainly seen a lot of them.

Every day seemed to bring him a new and interesting experience and he was glad he'd decided to make Atlanta his home. It wasn't as humid as he was used to but the temperature at this time of year was perfect and the greenery reminded him of his former home. Piedmont Park was his favourite place in the city and walking around different sections of this 75-hectare green space with its lake and plentiful foliage was always the perfect end to the day.

Chapter 13

Brighton, UK

Tom arrived at his desk earlier than usual on Thursday morning as he had a lot to do before jetting off on his corporate jolly the day after tomorrow. The company had given the four of them the day off on Friday as compensation for losing a day of their weekend flying to Atlanta and while there was an expectation that they would use it to plan their approach, Tom was planning to go on the beach all day and Irma had a list of jobs around the house for Martin to do before he left.

Tom walked across the large open-plan room like a rock star, saying 'good morning' to his legion of fans who were clearly envious of his new-found status as International Troubleshooter and Fire Putter-Outer. When he returned in a couple of weeks he would probably need to update his business cards to reflect his new level of awesome-ness. He might also need security to keep his fans at a distance too, although walking through the office this morning it seemed like most people were ignoring him. They were clearly starstruck.

"Hello mate," said Martin as he reached his desk.

"Hi Martin; all ready to go on Saturday?"

"Yep! I'm looking forward to it. We're having an early party for Irma tomorrow because it's her birthday next week and I won't be here."

"Cool. Have you bought her a present?"

"I'll pick something nice up in Atlanta but for the moment I bought her a new iron," said Martin.

"A what?!" asked Sue.

"A new iron. She needs one with the amount of ironing she does. The boys have so many clothes these days she's always at is," said Martin.

"Do you think that's the most romantic present you could get?" asked Katrina.

"I'll get her something in Atlanta too. She's always drinking Coke so I could get her a t-shirt from the Coca-Cola museum."

"Why not buy her some nice things in Atlanta and then wait until you get back before you give her the iron? That way you could hide the iron among the good presents," Tom suggested.

"That wouldn't really work," said Martin. "It always takes her a few goes before she gets the hang of using anything new so I want her to practice on her own clothes before she irons any of mine. I'll have a lot of ironing when I come back so I want her to know what she's doing."

The team were stunned into silence. Martin was clearly living back in the 1950s but there was no point in arguing with him as his domestic arrangements were none of their business; even so, Katrina and Sue both made mental notes to call Irma with details of potential new husbands while he was away.

"I'll need your number, Tom," said Katrina. "Keith and Lisa have asked for daily progress reports so we need to keep in touch."

"Okay," said Tom. "Don't call me when we're out partying though!"

"Hopefully you won't be partying, you'll be working."

"Of course. What time will you be calling?" asked Tom.

"The directors want to meet with me every lunchtime so once I've seen them, I'll call you to give you any new instructions and get an update from your end. It'll probably be just as you start work each day, around 8:30am your time."

"Why aren't we using the office phones?"

"Let's get some coffee," said Katrina, picking up her cup and beckoning Tom to follow her to the kitchen.

"What's going on?" asked Tom when they were alone.

"Keith isn't sure where the problem is. The data breach is likely to have been instigated by a third party but it may also have been internal, in which case it could have come from our end or their end. While you're over there we need you to check if there is anything unusual with their set-up."

"In what way?" asked Tom.

"Stuart and Bhavna have been told to look for anything unusual in the system but Keith wants you to keep your eyes open with the staff and the office in general. Don't tell

87

Martin, Karen or anyone else because we don't know if the data has been leaked from an internal source."

"So, I'm like an undercover agent as well?!" asked Tom, excitedly but in a hushed tone.

"Something like that. Just be available between 8am and 9am each morning to let me know what's happening in that area. Anything else can be discussed normally during the day."

"Okay Katrina," said Tom. "You can rely on me."

"I hope so. This could really elevate your standing in the company if it works out. There are a couple of very high profile programmes of work coming up that need a Programme Manager to oversee them. Let's not get ahead of ourselves yet, but this could be a really great opportunity for you if you get it done."

Tom and Katrina went back to their desks and back to their individual routines of analysis, checking emails and attending meetings. There was a meeting scheduled with HR for Tom, Martin, Stuart and Bhavna that afternoon to finalise the travel and accommodation arrangements and to clarify the expenses policy. Until then Tom and Martin just busied themselves as usual, with Tom making witty comments (most of which were inappropriate for work) and Martin listening to his 'Country Legends' playlist.

Occasionally Tom glanced at Martin's phone to see what track was playing - especially when Martin was nodding along to the music. It seemed that he was currently listening to a song about a man who built a car by stealing parts from the factory he worked at. That would be much cheaper than buying it from the dealership (or your cousin) but trying to put it all together might be tricky.

Tom turned back to his screen and saw an email from Karen; she was asking for his phone number too so she could get in touch when they were in Atlanta and make arrangements for Monday morning. Tom emailed his number to her and smiled because two women had now asked for his phone number so far today; he was becoming quite the ladies' man and nobody had stepped in any dog shit either.

These two requests had brought the total number of women who had asked for his number in the last year to three - although one of those was a neighbour who wanted him to look after her rabbit 'Foofoo' while she went away for a long weekend. Hopefully neither of these two current women would call him in the middle of the night to ask him to check on their foofoo.

Tom's phone buzzed and he saw the familiar green notification icon from his messaging app. It was an American number that he didn't recognise:

"Hi Tom, just letting you have my number. I'm in a ton of meetings today and I know you're off tomorrow so have a great flight on Saturday and we'll catch up soon. Do you guys want to meet up for lunch on Sunday? Let me know! Karen."

Tom stared at the screen for a few moments and was about to reply but then thought of the others on the team. Would they want to go or not? It didn't matter - the week-ends were their own time and they didn't need to spend it together so he replied:

"Hi Karen, that would be great! I'll certainly be there and I'll ask the others today. I'll let you know when we get to our hotel on Saturday night and we can organise something then. See you soon x."

He pressed 'Send' and then saw what he'd done. He'd absent-mindedly put a kiss on the end of his message. That wasn't very professional. Oh crap.

Just over 4000 miles away across the Atlantic, Karen saw the message come through and was pleased that she'd get to meet Tom and the others informally before the work started; it would make things far easier on Monday if they could get straight on with what they were doing without wasting time going through a bunch of awkward introductions.

She put her phone down. Then she picked it up again and re-read the message. What was that at the end? Oh man! Was that a kiss? Surely not. It must have been a typo. Or maybe he put them on every message he sent. Or maybe...no, it wasn't that. Was it? She didn't know at the moment - but she did know that it would bounce around in her head for the rest of the day.

Chapter 14

Brighton, UK

After a day at leisure on the beach and a relatively early night yesterday, it was now a cool, clear and dark Saturday morning that greeted Tom as he went to pick Martin up and take them both to Heathrow Airport. When he arrived at Martin's house, he asked Martin to double check that he had his passport and everything else he needed before setting off.

"I'm not that dopey," said Martin.

"I just don't want us to forget anything," said Tom.

"I went to Florida last month without you fussing over me," said Martin, immediately regretting it.

"I remember that," said Tom. "Did you forget anything?"

"Irma," said Martin. "But it wasn't my fault. She told me to put the suitcases in the car while she put the boys in their booster seats. She then got in the car and I heard her shut the door. When I finished, I just got in the car and drove off without looking across at the passenger seat. How was I supposed to know she'd gone back in the house for something? It was dark and I was half-asleep."

"Just like this morning?"

"Yeah...a bit," said Martin.

Tom checked Martin had everything he needed; passport, laptop, voltage adapter, phone and wallet. If he was missing anything else and he would have to go to Walmart and buy it. Maybe he could get himself a gun there as well. Once they were satisfied that they both had everything, Martin said goodbye to Irma and got in the car for their journey to the airport.

"Hold on," said Martin as they got to the end of his road. "I've forgotten something."

"What?"

"My camera; I need it to take pictures of the city because I'm entering a competition at the local photography club."

After going back and collecting Martin's new camera, they were finally on the road and headed north to the airport.

"What time do we get there, mate?" asked Martin as they drove north up the M23, passing Gatwick Airport as they approached the M25 that would lead them towards Heathrow.

"About 5:30pm I think. Which will be 10:30pm our time."

"That will be time for bed then," said Martin.

"Well, not really," said Tom. "We'll probably get to the hotel around 7 o'clock then I'm planning on going out for a beer and a burger. We might as well make the most of our first weekend."

"I suppose so," said Martin, feeling slightly unsure. The last time he and Tom had been out things hadn't ended well and Martin's luck on holiday had never been good.

"Are you still thinking back to that night in London last year?" asked Tom.

"Yeah. I have a lasting souvenir of it."

"But you always said you wanted a tattoo," said Tom.

"Not on my arse. And not of a pink unicorn."

"It was the only colour the guy had. It was quite late and he'd run out of all the normal colours."

"That's because we went back to his house. He probably had loads at his studio."

"But his studio wasn't open. It was 2am; you can't expect him to be open at 2am. Everyone needs some time away from work."

"Why didn't we wait until morning?" asked Martin.

"Because you were insistent you wanted a tattoo and didn't want to wait."

"I was drunk," said Martin. "You should have stopped me."

"I was drunk as well though."

"So was the tattoo artist."

"Yes - it didn't really look too much like a prancing horse did it?" laughed Tom.

"No it didn't. I wanted a majestic prancing horse - just like the Ferrari logo but in bright red," said Martin. "Instead, I got a pink fucking unicorn!"

Tom laughed. He could see out of the corner of his eye that Martin didn't share his mirth but continued anyway. "Irma liked it though," he said.

"Yeah...she did, to be fair. Once she'd stopped laughing," admitted Martin.

"Well there you go then. No harm done."

"I suppose not. But I'm not getting any tattoos in Atlanta."

"You say that now..." said Tom, but Martin had turned his head towards the side window and was no longer listening.

Tom continued driving and turned onto the M25 which would take them the remaining 30 miles or so northwest to Heathrow. They had arranged to meet Stuart and Bhavna outside the terminal as those two both lived in a different part of Sussex. Also, Stuart's beard had a strange smell to it and Tom didn't want it in his car.

"What do you think of the others?" asked Martin.

"Stuart and Bhavna? They're alright. Bhavna knows her stuff and works all the hours she can which will take the load off us. Stuart is very tenacious so if there's a problem with some code he'll find it," said Tom.

"They certainly picked the 'Dream Team' for this trip," said Martin.

"I just hope we don't have to eat with them too often."

"Why?"

"Well, Stuart's beard traps bits of food that drop out of his mouth and I never have the heart to tell him," said Tom.

"Perhaps he's saving it for a mid-afternoon snack?"

"Maybe, but his beard is like the roof of a thatched cottage. There could be all sorts of small animals living in it. I'm sure I saw a tiny mouse come out of it, grab a crumb of mince pie and then scuttle back in again at the last Christmas party," said Tom.

"I'm sure he wouldn't have a mouse living in his beard," said Martin. "It would be difficult to sleep at night with all the scurrying that mice do."

"True. I don't know if he's married or not but I wouldn't think he'd be able to attract too many women with a family of mice living in his beard. Some people can be a bit fussy about having rodents in their bed. I guess that's the problem with having a beard that's bigger than your own face."

"What about Bhavna?"

"I don't think she has a beard. Certainly not one that's bigger than her own face."

"I meant what annoying habits does she have?"

"None that I can remember. She's quite uptight though - and I think she might slurp her soup."

"Have you seen her slurp her soup?" asked Martin.

"No. I just think it's the type of thing she'd probably do. She has the mouth for it."

"I know what you mean. Let's make sure we don't eat with them too much," Martin agreed.

"Well, we'll be eating with Karen tomorrow. She's invited us out for lunch."

"Really? That's good," said Martin. "Has she invited all of us?"

"What do you mean?"

"It's no secret you two get on well - you're always laughing on the phone. We just wondered if you were planning some 'alone time' together?"

"Who is 'we'?" asked Tom, turning his head to look at Martin, who had his trademark stupid grin on his face.

"The team. We've got a sweepstake going."

"A sweepstake?"

"Yeah. Katrina thinks you'll ask her out and fall flat on your face, Sue thinks you'll ask her out but she'll realise you're a dick and Colin thinks she'll realise you're a dick before you ask her out."

"Well thanks, that really makes me feel good," said Tom. "And what about you? What have you got your money on?"

"I think you'll have sex with her and then she'll hate herself forever and it will make things so awkward that the project will be ruined and we'll all get sent home early," said Martin. "I've got £10 riding on that one."

"Thanks for your support," said Tom, slightly hurt but also pleased that Martin thought he'd be having sex with Karen. It wasn't something he'd thought about himself but the idea was now in his head and he'd certainly think about it while he was on the plane.

"I just want to get back as soon as possible," Martin added.

"Why do you want to get back early? This trip will be great - even if you don't win your bet about me getting together with Karen."

"I just want to be back with Irma and the boys. Well, the boys mainly."

"You're just rubbish at being on holiday," said Tom.

"Probably. I don't like going away because I'm too accident-prone. I feel safer at home."

"Do you have accidents at home?"

"Yeah...but Irma has a first aid kit so she fixes me up and there's a hospital just across the road if I get any serious injuries."

"How often are you in the A&E department?"

"No more than once a month usually," said Martin.

"That's quite a lot."

"At least I don't have my own seat in the waiting room like you have in HR," said Martin.

"That's probably for the best though."

"Why?"

"You'd probably fall off it and injure yourself."

The first signpost for the airport came into view as the sun rose across west London. Tom followed the satnav directions, turning the volume up to drown out any more conversation from Martin and they were soon pulling into the pre-booked airport car park. Tom brought the car to a stop so they could get out and get their luggage out and opened the boot. He looked at his bright green suitcase. He then looked at Martin's bright green suitcase right next to it.

"Why have you got the same suitcase as me?" asked Tom. "We're going to look like a right pair of idiots walking through the airport with matching luggage."

"You told me it was good when you bought it last year."

"I know. But I didn't expect you to buy one exactly the same."

"Well I didn't expect to be going away with you," said Martin. "I've got a yellow ribbon on mine to identify it on the baggage claim though."

"So have I," said Tom.

They took their cases out without further comment and made their way towards the bus stop and the bus that would soon arrive to take them to Terminal 3 where Stuart and Bhavna would be waiting. They would then check in and go for some breakfast. Tom reminded himself to sit next to Stuart rather than opposite him so his eye wasn't drawn to the food dropping down into his beard that would later be eaten by the family of tiny mice that undoubtedly lived there and were about to go on their first foreign trip.

The arrival of the bus jolted Tom out of his thoughts. There were a handful of other passengers ahead of them in the queue but they all eventually got on for the ten-minute ride to the terminal. As they approached the building, Stuart and Bhavna were waiting and greeted them warmly.

"Hey guys! Great to see you. How are things?" said Stuart.

"Good morning to you both," added Bhavna. "I am very pleased that we are all together now as I was worried that one half of the team might be delayed. Not us, of course as we were very well-prepared and have been here for some time."

"We're good thanks. Let's rock and roll," said Martin, without any clear intention to rock or roll.

"Morning all," said Tom. "How long have you been here?"

"Two and a half hours," said Stuart despondently.

"It is far better to be two hours early than one minute late," argued Bhavna.

"Two and a half," said Stuart.

"You could have got here half an hour early," suggested Tom.

"That's what I said," said Stuart.

"I see you have matching cases," said Bhavna, changing the subject. "We didn't get the memo did we Stuart?"

"No. I'm glad about that; it would have been embarrassing," Stuart added as they headed inside to find the check-in desks.

"I told you," said Tom, glaring at Martin. "I think one of us should buy a new case; probably you, because I had mine first."

"You won't be able to until we have passed through security and by then it will be too late," said Bhavna unhelpfully.

"Let's just get this done and get some food," said Tom, heading towards the check-in.

After check-in and bag drop came the usual rigmarole of security where they all removed their belts, jackets and shoes to go through the scanner. Tom noticed an attractive young female security agent and deliberately left some coins in the front pocket of his jeans. Hopefully the machine would beep and she'd come over to frisk him.

Beep.

"Over here please sir," said the attractive young female security agent to Tom after the machine had sounded its warning.

"Certainly!" said Tom and stepped smartly over to where she was standing.

"It'll just be a minute," she said as she called her colleague Sergei over.

Sergei arrived and towered over Tom. He was well over 6 feet tall and was built like a tank that had just swallowed another tank. Tom looked up and gulped. Where was the young female agent he'd been hoping would pat him down?

Sergei picked up an electronic body scanner and moved it up and down Tom's arms, legs and torso as his female colleague did the same with a female traveller a few feet away. After a rigorous pat down of some body parts that Tom had been hoping the female agent would be patting down, Sergei satisfied himself that this traveller was more of an idiot than a terrorist and waved him through, noticing that all of the other young men in the queue were suddenly emptying their pockets of any change that was likely to set off the metal detectors.

"I'm glad that's over," said Tom as he joined the others.

"Did you deliberately make the machine beep so a pretty young girl would touch you up?" asked Bhavna with a grin.

"No," said Tom defensively.

"You should know that they have agents of different genders for that very reason," she replied.

The rest of the team laughed as they walked off to find a restaurant leaving Tom wondering if he should have worn a dress. That way he could have been frisked by the female security agent, although the downside was that anyone who had seen his and

Martin's matching luggage would have thought they were a couple. Tom shuddered and caught up with the others as they went into one of the restaurants for breakfast.

Having arrived last, the only seat left was opposite Stuart and Tom reluctantly sat down, noticing a wry smile on Martin's face who could also see Stuart head-on. Breakfast was every bit as bad as they had feared with at least four pieces of scrambled egg and a generous portion of toast crumbs finding their way into Stuart's beard. That should keep the mouse family going for a couple of days.

Finishing their breakfasts, they eventually left the restaurant and made their way to the departure gate where they sat and waited for their flight to be called.

"Here we go," said Martin. "I'm on the early plane to Georgia," he half said and half sang.

"That doesn't have quite the same ring as the midnight train," said Tom.

"Well, no," said Martin.

"It would be impossible to go there by train from here," said Bhavna.

"We know," said Tom, thinking to himself that Bhavna was going to be hard work on this trip if she took everything so literally. Maybe there was a way that she could be sent somewhere else instead - like the moon. She sucked all of the atmosphere out of a room whenever she started talking so she'd fit right in there.

The four of them got up, joined the queue and boarded their flight to Atlanta. As Tom settled himself into his seat and looked out of the window, he wondered what lay ahead. Did the rest of his team really have a sweepstake on what would happen between him and Karen? Did he really send that message with a kiss at the end? She hadn't replied. That was a bad sign - or maybe a good one. Either way, he hoped he hadn't upset her. Thoughts of the work ahead of them, how they would spend their free time in Atlanta and who would win the bet about him and Karen swirled round his mind as his eyes began to close and sleep overtook him.

In the next seat, Martin had already plugged his headphones into his music player and was also about to drift off to sleep listening to tales of Louisville sluggers and golden fiddles. Two rows in front, Bhavna had instructed Stuart to swap seats with her so she could have the aisle seat so he was unceremoniously moved to the middle seat.

Bhavna began talking about the job they needed to do in Atlanta in great detail so Stuart closed his eyes and pretended to be asleep. Soon he actually was asleep, leaving Bhavna talking to herself as the plane took off.

PART TWO

Chapter 15

Atlanta, USA

It had been an uneventful Saturday morning in the IT department of Classic Country Clothing (UK) Inc. in Atlanta and Karen had found very little to do with her time other than stare at her co-worker's ugly coat that was currently resting on the back of the chair next to her. If the weather improved in the afternoon Delores would often leave it there - she claimed to forget but Karen was sure it was done deliberately just to annoy her - and the next morning Delores would turn up wearing something almost as ugly and then have to take two jackets home. That served her right.

One of the many other things that annoyed Karen about her daily life was having to work every second Saturday to provide IT support to those customers that were dumb enough to use the company's app on their smartphones. It was well below her pay grade and experience level so most of the time she just told them to restart their phones and hope they didn't call back. This generally worked, although she always made sure one of her colleagues took the call if the customer came back.

Since the recent data capture incident, however, she was tempted to look up their names on her spreadsheet and ask them what they liked doing with bananas and honey - although after having seen some of the data she knew she wouldn't enjoy some of the answers.

As morning turned to afternoon, Karen realised she was bored; this was partly because there was little she could do until the UK team came over and sorted the data capture issues out and partly out of apprehension. She was expecting the team to arrive just as she was going home for the night and would give Tom and the others a couple of hours to get to their hotel and settle down before she messaged them about meeting up tomorrow lunchtime. They were staying downtown so she'd probably arrange to meet them at their hotel and they could find somewhere for lunch from there.

As 5pm got closer, the skeleton staff they employed on Saturdays started to go home so Karen packed up and left too. Why was she so nervous? She got in her car and selected a different route back to her house. For the first time since Wendy arrived, she was actually glad her sister was staying with her as it would give her someone to talk to this evening. It would take her mind off of...what? The message from Tom with the kiss at the end still played on her mind; they got on well but surely that was all it was. Wasn't it?

The journey home passed uneventfully but Karen barely remembered any of the drive. Her mind was somewhere else and she almost walked into Wendy as she went through her front door.

"Hey sis! Watch where you're going!" said Wendy. "You nearly knocked me over!"

"Sorry Wendy. I'm not looking where I'm going."

"Is that because your British guy is coming over to see you?" Wendy teased, making kissing noises to annoy her older sister just a little bit more.

"No!" said Karen, meaning yes.

"When are y'all meeting up?"

"I'm going downtown to meet them all for lunch tomorrow. There are four of them coming over to rake through all our shit so it's all strictly professional."

"Are you happy about that?"

"Hell no! If it's got to be done then it's got to be done but I wish they'd trusted us to fix it first rather than sending a bunch of Brits over to get all up in our business."

"I bet there's one of them who you'd love to be getting all up in your business," laughed Wendy as she picked up one of her cats and deposited it in the kitchen where its food was waiting.

"I don't know what you're talking about," said Karen, blushing slightly. "You know, sometimes I wonder if we came from the same mother - what with you being all flighty and shit and me being all sensible and mature."

"You mean boring?" asked Wendy, extending the word boring for a good three seconds.

"Whatever," said Karen. "Just hurry up and make your stupid rabbit food so I can get in there and cook a nice juicy steak."

Wendy was about to reply when Karen's phone rang. She noticed Karen's face light up as she looked at the screen. It was an expression she hadn't seen since they were teenagers and she'd caught her sneaking a boy into her room late one night while their parents were sleeping.

"Hey! How are y'all doing?" said Karen. "Did you have a good flight?"

"Hi Karen. Yes thanks - we got in a bit early and are now at the hotel," said Tom.

"What's your hotel like?" asked Karen.

"It's not the best. There's a car park outside with some big bins outside and a few homeless people sitting by them."

"Oh man!" Karen's booming laugh erupted across her living room, taking Wendy by surprise and scaring those cats that hadn't yet realised their food was waiting for them in the kitchen.

"Where is it?"

"I don't know but it's a couple of streets behind a big Ferris wheel."

"That's the Skyview. And we call them 'blocks' over here," said Karen. "Those bins you see are called dumpsters," she added, seeing Wendy pretending to kiss an imaginary person in front of her.

"One of them is on fire," said Tom.

"That sounds like some fancy ass hotel you've been given there. Don't worry about it; I know someone whose whole life is one big dumpster fire," laughed Karen, turning her head to look straight at Wendy like a velociraptor eyeing its prey.

"The inside of the hotel isn't great either and there are a lot of flies in the rooms."

"Ewww. That ain't good," said Karen. "It sounds like the company is sparing no expense with you guys."

"Yeah, it's a bit disappointing. Anyway, I have a question."

"Shoot," said Karen.

"We're all meant to be meeting up tomorrow but are you free tonight?" asked Tom. "The other three aren't exactly party animals and I'm going to struggle to get them to leave the hotel unless I pull the fire alarm or throw them out of their bedroom windows."

Karen paused for a second or two. She hadn't been expecting this but she had no plans for the evening and it would at least get the awkward introductions out of the way sooner rather than later so she gestured to Wendy to invite her along too.

"That'll be awesome sis!" said Wendy excitedly. "Do you want me to come?"

"Hey Tom, how do you feel about my dumbass sister coming down too?"

"Wendy? That'll be great! She does know we're foreigners doesn't she?"

"Yeah, I told her you're just like Americans but a lot quieter. Like a 'lite' version of a soda so she thinks she'll be able to cope."

"That sounds good," said Tom.

"We'll meet you at the Skyview Ferris wheel at eight and then grab some food somewhere," said Karen.

"Cool! I'll tell the others and we'll see you at eight!"

Karen looked at Wendy who was now dancing around the room with one of her cats singing a made-up song that seemed to only have one line - 'Karen's gonna get it tonight, oh yes she is, she's gonna get it real good.'

"Wendy?" said Karen.

"Yes sis?"

"Go fuck yourself," Karen told her and went upstairs to get ready. This wasn't how she thought her night would pan out when she'd left the office just over an hour ago but she was excited to meet the others - and at least it would be a night away from Wendy's damned cats.

"Why did you invite me along?" Wendy shouted up the stairs. "You know I have a phobia of foreigners."

"They used to own this country a couple of hundred years ago so just think of them as distant cousins."

"I can do that but I thought you'd want to go and meet Tom alone."

"If you think I'm going down there to meet these fools on my own you're dead wrong so just get your lazy ass ready."

***

Just over an hour later, the two warring sisters got out of Karen's car in downtown Atlanta and walked along the main road towards the Skyview where Tom and the others were supposed to be waiting, although when Karen and Wendy arrived, they were nowhere to be seen.

"So where are these damned fools at?" Karen said as they stood waiting and looking around.

"Maybe they have a phobia of being on time," suggested Wendy. "Do you know what they look like?"

"Yeah, Tom and I are connected on LinkedIn so I've seen his picture."

"Hey Karen!"

Karen and Wendy looked round to where the voice had come from and saw two excited people getting out of one of the cars on the Ferris wheel and heading towards them; they were followed by two other people who looked slightly unwell.

"Hey guys! How are y'all doing tonight?" said Karen warmly as the two groups approached each other.

"We're great! Well I am and so is Bhavna but Martin and Stuart didn't like the Ferris wheel," Tom laughed as he extended his hand towards her.

"What the fuck's that?" asked Karen, looking at Tom's hand and giving him a hug instead.

"Woah!" said Tom as they embraced, noticing Wendy had a grin on her face.

"That's how you greet people Southern-style," said Karen and started to laugh.

Everyone introduced themselves with hugs apart from Stuart whose face had turned green from a combination of jet lag, the Ferris wheel and Bhavna talking his ears off at 39,000 feet for most of their nine-hour flight. Karen then led them all down a side street towards a restaurant she and Wendy used to go to when they both worked in the downtown area a few years ago.

"What do you think of Atlanta so far?" asked Wendy.

"I feel sick," said Stuart.

"I took the time and trouble to read up on the city and familiarise myself with the layout and the history so there have been no surprises for me," said Bhavna.

"I want to visit the College Football Hall of Fame," said Martin. "I also need to buy my wife Irma a Coca-Cola t-shirt for her birthday."

"Is that her main gift?" asked Wendy.

"No, he bought her an iron before we came away," said Tom, laughing his head off. "How did she take it, Martin?"

"She wasn't impressed but it might grow on her," said Martin to raucous laughter. "Unfortunately, I'm not allowed to spend too much money without telling her what I'm spending it on."

"Why not?" Wendy asked.

"When we got married, she said we should each have a discretionary spend limit each month so we can buy things up to that limit without telling the other one what they are."

"That sounds fun! How much is the limit?"

"Her limit is £500."

"That could buy a lot more than an iron."

"That's her limit...my limit is £40."

"Oh man! You should have saved your allowance up for a few months because she's gonna ram that thing right up your ass when you get home," said Karen as her booming laugh filled the night air for six blocks in every direction.

The group reached the restaurant still laughing and were soon seated at a large round table in the window. The place had clearly seen better days but it had been a favourite of Karen's so Tom didn't question it. Also, Stuart had perked up a little and his beard seemed to have come back to life. Luckily for Tom he was sitting next to Stuart so he didn't have to see the beard while he ate, although being that close did mean that if there were any small creatures living in it they might take an interest in Tom's food too.

"Why don't we all tell everybody something random and embarrassing about ourselves," Wendy suggested after they'd all ordered.

"Hell no!" said Karen. "These good people don't want to know that shit about us."

"I don't mind," said Tom. "Although it might be more fun if we told the group something about somebody else."

"Now we're talking," said Karen.

"Oh shit," said Martin, knowing exactly what Tom's story would be about.

"Who agrees?" asked Wendy.

Tom and Karen said 'yes' but everyone else looked down at the table so they went with Wendy's original plan of saying something about themselves.

"That's a bit of a shame," said Tom, seeing the relief on Martin's face. "But never mind. I was once with someone who paid £2,000 for a £1,500 car!"

"Oh, fuck off!" said Martin as the table exploded into laughter.

"Oh man! You've got to tell us who this fool was," said Karen excitedly, already guessing his identity.

"It was me," admitted Martin. "It was years ago and it sort of slipped out while I was trying to buy a car from my cousin."

"What was the vehicle like?" asked Bhavna. "Were you ultimately pleased with its performance despite the actual price you paid being considerably higher than the price you needed to pay?"

"It was okay."

"He crashed it three times on the first day doing a two-mile drive," said Tom.

"Oh my! This is too funny," said Wendy, sitting next to Martin with tears streaming down her face. "You're a legend, Martin," she said and gave him a big hug.

"Thanks. At least I don't borrow my neighbour's dog to go to the park and pick up women."

"Who does that?!" screamed Karen

"Tom does," said Martin. "It doesn't work because any woman who's unlucky enough to be approached by him ends up with shit in her shoes because he doesn't clean up after his dog."

"It's not technically my dog. Or my shit."

More laughter erupted as the food arrived and the table then descended into relative quiet. As is usual when groups go out to eat, everyone started looking at everyone else's plates.

"What have you got there Wendy?" Tom asked.

"It's a vegan-friendly meal of tomatoes, corn and mushrooms," she said proudly.

"I told you Wendy's a vegan and it turns out that she has a phobia of the colour green so she can't eat like 90% of the vegetables in the world."

"I get by, sis," said Wendy.

"Only just. There ain't nothing of you. What do you weigh, about 30 pounds?"

"A bit more than that," Wendy said indignantly but with a laugh. "Maybe we should go back to telling each other something about ourselves rather than other people?"

"Okay. Well I am 32 and I'm single," said Tom, meeting Karen's eye opposite him and noticing her looking away quickly. "I have been in my current job for four years and outside work I love travelling and video games. I also watch a lot of sport on TV because I'm too lazy to play it."

"But you like walking your neighbour's dog?" said Wendy.

"Yeah, but the park is literally next door to his house," said Martin. "And that's only to pick up women and it doesn't work."

"I think we are getting a flavour of Tom now," said Bhavna. "I will go next. I am 29 years old and I am originally from India. I love computer programming and coding and I am a very hard worker."

"What do you do for fun?" asked Wendy.

"Like I said, I love computer programming and coding. I find it immensely fulfilling and love to code late into the night. I have three cats, however, and love spending time with them too."

"I have four cats!" exclaimed Wendy. "My girls are wonderful!"

"Except one of them is a boy," said Karen.

"Technically, yes, but he's still a girl. Like that Sadie I met at the phobia workshop. She's a girl that used to be a boy but she's now a girl. I'm sure it's the same with cats."

"But your cat hasn't had a sex change," said Karen.

"Well, no. Not yet, but I'm looking into it."

It was the group's turn to laugh at Wendy now as the waiter arrived with dessert menus. Karen turned to take one from him and as she did so, she looked out of the window and saw two police officers escorting a woman to a patrol car parked just across the street from the restaurant. That woman was wearing one ugly ass coat she thought to herself. The coat reminded her of the one Delores wore to work - in fact, now that she looked, it was Delores from work.

"Hey guys, you know I mentioned one of my co-workers always wears a real ugly purple and mustard patterned jacket?"

"Yes," said Tom. "I can't wait to see it on Monday."

"You can see it now - she's just gone and gotten herself arrested outside."

Everyone at the table (including the waiter) turned to look out of the window and right across the street was a woman wearing the ugliest jacket they'd ever seen slowly disappearing into the back of a police car.

"I wonder what she got arrested for," said Tom.

"Probably wearing that jacket in public. That'd be a misdemeanour without her having to commit any actual crime," said Karen as her laugh boomed around the restaurant.

"Irma's got a coat like that," said Martin to howls of laughter from everyone else.

"Her taste in men isn't much better," said Tom.

"Don't be so mean to him," chided Wendy. "Martin, tell us more about yourself."

"I'm married to Irma and we have two boys aged one and three. I do data analysis at work but I love taking pictures of things so I've brought my camera over. I want to go out late at night and take some photos of the empty city streets and the buildings."

"Just be careful, Martin. It can be dangerous in some areas," warned Wendy. "Why not take Tom with you?"

"I don't want to get shot!" Tom protested.

"You probably won't get shot," said Wendy.

"Probably?"

"Well, almost definitely."

"Can you guarantee it?"

"Not totally."

"There you are then. Anyway, Martin has already nearly been killed once today. As we left the hotel, we started to cross the street but he forgot to look the right way and got blasted by an ambulance so he probably won't survive long enough to worry about getting shot later."

"At least he would have been in good hands if he'd been hit by an ambulance," said Stuart.

"You are correct but the American healthcare system is very different from our own and he would have needed to pay for his treatment, however minor it may have been," added Bhavna.

Tom, Martin and Stuart looked down at the table to see if there were any bread rolls remaining that they could wedge into Bhavna's mouth to stop her from talking. Luckily for Bhavna there weren't and the desserts arrived to distract everybody again.

As the group started on their desserts, Martin told them about his love of country music and food before boring them all to death (in Tom's opinion) with tales of his kids. Stuart then took over and gave them all some dull facts about his life before the four from the UK office turned to the two locals.

"So, you all know I'm Karen and I'm the IT Manager..."

"...and single," interrupted a slightly drunk Wendy who was now on her fourth whiskey.

"As I was trying to say, I've been working for this dumb British company that sells a range of ugly, poor quality, green and brown coats, hats and other shit," she continued to much laughter.

"Go Karen!" said Wendy, almost on the floor now. "But don't go getting me one of those green coats. It would probably explode my head."

"As I was saying, AGAIN, I love nature and walking in the forest. I also used to enjoy the peace and quiet of living alone until my dumbass sister lost her damned job, couldn't pay her rent and had to move in with me."

"I love you sis," dribbled Wendy into her now empty whiskey glass.

"How about you show me how much you love me by getting yourself a job and moving into a place of your own?"

Wendy was now face down on the table so Karen said she'd have to take her home. Tom and the others were also beginning to fade as the time difference was beginning to hit them so they left the restaurant with Stuart and Martin helping to support Wendy on the way to Karen's car.

"Are we going to meet up tomorrow as well?" asked Karen.

"If that's alright with you, I'd love to," said Tom. "We want to go to see a few of the touristy things in the morning though so could we meet later in the day?"

"That works for me. Wendy won't be awake until noon if she's drunk. How about we meet y'all at 3 o'clock? We could go to Piedmont Park for some fresh air. There's a nice tavern there too so we can eat."

"Sounds perfect," said Tom as they reached Karen's car.

"Right, just let me get this drunk ass reprobate home and I'll call you tomorrow," said Karen and gave Tom another hug - this one slightly longer and slightly tighter.

"Cool. I'm getting excited already," said Tom.

"I know," said Karen as she pulled away.

The group said goodbye and the four visitors watched Karen drive off with a severely inebriated Wendy waving out of the passenger window and screaming unintelligible things to anyone in earshot. They then turned round and went to find their hotel. It was only just after ten but they were all exhausted and looking forward to a good night's rest - hopefully without too many flies buzzing around them as they slept. Maybe they'd all settle down for the night in Stuart's beard, Tom thought,

Chapter 16

Atlanta USA

Sunday had always been one of Tom's two favourite days of the week and he never understood why office workers the world over loved Fridays when they were a day of work when Saturdays and Sundays were days of rest and nights of partying. Friday nights were good, obviously, but the day part still sucked as much as any other work day. Weekends were awesome - Saturdays were obviously better but Sundays were sort of okay as well.

This Sunday morning he woke up in a strange bed in a strange place and it took him a second or two to remember where he was. Atlanta. Did he really go out with a group of work colleagues and Karen and her sister last night? It was still a bit of a blur so he'd ask Martin at breakfast; he might have taken pictures.

Tom showered and got dressed and then went to find Martin's room at the other end of the hotel corridor. He banged on the door and when Martin opened it Tom saw he was as annoyingly bright-eyed and enthusiastic as he always was in the mornings.

"Morning!" said Martin.

"Alright," mumbled Tom, slightly tired but not too badly hungover.

"Are you going down for breakfast?"

"Yeah...let's get the others. I told Karen we'd meet them at 3 o'clock today so we can go to the aquarium and Coca-Cola first."

"Okay - where are we going?"

"Some bar near a place called Piedmont Park. Apparently, it does food and then we can chill out in the park after."

"Sounds good. Let's grab the others and get some food inside us."

"How do you feel?"

"I'm okay - although I'm not sure what we ate last night. I was in the toilet a couple of times."

"Really? Me too."

"Maybe it was just jet lag and excitement," said Martin.

The two friends found the stairs and went down one floor to where Stuart and Bhavna had their rooms. Tom knocked on Bhavna's door while Martin knocked on Stuart's door directly opposite but neither got a reply so they knocked again. Still no replies.

"They're probably downstairs already," said Tom.

"I hope there's a buffet," said Martin as they went down the remaining stairs to the hotel lobby.

As they walked into the restaurant Tom looked around but could see no sign of Stuart or Bhavna anywhere. Martin headed to the buffet while Tom found a four-top table for them all. As Martin came back with his first plate, Tom's phone buzzed and he saw a message from Stuart.

"Hi guys. I'm not sure what I ate last night but I am really ill and think it might be food poisoning. I heard someone else throwing up all night across the corridor from me - it might be Bhavna. I'm staying in bed today. Stuart."

"Stuart says he's got food poisoning and is staying in bed all day," Tom informed Martin. "Bhavna might be ill too."

"Shit. That's not good. What did they have to eat?"

"Wasn't it some kind of Thai curry?"

"That's it - they both had the same because Stuart complained Bhavna's portion was bigger than his and she laughed at him," said Martin.

"Well, if that's what did it, she won't be laughing now. I'll message her."

Tom sent a message to Stuart telling him to look after himself and message him if he needed anything then sent one to Bhavna before visiting the buffet. As he sat back down, a message came in from Bhavna.

"Good morning. I am very sorry but I am feeling a little poorly today. I think there were some issues with the food I ate last night so I will get some rest here today and try to join you this evening. Warmest regards, Bhavna."

Tom had a mouthful of food so he held his phone up to show Martin the message. It looked like today would be just like old times now there were only two of them. Good, he thought. Stuart was boring and Bhavna was a pain in the arse - at least Martin was fun. And his accident-prone nature meant that there was always a chance he'd fall down a sinkhole or get hit by a mini-tornado and hurled into a trailer park.

As they continued their breakfast, Karen called to check they had all got back safely and Tom explained that Stuart and Bhavna were ill so there'd just be two of them later on.

"Oh man! What did those two eat last night?" asked Karen.

"They both had Thai curry. Maybe there was something wrong with it; although we both suffered a bit in the night too."

"You did? I'm sorry to hear that. I'm fine but Wendy is still hungover on the couch with two of her cats."

"Are the cats hungover as well?"

"No, they aren't. What kind of a dumb question is that?!" Karen laughed. "You Brits have some strange habits if you take your cats out drinking with you; there's laws against that kind of stuff over here."

Martin looked up as Karen's laugh came through Tom's phone and across the table. It was just like being at work and he wondered if he'd win the office sweepstake about Tom trying to get into Karen's bed. Stuart was the official adjudicator because Katrina and the rest of the team said there'd be a conflict of interests if Martin was reporting on what happened and also had money on one of the outcomes. Although with Stuart confined to his room, Martin would have to let them all know what transpired and wondered if he should take some pictures - although that might be seen as a bit creepy.

Tom finished his call with Karen and turned back to Martin, who was now messaging Irma and had received a photo from her of the two boys playing with a hosepipe in the garden. It looked like total carnage with everything covered in water and while he was sad he wasn't with them all, it looked a real mess and he knew who'd be in charge of cleaning everything up if he were there.

"What's this?" Martin asked, pointing at a porridge-like substance on his plate.

"I've no idea," said Tom. "It doesn't look very nice though."

"A woman at the buffet said it was called grits and I should try it because it's a true Southern food. She said I'd love it."

"Do you love it?"

"No, it's disgusting."

"What does it taste like?"

"It's gooey and bland. It tastes like disappointment."

"Maybe we should find her and ask her why she hates you so much."

"I'll just leave it here; maybe they can use it to fill in that hole in the wall behind you before they paint over it."

"Let's make our escape and get started," said Tom. "We'll head over to the aquarium and then the Coca-Cola museum next door."

"What about the College Football Hall of Fame?"

"Maybe next weekend? We've got two days so we could do that and also see CNN; they do tours, I think. Then on Sunday we can head out to Stone Mountain; it's a big old rock in the middle of nowhere with a cable car that takes you to the top."

"That sounds like a plan," Martin agreed as they left the restaurant. "I'll go up and get my camera then meet you here in a few minutes," he said as he disappeared up the stairs, glad that Tom would be handling their entertainment arrangements.

Martin had never trusted lifts - or elevators as they called them over here - since that time in Spain when he, Tom and a couple of their friends were on their first 'lads' holiday. After using the very slow lifts for the first few days, they all decided that running down the stairs would be quicker from the ninth floor that their room was on. Martin was chosen to be the 'control group' and take the lift so they could see which was quicker.

As the lift opened, Martin got in and laughed as the others started their descent on foot. Martin fully expected to win and probably would have done if the lift hadn't have got stuck between the third and second floors. The others reached the lobby and celebrated their victory while waiting for Martin's lift to arrive but, when he didn't, they looked at the lift display and could see it was held on the third floor and eventually told the manager who then called the local fire department. Two hours later, Martin was rescued and walked through the lobby to find them drunk and laughing in the bar.

"It's not funny," said Martin as he stormed up to where they were sitting.

"It is mate...it's hilarious!" said Tom.

"Maybe for you bastards it is. Get me a beer."

As the bartender went to get Martin a bottle of beer, he found that the door of the glass-fronted refrigerator they were kept in was stuck. This brought even more laughter from the group so Martin promptly left the hotel and went to another bar just around the corner where he sat on a bar stool and didn't leave for the rest of the day. Tom was still thinking about that - and all the other times life had conspired to mess with Martin

- as he saw him come back down from his room with his new camera. He'd probably lose it at some point on this trip.

Within a few seconds they were both outside in the mid-morning sunshine, ready to head over to the far side of Centennial Park to see the wonders of the aquatic world at the Georgia Aquarium and then buy Irma a t-shirt with the name of her favourite soft fizzy drink on. It was not the most inspiring of birthday presents, Tom thought, but this was Captain Dumbfuck and at least it was better than the iron he'd already bought her. Marginally.

"Martin, have you thought about how thrilled Irma is going to be when she uses her new iron on her new Coca-Cola t-shirt?" asked Tom.

"No, I hadn't thought of that. It's a good point though."

"She'll be ecstatic seeing both of her birthday presents working in harmony with one another."

"Yeah, she will," said Martin enthusiastically.

"I wouldn't be surprised if there's an addition to the family in nine months."

"Really? Do you think she'll be that pleased? I hadn't thought about that," said Martin. "Maybe I'll get her a keyring instead."

"Why? Don't you want any more mini versions of you in the world?"

"Not really," said Martin. "Three of us is probably enough."

Tom started to laugh as they walked past the Fountain of Rings where a dozen or more young children were running in and out of the water.

"If the boys were here now, Max would probably be waterboarding Ben in those fountains," Martin said grimly as they walked past and headed across the green towards the aquarium.

"From what you say they can be a bit of a handful."

"Ben's okay; it's Max. He's mad."

"I'm trying to think of a nickname for him now," said Tom.

"Yeah, I know. We call him that. There's something not quite right about his temperament and I think we might need to seek professional help."

"What, like a hitman?"

"No! A child psychologist. Although your idea might be cheaper in the long run because Irma thinks it will take months of work. And of course, she won't let one boy do anything without the other one doing it too."

"I thought that was just clothes?"

"No, it's everything. If one of them has a shit the other one gets taken up to have one as well."

"That's a bit weird," said Tom.

"Yeah...I'm worried that if we take Max and get him sorted out, Irma will insist on taking Ben too and we'll mess him up."

"That might happen. Have you thought about eBay?"

"What? To find a child psychologist? I don't think you can buy one of those on there."

"No, to sell Max. I think there is a category especially for small pets and unwanted family members. Normally it's just for grandparents that have outlived their usefulness and don't have any more stories about the wars they've fought in but you might be able to put Max on there."

"I'll have a look," said Martin. "But I'm not sure how Irma would react. She thinks more of the boys than she does of me."

"That's probably natural."

"For all women - or just for the one I'm with?" asked Martin, now looking at Tom.

"Oh look, we're here," said Tom brightly and joined the queue to buy tickets from the machine outside the main building.

After purchasing their tickets, they joined the queue for entrance to the aquarium and what Tom was convinced would be the highlight of his trip to Atlanta. Martin enjoyed anything from the natural world and while he wasn't the world's biggest fan of animal captivity, he was happy to be out and about doing something different and he could buy some soft toys for the boys while he was there.

***

Just over 12 miles north of the Georgia Aquarium in a small three-bedroomed house belonging to her sister, Wendy was gradually regaining consciousness face-down on Karen's couch with one of her cats licking her ear. She struggled to open her eyes but eventually she did and was greeted with a small furry face less than an inch from her nose, followed by another one and then a third. The final cat then jumped up on her legs and startled her.

"Ouch! Leave me alone, girls."

"They've been bothering me all morning sleepy-head," said Karen from the chair opposite.

"What time is it? Why am I down here?"

"It's just after eleven and your drunk ass passed out on my couch last night,"

"Did I have a good time?"

"Hell yeah, certainly if you count it by the number of empty whiskey glasses in front of you on the table."

"Did I do anything stupid?"

Karen looked at her and said nothing but Wendy knew her sister well enough to know there had been something.

"What did I do?" asked Wendy.

"Well, first you hugged one of those Brits that you're supposed to have a phobia about, then you got drunk and passed out on the table and told everyone I was single."

"Maybe my phobia is gone. That's a good thing, right?"

"That's if it was even there in the first damned place. I'm thinking of feeding you some green beans later to find out if that phobia is real too," Karen said, only half joking.

"They're all real. What else did I do? Why have I only got one shoe on?"

"We pulled up at a stop light and you saw a guy you liked the look of coming out of a liquor store," said Karen. "You shouted some unintelligible shit about being Cinderella and threw your shoe at him; you told him if he could find you and bring your shoe back then you'd marry his ass."

"That doesn't sound like me," said Wendy.

"You sure as hell did it though."

"What did he say?"

"He said you were a drunk, crazy bitch who should go home and sleep it off."

"That part sounds like me," Wendy admitted.

117

"Then he threw your shoe at the car as we drove off and it hit my back window."

"He's got a good aim."

Karen got up to make some coffee while Wendy sat up on the couch and started to talk to her cats. Coffee would be welcome and then a shower.

"Here's your coffee," said Karen, handing her a hot drink in a green mug.

"It's green. You know I have a phobia about the colour green."

"Yeah, right. I also know you have a phobia of foreigners but you had a good time last night so just drink it. You need to wake yourself up because we're going out this afternoon."

"Where are we going?"

"We're meeting the others for a late lunch in a bar near Piedmont Park."

"I'm not sure if I can make that," said Wendy. "I'm meant to be seeing Sadie and Dave from the phobia workshop later."

"Well bring them along; unless they've got phobias of meeting people's sisters?"

"Dave doesn't get on well with water," said Wendy.

"We won't push him in the lake then."

"I'm not sure I can just change the plans at short notice."

"You sure can. Just tell them to meet us at that bar outside Piedmont Park at three o'clock. Two of the Brits won't be coming because they've got some kind of food poisoning shit going on today. They've just got weak ass stomachs if you ask me."

"Which two are coming?" asked Wendy with a slight smile. "Will Tom be there?"

"Yes, he will. Martin will be there too but the others are sick."

"Good," said Wendy as she got up and went upstairs to get dressed and message Sadie and Dave with details of the new plan.

Chapter 17

Atlanta, USA

Martin left the aquarium laden down with soft toys and t-shirts for his two boys. His camera had also had a good workout and apart from a small number of shots of the inside of the lens cap that should have been pictures of African Penguins, he was happy with his morning's work. Tom was also happy because he'd seen some dolphins and some turtles and had got talking to an attractive young woman in the gift shop who'd given him her number.

"What did you think?" Tom asked Martin as they walked the short distance across Pemberton Place to their next destination.

"It was brilliant; I enjoyed it a lot more than I thought I would. I like anything to do with animals and fish. Not birds though - they're a bit annoying."

"I meant Lucille in the gift shop."

"She sounds like the type of woman who'd leave you with 400 children and a crop in the field," Martin laughed.

"What do you mean?"

"You know the old song where everyone thought the words were 400 children instead of four hungry children?"

"I have no idea, Martin. You probably need to listen to some more modern music."

"I like what I like."

"What about Lucille then?"

"She looked okay. Quite tall though."

"She gave me her number," said Tom, showing Martin his phone.

Martin stopped in mid-stride and took the phone. He looked at the screen then gave it back to Tom and started to laugh uncontrollably.

"What's going on?" asked Tom.

"Oh mate! It's hilarious. I can't wait to tell Karen and Wendy later!" laughed Martin. "Do you see the area code 555?"

"Yes," said Tom looking at his phone.

"Do you ever pay attention to American TV programmes or films? If you did, you'd see they always give out numbers with 555 in them. It's to stop people calling the numbers in real life."

"Oh," said Tom disappointedly.

"And to give young, innocent American girls protection against horny British visitors."

"Well at least I didn't take lots of pictures with the lens cap on."

"Yeah...I thought I might have done that. One good thing has come out of this though."

"What's that?" asked Tom suspiciously as they entered the Coca-Cola Museum.

"The next time you talk to a random woman and she gives you a number with '555' in it you'll know she's not interested immediately rather than having to wait until you call her and get the 'out of service' tone."

"Good point. It'll save a bit of time so I might consider that a win."

Martin rolled his eyes and walked off wondering which one of them was the more worthy of the name 'Captain Dumbfuck'. He'd always known it was him but sometimes Tom seemed to be just as deserving.

***

Karen and Wendy were getting ready for their afternoon out and were arguing about bathroom usage, who should feed the cats and which one of them was going to drive when Wendy's phone buzzed. It was a message from Sadie confirming she and Dave would meet them at the bar later and were looking forward to meeting Karen and the two English guys.

The message went on to say that neither of them had ever met anyone from England before and that Dave wanted to know if they spoke English. Wendy messaged back that they did and that they were good guys so it should be a fun afternoon. She then read the message again.

"Hey sis, look at this," said Wendy, showing Karen her phone.

"What's that?" Karen asked.

"It's this message from Sadie. She says that she will be there with Dave at three o'clock today."

"Well that's good isn't it?"

"I guess. But she's answering for Dave when he's not even there."

"Well maybe she's with him and they're coming together."

"But..." Wendy began.

"Maybe they've hooked up," suggested Karen, catching the look of disappointment on Wendy's face as she turned away and headed into the bathroom.

"It's possible, I guess. They do go well together - almost as well as a certain sister of mine and a certain British guy."

"What are you talking about?!" Karen shouted from the bathroom.

"I saw the way he kept looking at you."

"Oh man! He looks at everyone like that. He looked at the server like that, the hostess and a couple of women on the table next to us. Hell, he'd probably even look at one of your damned cats like that."

Karen's laughter carried across the hallway as she walked back to her bedroom to finish getting ready, leaving Wendy to wonder what whoever was controlling her romantic life had in store for her now that Dave was probably with Sadie. Hopefully there would be some new weirdos for her to talk to at the next phobia workshop. Or she could just get there before Sadie and shut all the doors so she couldn't get in.

***

"That was good," said Martin. "And I got Irma a t-shirt for her birthday."

"Did you get the right size?" asked Tom as they waited to be served in the gift shop.

"Yeah...I think so. Why?"

"Well, Irma's got big boobs. Is that t-shirt going to hold them in?"

"For fucks sake! Why are you looking at my wife's boobs?!" said Martin.

"Well it's difficult not to."

"True. She's certainly well-endowed. Maybe I'll get the next size up."

"Don't you know what size your own wife takes in clothing?"

121

"No. That's why I usually buy her household appliances. I got her a microwave for Christmas."

"What did she say?" asked Tom, expecting something quite insulting.

"Nothing."

"Nothing?"

"Yeah...she just threw the box at me."

"Why don't you buy her some jewellery or something personal for her to cherish?"

"She spends so much time doing stuff around the house and looking after the kids she says she never wants anything fancy," Martin explained.

"Well that's exactly why you should buy her something nice...to show her that she's more than a wife and a mother. Let's speak to Karen and find out if there's a nice jewellery shop locally so you can surprise Irma when you get back."

"That's a good idea. Although she'll probably expect the same next year and I don't want to set a precedent."

They left the museum and took a long walk around Centennial Park on the way back to their hotel. Martin took a few pictures of the fountains, the College Football Hall of Fame and the Ferris wheel from a distance before crossing over to the CNN building. Just as he stepped into the road, he heard some people shouting.

"What the fuck, man?!" came one voice.

"Move your ass!" said another.

Martin spun round to see two burly young men on cycles heading straight for him and felt a hand grab his arm and pull him towards the kerb.

"You're going to get yourself killed if you don't look the right way," said Tom. "That's twice you've nearly been killed and we've only been here a day."

"Yeah...the cyclists seem a bit militant over here," said Martin sheepishly.

"If you want to get yourself killed, at least wait until we've sorted this data breach out."

"Is that the only reason?" asked Martin.

"It's the main reason. Also, I don't want to have to tell Irma that you got killed by a bloke on a bike. Getting shot is one thing, but being hit by a bike is a bit lame."

"You're right."

"It's not the most glorious of deaths is it? Although I could invent something a bit more heroic if you wanted."

"You're loving this aren't you?"

"I just don't want to have to go round to your house and tell Irma that you got hit by a toddler on a tricycle and died."

"You just want to go round and stare at her boobs."

"I hadn't thought of that," said Tom. "Maybe I should stop saving your life so it will give me an excuse to go round there. For the moment, though, let's just go back to the hotel so you can dump your stuff and we can get a taxi to the bar and meet the others. Karen just sent me the details."

***

The sun was high in the sky and the temperature was hotter than either Tom or Martin had expected as their Uber pulled up outside the bar Karen had suggested they meet at. As they got out, they both immediately made for the shade of some nearby trees.

"This is seriously warm," said Tom, not necessarily to Martin but he answered anyway.

"Yeah...I had a message from Irma a few minutes ago. She says it's raining at home."

"That's good," said Tom. "I hate it when I go on holiday and the weather at home is nice. You get everyone saying 'the weather was great here; you should have stayed at home' even though I've been sightseeing all day and partying all night while they've been chained to their desks."

"That's what you said to me when I came back from Florida," Martin pointed out.

"Did I?"

"Yeah...you said you'd had hot sunny weather all day, every day and I'd have been better off not going to Orlando."

"Well...was I right?"

"Yes," said Martin. "I didn't really enjoy it with Irma's family but that's not the point; the weather was good."

"But the holiday was crap."

"Yeah...a bit."

"I still think it's you; you're just rubbish at being on holiday."

"Hey y'all!" came a loud American voice from behind them.

"Hi Karen! Hi Wendy! How are you both today?" said Tom, turning to face the two women who were walking towards them.

"Hi girls," said Martin as they all embraced.

"Apparently it's raining in England," said Tom.

"No shit! It's always raining over there," said Karen, her laugh not seeming quite as loud now they were outside.

"We had a hot summer in 1976," said Tom.

"And are y'all still talking about it like a hundred years later?"

"Yeah," said Tom and Martin in unison to more laughter from Karen, with Wendy joining in too.

Looking at the four of them as they walked to the bar, anyone passing would have thought they were two couples who had been friends for years. The laughter and the smiles appeared so easily whenever one of them said anything and there were now playful arm punches and slaps between one of the 'couples' too.

"What happened to Stuart and Bhavna?" asked Karen as they entered the bar.

"They both seem to have food poisoning," said Tom.

"Are you sure they ain't hooking up?" Karen asked wickedly.

"I hadn't thought of that," said Tom. "What about you, Martin?"

"I doubt it; Bhavna is hard work and Stuart isn't much fun. They just seem to bicker all the time."

"Well that's it then. They're just like an old married couple," said Wendy. "I bet they're at it right now," she added to a combination of laughter and disgust.

"Ewww," said Tom. "Can you imagine that beard?"

"Oh, shut up!" said Karen. "I'm going to eat soon; I don't want to be thinking about that damned thing going anywhere near anyone."

More laughter filled the bar as the hostess escorted them to their table.

"I'm sorry but we'll need a bigger table," said Wendy. "We have two more coming soon."

"Two more?" asked Tom as they were escorted to another part of the bar.

"Yes, I met a couple of really cool people at my phobia workshop last week so I invited them along. You'll love them!"

"Cool. The more the merrier!"

As the hostess showed them to a more suitable table, Dave and Sadie were making their way through Piedmont Park. They had spent the night together, but not in the traditional way; they had both been arrested in separate locations and had been taken to the same police station downtown where they'd both been held overnight. When Sadie had been released this morning, she'd seen Dave standing outside and had gone over to him.

"Hey Dave! It's so great to see you! What were you in for?" she asked.

"Hi Sadie! Just the usual drunk and disorderly conduct. No big deal. What about you?"

"I got caught in the parking lot near the stadium. There's a new bunch of homeless guys living under the bridge so I thought I'd make their Friday night for them."

"And you got arrested?"

"Yeah, it's a bummer but they're really friendly at this station, aren't they? Michael is really cool and so is Lauren."

"You know them by name?" asked Dave.

"I've been here a lot," admitted Sadie. "They even know how many sugars I take in my coffee."

"I guess that's one benefit from being a regular. I'm not usually downtown on Saturday nights; I normally only get brought here on Sundays."

"Maybe we'll see each other tonight then?" Sadie began to laugh but then suddenly stopped as her attention was caught by someone else coming out of the police station.

"What is it?" asked Dave.

"Did you see that woman's coat? That is the most disgusting thing I've ever seen," said Sadie.

"The purple and mustard patterned one over there? I wish I hadn't seen that; I'm still hungover and I think I'm going to be sick now."

"Do you think she got arrested for wearing that jacket?" asked Sadie.

"No. If she had they would have kept it as evidence and destroyed it."

They were both laughing and about to go off their separate ways when Wendy's message had come through. Sadie had responded on behalf of both of them and Dave had invited her back to his parents' basement.

"I live quite close to that bar. We could both go back to my basement and you could take a shower and get freshened up there."

"You're inviting me back to your basement? That sounds a bit creepy," Sadie laughed.

"I know," said Dave. "It sounded alright in my head though."

"It's okay. I've got some clothes in my bag; it will be quicker than going back to where I've been staying this week."

They took a bus to Midtown where Dave's parents lived and walked the rest of the way swapping stories of arrest, the standard of coffee in the different police stations they'd been taken to and the level of fines they'd each had to pay. Once they'd reached Dave's basement, showered and made themselves presentable, these two people who'd only met four days earlier started to walk through Piedmont Park towards a bar to meet up with someone else they'd only known for four days and three random people they'd never met - two of whom were British. What a strange world, Sadie thought as she stood at the entrance to the bar and waited for Dave to open the door for her.

Chapter 18

Atlanta, USA

Dave let Sadie into the bar and they made themselves known to the hostess. They could hear Wendy and the others before they saw them and Wendy immediately got up and greeted them both like old friends.

"Hey! How are you guys?!" she immediately asked them both.

"I'm good thanks but I can't speak for Sadie," said Dave.

"I'm good too!" said Sadie. "We were both in the same jail last night. What a coincidence!"

"That's so cool!" said Wendy, slightly relieved that Sadie and Dave weren't properly together but still upset at the level of comfort they already seemed to have with one another.

Undeterred, Wendy introduced them both to the rest of the group.

"That's my big sister Karen, who suggested I come and stay with her."

"What are you talking about?" asked Karen a split second ahead of her booming laugh. "I never invited you Wendy, you invited yourself. And you brought a houseful of stupid cats with you."

"Anyway...sitting suspiciously close to my wonderful sister Karen is Tom from England and this is Martin who works with Tom and they've also been friends since kindergarten. Do you guys have kindergarten over there?"

"Yes, but we call it infant school," said Tom as he got up to shake hands with the newcomers.

Dave and Sadie introduced themselves then sat down in the booth with the others. Wendy was happy that Dave sat next to her and she was now in between two men and opposite her sister.

"So, tell us about your jail time last night," said Karen.

"I got arrested for being a bit too drunk - as usual," Dave said laughing. "I think I should get some kind of loyalty card from the Atlanta Police so every time I get arrested, I get a stamp on it."

"What would happen after you get arrested ten times?" asked Tom.

"I haven't thought that through yet - maybe I get a free go in the electric chair? At low voltage of course. I don't like too much pain."

As everybody laughed, Tom looked at Dave and saw what he thought was a typical American redneck - a baseball cap, faded jeans, white t-shirt and a few days of beard growth. He also got drunk and arrested a lot. He decided he liked him and then looked along the line at Sadie, who used to be a redneck truck driver in a former life according to Wendy. She kept looking at Dave and laughing at his comments so she probably liked him too - but in a different way. They were probably at it, he thought. Or soon would be.

"I got arrested down behind the stadium giving some much-needed comfort to some of Atlanta's homeless men," said Sadie.

"Oh my!" said Tom, shocked at this admission. "That doesn't sound right."

"I know!" said Sadie, completely missing Tom's meaning. "I offered the policemen something special if they'd let me go but they wouldn't go for it. Boring cops."

"Maybe they just want to protect and serve?" suggested Karen.

"Maybe," said Sadie. "It's still a bummer though and I have to pay a fine."

A goth waitress came over and took their drink orders while they started to look at the menus.

"So how are you two liking Atlanta so far?" Sadie asked Martin and Tom.

"It's cool," said Martin. "There are four of us here but the others got food poisoning last night so they're recovering in the hotel. I'm enjoying it so far, although we have to work tomorrow so it'll be a bit less fun then.

"Me too," added Tom. "I just love the place and the people I've met so far. It's such a vibrant city and there's so much to see and do."

"It is pretty cool here," Dave agreed.

"We went to the aquarium and the Coca-Cola museum earlier and Martin got his wife a t-shirt for her birthday."

"A t-shirt?" asked Dave. "Is that all?"

Tom, Karen and Wendy began to laugh as they knew what was coming next.

"I bought her an iron before I came over," said Martin gingerly, expecting the worst and getting it.

"An iron! That's awesome!" said Dave, although hardly anyone heard him over the laughter and the arrival of the waitress with their drinks.

"I'll probably have to get her something else as well," Martin admitted.

"You think?!" said Dave.

"That's if he makes it home," said Tom. "He keeps forgetting to look the right way when we cross the road and has nearly been laid out twice. We only got here last night."

"That's so funny!" said Sadie. "Has anyone else ever done something really dumb that made their partner mad?"

"Well," Dave began. "I was married once. My wife was putting on a dress she hadn't worn for a few months and asked me if it still fitted her properly."

"Oh man! You didn't say 'no' did you?" asked Karen, already beginning to sense how this was going to end.

"No of course not - I'm not that stupid. But I did hesitate a bit."

"Uh-oh," said Karen.

"It was only for a fraction of a second!"

"That'll do it. What happened?"

"She went apeshit and threw her shoes at me. One of her heels caught me in the eye and it started bleeding and we had to call 911," said Dave, beginning to laugh.

"You got off easy," said Tom. "My old boss did that once. His wife got angry and he told her to calm down."

"Big mistake," said Karen and Wendy together.

"They never did find all his body parts."

"Oh man! That serves him right if you ask me," Karen said, turning towards him and realising their faces were now only inches apart.

The waitress returned with their food order and the noise level began to reduce as they started to eat - much to the relief of the rest of the people in the bar.

"Martin's worried about getting shot while we're over here," said Tom, who didn't like awkward silences and was always ready to embarrass Martin if he could.

"No way," said Dave. "You should be fine until June 1st."

"What happens then?" asked Martin, now getting slightly worried.

"That's shooting season. All Brits and Europeans become fair game."

"Do they?" asked Martin.

"Sure. We give y'all special t-shirts to wear with archery targets on them to make it easier for us to spot you. And for scoring purposes."

"Scoring?"

"Yeah. We get ten points for the heart, 9 points for a vital organ...and so on."

"Shit," said Martin, looking down at the steak he'd ordered. "We'd better get this work finished soon."

As he looked back up, he was just in time to see five faces exploding with laughter at him as he realised he'd been pranked. Standing right behind them was their waitress who was beginning to regret coming into work today.

"What about getting run over by a bike?" asked Tom. "Martin nearly got hit by two cyclists this morning outside the CNN building."

"Did he?" asked Wendy. "You poor thing," she said to Martin and briefly squeezed his knee under the table.

"At least he would have made the news. If something happened outside their front door, they'd probably run the story all day," said Dave.

"I once saw a guy with one leg in a cycle store," said Sadie.

"Was he buying a bike?" asked Tom. "Surely he'd just ride round in circles?"

"I don't know; I was in there trying to pick up some paying clients. The homeless guys are very grateful but they don't have any money. I need to get some paying clients soon and make some money or I'll be couch-surfing forever."

"Or you could get a boyfriend?" suggested Dave.

"Oh, I had a boyfriend for a while but that ended a few weeks back."

"What happened?"

"I dumped him when he told me he had a phobia of opening doors too. We can't both have the same phobia or we'd never be able to go anywhere. Not anywhere that had a door anyway."

"Hey Wendy, what happened to that guy you were dating a few months ago? Wasn't he a police detective?" asked Karen.

"Schroedinger? He wasn't really that talkative unfortunately. I like a guy who talks a lot but he was almost monosyllabic and hardly spoke at all unless it was about work so I ended it."

"What did he say?" asked Tom.

"Nothing."

"Nothing at all?"

"Nope. He just walked out the door. He never was a big talker."

"Did he have a first name?"

"I found out near the end that it was Pete. I only knew his surname for most of the relationship."

"How did you know his last name was Schroedinger?" asked Martin.

"I saw it on the citation he gave me when he stopped me for jay-walking while intoxicated."

"She dated him for two months and never knew his first name!" said Karen. "That is typical Wendy," she added as she began to laugh again.

"He wasn't a detective at the time. He was just a regular cop but he was so nice to me I asked him out."

"Did he say anything?" asked Tom, to more laughter from Karen.

"Not at the time, but he did call me later that day and we went out a few times."

"That's nice," said Sadie.

"It was cool for a couple of months but then he went for a promotion to detective and became even more serious so I dumped him. He got the promotion a few days after so maybe I was his lucky charm," said Wendy with a smile. "If I ever went out with another cop I'd want someone who was more senior."

"Maybe you should knock off a bank," suggested Tom.

"That would work."

"Good grief," mumbled the waitress under her breath as she put some more napkins on the table for them on her way back to the kitchen.

***

Less than a mile away from where this unlikely group of new friends were enjoying their late afternoon lunch, Norman Henry Normanson was enjoying his afternoon coffee. It was a ritual he had been enjoying for the last few weeks because it helped keep his bowel regular and today's coffee was just as welcome as every other cup he'd had.

Norman was sitting in the same chair he always sat in and was watching the same channel on TV that he always watched. The birds were singing in the garden outside the open window to his left and everything was normal. He'd shortly be going out for his late afternoon walk and then he'd come back, have a late dinner and settle down in front of the TV for the rest of the evening.

Most days he'd walk around Piedmont Park as he loved to watch people enjoying themselves in the warm sunshine. On cooler days he'd sometimes walk along the Beltline, although it had a lack of benches to sit on and fewer trees to take shade beneath so that was a walk he only took when he wanted a change of scenery. He had already decided that it would be Piedmont Park today.

Norman thought about the calm, smooth routine his life had recently settled into. He got up each morning, enjoyed a light breakfast, watched some TV before lunch and then watched some more in the afternoon before going for his walk. Some people would call it dull, but he enjoyed it and it brought him peace. This evening, however, Norman's life was about to get a whole lot more exciting.

It was also going to end.

***

"How's it going at table six this afternoon Becci?" asked the duty manager.

"It's okay, I guess. They're a bit loud though and they just laugh all the time. It's pissing me off."

"You don't like people laughing?"

"I'm a goth."

"I see. Are they celebrating something?"

"No," said Becci. "From what I can tell there are two arguing sisters - one of whom has a bunch of cats that the other one doesn't like, a transgender hooker, a drunken jailbird and a couple of guys from Britain."

"Two British guys? That sucks. Make sure you don't give them the check."

"Why?"

"Because they don't have the same tipping culture in the UK so you won't make much if they pay it. Give it to the two warring sisters - hopefully they'll fight so much over who's paying they'll pay twice."

Becci took the bill and the credit card machine over to table six and checked once again that everything had been alright with their meals. As she reached the table, she caught the tail end of what seemed to be a horrific story that she would forever remember as 'grand theft baby'. What the hell did people in Britain get up to in their spare time?!

"You got banned from all of the grocery stores across the whole country?" asked Sadie.

"Yes!" said Tom, looking pleased with himself. "Although you have to understand that it was only from one chain of stores. We do have several others so I'm not going to starve."

"That's good to know. What did you do? Was it something really gross with the fresh produce?"

"No, nothing like that."

"That's a shame," said Dave to much laughter from the table and increasing levels of concern from Becci as she stood there not wanting to listen any further but not wanting to stop listening.

"Well, you know how you sometimes grab something out of a random person's trolley and put it in somebody else's trolley for a laugh..." Tom began.

"No," said the whole table in unison. ('What the fuck?' thought Becci).

"Oh, you must have done it!"

"I haven't," said Dave. "And I've done some pretty messed up stuff in my time."

"Me neither," said Sadie.

"What about you Wendy?" asked Karen.

"I don't think so...but I don't want to confirm or deny anything at this stage. Tom, by 'trolley' do you mean shopping cart?"

"Yes, I do," said Tom. "Anyway, I was on a dare from somebody who gave me ten seconds to grab something from the trolley of a woman in a blue dress who had just passed us."

"Did you do it?" asked Dave.

"Well...she'd only just started her shopping so there wasn't much in her trolley. I panicked and grabbed the first thing I could."

"What was it?" asked Karen, as the eyes of the Americans were all on Tom, including Becci's.

"It was her baby. It was sitting in that little trolley seat they have so I just picked it up and put it in another woman's trolley."

"What??!!"

An explosion of laughter from the people seated around the table reverberated around the bar while Becci stood frozen to the spot in horror, as if she had stared at Medusa's face for slightly longer than the recommended time limit.

"I made sure I put it in the trolley of another woman rather than some paedo or something," said Tom, trying to justify his actions.

"What happened next?" asked Wendy.

"A security guard was called and he showed us to the door. I'm not allowed to shop there ever again," said Tom dejectedly. "It's a shame because it's only a couple of minutes from my house."

"What about the woman with the baby?" asked Karen.

"Oh, she's still allowed to shop in there. I often see her while I'm walking past."

"Does she recognise you?"

"I don't know...but she runs every time she sees me so it's possible."

"I don't blame her," said Wendy.

"I blame the person who dared me," said Tom.

"Who was that?" asked Karen.

Tom went quiet and looked at the person directly opposite him, who had remained quiet during the telling of this whole story. He could also see the waitress hadn't left as she clearly wanted to know who'd set him up too.

"It's not my fault," said Martin. "I meant another woman who was wearing a blue dress. The one with loads of stuff in her trolley already. She wouldn't have missed a tin of soup. If you'd have done it properly, we wouldn't have both been banned."

"Have you been banned too?" asked Karen in mid-laugh.

"Yes. They have a superstore close to where I live but they have my picture on the door to let the staff know I'm not allowed in."

As the idiots at table six began to laugh at each other once again, Becci went back to her station and told her duty manager she was traumatised and wanted to lie down. The duty manager went over to table six to take payment and purposely looked back and forth between the two sisters as the group discussed their options.

Eventually, the older of the two women pulled out her credit card and muttered something that sounded like "it's time you got yourself a damned job" to the woman opposite her. Once the transaction was complete and they began to leave, the duty manager saw that they had left a very healthy tip. That should make Becci smile, he thought. Although being a goth, it probably wouldn't.

Chapter 19

Atlanta, USA

Piedmont Park has been enjoyed by the good people of Atlanta and its visitors since 1887. It is situated just over a mile north-east of downtown Atlanta and was originally opened to host two major expositions, ultimately housing the first professional baseball team in the city and also serving as a major athletic centre. Over the years, it has been expanded and improved and was now a popular choice for both locals and visitors to relax in. It had also become Norman Henry Normanson's favourite place to walk before his evening meal.

Whenever he chose Piedmont Park for his walk, he would walk up the street, turn left at the high school, then turn right, cross over the main road and he was there. He loved the green space, the lake and the trees and seeing young families playing and cycling gave him pleasure as he reminisced on his own life, his youth, the choices he'd made and the chances he'd taken. They had all led him to this point; his final day on earth.

Norman reached the park and began to walk towards Lake Clara Meer - his favourite spot in the whole of Atlanta. The park wasn't as busy as usual but as he continued his slow walk around the lake, he could hear the sound of a group of high-spirited young people. He looked to his left and saw what looked like five - no, it was six - people sitting on the grass talking and laughing. They were clearly having a good time, he thought. It also sounded like they'd been in the bar.

As a reformed alcoholic, Norman had not had a drink for over 20 years. He'd been tempted a few times of course, but had never succumbed. He wasn't anti-alcohol and could understand why people enjoyed it, but it wasn't something he wanted or needed in his life. Besides, some people made complete fools of themselves after too much alcohol and he had seen enough drink-fuelled fights in his younger days to last a life-time. To be fair, Norman had started most of them, but he still counted them as fights he'd seen.

The six young people Norman had briefly studied began to fade into his memory as he walked round the lake to look for a bench to rest on. At his age he was no longer young and sprightly and although getting old was bad, the alternative was worse. He envied the young people with their whole lives ahead of them but the group of six people he'd just seen were certainly living their lives to the full. Norman approved of this. But did they have to be quite so loud about it?

The bench that appeared a short way ahead of him was a very welcome sight and he sat down to survey the scene. Norman sat for longer than he normally did and continued to look back on his life. Maybe it was the group of young people he'd just seen, but he suddenly missed his youth and would give anything to be back in his 20s or 30s again, but with all of the opportunities today's young people had. He would certainly want to have a lot more sex than he'd had the first time around.

After a few more minutes of reverie, Norman got up and made his way back to the house he lived in. The sun would later be setting on both Atlanta and on his life - although at this point he was only expecting one of those things to happen. He turned to look back at the park for what would prove to be his final time and headed home.

***

"Did you see that old guy looking at us?" Sadie asked the group as they sat in the middle of the park.

"No," said Tom. "Which old guy?"

"Just some random dude walking past. He stopped and looked at us for a few minutes and then walked off," said Wendy. "He had a small head."

"Did he have a small body to match?"

"Not especially. He was kind of average build, quite tall but with a small head. He had a cap on that looked way too big for him."

"How do you know he had a small head?" asked Tom.

"He took his cap off for a second and I saw his head. It just seemed smaller than normal."

"I didn't see him. Was he looking at all of us?"

"I think so. He just looked at us and then moved on. I don't think it was in a creepy way."

"Perhaps he was just looking at Karen," Wendy suggested. "You've got some competition now Tom!"

"What the hell do you mean?!" asked Karen.

137

"Oh, come on sis! I'm sure you only caused that problem at work so you could get Tom over here," she laughed, taking another drink from her water bottle that Karen was beginning to suspect didn't have water in it.

"Just you shut your mouth or you and your stupid cats can move out," said Karen. "Maybe you can go and move in with that creepy old guy that just walked past. Although I wouldn't wish that on anyone," she said, laughing as she did so.

"I was just saying, that's all."

"Well maybe you should wait until you've got something important to say like you've got yourself a job and you're moving out."

"What job are you looking for?" asked Sadie.

"She used to be a telephone operator at one of the museums here but she has a phobia of speaking to strangers on the damned phone so she got her ass fired," Karen told them.

"I need something more exciting," said Wendy. "But I don't know what."

"Maybe we could think of something for you. What do you like doing?" asked Sadie.

"She likes being a pain in the ass, eating my food, pointing at shit, telling people how to live their lives and having her head up in the clouds the whole time. What kind of job fits that particular set of qualifications?"

"If she likes pointing at things, she could be a weather presenter on TV," suggested Martin. "All they do is stand there and point at stuff. It's probably quite easy over here where it's sunny and warm most of the time."

"Scorchio," said Tom.

Martin and Tom both laughed but four pairs of eyes looked at them blankly and this made them laugh even more.

"What?" asked Karen.

"Sorry, it's a catchphrase from a TV show in the UK," Tom explained. "But Martin's right about being a weather presenter. If Wendy likes pointing at things it could be the perfect job for her."

"She could also be in Marketing. They've always got their heads in the clouds," suggest Martin, suddenly full of good ideas. "Or a food taster."

"What about a job for someone who's got their head up their ass the whole time?" Wendy asked, laughing and looking at Karen.

"You think you're so funny," Karen said with a fake smile.

"Maybe Karen could be a courtroom judge because she likes bossing people about," Wendy continued, getting into her stride now that the attention was turned on her sister.

"You're such a disappointment," said Karen. "Come on, let's go for a walk. I'm seizing up sitting here."

"I'd like to take some pictures of the park and the skyline as the sun goes down," said Martin.

"Well, don't walk too far because there's a road that goes through the park up there. Tom says you keep getting run down by trucks and bikes."

"I don't keep getting run over. I keep nearly getting run over. There's a big difference."

Everyone got up and gathered their belongings so Karen could show them round the park. As a nature lover she enjoyed nothing more than being outside amongst the trees, lakes and open spaces. It was normally so peaceful but today she had these fools with her so she wasn't sure if she would enjoy it as much.

Making their way around the park was slow because Martin kept stopping to take pictures. He took pictures of the lake, the skyline and the group of them; he also managed a few shots of the inside of his lens cap, much to everyone's hilarity. They could see the lens cap on the lens as he lined up the first shot but just as Wendy was about to warn him Tom had nudged her to keep quiet.

Word soon reached Sadie and Dave what was going on and every time Martin lined them all up the laughter increased. Martin wondered about the hilarity but assumed it had been caused by the beer and whatever it was in Wendy's water bottle. Eventually Tom told him so he could get some actual pictures of them and not just the inside of a lens cap - not necessarily for Martin's sake but because he wanted some pictures to remind him of their trip and the new friends they'd made and couldn't be bothered to take any himself.

***

A few streets away from this happy band of new friends, Norman Henry Normanson had just finished his final meal.

"Hey Wendy," said Sadie as they walked past the tennis courts in the northern section of the park. "What's the worst job you've ever had?"

"Probably having Karen as my older sister. That's really hard work," Wendy replied.

"That's almost as hard as being your older sister," said Karen.

"Seriously, what's the worst job you've had?"

"Probably working in a fast-food shop late at night and dealing with all the drunks. No offence, Dave."

"None taken," said Dave with a smile. "I've been known to tear it up a bit when I've had a few too many. It can't be easy working in those places, especially when people like me come in."

"Do you ever go back the next day and apologise?" asked Tom. "We apologise for everything in the UK even if we didn't do anything. We're a bit like Canada."

"I would do, but I can't always remember anything about where I've been or what I've gotten up when I wake up in jail the next morning."

"That's fair enough," said Tom.

"I worked in a fast-food restaurant once," Martin added while getting his camera ready to take some more pictures.

"They called him 'Johnny No Stars' while he was there," Tom added.

"I'd forgotten about that," Martin admitted.

"Why did they call you that?" asked Wendy.

"You know they all have stars on their name badges to show how proficient they are? I was there for three years and didn't earn any stars."

"But they give you a star for making it through the first day without setting fire to the place, don't they?" Wendy asked.

"Yeah...about that," Martin began but couldn't finish due to the laughter coming from all sides.

"Guys, I've known Martin for 25 years and I've discovered that he has a unique level of stupidity in some things. It's not something you can teach. He was born with it."

"It's a natural gift," Martin agreed.

The six of them continued their walk around the park swapping stories of all the bad jobs they'd had as the sun began to set.

"I was once a tattoo artist," Dave began as they sat on the steps in front of the gates that separated Piedmont Park from the Atlanta Botanical Gardens.

"You could get another tattoo, Martin," Tom suggested.

"No thanks," said Martin.

"Did you enjoy it Dave?" asked Sadie.

"Yeah, I did but I had to leave."

"Why?"

"It wasn't my fault...really," said Dave with a grin.

"Tell us more!" Sadie begged.

"A guy came in one day and wanted a tattoo of a teardrop. I was quite new so the owner said I could do it because teardrops are easy."

"Don't they signify you've killed someone?" asked Karen.

"Yeah, the guy had just come out of prison for killing his boss for asking him to do overtime on a Saturday."

"I think we could have all been there at some point," said Karen.

"I hear you. But this guy had a really bad stutter and I'd just come back from my lunch break in the bar next door."

"What happened?" asked Sadie.

"I was a bit drunk and he was stuttering and asked for a teardrop like 17 times. So, I gave him 17 teardrops."

"Oh man!" said Karen.

"Yeah...he was on his phone and wasn't really concentrating. And I was drunk so I wasn't really concentrating either. When I finished and he saw what he'd got he went mad and shouted 'I look like a fucking serial killer now!' and walked out without paying. I didn't get a tip either."

"What did the owner say?"

"He fired me and told me if he ever saw me again he'd be the one needing a teardrop tattoo."

Darkness was now beginning to engulf them as Martin and Tom let the others go on ahead of them so Martin could continue taking pictures of the trees silhouetted against the skyline of the buildings in Midtown. The sky had turned from light blue to orange as the sun went down and was now a deep blue as night approached.

Martin had a look of frustration on his face that could only mean one thing. He was struggling with something that most normal people would have no problems at all doing.

"Are you alright Martin?"

"Yeah, mate...it's just my hands have been a bit sweaty because of this heat and every time I go to adjust my camera or put it in its case, I accidentally press the button and take a picture. It's really annoying."

"Aren't cameras all very similar?"

"Mostly, yes, but this is new and I haven't got used to it yet. It's too easy to press the button and accidentally take a picture but I'll be alright in a few days."

"What do you think of it other than that?"

"It's the second one I've had that's got an SD card. I used to prefer old-fashioned film but with this one I can take a lot more shots in case I mess a few up."

"Or take a few with the lens cap on."

"Yeah, that too," Martin agreed.

"Isn't it too dark now for landscape shots?"

"It is a bit."

"Can you take a couple of me so I can use them on my online dating profile when I get home? I want people to think I'm well-travelled and sophisticated and this twilight will make me look dark and mysterious."

"But you're none of those things."

"I know, but I still want people to think I am."

"Okay, stand over there under that lamppost by this wall and I'll..."

"WHAT THE FUCK??!!" shouted Tom, grabbing Martin and pulling him onto the path.

"SHIT!!"

As Martin had stepped back onto one of the internal roads in the park to take the pictures Tom had asked for, a car came hurtling around the corner and almost ran them both down. Martin had seen Tom jump forward to grab him and had also jumped back instinctively and fallen over a small stone wall as the car disappeared into the night.

"How fast was he going?!" asked Martin. "He could have killed us both."

"I know," said Tom as the others turned back to see what the commotion was about.

"Hey y'all. Are you guys okay?" shouted Karen as they approached.

"I think so. Some maniac in a car tried to kill us!" said Tom.

"I'm sure they didn't try to kill you on purpose. They don't know you well enough yet," said Karen.

"That's true," Tom agreed.

"Give them a few days and then you'd better be worried."

"Thanks Karen. That makes us feel a lot better," said Tom with a smile.

"I'm just messing with y'all," she replied. "Come on, let's get out of here so you can get back to your hotel. Try not to get assassinated on the way back."

"That's good advice in any situation," said Tom as they made their way back through the park.

In the excitement of nearly being hit by a speeding car Martin had dropped his camera and was anxious to get back to the hotel to check it was still working. He also remembered that he'd promised to call Irma but hadn't had the chance. She wouldn't be happy but at least he was halfway around the world from her; if they were in the same room and he hadn't done something she'd told him to then a broken camera would be the least of his worries.

"Hey guys, what's that?" asked Wendy. "Just there by the water. It looks like..."

"Where?" asked Dave.

"I see it," said Karen.

"It looks like..."

"A body. A dead one." said Dave.

"Is it a dead hooker?!" asked Tom excitedly. "I've heard a lot about them."

"No, sadly," said Dave.

"What do you mean 'sadly'?" asked Sadie, getting upset. "Are you a fan of dead hookers?"

"No, of course not. I meant it would be a shame for Tom if he's always wanted to see one."

"Oh yeah, definitely. That is a shame."

"I haven't always wanted to see one...it's just something you hear a lot about on TV cop shows and in the movies," said Tom. "I'd be almost as happy not to see one."

"That's not what you said on the plane," said Martin.

"Is that the thanks I get for saving your life three times since we've been here?"

"It's only twice; the first time you just laughed and the second time you were more interested in going round to tell Irma's boobs that I'd been killed by a kid on a tricycle."

Dave and Wendy approached the edge of the lake to get closer to the object that looked like a dead body and found that it was. It also had a smaller than average head.

"I know it's quite dark but it looks like he's got a small head," said Dave.

"Maybe it's that creepy old guy from earlier," suggested Sadie.

"Whoever it is, we'd better call the cops," said Karen and reached for her phone.

Chapter 20

Atlanta, USA

The warm, yellow glow of the ornamental lamp posts in Piedmont Park was punctured by the flashing blue lights of two dark blue patrol cars as they made their way across a small bridge that led from the city streets to the centre of the park. As they stopped their vehicles and got out, the four uniformed officers were greeted by six civilians and what looked like a corpse just behind them.

"Can somebody tell me what happened here?" asked the first officer to reach the group.

"We were just walking through the park and we stumbled across this body," said Karen, electing herself as the official spokesperson.

"I see," said the officer. "Go on."

"We've been out for lunch, walking around and generally having a good time. As soon as we decided to leave, we saw what looked like a body and called you guys."

"Did you notice anything suspicious at the time?" asked a second officer, leaning over the body for a closer look.

"Not really. Although these two guys nearly got mowed down by a speeding car just before we found it," said Karen, pointing at Tom and Martin.

"What was that?" said the first officer again, who was about to examine the body but stopped and turned to face the group.

"We were hanging back a bit checking out my camera when someone came speeding towards us and nearly killed us," said Martin. "We jumped back and fell over that wall back there," he added.

"I saved his life," said Tom. "That's twice today so far. I think I should get a medal."

"How long was it between this incident and your discovery of the body?" asked the first officer, trying to keep the conversation on track.

"A couple of minutes, I think. The car came from down this way and then headed off in the direction you came from," said Martin.

"To confirm, you're saying that while you were back there, a car came from this direction at high speed and almost ran you down. Then you caught up with your friends to continue your walk and came across the body a couple of minutes later?"

"Yes," said Martin.

"Did you get a look at the vehicle?"

"Not really. It all happened so fast but it looked like an old car. Like one of those classic American cars from the 1950s. It wasn't anything we'd have in the UK," said Tom.

"Did you get a colour?"

"It was a dark colour; maybe black or brown or a dark blue or green. Sorry, I didn't really see it clearly."

"And what about you?"

"Sorry," said Martin. "I was facing the other way as it came around the corner from behind me. I didn't see it until it was practically on top of us. It wasn't a Cadillac though."

"How do you know that?"

"It didn't have any tail fins. Apparently, Cadillacs have tail fins according to that Johnny Cash song."

"Okay. Thank you...I think," said the first officer before turning to address the rest of the group. "Does anyone have anything else to add at this time? Anything useful."

The six of them looked at each other and mumbled incoherently before confirming they didn't have any other information apart from noticing that the victim looked like he had quite a small head and they'd seen a man walking around the park earlier with a small head.

"Can you describe the man you saw earlier? Was he doing anything suspicious?" asked the first officer.

"He was just walking round the park. He stopped and looked across at us from the path but then moved on," said Wendy. "He took his cap off and I noticed his head was quite small."

"Did you get a good look at him?"

"Not really, he was too far away to see his face clearly, although he seemed quite tall and looked old. We did have a look at the dead guy here but his face is pretty bashed in so I can't tell if it's the same guy or not."

"The victim does appear to be an elderly gentleman and - if it's the same person - it might indicate that he lived locally and had walked to the park. We'll investigate this but we'll need you all to come to the station so we can take statements."

"Cool," said Tom. I've never been in a police station."

"They're so cool," said Sadie. "I'm thinking of reviewing them on Trip Advisor. I could score them on friendliness, space in the cells and the quality of the coffee."

"What about free Wi-Fi?" asked Dave. "That's always good to know."

"Oh yes! Of course."

"Why would you want to review police stations?" asked the second police officer.

"Well, it would let people know the best places to get arrested. It would also help the local economy," Sadie added.

"How would it help the local economy?" asked the same officer.

"Easy," said Dave. "I get arrested a lot for being drunk and I get taken to the nearest police station. If I knew which police stations were the nicest..."

"...the most perp-friendly?" asked the same officer.

"Yes! If I knew which ones were the most welcoming, I'd make sure I drank in the bars closest to that particular station."

"I hate to admit it, but that's a good point," said the officer.

"We could run 'Officer of the Month' contests from the perspective of the public," said Sadie.

"Do we get to vote out the ones we don't like?" asked Dave.

"That would be even better. There's one officer that books me in sometimes who's always so mean. She treats me like a criminal."

"If you're arrested and charged with a crime that would technically make you a criminal. There's a clue in the word," said the first officer.

"I know, but they don't have to be so mean about it."

"Have you tried not committing crimes?"

"I'd miss the free coffee."

***

The two officers from the second patrol car were sealing off the crime scene as the medical examiner arrived. He went to investigate the body and immediately advised the uniformed officers that the cause of death appeared to be blunt force trauma to the head, although there were some inconsistencies in terms of the shape of the murder weapon and the depth of some of the wound indentations. Also, the victim had a smaller than average head.

"What do you think could have caused the injuries?" asked the first officer.

"It's hard to say. There are quite a lot of indentations but usually I would expect them to be of a similar shape and size. This victim has a lot of fairly shallow wounds - and I mean a lot - as well as a few different wounds. It's likely he was struck by two different objects," said Dr Brownstein.

"Really?"

"Yes. I'm not sure why the murderer needed to give him so many blows to the head. Normally one or two would suffice. I'm guessing here, but I'd say whoever did this wasn't very strong so they had to hit him multiple times."

"A woman then?"

"It's possible. Or someone very young; or even someone old. The sheer number of shallow blows suggests somebody really hated the victim but there's a second pattern that must have been caused by another weapon."

"Could two people have killed him, doc?"

"Again, anything is possible," Dr Brownstein advised

"I'll call it in so they can assign a detective to the case and take the witness statements at the station."

"Don't worry officer, I already have. Detective Schroedinger will be here shortly."

The medical examiner continued to review the body while the four officers secured the scene and checked the immediate area. There were no tyre tracks, no discarded personal items and nothing unusual. They would stay and work through the night but weren't confident of spotting anything until daylight which was still several hours away.

As the officers alternated between speaking to Dr Brownstein, securing the area and searching for clues, Tom, Martin and the others waited by a bench a few yards from the scene and were the first to see the lights of more patrol cars emerge from the darkness. Once the vehicles had stopped it was clear that there were three of them.

"How many police officers do they need?" asked Tom. "It's just like in the movies where they bring two hundred cars and a thousand officers to arrest someone who has gone up and taken a free drinks refill in a restaurant that doesn't offer them."

"They like to be thorough over here," said Dave. "Whenever I get arrested there are usually at least six officers present."

"Why do they need so many?"

"Well...I don't tend to go quietly. When I've had my fill, I get a bit on the rambunctious side so if they try to arrest me I fight back."

"Do you assault the officers?" asked Wendy.

"I try to, but I don't usually succeed because I'm usually too wasted to know what I'm doing. I've punched myself in the face a few times by mistake," Dave explained and started to laugh.

"That's brilliant!" said Tom. "That's the type of thing you'd do Martin."

"I've done it before," Martin admitted. "Normally when Irma is helping me out of a tight t-shirt or sweatshirt. Sometimes she pulls the sleeves and I'm pulling my arms and I smack myself in the face by accident."

"You two are awesome!" said Wendy. "This has been such a great day."

"Apart from the dead guy," Karen reminded her. "It's probably not been a great day for him."

"I guess not," said Wendy. "But I'm sure he's laughing with us wherever he is."

"He's up there under a tarpaulin. I don't hear him laughing."

"He's probably laughing on the inside," said Wendy, reaching for her water bottle again.

"Good evening," said a loud voice approaching the bench where they were congregated.

"Hey Pete!" said Wendy, getting up from her seat. "How are you doing?"

"Oh. Hi Wendy," said Detective Schroedinger. "I'm good thanks. How are you?"

"We're all cool. This is my sister Karen, her friends Tom and Martin from England and these two are Dave and Sadie who I met at a phobia workshop."

"Good evening everybody. I am Detective Schroedinger from Atlanta PD and I will be leading the investigation on this case. I understand you found the body?"

"We sure did, Pete," said Wendy.

"Wendy, as this is official business, I'll need you to call me by my proper title. How did you know my first name anyway?"

"I looked in your wallet and checked your ID one morning while you were in the shower. Also, why do you still have a Blockbuster Video membership card?"

"Let's get on with trying to find out what happened here. Can one of you tell me what happened and what you saw from the time you arrived at the park until the time you found the body of the victim? Not you, Wendy."

"Sorry Pete. Just one thing though - why are they called victims and not 'murderees'? It would make more sense if you have a murderer and a murderee. Just like employers and employees."

"Can somebody please go through your movements for the afternoon," said an increasingly exasperated Schroedinger.

"Hey Detective, I'm Karen. The six of us had been out for the afternoon and we'd had lunch at the bar at the entrance of the park and then just sat around and walked and talked."

"Do you have a receipt for your lunch?"

"Yes I do. We were there until sometime after five o'clock and then just sat around in the park enjoying the sunshine."

Schroedinger started to take notes as Karen told the story of their afternoon with the occasional interruption from Wendy. She then handed over to Tom to tell the part of the story where he and Martin had nearly been hit by the speeding car before Wendy took over to finish the story and explain how she had been the first one to see the body and had pointed it out to the others. She also mentioned her cats were good at solving murders as they often hissed at people on TV shows and at least part of the time the person they'd hissed at had proved to be the murderer.

The detective let them speak without asking questions and took copious notes. He was a methodical man, taller than each of them and a lot more serious. He had short black hair and a Latino complexion and, as he was talking, Karen could see that he and Wendy would not have been a good match. Whatever complaints her sister may have had about him being too quiet and serious, he would have had the same number of issues about her being too loud and flighty.

"Thank you all," Schroedinger said when they had finished. "I will need you all to attend the police station in Midtown tomorrow to give formal statements but in the meantime I will need your contact details."

"We are staying at The Ocean Hotel," said Martin.

"That sucks," said Schroedinger. "Room numbers?"

"I'm in 204 and Tom's in 212."

"Thanks."

"I'm staying with Karen in Cumberland," said Wendy as she gave Schroedinger the address.

"I'm staying with Dave in Virginia-Hyland," said Sadie.

"Are you?" asked Dave.

"It would be much easier. Especially since we can't skip town now because we're witnesses to a major crime."

"Okay," said Dave. "I live with my parents in their basement."

"You all live in their basement?"

"No. They live upstairs. I live in the basement."

"He invited me to his basement earlier - but not in a creepy way," said Sadie as Dave showed Detective Schroedinger his ID with the address on it.

"Thanks," said Schroedinger. "That will be enough for tonight. I need you all at the Midtown police station at 8am tomorrow. Have a good night."

Detective Schroedinger walked back towards the flashing lights of the patrol cars to rejoin his uniformed colleagues and the medical examiner as they were clearing the scene, leaving the six witnesses sitting together in an eerie silence.

"It's been quite an interesting day," said Tom.

"Yep," agreed Martin. "Aren't we supposed to be at work tomorrow sorting the data breach out?"

"Probably. But this is more important I think."

"Katrina will go mad."

"She will."

"Just tell her that you're both at the police station. It won't be a big surprise," said Karen, using her laugh for the first time in a couple of hours.

"I did think we might end up in jail at some point on this trip," Tom admitted. "But I thought it might be for one of us killing Bhavna."

"Hell yeah! You know she'd be complaining about how you weren't doing it in the most efficient way while you were murdering her though, don't you?"

"She'd be all like 'if you severed my carotid artery with a steak knife instead of trying to beat me to death with a can of diet cola it would be much quicker for both of us' while Googling if there were any other methods that were even more efficient."

"Can you beat someone to death with a can of Coke?" asked Martin as the laughter intensified.

"I had a buddy who knocked himself out with a beer can once," said Dave.

"That's cool," said Tom.

"Not really. Frank was driving his truck and was coming to pick me up to go fishing. He'd had a couple of beers on the way over and as he got close to where I was standing, he smacked an empty can against his forehead to crush it; unfortunately, the fool wasn't concentrating and picked up a full can; he hit himself too hard and got a concussion."

"That's terrible!" said Sadie. "Was he alright?"

"He was, but I wasn't. When he knocked himself out, he lost control of his truck and it started to head straight towards me. I ran away but the truck kept coming so I jumped over a fence into somebody's yard and got chased by their dog. I was getting bitten by this damned mutt while unconscious Frank and his stupid truck rolled right on past me into the river without a care in the world."

Laughter once again filled the air a few yards away from where Schroedinger and his team were discussing the body. The police considered murder a serious business even if this bunch of drunks and misfits didn't. He felt confident he and his team would get to the bottom of this crime and it would then be another step on the way to his next promotion, although finding out his ex-girlfriend was one of the key witnesses (or was she a suspect?) was not something he would have chosen himself.

Maybe he could just pin the murder on her and her friends? Wendy and her laughing sister would go away for a long time, the other two Americans looked like they already knew what the inside of a jail cell looked like anyway and the two British guys could be sent back home to the Kingdom of United Britain-land or whatever those people called themselves over there.

As Schroedinger smiled to himself he could see in the distance that this group of drunks and misfits had got up from their bench and were now making their way out of the park. He was left with a team of uniformed officers and now had the task of establishing the identity, last movements and murderer of the victim they had just sent to the city morgue.

The medical examiner's vehicle pulled away from the crime scene and the body of 81 year-old Norman Henry Normanson left its favourite place in Atlanta for the final time.

Chapter 21

Atlanta, USA

Karen had offered to drive Tom and Martin back to their hotel to save them calling a taxi so they said goodbye to Dave and Sadie at the edge of the park and walked to Karen's car.

"I need to get some gas first," she said as they reached the vehicle.

"I've never been to American petrol station," said Tom. "What are they like?"

"Just the same as yours I guess. You pump your gas and you can buy all sorts of over-priced shit that you don't need in the store."

"Some of them sell food," added Wendy. "Although the quality varies. I remember being invited over to meet Pete's parents for the first time at a potluck lunch."

"What's that?" asked Martin.

"Oh my! Don't you have them over there?"

"We might call it something different."

"Well, y'all get together and each bring a dish of homemade food for everyone to en-joy," Wendy explained.

"I think we do that informally but it doesn't really have a name."

"It's so much fun!" said Wendy.

"Do you guys want to know how it all turned out?" asked Karen, threatening to deafen them all with her laugh. "Tell them, Wendy."

"It wasn't all my fault. I was running out of time so I bought some sushi from the gas station."

"Gas station sushi?" asked Tom. "That doesn't sound good."

"It wasn't the best," Wendy admitted. "Everybody got food poisoning and Pete was off work for a week in the middle of a big murder investigation. I think the killer got away but I'm sure they'll catch him next time. I hope so, anyway."

"What about you?"

"Oh, I was okay because I don't eat sushi."

Karen pulled up at the pump and noticed the woman opposite was checking the display before paying.

"That woman there has just put $1 of gas in at pump two. Where the fuck is she going on that? Pump three?"

"Maybe she's poor?" Martin suggested.

"She's driving a big-ass truck for a poor person."

"Maybe she stole it?"

"Well she ain't going to get far on a dollar of gas if the police start chasing her. I'd be filling up so I could make it to the state border."

Karen sighed with frustration and got out of the car. Tom noticed that she filled up and thought it was a good idea - especially if the police thought they'd had anything to do with the murder of that man with the small head.

"Stuart and Bhavna won't be very happy to have missed all the excitement," said Martin as Karen returned to the car and they headed downtown to the hotel.

"Maybe they killed him. We haven't seen them all day," said Tom.

"Why would they kill some random man in a foreign country?"

"Maybe he wouldn't accept Bhavna's opinion on something trivial."

"The medical examiner said there were different shaped wounds on his head. Maybe Bhavna hit him a few times with her shoe and then Stuart finished him off with his laptop," Martin suggested.

"Hey y'all. Do you need me to pick you up tomorrow morning or are you going to make your own way to the police station?" Karen asked as she returned to the car.

"We'll get a taxi," said Tom. "I don't want you to have to come downtown in all the traffic. We'll see you there at 8am."

"Okay, that's cool."

The car soon pulled up by the hotel and the two visitors got out. Tom went to the driver's window and thanked Karen for driving them back. Her arm was leaning on the door through the open window so he squeezed it for a second; she laid her other hand on his and smiled. It had been a fun day - maybe not so much for the guy that had died

- but certainly for the rest of them and she was looking forward to seeing him again tomorrow.

Tom and Martin said goodnight and walked into their hotel lobby as Karen and Wendy drove home. Stuart and Bhavna were sitting in the bar and looked up as they walked in. Neither of them looked particularly happy - or particularly healthy - but at least they'd left their rooms.

"Hey guys! How are you feeling?" asked Tom brightly as he went to sit down with them.

"We do not feel very good and we are also unhappy," said Bhavna.

"Why is that?" asked Tom as he sent Martin to the bar to order some beers.

"The food last night was terrible and we have wasted the day in bed today. We came down to the bar this evening and I have been talking to Stuart about the work we have to do this week but he says he feels worse now."

"It's true," Stuart agreed. "I feel a lot worse after having to listen to Bhavna talking to me about work for four hours on a Sunday."

"I am very disappointed that you two were not here to listen to my plans to resolve this problem."

"It's been a long day Bhavna. Also, I'm the Project Manager so you report to me for this and there is no way I am going to get into a long discussion about work on our day off. If I'd been here this evening I would have felt just as bad as Stuart having to listen to you talk about work all night."

"Also, we were involved in a murder," Martin added cheerfully.

"What?!" said Stuart. "You're kidding."

"We were in the park with Karen and some others and found a dead body. The police were called and asked us loads of questions. We've got to go to the police station to-morrow to give formal statements," said Tom.

"I'm not sure I believe this story," said Bhavna.

"Well here is Detective Schroedinger's card and the address of the police station we have to go to tomorrow."

"With a name like Schroedinger how do we know he even exists?"

"I'll ask him for a picture of his cat tomorrow if that helps."

"What are we doing tomorrow?" Stuart asked.

"We need to get to the police station at 8 o'clock and then I presume Karen will take us to work from there. Maybe you guys should go on ahead and have a look at some of the data first and we'll meet you when we're done.

"That sounds good," said Stuart, looking straight at Bhavna. "And it didn't take you four hours to give us our instructions."

"Tell us about this so-called murder you say that you were involved in," said Bhavna, deliberately not returning Stuart's gaze.

Tom and Martin looked at one another, took sips of their drinks and began the story of their day, from the aquarium and the museum in the morning to the long lunch and the walk around Piedmont Park in the afternoon. No detail was spared and Stuart began to think that Tom and Martin were just a bit too excited telling it - especially considering an old man had lost his life earlier that day.

When they finished the story, Bhavna sat there open-mouthed and Stuart had a blank look on his face. Tom went to order some more beers and when he returned was faced with a barrage of questions from Bhavna. Once she was satisfied that she knew as much about their day as they did, the conversation slowed down so they made arrangements to meet at breakfast the next day and then went upstairs and into their separate rooms for the night.

***

The Georgia sun was shining through the Atlanta skyscrapers on Monday morning as Tom and the others woke and began to look forward to the day ahead. For Tom and Martin, it was a trip to the police station to give witness statements while Stuart and Bhavna would be going straight to the Atlanta office of Classic Country Clothing (UK) Inc. to start work.

It was clear from the night before that Bhavna didn't believe there had even been a murder but hopefully with Karen to corroborate his and Martin's story she would have to believe them. Or maybe she still wouldn't - although it didn't really matter what she thought because it had been a great day yesterday (for most people) and Tom was look-ing forward to seeing what today would bring.

"Morning!" shouted Martin from the hotel corridor as he knocked as he knocked on Tom's door.

"Just give me a minute to get my shit together," Tom replied. "I had a bit of a restless night."

"Me too. It's probably due to all the excitement we had yesterday. I'll grab the others and meet you at breakfast," shouted Martin, much to the annoyance of the guests still sleeping in the nearby rooms.

Tom finished his morning ablutions and made his way downstairs. He had a slight pain in his foot from an accident the night before as he got into bed but was hoping it wouldn't need a trip to the hospital. If it did, all he'd need is for the hotel to catch fire and he'd then have the full set of meetings with the emergency services.

"Are you okay?" asked Stuart as he saw Tom limping slightly.

"Yes. Just a slight accident last night," said Tom as he joined them all at the breakfast table.

"What happened to you?" asked Bhavna.

"I banged my toe against the bed. I banged it so hard it's demanding I take it out for dinner and drinks retrospectively."

Tom looked at the three blank faces staring back at him. I'm wasted on these people, he thought as the waitress came over to take their order.

"What's the plan today?" asked Martin.

"Karen and the others will be meeting us at the police station while Stuart and Bhavna will go straight to the office and meet with Delores and her delightful jacket."

"What time do you think you will be joining us?" Bhavna asked, still not quite sure if there had been an actual murder or not.

"I wouldn't think it would take more than a couple of hours but they might interview each of us separately to see if our stories match."

"Do you think we should go over our stories first?" asked Martin, looking worried.

"No. We'll just tell them what we saw. Our experience will be slightly different from the others because we've got the car to talk about."

"Okay, you're probably right."

"It seems that you will be having fun at the police station with your friends while you send Stuart and I go on ahead to do all the work," said Bhavna.

"I don't make the rules," said Tom.

"You literally just made that rule," said Stuart.

"It's just common sense. There's no point in you two hanging around here waiting for us. Just crack on and we'll be with you as soon as possible."

After finishing their breakfast, they made their way upstairs to collect their laptops and bags and then asked reception to call them two taxis. As Tom watched Stuart and Bhavna get into the first taxi he couldn't help but wonder if Bhavna would survive this trip.

"She's a pain in the arse isn't she?"

"Definitely," Martin agreed. "But she knows her stuff."

"I know that once she gets cracking we won't hear another word from her until the end of the day but at the moment she's just doing my head in."

"Could we get her a dodgy kebab for lunch so she'll get food poisoning again?"

"I like your thinking but we need her," said Tom. "I wish they'd sent Sarah instead."

"Which one's she?"

"The one with the big boobs," said Tom.

"I think you mean the one with the excellent computer skills," said Martin.

"But she's got big boobs as well. It's just my way of identifying her from the rest of the people on that team."

"All the rest of her team are men."

"And none of them have got big boobs. I rest my case."

"What about Gordon? He's got big man boobs."

"Fair point," said Tom.

"I'll just drop this mic here," Martin chuckled as they walked outside.

The taxi arrived and soon deposited them at the police station in Midtown where Karen, Wendy, Dave and Sadie were outside waiting. They'd all had a restless night and an early start so their greetings were more muted than before and they immediately headed inside and reported to the reception desk.

The officer took their names and pointed to a waiting area where they were told to sit and wait for Detective Schroedinger to arrive. Tom chose the seat by a plant because it reminded him of his seat in the HR waiting room. Hopefully the coffee here would be as good as it was in HR.

"Thank you all for coming this morning," said a deep voice to his right. "Please could you follow me to the interview rooms."

"Sure," said Wendy. "It's good to see you again, Detective," said Wendy, emphasizing the last word in response to Schroedinger's insistence that she stopped calling him Pete.

Schroedinger led the six witnesses (or suspects) through a door and ushered Tom and Martin into one room and the four Americans into another room where a colleague was waiting. Turning back to the first room, Schroedinger joined Tom and Martin and told them to sit down. A young uniformed officer asked if they wanted coffee and they all said yes.

"I believe you two were slightly behind the rest of the group leading up to the time that the victim was discovered?"

"Yes we were," said Tom, deciding it would be better if he did all the talking. Martin wasn't as dopey as he had been when they were younger but if he let him say too much there was a good chance he'd say something stupid and they'd both be in the electric chair by the end of the day.

"What is your relationship with the others?" asked Schroedinger.

"We work for a company in England and have been sent over to investigate a data breach that has affected the Atlanta office. Karen is our contact there so we decided to meet up on Saturday night for a beer to get to know each other. We had a great time so decided to meet up again yesterday for lunch."

"Is the company called Classic Country Clothing (UK) Inc.?" asked Schroedinger, referring to a notepad on the desk in front of him.

"Yes. There's been a data breach and we have guys in the UK looking at the technical side of it but we've been sent over here to check the data, find out what went wrong and implement some new controls."

"I hope you'll be vigilant because I bought one of your coats online and I take my data privacy very seriously. In fact, I take everything very seriously."

"We will be," said Tom, making a mental note to check out Detective Schroedinger's browsing history when he got to the office and see what kind of things he'd been looking at.

"So, you work with Karen - what about the others?" asked Schroedinger, turning his gaze towards Martin for the first time.

"Wendy is Karen's sister. She came along on Saturday night but the other two are friends of hers and we met them for the first time yesterday."

"Are there any other people in the group that travelled over here?"

"Yes. We have two people who came with us but they both got food poisoning on Saturday night so they didn't come with us on Sunday."

"I see," Schroedinger paused to take some notes. "Tell me what happened from the time you met Wendy and the others until the time the police arrived."

Their coffees arrived and Tom gave Detective Schroedinger a detailed explanation of the day with Martin chipping in anytime Tom took a sip. So far, so good. There was no electric chair in sight but they had only reached the part where the car had nearly hit them so there was plenty of time for Martin to say something that would condemn them both to a shocking but possibly half-deserved end. Maybe Georgia didn't have the death penalty? He probably should have researched this before they'd come over. You could never be certain of getting home in one piece when you went anywhere with Martin.

"You said last night that the car was a dark colour. Do you remember any more details?"

"Sorry, but no. It was definitely an old car and I'd say it was black or dark blue but I don't want to rule out anything."

"That's okay. We'll check the database and see if we can match classic vehicles in the Atlanta area. Did you see the driver or the licence plate?"

"Sorry again. It all happened so fast and the headlights were full on. Martin was taking some photos of me for my dating profile when we got home so I probably saw more than he did but I didn't see much."

"You looked like a serial killer in the first photo I took," Martin added. "You should smile more."

"But then I look like a psychopath."

"True."

"Please continue telling me what happened during the rest of the evening," said Schroedinger, hoping their coffees had 'accidentally' been poisoned.

Martin picked up the story with Tom interjecting this time. They reached the part where Wendy had called them over to check the body when Detective Schroedinger stopped them.

161

"Was it definitely Wendy who called out to you?"

"Yes. And then the others. We were only about 20 metres away from them," said Tom.

"20 metres? That's about 65 feet?"

"I'm not sure, but it sounds about right."

"So, you both joined the others, saw the body and called 911. Is that right?"

"Yes. Karen called the police and we just stood and waited for them to arrive," said Tom.

"Do you think the incidents are connected? asked Martin.

"Almost certainly. It's likely that the perpetrator had just committed the crime and was fleeing the scene as you all arrived. That would explain the vehicle travelling at high speed towards you. If someone commits a crime, they don't usually keep to the posted speed limits - especially when leaving the crime scene."

"It could have been a triple homicide - as you guys say over here," suggested Tom.

"If you had both been hit by the vehicle, potentially yes."

"Cool," said Tom.

Detective Schroedinger looked at Tom in the way a cat might look at a cucumber. Were they all like this where these two came from? His cousin was a big fan of the Beatles and had once visited Liverpool to soak up the history of the city they came from. When he returned to Atlanta, he'd complained that he couldn't understand a word anyone was saying. Schroedinger could certainly understand what Tom was saying - he just couldn't understand why he was saying it.

"Thank you for your time. We have your contact details on file and I will be in touch again if we need anything else. If you think of anything else in the meantime, please contact me."

"We will," said Tom.

"How long are you here for?" asked Schroedinger.

"Two weeks initially."

"Okay. I won't be able to let you leave the country without agreement so if we haven't spoken again, please check in before you plan to leave. You will need authorisation from us or they will stop you at the airport."

"Awesome. Are we free to go?"

"Sure, but please call if you remember anything else, no matter how insignificant it may appear."

Chapter 22

Atlanta, USA

Tom and Martin were shown out of the police station and sat on a wall outside to wait for the others. Tom's phone had buzzed a few times while they were in with Detective Schroedinger and he now finally had the chance to check it. Three missed calls from Katrina on his messaging app. He called her back immediately.

"Good morning to you. How was the flight and hotel?" asked Katrina.

"Hi Katrina. The flight was good but the hotel isn't the best; they said it's being demolished in a few weeks due to repeated public health code violations."

"I'm sorry to hear that, but you know what the company is like when it comes to spending money on anything. How are you all getting on?"

"It's been great so far. We're at the police station at the moment," Tom replied.

"What?!"

"We're at the police station. I'm with Martin and Karen, plus her sister and two of her friends."

"What the fuck are you doing at the police station?! It's only your second full day there. Couldn't you keep out of trouble for five minutes?!"

"It's not us. We're witnesses to a murder," said Tom, brightly.

"Did one of you kill Bhavna? We thought it might be a possibility so we started a sweepstake. I've got £10 on Stuart."

"No, we were in the park yesterday and found a dead body so we reported it and the police have taken statements from us this morning. Stuart and Bhavna weren't involved because they had food poisoning. They've gone on ahead and should be at the office. Unless he's killed her."

"When will you be doing some actual work?" asked Katrina, slightly calmer now she knew that two of the team hadn't been arrested and the third one hadn't killed the fourth one.

"We're waiting for Karen and should be going up soon. It's just after 9am here and it's only a few minutes' drive."

"Okay," said Katrina. "I'll call you tomorrow but let me know if you find anything out before then."

"I will," said Tom as Karen and the others came out of the police station.

Tom ended the call and walked back over to Martin. Karen had already offered to drive them to the office while Wendy, Dave and Sadie stayed downtown so they all said good-bye.

"Are we all meeting up tonight?" asked Sadie. "It's Dave's birthday!"

"Hey! Happy birthday Dave," said Wendy, followed by a chorus of 'Happy Birthdays' from the others.

"It's no big deal," said Dave. "I mean, why do we congratulate someone for not doing anything dumb enough to get themselves killed over the last 12 months?"

"From what you've said it's a big deal for you to not get yourself killed over the last year," said Sadie.

"Yeah...you've got me there."

"It's a big deal for Martin as well," Tom added. "He's always falling over, breaking himself or getting stuck in mechanical things. I was trying to stop him saying too much during the interview in case we ended up in the electric chair."

"We do it by lethal injection these days," said Karen. "It's more humane."

"Why do they care about being humane when they're killing someone?" asked Martin.

"They just do. Something about lawsuits probably. Or maybe they didn't pay their power bill."

"The one about the power bill makes sense," said Tom. "You wouldn't want to pull the switch and only 15 volts came out. It would take forever to fry someone with that."

"Oh man! Where did you come from?!" laughed Karen. "Is everyone in England like you? I'm going to have to come over and visit someday."

"Most people aren't like him," said Martin. "Most people are normal."

"Maybe I'll have to come over and see for myself one day," said Karen. "But in the meantime, we've got to get to work. I'll call you later Wendy. It would be great to go out tonight for Dave's birthday if everyone's free?"

"I'm not free," said Dave. "I have to do family shit. But tomorrow would be good."

"That's fine. Let's talk about it later and we can meet up tomorrow. And let's hope we don't find any more dead bodies or the police will start thinking these two have come over on some kind of murdering spree," said Karen. "We thought we'd got rid of them in Boston by throwing all their tea in the harbour but the fools keep coming back."

"We want revenge," said Tom. "We take our tea very seriously in Britain."

Looking down at the six from the vantage point of an upstairs window, Detective Schroedinger couldn't imagine any of them as murderers. All they seemed to do was just talk and laugh the whole time and he couldn't see any of them being serious enough for long enough to actually do something as grave as murder. He could see them annoying someone to death but bludgeoning them seemed unlikely.

Down on the street, totally unaware of Schroedinger's favourable appraisal of them, the group of six separated into two groups of three and parted company. Wendy, Dave and Sadie went to get some breakfast while Karen led Tom and Martin to her car ready for the short drive north to the office.

***

Stuart and Bhavna were busy interrogating the internal code of the system that had caused the company so much trouble when the others arrived. They were totally absorbed in their task and Bhavna was particularly pleased to be doing some actual work rather than having to socialise with the others. She knew she was the odd one out in terms of her work ethic but doing a good job meant more to her than going out and filling her face with food and drink - especially after the food poisoning incident on Saturday night.

Stuart was less pleased to be working but from the sound of what was happening with Tom, Martin and Karen he was much safer in front of a computer than he would be in the bars of Atlanta and had already thought of his excuse for the next time they invited him out. He never thought that people working in IT could be so noisy; normally the only noise that came from them was the tapping of their keyboards. As if to prove his point, the main door suddenly opened to a cacophony of noise and laughter as Karen breezed in, followed by Tom and Martin.

"Hey y'all! Happy Monday everyone!" shouted Karen as she walked across the office.

"Good morning Karen," said Bhavna as she approached the desks where she and Stuart were sitting. "I understand that there may have been an incident yesterday?"

"Hell yeah! A real live dead body right in front of us! Can you imagine that?"

"I cannot."

"What?"

"I cannot imagine a real live dead body. A dead body is, by its very definition, dead and I cannot imagine a live dead one."

Karen went to the kitchen to make some coffee and offered to give Tom and Martin a tour of the building. As she went past, Bhavna thought she heard words that sounded very much like 'fuck you' but they were very faint. Perhaps she would ask Karen about this when she had returned from showing the other two around the building.

"What the hell is wrong with that woman?" Karen asked Tom once they were out of earshot.

"She's a bit pedantic, isn't she?"

"More than a bit."

"She's just as bad in England," offered Martin. "She's great at her job but a bit too serious."

"If she took that stick out of her ass she might be okay," Karen agreed. "But I doubt it."

A few minutes after leaving the main office, Tom and Martin re-appeared and went to sit at some spare desks near Stuart and Bhavna. As the American division of the company was still growing, there was still plenty of space in the main office where most people sat and spare desks were easy to find. In a few months it was hoped that the whole of the ground floor - or the first floor as Karen had called it - would be occupied and they would then need to move the directors and senior managers upstairs to the second floor (or the first floor, as Tom and Martin had called it).

"How is it going?" asked Tom as he and Martin sat down.

"We're just getting into the system now and it does seem to be capturing a lot more data than we would expect," said Stuart. "We can isolate certain fields and tell the system not to capture them in future, but why this happened is a mystery."

"It sounds like Johnny Pervert wanted to know a bit more about his customers than he had any right to," said Tom.

"Firing him was the best thing they did. Do they think he could be behind the data breach?"

"I don't know. Keith is dealing with that but they're not ruling anything out."

"How did the meeting at the police station go?" asked Bhavna, seemingly satisfied that there had in fact been a murder now that Karen had confirmed it.

"It was okay. They just asked for our statements and we told them what we saw - or rather didn't see. It was so dark and all we could give them was a dark car whizzing past us and a dead body by the lake."

"I am sure the police will do their work and establish the identity of the murderer."

"Let's hope so. If they saw us, then we might be next," said Tom.

"What do you mean?" said a suddenly worried Martin.

"Well, you know how it is. Murderers like to tie up all the loose ends. We should probably avoid that park for the rest of our trip."

"Yeah...probably. I told you we should have brought some guns with us."

"You did," said Tom. "Maybe I should listen to you occasionally. Not often, but occasionally."

Martin laughed and set up his laptop. Karen came over and logged them in to spare computers and gave them both USB data sticks to allow them to transfer data from the main computers to their laptops and then went back to her desk to speak to Delores, whose trademark purple and mustard jacket was thankfully missing due to the warm weather. Karen hoped she wouldn't have to see it again until October.

"Hey Delores. Did you have a good weekend?"

"Just the usual," Delores said, not looking up.

"You get arrested every weekend?!"

"What do you mean by that?"

"We were all in a restaurant downtown and saw you being bundled into the back of a squad car."

"What made you think that was me?" Delores asked, becoming defensive.

"You were wearing that ugly ass coat of yours. Nobody else has got a coat like that."

"That's because nobody else has the same taste in clothes as me."

"You got that right," laughed Karen. "What did they arrest you for? As your manager I need to be sure you're not some kind of master criminal."

"It was nothing. I had some two-dollar bills and I went to pay for some medicine with them. The cashier at the drug store refused to take them and I got angry because I needed the meds."

"Two-dollar bills are legal tender though."

"That's what I said. But they accused me of fraud and called the cops."

"What happened then?"

"The cops came and they also disputed that two-dollar bills were legal tender so they put me in the back of a patrol car. Once we got to the station the sergeant on duty told them that two-dollar bills were legal and they had to let me go. They were about to let me go but one of them made a comment about my coat."

"Was it a positive comment?" asked Karen, trying not to laugh.

"No, it was not a positive comment. It was a negative comment. He said I shouldn't wear it near a school in case I scared the kids and gave them mental trauma."

"What did you do?"

"I slapped that young man right around his head. That's when they arrested me and kept me in overnight."

Across the other side of the room, Tom and the others were busy looking at different sets of computer data when the explosion of laughter reached them. It was impossible to concentrate when Karen was laughing and - after being at work for almost ten minutes - Tom was already in need of a break and walked over to find out what was going on. Delores explained the story of her arrest and what the police officer had said about her coat and Tom duly relayed this to the others when he got back to his desk.

Martin and Stuart both found the tale amusing but Bhavna was either not impressed or had left her sense of humour at home and immediately put her headphones back in; she was another one still using wires Tom thought. What was wrong with these people? Tom got out his wireless headphones, logged in to the company's Wi-Fi network and followed the rest of the team in getting down to what it was they were being paid to do. He did wonder about the murder though and hoped they hadn't heard the last of it.

***

Across the city, Wendy was spending the afternoon at The King Center with her new friends Dave and Sadie. Sitting on a bench by the cobalt blue waters of the reflecting pool Wendy felt a sense of much-needed calm and tranquility. She saw herself as a free spirit and while she had a list of phobias as long as the terms and conditions in an iPhone software update, she tried not to let things get to her. This felt different, however, and brought with it a huge sense of loss that seemed somehow personal.

Two weeks ago, Wendy had been working in a museum and living in her own apartment. Since then she had lost her job, been forced to give up her apartment to move in with her sister and had now seen the body of a man who had just lost his life. Seeing Pete Schroedinger again had brought back the memories of her relationship with him and its eventual end - resulting in more loss. Living with Karen couldn't last forever and she knew that once the excitement of the murder had subsided and the British guys had gone home there'd be another hole in both their lives.

Wendy gazed into the peaceful waters surrounding Martin Luther King's tomb as she waited for Dave and Sadie to come back from the gift shop and still wasn't totally sure if the other two were hooking up or not. They certainly seemed to get on well, but then all three of them got on well so it was hard to tell, although with Sadie now effectively living with Dave there was a fair chance they were becoming a couple.

She was snapped out of her thoughts by a group of tourists asking her to take a picture of them by the Eternal Flame that burned in a small area opposite Dr King's tomb. As Wendy got up to take the photo for them she wondered if this was where the Bangles had written their hit song.

"Hey Wendy!" came a male voice from behind her.

"Hi Dave. Where's Sadie?"

"She's in the bathroom. She's been there a while so she's either taking a huge dump or she's waiting for somebody to open the door for her," said Dave. "We were going to get something to eat soon if you want to come along. It's a bit early but I've got this birthday thing later with my folks so I need to get some food in my stomach to soak up all the beer I'll be forced to drink."

"Forced?" asked Wendy with a raised eyebrow.

"Well, no," Dave laughed. "I'm always quite happy to drink beer. I'm pretty good at it too."

"Normally I'd say yes but the last couple of days have been a bit full on so I think I'll just head home and get an early night."

"What's up Wendy?" asked Sadie, arriving from the bathroom.

"I'm thinking of heading home and crashing on the couch for the evening. Last night was a bit intense."

"It was cool wasn't it?" Sadie said excitedly.

"That's not the word I would have used."

"I guess not.   But it's been a while since I've seen a dead body. I'm trying to clean up my life a bit and get away from that world if I can."

"That's great news," said Wendy.

"I'm helping her," said Dave, blushing as Sadie squeezed his arm.

"Well you two kids have fun now," Wendy said. "I'm going to call an Uber and go back to Karen's and drink the biggest bottle of wine I can find."

Sadie and Dave both hugged Wendy and watched her walk back up the slope that ran alongside the reflecting pool to the exit before deciding where they were going to eat.

Chapter 23

Atlanta, USA

It was late afternoon and Detective Schroedinger was going over the notes from the two sets of interviews earlier that day. Having interviewed the two British guys himself he'd picked up on the nuances of speech and body language and could just about conclusively prove they were too immature to have been involved in anything like this. He also knew Wendy was not capable of murder and her sister Karen seemed like the only sensible one in the whole group so he could probably rule her out too.

The other two - Dave and Sadie - each had a list of arrests for minor misdemeanours but again, nothing that would point to murder and he was sure that even if they had been involved, at least one of the others would have slipped up and said something. It looked like this was a genuine case of six idiots finding a dead body in a park. It was not an everyday occurrence in this city but it probably did happen somewhere. Maybe in Britain? Any country that drives on the wrong side of the road must have something wrong with it.

As Schroedinger re-focused on his case notes he looked again at the coroner's report. The autopsy had been performed but nothing conclusive had yet come back. The head wounds were clearly inflicted by two separate objects and, according to Dr Brownstein, there were more than 20 shallow indentations in the victim's head in the shape of what appeared to be a cooking ladle. Who kills somebody with a giant spoon?

The other wounds were deeper and there were only two of them - one to the face and the other to the side of the head. It looked like whoever had tried to kill the victim with a ladle had either found something more substantial to finish the job off with or had received help from someone with an altogether more serious approach to bashing people's heads in.

Detective Schroedinger got up and looked out the window to clear his head for a second. The streets were beginning to fill up with the evening traffic as the commuters from downtown made their way back home to their families in the suburbs. Living alone, Schroedinger often felt lonely and having his own office cut him off from the rest of the department which made it worse. He wasn't the most talkative of people but did miss the company of others, even if it was just to pass the time of day or talk about the latest sports game. He didn't miss their inane chatter though.

The phone on his desk rang and the number on the display showed him the caller was either Dr Brownstein or one of his team.

"Schroedinger."

"Hey Pete, it's Bill."

"Hi Bill. What have you got for me?

"This guy with the small head and the multiple murder weapons..." Brownstein began.

"Yes?"

"We think we know what the second weapon was."

"That's good progress. What is it?"

"It's a sandwich grill."

"A sandwich grill?"

"You know, you get some bread, add a little cheese and tomato and then grill it. My wife bought one a while back and makes the best toasted sandwiches and paninis."

"I know what it is. I have one too, although I'm not sure I ever want to use it again now I know it was one of the murder weapons."

"Yeah, about that. It looks like somebody attacked the victim with the ladle and bashed his head in pretty well with multiple blows to the back, the side and the front of the head. The sandwich grill was used afterwards; probably to finish him off when they realised the ladle wasn't quite going to do it for them. We've got some iron fragments in the skull from the ladle and plastic fragments from the sandwich grill."

"Are you sure?"

"Almost 100%. Technically the sandwich grill is the murder weapon as there were no wounds inflicted post mortem."

"So, let me think," said Schroedinger. "Both of these items are kitchen implements so we could work on the possibility that the murder happened in the home - most likely the kitchen."

"That would be my guess too," agreed Dr Brownstein.

"The wounds are shallow and there are a lot of them. This would indicate someone without a lot of strength but with a lot of anger."

"That makes sense, although they did have the strength to carry the body from the house - if he was killed in a house - to the car and then from the car to the side of the river."

"That's confusing."

"It is," Brownstein agreed. "It seems you could be looking for someone strong enough to move a body but nor strong enough to kill in a single blow."

"Or two people," said Schroedinger.

"Or multiple people," Dr Brownstein added.

"True. The victim was a senior citizen and if we think that the murder probably took place in the home, it could mean the killer was his wife or another family member?"

"That would be the first place I'd look. You could be looking at a family where one person beat the guy up with a ladle - probably the wife as the wounds are quite shallow - and then another family member cleans his clock with a sandwich grill and disposes of the body."

"That works," said Dr Brownstein. "Do you have an ID on the victim yet?"

"Nothing at all."

"Why not?"

"He's not in the system. He had no ID on him, no wallet, no cellphone...nothing. Dental records have come up with nothing too."

"Is he a US citizen? His skin showed signs of sun damage."

"This is what I'm thinking. He was clearly a Caucasian but doesn't seem to have spent any time at all in the US."

"What's he doing here in Atlanta? Surely he didn't just move here in the hope of getting killed by a combination of a ladle and a sandwich grill?"

"It's unlikely. But we've got the corpse of an old man in his 70s or 80s who clearly lived here because witnesses saw him walking round the same park a few hours earlier in the day."

"Are we sure it's the same guy?" asked Brownstein.

"Pretty sure. The height, age and description of a smaller than average head suggests it is."

"You're probably looking at an old white guy who has suddenly moved to Atlanta after spending most of his life in another country. He lives close enough to Piedmont Park to walk there in the afternoon and then finds himself dead in the evening."

"That's about it. Although he could have driven to the park in the afternoon and then gone for a walk," Schroedinger added. "He could have lived just about anywhere."

"Good point. I'm glad you're the one that has to solve this and not me," Brownstein chuckled.

"Thanks. Just one more thing. How do you know it was a sandwich grill that killed him and not something like a toaster?"

"The two final blows to the victim's head left two distinct impressions. One was the corner of the grill and the other was the patterned ridges inside. It looks like the top half may have broken off with the impact of the first blow and the second blow was with the inside of the machine. The pattern is very clear. I can even tell you the brand and model number but I'll put it all in my report and email it to you by the end of the day."

"Thanks Bill, I really appreciate it."

"No problem, Pete. Have a good evening."

Schroedinger put the phone down, left his office and headed to the kitchen to make some more coffee. On his way there he thought about what Bill had told him. Who kills somebody with a spoon and a sandwich grill? What happened to the old days when a couple of slugs to the chest would normally do it? Were today's murderers becoming more creative? Or was it some kind of environmentally responsible way of killing people by not using bullets in case they depleted the ozone layer?

He reached the coffee pot and poured the strong black liquid into his mug. He'd got this for Christmas from Wendy. She'd had it personalised to say 'My Favorite Detective' and it had a picture of some handcuffs on it. He wasn't sure whether the picture referred to his job or their personal life but it made him smile. If only Wendy hadn't been such an airhead, their relationship could have gone somewhere. He needed someone who took life as seriously as he did but Wendy wasn't that person, although seeing her twice in two days had made him think about her again.

Schroedinger walked back to his office and turned his mind back to the case. From what he'd seen and from what Bill had told him, it sounded like a simple domestic homicide. In cases like this a family member would ordinarily be the chief suspect - particularly given the victim's age - but unfortunately he currently had no idea who the victim was.

"Hey sis! How was your day?" asked Wendy as soon as she saw Karen walk through the front door.

"Hi Wendy, it was good thanks. The British guys have been staring at computer data all day so I just got on with my regular work," said Karen.

"I went out with Dave and Sadie today. We didn't find any more dead bodies unfortunately."

"Well that's a blessing," laughed Karen. "Try not to find too many more or your ex-boyfriend will think you're a serial killer."

"How can I be a serial killer? I haven't even killed one person yet."

"Try to keep it like that."

"I will. But it's probably best if you don't annoy me - just in case," said Wendy, picking up one of her cats and stroking its head.

"What random shit are you having for your dinner tonight?"

"Tofu."

"What the hell is tofu?" asked Karen. "Is that some kind of hippie vegan stuff?"

"It's coagulated soy milk."

"What the..? Never mind. I don't even want to know. I'm just going to enjoy a meat feast pizza."

"Are you seeing Tom and the others tonight?" Wendy asked as they made their way into the kitchen to prepare their separate meals.

"No, I've been stuck looking at these fools most of the day so I don't really want to see them tonight as well."

"Are we going out with Dave and Sadie tomorrow?"

"Sure. I'll ask the others but I'll wait until Tom and Martin are alone."

"What's wrong with the other Brits?" asked Wendy.

"The woman - Bhavna - is so pedantic; if you say something simple she'll correct you to fifteen decimal places and Stuart has a beard twice the size of my head. Tom says he's seen insects and small rodents moving about in it."

Karen's laugh scared two of Wendy's cats out of the kitchen so Wendy went to collect them. As she went to find them, she checked her phone and saw a missed call from Pete - or Detective Schroedinger as he now wanted to be called. She took the phone up to her bedroom and called him back.

There was no answer at first so she went back downstairs, checked to make sure Karen wasn't trying to scare her cats with her laugh and tried again. Still no answer.

"What's up?" asked Karen.

"Pete called but now he won't answer my calls. I'll have to keep trying."

"Why can't you just leave him?"

"He wouldn't call if it wasn't important and I don't want him to think I'm ignoring him. He might need my help to solve the case."

"Do you think it will be about the murder or about the two of you?"

"It could be either. He wasn't the most talkative person when I was dating him so he's difficult to read. Hold on, my phone's ringing."

"Hi Pete, how are you?"

"I'm good thanks, Wendy. I was thinking about something you said yesterday about meeting Dave and Sadie at a phobia workshop."

"Yes, that's right."

"How long ago did you meet them?"

"Last week. It was my first session."

"I was thinking about coming along. What day does it run?"

"Tuesdays and Fridays. We'll be going tomorrow."

"That works for me. Tuesday is my day off. Can you text me the details?"

"Sure Pete. It's up near the Braves stadium; I'll text you the address and the time."

"Thanks Wendy. I'll see you tomorrow," said Schroedinger as he ended the call.

"Hey sis! Pete's coming to the phobia workshop tomorrow. Maybe I can get some details of the murder from him."

"What's he got a phobia of? Apart from dumbasses like you," laughed Karen, causing Wendy to look at her cats and prepare to reassure them.

"The only one I know of is loud noises, but he might have more."

"Maybe you two fools are made for one another after all," said Karen as she took her pizza out of the oven and carried it to the table.

"You eat a lot of pizza."

"I like pizza."

"You'll end up looking like a pizza soon," said Wendy.

"And if you don't shut your damned mouth you'll end up looking like that guy we found in the park yesterday."

***

The Ocean Hotel was a small hotel with a terrible reputation in the heart of downtown Atlanta. It was about to be demolished and the owner was trying to make as much money as he could before that happened. Tonight was the third consecutive night that a group of noisy and slightly clueless business travellers from Britain had been staying and it looked like this would be the first time they would be spending the whole evening in the bar.

Stuart bought the first round and the conversation started with the data analysis work Martin had been doing and flowed into Stuart and Bhavna's investigation of the data storage problems.

"What can you tell us then Martin?" Tom asked once they had all settled down at the table with their drinks and their laptops.

"Well, mate, it looks like the program Johnny Pervert installed was grabbing literally every piece of data from the user's phone if they had the app."

"I believe that the gentleman's name was actually Johnathan Perver," said Bhavna.

"We know," said Tom. "But given what we know about him and the data being collected by the software he recommended, bought and oversaw we're calling him Johnny Perver."

"That is totally fair," Bhavna agreed. "Please continue, Martin."

"If a user installed the app it would monitor everything they browsed, typed, messaged or looked at and then it would capture it and store it on the database. There are thousands of photos on there, copies of emails, texts and browsing logs."

"Are there loads of annoying pictures of people's kids eating their dinner?" asked Tom.

"Of course," replied Martin, the inference completely going over his head. "Every social media account post was captured from the time they installed the app. To be honest, it's horrifying."

"If this ever gets out it will be worse than that Facebook scandal a while back," said Stuart.

"Let's make sure it doesn't get out then," said Tom.

"I need to get some food soon," said Martin and got up to retrieve some menus from the bar.

"How about you guys?" asked Tom. "What did you find?"

"We found a lot of random data stored on the database on the server. All the stuff Martin found is on there. It's not great news but we can certainly delete it."

"That would clearly be the most favourable option," Bhavna added.

"Can you break it down into categories so I can go to the directors and the data security team to agree what needs to be deleted and what can stay?" asked Tom.

"Yes of course. It is sorted by app so it should be simple enough to delete anything it took from other apps such as social media, texts, emails and browsers and just keep the data taken from our own app."

Martin returned with the menus and another round of drinks for everyone and they took a few moments to decide what they were each having to eat before the server came over and took their orders.

"Bhavna just said the data is stored according to the app it was taken from. Is that how you see it too?" Tom asked Martin when the server had left.

"Yeah...whenever the user opens an app, the program hidden in our app just seems to scrape all the data from the new app and store it somewhere."

"It stores it neatly in app folders so we could easily just set up a list of apps we want to keep data from and remove the rest," added Stuart.

"What apps would we need to keep data from?"

"Firstly, our own app so we know what they've looked at and bought already but also any others from similar retailers. If the customer looks at our app, browses hats for example and then buys a hat from a competitor we could keep that data and send them offers on hats so they buy their next hat from us instead."

"Okay, that sounds sensible. What about internet browsing?"

"We could set it up so it only captures data from other retailers and holiday websites."

"Holiday websites?"

"If a customer looks at a yachting holiday website we could capture that and send them offers for extreme wet weather clothes - anything that might be useful on a boat."

"That sounds good," said Tom. "Can you give me a list of the type of apps we should keep data from and I'll speak to the directors tomorrow?"

"I can do that for you," said Bhavna.

"Thanks," said Tom as the food arrived and the conversation moved away from work and onto the murder as Stuart wanted to know every detail of the police interviews that morning.

Chapter 24

Atlanta, USA

The Tuesday morning sun shone down on Atlanta as Tom, Martin, Stuart and Bhavna made their way by taxi to the offices of Classic Country Clothing (UK) Inc. As the taxi pulled up outside the building Tom's phone rang so he excused himself while the others went inside.

"Hi Katrina, how are you?"

"Hi Tom. I'm good thanks - I hope you're not in police custody again?!" she teased.

"Not yet - although the day is still young over here and we're all going out tonight so who knows."

"Please don't get arrested," said Katrina.

"I'll try not to. Anyway, we've made good progress and we now know that the software powering the app was effectively scraping every bit of data from people's phones and storing it in folders on the database."

"Everything?" asked Katrina.

"Literally everything - from photos of their kids to private texts to their wives or husbands."

"Or somebody else's wife or husband."

"Exactly."

"It's every bit as bad as we'd feared," said Katrina.

"Yes, it is, but the good news is the data is stored very simply and Stuart can remove it from the database just as simply. We just need the directors' permission to capture data from certain apps but ignore data from others. I'll email you a summary when I'm set up at my desk."

"That will be great, thanks. Do you just need a yes or no against each app or type of app and we can delete the data we've captured and stop it from capturing any more?"

"Yes. If we don't want data from their banking app or their emails just let me know and what we've got already will be deleted and we won't capture any more in the future."

"That's a huge weight off my mind. I know Lisa and Keith will be pleased. Have you managed to find anything else out?"

"Nothing at all. Everyone here is just as surprised as we were and none of them seem the type to do anything like that. Half of them aren't bright enough to be honest."

"What about Karen?"

"She's indifferent to the whole thing. She wasn't involved in any of the setting up of the app or the software and doesn't care enough about the company either way to be bothered if it steals people's data or not. I've asked Stuart and Bhavna to stay late tonight and delve into everyone's computers when they've all gone home so we should find out if there is anything amiss."

"That's good. Well done Tom. I knew I could trust you to do a good job on this."

"Thanks Katrina. Maybe we'll solve the murder too while we're at it."

"Maybe, but please focus on the data breach first," Katrina laughed as they then said goodbye and Tom made his way into the building where the others were waiting.

***

"Good morning to you sir. My name is Lloyd. Are you here for the phobia workshop?"

"Yes. I'm quite nervous though," said the heavy-set young man before him with brown hair and fierce eyes. "I'm Vinny and I have a phobia of groups of people. I'm from Brooklyn originally but it was too crowded there so I moved down here to Atlanta."

"It's good to meet you Vinny. We are all friends here so please don't be nervous. There is no judgement," said Lloyd, trying to reassure the newest member of the group.

"Thanks Lloyd. I'm sorry I'm a few minutes early but I've got a phobia of being late."

"That is perfectly acceptable. The others will no doubt be joining us shortly."

"I hope they're not late because I've also got a phobia of other people being late."

"I'm sure they'll be here on time," said Lloyd.

"I hope so," Vinny growled. "For their sakes."

"Please help yourself to refreshments and take a seat. We have coffee, tea and water on the table over there next to the fire exit."

"Thanks," said Vinny as he went to pour himself some coffee before finding a seat.

Outside the building, Sadie and Dave were waiting for Wendy. When she arrived, she told them that Detective Schroedinger would be joining them so they waited for him. A few minutes later, a shiny black car pulled up and Schroedinger got out.

"Hey Pete! You made it," said Wendy as the detective approached the group.

"Good morning to you all. I'm sorry if I'm late."

"Good morning everybody," said a deep voice behind them. "I recognise three of you but you, sir, are one of our new friends, I take it? My name is Lloyd and I run these workshops."

"Good day Lloyd. I am Detective Pete Schroedinger."

"My word, Detective! We are not in any kind of trouble are we?"

"Not at all. I am just here for the workshop. Wendy suggested I come."

"Well that is a relief," said Lloyd leading them into the building. "We have another new friend who has already arrived. His name is Vinny and he has a phobia of groups of people so please be kind to him."

"Is that him running out of the fire exit?" asked Wendy.

"Yes...that was him," said Lloyd sadly. "Anyway, please help yourselves to the refreshments on the table that Vinny almost knocked over in his haste to leave and we will begin."

The four of them poured themselves some coffee and returned to the centre of the room where the seats had been set out. As Lloyd watched them, he wondered if he could move to a remote village in another country far away and change his name so nobody could ever find him. The session last Friday had been curtailed after only ten minutes due to the fire alarm accidentally going off and causing them to evacuate the building. He could only hope the alarm would go off again today - although maybe the calming presence of a police detective would bring some normality to proceedings this time.

"Good morning everyone and welcome to today's phobia workshop. As you all know, my name is Lloyd and while I always start by saying we are all friends, it seems that this is particularly true this week. You all know each other from this workshop or from outside in the real world so maybe we should begin immediately."

"Good morning Lloyd," said the group.

"As we have one new friend with us, maybe you could go first. Please tell me why you are here and what you have a phobia of."

"Certainly," said Schroedinger, clearing his throat. "I have a fear of loud noises which has proved to be limiting in my line of work."

"In what way?" Lloyd asked.

"I don't like gunfire so I prefer not to fire my weapon if at all possible."

"Well that's admirable Detective Schroedinger. Or may I call you Pete?"

"Pete is fine," said Schroedinger. "But only when I'm off duty," he added, looking sternly at Wendy, Dave and Sadie.

"Right-o Petey boy!" said Wendy as Schroedinger groaned and rolled his eyes.

"This is called phonophobia, Pete; do you know when your fear of loud noises began?" Lloyd asked, trying to get the conversation back to this fairly common phobia.

"A few years ago. When I was a rookie, one of the senior officers in my division was killed in the performance of his duty so there was a full police funeral with a guard of honour and a three-volley salute."

"I'm sorry, Pete. I'm not familiar with that term."

"Funerals of senior officers and those that served our country usually incorporate a three-volley salute where three rounds of ammunition are fired into the air to represent duty, honour and sacrifice."

"Thank you. Please continue."

"I was one of the officers taking part in the salute but I was slow to raise my rifle."

"What happened?"

"The rest of my team fired before I was ready and the noise of their shots gave me a start. I accidentally discharged my rifle and the bullet went into the coffin of the deceased officer."

"I see."

"Everyone said the bullet would have killed him if he hadn't been dead already."

"I see," said Lloyd again. Who exactly was this guy protecting and serving?

"Ever since then, loud noises have bothered me," said Schroedinger.

"I can understand that. Is there anything else?"

"Not at the moment."

The fire exit suddenly opened and a heavy-set young man gingerly put his head into the room.

"Is that Vinny again?" asked Wendy.

"It appears so," said Lloyd. "Vinny! Won't you come and join us?"

"I'm sorry Lloyd. There are too many of you. I'll come back next week - unless you do one to one sessions?"

"I'm sorry, Vinny. These are strictly group sessions on Tuesdays and Fridays."

"Okay, I'm sorry. There's a guy out here that wants to come in but he says he's scared of chairs and wants to stand up. What should I tell him?"

"You may tell him that he is welcome to come in and stand with us."

"But he's also scared of being late - just like me. That's how we got to talking."

"How long have you two been talking?"

"I saw him here when I ran out and we just started talking about being late."

"So he was on time until he met you?"

"Sure," said Vinny. "But then we started talking and now he's late."

"That doesn't matter; tell him that he is welcome to attend and can stand up if he prefers."

"I'll try but I don't know what he'll say. Also, he's late. In Brooklyn we wouldn't allow this type of thing,"

"Please tell him to come in."

"He said he's happy to stand up but he's scared you'll give him a hard time because he's late."

"You can assure him that we won't give him a hard time."

"I'd give him a hard time if I were you."

"But you are not me, Vinny. Please tell our friend he is more than welcome to come in."

185

"You want me to bust his ass for being late?"

"Why would I want a thing like that?" asked Lloyd, wondering how his day had taken such a wrong turn.

"To teach him a lesson for being late."

"But he has a phobia of being late."

"Maybe if I bust his ass he won't be able to sit down and that will cure two problems at once."

"Vinny, we are here to help each other not criticise or bust people's asses. I'm sure he's sorry he's late – even though it wasn't technically his fault."

"He doesn't look too repentant," said Vinny. "Do you want me to whack him?"

"No! I do not want you to whack him."

"You got anyone else you want me to whack?"

"No! I don't want you to whack anyone."

"They'd have to be on their own; I wouldn't be able to take anyone out who was part of a group."

Detective Schroedinger stood up and walked towards the fire exit where Vinny was gesticulating to a timid looking man standing by a dumpster. It looked like he was dragging his finger across his throat while his target was frozen to the spot in fear. Schroedinger showed Vinny his badge.

"Listen to me, sir. I need you to go home right now or I will arrest you for threatening behaviour."

"I ain't done nothing," Vinny protested. "Are you really going to arrest me for nothing?"

"Maybe I won't arrest you," said Schroedinger. "Maybe I'll do something far worse."

"Like what?"

"See that structure over there? That's Truist Park where the Atlanta Braves play baseball. Later today, that place will be teeming with thousands of people going to the game. How about I take you there and leave you in the middle of the crowd?"

"No way!" said Vinny. "I'm going. I won't cause you any trouble."

"Good."

"Do you know what time the Friday session is?"

"Just go and don't come back or I'll take you out to the ball game."

Vinny ran off. The timid man had already disappeared in the opposite direction so Schroedinger went back through the fire exit and into the room. As soon as he entered, he could see there was someone missing. It was Lloyd.

"Where did Lloyd go?"

"He said he had to leave urgently," said Dave.

"They weren't his exact words Dave," said Wendy. "His exact words were 'what the fuck is wrong with you people?' and then he walked out."

"Does that mean there won't be a workshop on Friday?"

"Probably not. He looked like he was going to lock himself away in a dark room for the rest of the day."

"Maybe he has a phobia of people with phobias," suggested Sadie. "That would be fun."

"But then he'd be afraid of himself, if he also had a phobia," said Dave.

"That would suck," said Sadie. "No wonder he had to leave."

"I need to go," said Schroedinger.

"How's the case going, Detective?" asked Sadie.

"You know I can't really talk about active investigations but we do have an idea of the two murder weapons."

"That's a good start isn't it?" asked Dave.

"Yes, but unfortunately we don't have any concrete leads and we can't ID the victim because he's not in the system.

"What does that mean, Pete? I mean 'Detective'" asked Wendy.

"It means he was probably a foreign national. Look, I'll be honest with you Wendy. We have no idea who he is or where he came from so unless someone reports him missing, I can see the case sliding down the list of priorities. I'm sorry but that's just the way it is."

"That doesn't seem fair."

"I know, but this appears to be a one-off crime, possibly a domestic homicide. If that's true then we wouldn't expect any further killings. Currently he's just another John Doe that will be buried at the city's expense. It's harsh but we don't have much to go on at the moment."

"Did you say there were two murder weapons?" asked Dave.

"Yes. Strictly between us - and I'm counting on you to not spread this around Wendy - he was attacked multiple times with a large metal spoon or ladle and finally killed with a sandwich grill."

"A sandwich grill?"

"Yes."

"One of those appliances that are advertised on TV shopping channels that old people buy, use once and then put at the back of the cabinet?"

"Yes."

"Old people are great, aren't they?" Sadie laughed.

"They're like young people but they've been around a long time," said Dave. "Like dinosaurs."

"Would dinosaurs use a sandwich grill?" Wendy asked.

"Not the T-Rex," answered Dave, clearly considering the matter. "They've only got little arms so I doubt they'd be able to plug it in."

"Good point," said Sadie. "Did they have electricity when the dinosaurs were around?"

"I'm not sure, but even if they did, the sandwich grill wouldn't have been much use to them if they had small arms."

"And if they didn't have electricity, they wouldn't have been able to buy one anyway because there would have been no TV without electricity," Wendy added.

"You're right. Although only old people buy them and I'm not sure they would have moved into a retirement community near a dinosaur habitat," said Dave.

"Can we stop talking about dinosaurs?!" said Schroedinger. "Some of us have work to do."

"Detective?"

"Yes Dave."

"Seeing as we're all key components for a major Georgia murder investigation would you be able to help me out with some outstanding citations?"

"No."

"My brother used to date a police officer up in Cobb County and I used to ask him all the time to get her to help me get out of tickets."

"And did she?"

"No, sir, she did not. I was a bit disappointed to be truthful. I always thought that having a cop in the family would help me get out of jail."

"The best way to get out of jail is to not be in jail in the first place and the best way to achieve that is to not commit petty crimes."

"Are you sure, Detective?"

"Positive. Without people like you we'd have a lot less to do."

"So you'd be bored?"

"I have to go," said an exasperated Schroedinger. How did he keep getting into these random conversations? Maybe he would pin the murder on them after all, for the sake of his own sanity. He'd ask the District Attorney for the death penalty and administer the injection himself if he had to. And on his day off if needed.

"See you later, Pete. Maybe we can talk some time?"

"Sure, Wendy. Have a good day everyone."

Detective Schroedinger made his way across the room, went through the door and headed back to the sanctuary of his car. Wendy, Dave and Sadie were now alone in a room that was meant to be alive with people discussing their phobias and trying to come up with coping mechanisms for each other but which now felt curiously empty without Lloyd.

"Do you think Lloyd will be back on Friday?" asked Sadie optimistically.

"I can't be sure," said Wendy. "He didn't seem very happy when he left. When he was talking to Vinny it looked like all the life was slowly draining out of him."

"I think I saw his soul leave his body when Vinny offered to whack that other guy."

"I saw that too," said Sadie. "I need to get all my things from various friends and move them to your basement if that's okay Dave?"

189

"Sure. Just be back by seven o'clock so we can all go out," Dave replied. "We are still going out tonight aren't we?"

"Definitely," said Sadie.

"I'll call Karen and her two British friends to see what they're doing tonight. Shall we go back to that bar we were at on Sunday? It could be our tribute to the guy that got murdered."

"Sounds great," said Dave as they made their way out of the building.

As they went their separate ways, somewhere across the city a goth waitress was getting ready for her first shift back at work after what had been a particularly traumatic Sunday afternoon. At least that group from table six wouldn't be there again. She looked in the mirror as she applied her make-up and practised her best resting bitch face.

Chapter 25

Atlanta, USA

Stuart and Bhavna were working through the data that had been stored on the server and had separated it into two types - data that should be kept and data that should be deleted. Emails had been going backwards and forwards between Tom and Katrina all morning and just after lunch they had received the confirmation they needed to delete all of the unnecessary and highly sensitive data.

"I've just forwarded you confirmation from Lisa to delete everything captured from browsers, phone calls, texts, messaging programs and social media accounts," said Tom.

"Thanks," said Stuart. "I'll do that right away."

"Before you do, I need to check something."

"Sure. What do you need?"

"That Detective told me he bought something from us so I think we should use him as a test case. A sort of 'before and after' snapshot."

"That makes a lot of sense to perform this test," agreed Bhavna. "But why do you wish to use him as the test subject? Are you hoping to find out more about him?"

"Of course."

"Sounds like a plan," said Stuart. "Let's have a look. What's his name?"

"Pete Schroedinger. I presume he lives in Atlanta."

"Found him."

"That was quick," said Tom, surprised and pleased at the same time.

"It's an unusual name."

"Let's see what he's interested in."

"Well, he doesn't have a cat which is a bit of a shame. He's single, 40 years old and his hobbies are...." Stuart tailed off.

"Is it that juicy?!" said Tom, moving closer to the computer screen.

"No, quite the opposite. He likes hiking and camping from the looks of this. Everything about him is just about average and there's nothing salacious at all. He also likes the Atlanta Braves baseball team, Star Wars and Leeds United. That's odd."

"How did some boring American cop hear about the mighty Leeds?" asked Tom. "I didn't think football was that big over here."

"Exactly. Well it will give you two something to talk about."

"I know, although I won't mention his support or he'll know we've looked into him. I'll just mention it casually."

"Why are you trying to befriend this police detective?" asked Bhavna.

"We all just want to help if we can; we found the body, after all. If we help him out, we might get a Purple Heart or something."

"I think that's just for American military personnel who are killed or wounded in the line of duty?"

"There must be a similar medal for civilians?"

"Perhaps there is, but you would have to do a lot more than snoop through a detective's browsing history to earn it."

"You're probably right Bhavna, but it's worth a try."

Stuart and Bhavna buried themselves in their work and Tom went over to talk to Karen. Why did the woman sitting next to her still need to bring that disgusting purple and mustard patterned jacket in when the weather was so warm? She must be doing it to annoy Karen.

"Hey Delores. That's a nice coat you've got there."

"Why thank you honey, it's good of you to notice. At least somebody in this office shares the same taste in high quality garments that I do."

"Well bless your heart, Delores."

"Excuse me?!"

"It's a British phrase. It means I'm in agreement with you."

"Well that's good then. It means something different over here, but I guess you wouldn't have known that."

"Shall we get a coffee and have an update?" Karen asked, stifling her laughter as she got up.

"Good idea," said Tom and followed her to the kitchen.

"I know you know exactly what 'bless your heart' means down here and I know you hate that ugly ass jacket just as much as we all do," laughed Karen as they reached the kitchen.

"I was just trying to be friendly," said Tom with a cheeky grin.

"You make me laugh so much. It's so great having you over here."

"I love it here. I wish I could stay forever. We're getting through the work much quicker than expected and the murder was fun."

"Fun?" laughed Karen. "Maybe for some people but certainly not for the guy we found with his head bashed in by a sandwich grill."

"What's that?"

"Don't you have those over there? It's a small appliance that you put bread and shit in and it makes a grilled sandwich for you."

"Like a toasted sandwich maker?"

"Does that do the same thing?"

"I think so."

"Well that's apparently what killed the poor guy. Wendy just messaged. She said Schroedinger told them the guy was beaten up with a metal ladle and a sandwich grill. The spoon would have softened him up a bit and then the sandwich grill finished the job."

"Ouch."

"Yeah, that would have hurt. She's been trying to find out all the juicy details from Schroedinger."

"Cool. What else did she find out?"

"She said she'd tell us tonight. Are you guys still on for Dave's birthday night out? Wendy says they're going to the same bar we went to on Sunday."

"Definitely, although I've got some stuff for Stuart and Bhavna to do tonight so they won't be able to make it."

"That's good," said Karen with a laugh as she turned to leave the kitchen. "We wouldn't want to spoil Bhavna's fun by taking her away from her work."

"Or spoil our fun by having her with us."

"We are definitely on the same page. Let's finish up here and we'll meet you at the bar later if that's okay?"

"Sounds great. I'll tell Martin when the others aren't around."

Tom and Karen went back to the main office and Tom called a meeting with his UK team to go through what progress they'd made so far. Stuart told them that he'd now deleted the sensitive data from the database and would test the 'before and after' scenarios with customers that were currently using the app once the directors had told them where they could capture the data from moving forwards.

Martin then added that he'd removed some of the storage folders on the database so there was nowhere for the software to store the data even if it did capture it again and Bhavna confirmed that her and Stuart would be able to prevent the data being captured in future.

"It looks like we're in a good place so far. Martin, could you send an email to Katrina asking her if we can have the list of approved apps tomorrow morning?"

"No problem. I'll go and do it now," he replied and walked back to his desk where he'd left his laptop.

"Guys, are you two happy to stay on tonight and check the systems here as we said? I'm not allowed to tell Martin, Karen or anyone else - not even that woman with the disgusting jacket."

"It would be a pleasure to complete this task to establish which of these American staff is a cyber-criminal. It should not take too long," said Bhavna.

"Thanks," said Tom. "Let me know tomorrow what you find. Send me an email confirming it so we have a trail and copy Katrina and Keith in."

"Sure," said Stuart. "What are you two up to tonight?"

"We're going out with Karen and Wendy for an hour or so," said Tom, trying to play it down. "It was Dave's birthday yesterday - he was one of the people with us when we found that body."

"Well don't get too drunk. We'll probably just be in the bar once we're done here."

Martin returned to the meeting table they were using and confirmed the email had been sent and he was ready to go. They all returned to their desks and Tom and Martin shut down their laptops and got ready to leave.

"Bhavna and Stuart are staying late to finish some stuff and we're meeting Karen and the others at the bar later. It's the place we were at on Sunday; Wendy wants it to be a tribute to the dead man."

"That sounds a bit creepy," said Martin.

"It does, but it's food and beer so I'm not complaining."

"Food and beer are always good," Martin agreed as they waved goodbye to everyone in the office and waited outside for the taxi to take them back to their hotel.

***

Becci had just finished her break and had enjoyed her shift so far. The bar hadn't been too busy and most of the customers were senior citizens who didn't normally cause any trouble. She liked working weekdays - not that anyone could tell by looking at her - but inwardly she was happy. She was working until 10pm tonight and was planning to then meet some of her goth friends at a club and stand moodily in the corner scowling at everyone.

As she walked from the recessed area by the kitchen where the staff took their breaks back to the bar she froze in her tracks.

"Hey Becci," said the duty manager. "Can you seat this group in your section? They've asked to sit by the window."

"Sure," said Becci. "Good evening. Didn't I see you all here on Sunday?" she added, although it was more of an accusation than a welcome.

"Yes," said Wendy. "After we left, we found a dead body so we thought we'd come back and honour the dead guy's memory."

"By eating, drinking and getting loud?"

"Exactly."

"Follow me," said Becci and reluctantly led them to a round table by the window, wishing she could lead them to another bar instead.

The group made their way around the table to sit down and Martin was about to sit next to Karen when he felt his shirt being pulled from behind. He knew Tom well enough to know what that meant so he took another seat, leaving an empty space next to Karen. As Tom sat down, he noticed Karen move her chair slightly closer to his.

"Can I get you some drinks?" came a sullen voice from behind them.

"Shall we get a bucket of beers?" said Dave. "It's my birthday week so I feel like celebrating."

"That sounds perfect," Sadie added. "Let's get 12 to start with."

"Let's get a bucket of 20 instead," said Dave. "That way we can have a couple for the dead guy with the small head."

"Good idea. Do you think having a small head would stop him from drinking as much beer as other people?" Sadie asked.

"I don't think so," said Tom. "Every other part of him was regularly sized."

"True," Dave admitted.

"I'd imagine his ass being dead would stop him from drinking beer more than the size of his head would," said Karen to laughter from the group and panic from Becci.

"I'll be right back with your drinks."

"Is that the same table of weirdos you served on Sunday?" asked the duty manager.

"Yes. They've come back to honour a dead guy they found in the park by having a bucket of beers."

"What?"

"I want to go home."

"They gave you a $30 tip last time."

"I know. I'm putting it towards a therapy session."

"Maybe they'll give you another big tip tonight? That would help you pay for the whole session so these people could be a positive thing."

"They're causing the issues that I need therapy for. I think I have a phobia of people."

"My neighbour runs a phobia workshop up in Cumberland near Truist Park. He might be able to help. It's free."

"Maybe I'll give it a go. I just don't want to see any of these people ever again after tonight."

Becci and the duty manager carried the bucket of beers to the table by the window and set them down. The six customers eagerly grabbed a beer each and one of them proposed a toast.

"To the dead guy!" said Dave. "Whoever the fuck he was!"

"I see what you mean," said the duty manager as he and Becci turned away.

"To Dave!" said Sadie. "Happy birthday for yesterday."

"To the dead guy and Dave!" said Wendy.

"Can't I be first?" asked Dave, looking hurt. "I'm still alive."

"To Dave and the dead guy," they all said, just as Becci returned to take their orders.

After they had ordered their food and some of them had reached into the bucket of beers for a second time, the conversation turned to the murder as Wendy was keen to tell Karen, Tom and Martin what Detective Schroedinger had told her at the phobia workshop.

"Pete said they don't know who he is yet but they know he was killed by a combination of a ladle and a sandwich grill."

"What a way to go," said Tom. "I think I'd rather be shot in the back of the head by a sniper just as I'm about to do something I don't want to do."

"Why is that?" asked Martin.

"Well, I wouldn't see the bullet coming if it was behind me and half a mile away and I'd get out of having to do whatever it was I didn't want to do."

"Maybe you could hire someone to follow you round and shoot you if they see you doing something you don't want to do."

"Hmmm...but how would they know I didn't want to do it?" Tom asked.

"You could agree on some hand signals," Dave suggested. "If you wanted to be shot you could just scratch your right ear or something."

"But what if I just scratched my ear in normal life?"

"That's a chance you'd have to take I guess," Dave conceded. "You'd have to hope the sniper either didn't spot it or it was his day off."

"He wouldn't be a very good assassin if he wasn't concentrating and couldn't spot a signal," said Martin. "And what if the target was only available on that one day? Taking that day off would mean he'd miss his chance."

"True. We need to think about this a bit more," said Dave. "For Tom's sake."

"Thanks," said Tom. "I think."

"You get what you pay for with contract killers I think," said Martin.

"I don't want to pay too much," Tom said.

"But you'd soon be dead so you wouldn't need any money."

"You may be right there, Martin."

Becci had recently arrived with their food and was passing the plates to each of them. As seemed to be the case every time she approached this table, the six of them were engaged in a surreal conversation that seemed to go everywhere but nowhere. As she left, she scratched her right ear and hoped that somewhere across the park a sniper would see her signal and grant her a sweet release. While she waited for that blissful moment, she could hear the conversation starting up again behind her.

"Do you have anyone actively trying to kill you?" asked Dave. "That would complicate things a bit if there were two potential assassins. They'd get in each other's way."

"I don't think so," said Tom.

"Sometimes the people at work want to kill him," said Martin.

"Do they?" asked Karen. "I can believe that. What's stopping them?"

"Money. We've looked it up online and it costs too much. We had a collection one day and were still a bit short."

"How much were you short?" asked Tom, now becoming slightly concerned.

"Quite a bit. We're now looking to crowdfund it."

"Pete was nearly murdered once," said Wendy.

"But he's a police officer; that goes with the job over here doesn't it?" asked Tom. "At least his own work colleagues aren't trying to kill him."

"In this case they were. Pete used to get a couple of donuts each morning and take them in for his breakfast. One day he arrested a guy dressed up as Santa in the local mall for selling drugs to the parents of the kids who were going in to see him. Mrs. Claus was a cop and didn't take it too well."

"What did she do?"

"She got some poison and injected it into Pete's donuts while he went to make his coffee."

"What happened?" asked Tom.

"Pete came back with his coffee, picked up his donuts and went into his office. He shut the door behind him. There were no internal windows so the rest of the department were left wondering if he'd eaten the donuts or not. They took wagers on it; some said he was dead and some said he was alive. One of the brainy forensic guys said he was technically both dead and alive until we knew for sure, although that wasn't one of the options."

"Did Schroedinger eat the donuts?"

"No. Luckily somebody got murdered right across the street so he had to run out and deal with that instead."

"That was lucky," Tom agreed as Becci walked away shaking her head.

Chapter 26

Detective Schroedinger was working late and had just come off the phone to Bill Brown-stein, the medical examiner dealing with the dead body found in Piedmont Park. Bill had completed his final examination and had nothing further to report other than traces of an anti-malarial drug in the victim's system. Bill had said it was likely the victim had spent some time in the southern hemisphere recently but couldn't be more specific - although if he'd spent much of his life there it could explain why he wasn't anywhere on any of the US databases.

Schroedinger looked at the pile of cases on his desk. He still preferred paper files de-spite the move towards greener working practices and was well-known for printing off every email, report or document anybody sent him. It infuriated his colleagues but it allowed him to make notes; if there was one thing Schroedinger enjoyed it was making notes.

The murder of a visiting foreign businessman and two of his staff that morning had now taken precedence and this case had officially been classed as low priority. As a perfec-tionist, he wanted to solve every case that came across his desk but the department had been told to focus on more important matters so it looked like this would be left until they had more time, which he knew would be never.

The clock in Schroedinger's office struck nine and he got up to leave. He took one final look at the picture of the victim. Who would kill someone with a sandwich grill? What was it that Wendy's friend Dave had said earlier? Something about sandwich grills be-ing bought by old people on TV shopping channels. That would fit with his theory that the murderer was not a strong individual and it was a domestic homicide so it was more than likely that it was the guy's wife who'd killed him.

Schroedinger checked the autopsy report and the photos; there was no mention of a wedding ring and no differences in the colour of the skin of the victim's ring finger. Did somebody else's wife kill him? Or maybe the husband of someone he was having an affair with? Did people in their late 70s or early 80s even have affairs?

He got up from his desk and made his way towards the door, leaving the file open as a reminder to have another look at it tomorrow. He wanted to solve the case for Wendy too as he realised that he missed her. Given the choice, he'd rather not have her or any of her friends anywhere near one of his investigations but seeing her again this week had stirred something inside him. Instead of being a vacuous airhead, perhaps she just had a happy-go-lucky side to her? His parents were always telling him to lighten up and maybe this was the type of woman he needed. Although she might not be as interested if he told her that he'd dropped the case.

***

The noise levels were increasing at the table in the window. Becci the goth waitress had tried to pass the table to a colleague but all of the other servers had declined either politely ('that's okay, honey, you keep it') or more directly ('fuck no') and as she approached the table with another round of drinks she was wondering if she could fake her own death.

"I've always wanted to go to England," said Dave. "Would I get to see any of the Royal Family?"

"Probably not," said Tom. "They don't tend to socialise with us commoners much."

"Oh, that's a real shame. I love that the place is so old and historic."

"We've got loads of castles and old buildings everywhere. Where we live there is a massive palace with onion domes on the roof. It was built as a seaside retreat for a Prince George who later became King George IV."

"Was he the mad one?" asked Karen.

"Not as much as some of the others. He was a bit mad but not as much as his father George III was. He was the one that lost America."

"So, if George III wasn't mad, we'd belong to you still?" asked Wendy.

"Who knows?" said Tom. "It would be fun to have my very own American though."

"Yes sir, your royal awesomeness," said Dave, mockingly tugging his forelock as they all laughed.

"You could all be my butlers."

"If you think I'm going to wait on you like a servant you're mistaken," said Karen. "I'd give it a week at the most."

"Until what?" Tom asked.

"Until I whooped your sorry ass and buried you in an unmarked grave."

"Is murder common over there?" asked Dave

"Not as much as it is here, but we don't have the death penalty."

"So, they don't take it as seriously as we do and you could sort of get away with it a bit more?"

"Oh no, it's still frowned upon. If you murdered someone, you'd probably have your golf club membership cancelled and you wouldn't be invited to certain social gatherings."

"I get it," said Dave. "I've got a cousin like that in Tennessee. Nobody talks to him any more since that time with the preacher's daughter down by the river one Saturday night."

"What happened?" asked Sadie.

"Well, Cletus - that's my cousin - he'd just got himself married to Mary-Beth - that's another cousin but she lived in a different county so that was alright. On their wedding night they agreed to meet down by the river because they didn't have a place of their own yet so were staying with Cletus's parents and wanted some privacy."

"That's understandable," said Tom.

"I know, right? Well, Cletus was at the river and it was dusk and he saw her standing by the riverbank. He just went right up behind her and had his way with her right there."

"That is so romantic!" said Wendy.

"Yeah, but his phone kept ringing while he was doing the deed and he ignored it."

"Well, you would, wouldn't you?" said Tom.

"Yeah, but it was Mary-Beth calling him from the other side of the river; she could see exactly what he was doing."

"Oh my!" Wendy exclaimed. "And the woman he was with was the preacher's daughter?"

"Yep. Mary-Beth wanted to know why he'd ignored her calls because her name and picture came up on his screen and she saw him look at his phone every time it rang."

"Ouch!" said Tom. "That's not easy to explain away."

"That wasn't the worst part. The preacher's daughter was tall, skinny and blonde while Mary-Beth was short, dark and pregnant. Even a blind man with a bag over his head in a dark room in the middle of the night could have told those two apart."

"Oh man! What happened to them?" Karen asked. Even Becci - now rooted to the spot just behind Dave - wanted to know how this ended.

"Well, Mary-Beth had her baby in the winter," said Dave. "The preacher's daughter had her baby in the spring."

"What the actual fuck?!" said Becci.

"They both had their babies within a few months of one another," said Dave, turning round to address this additional audience member. "Cletus and Mary-Beth patched things up and he goes over to see his other family at the weekend. The whole town have turned their backs on him and the family doesn't talk to him either."

"I'm sorry," said a flustered Becci and quickly made her way to the kitchen, took off her apron and continued her journey out of the back door and across the street to her car. Ten minutes later she was at home vowing to never go back.

"I'm not sure I would ever want to get married," said Tom.

"I'm married," said Martin. "It's alright."

"What's good about it?" Wendy asked.

"You get someone to talk to and hang out with when all your friends are busy."

"Why would your friends be busy?" asked Dave.

"Well, they might be out," said Martin, slightly unsure.

"Yes. We're out enjoying ourselves because we're not married. We just didn't always invite you because we know what Irma will say. We fear for your safety sometimes."

"That's a fair point. She can be a bit fierce," Martin admitted. "To be honest, I didn't know there was a wrong way to put milk back in the fridge until I got married."

"Or have your hair cut?" Tom added.

"Yeah, that too."

"Being single and able to mingle is the way forward."

"It's not all it's cracked up to be though. What happened the last time you went out on a date?"

"Nothing."

"Exactly. At least I'm in with a chance of getting some every night."

"And do you get some every night?" asked Wendy.

"Not usually, no," said Martin to much mirth. "We've got two kids and she won't let me near her again until I've had the snip."

"There you go then. Single people often have sex more than married people."

"You might be right. Although I remember that last date you told me about didn't go too well."

"Which one?"

"The girl whose family were all in the navy."

"What happened Tom?" asked Karen, loving the way Martin was making him squirm.

"I was sitting with her in a pizza restaurant and she blinked a lot; I thought she had something wrong with her eyes."

"Did she?" Karen probed, sensing her booming laugh building inside her.

"No," said Martin. "She was blinking the words 'help me' in Morse code to an old man sitting close to them hoping he'd understand it and rescue her."

"Oh man!" said Karen, spitting part of her drink out across the table. "Oh shit! I'm so sorry guys."

Nobody could hear Karen's apology through the laughter that was now making its way across the bar from their table. Becci was now safely at home so was spared this latest episode but the rest of the staff and most of the customers started to wonder what else might have been in that table's buckets aside from the beer.

"What was the worst relationship you've ever had Tom?" Wendy asked once Karen had cleaned up the beer she'd inadvertently sprayed all over the table.

"Probably the last one. It was a few months ago but it didn't end well."

"What happened? I'm sure we'd all like to know," Wendy said, looking directly across at Karen.

"It wasn't my fault," Tom began but was interrupted by laughter from the group as even the Americans knew him well enough to guess that it almost certainly would have been his fault.

"You know how women wear your t-shirts and underwear?"

"Irma always wears my stuff," Martin agreed. "It annoys me a bit because she pushes out the front of my t-shirts with her massive boobs."

"Personally, I'd count that as a win," said Dave.

"Well, my last girlfriend was always wearing my things because she said it was romantic and would bring us closer together."

"You broke up because of that?!" said Karen.

"Not exactly. I decided to teach her one day a lesson and see how she'd feel if it was the other way round."

"You didn't?"

"All I'm saying is it's okay when a woman wears your clothes and underwear but when you wear hers then you 'have to have a little talk' apparently."

"I'm getting a bit worried about you mate," said Martin through the laughter that had taken over once again.

"I'm getting a bit worried about me as well," said Tom. "To be fair she was a bit of a floozy so I was glad to be out of it. I just want someone decent, kind and funny who wants to be my girl."

"Does such a woman exist in England?" asked Martin. "There are a few decent ones but it might be tough trying to find one who would actually want to go out with you."

"I think you're right. I certainly haven't found one yet."

"Maybe you should look further afield," suggested Wendy, looking at Tom and then at Karen.

"Maybe."

"I'd prefer a floozy," said Dave. "They sound way more fun."

"I want somebody nice but who also wants to live their life and take some chances. That last girlfriend I had was very enthusiastic about everything. In the UK we call them eager beavers."

"I'd sure love me an eager beaver," Dave agreed.

The duty manager appeared at the table with the credit card machine to take their payment and was dismayed to see it was one of the British guys that was about to pay.

This meant they'd not be leaving much of a tip, although now that Becci had quit all her tips were going to him so he'd take whatever he got.

Tom paid the bill using the company credit card they'd given him to use while he was here. He wasn't sure if it was meant to be used to pay for the food and drinks of non-employees but he could tell them that Stuart and Bhavna had come out. Also, he knew that solving the computer data breach problem would result in them erecting a statue of him in the company car park so a few extra dollars on a meal wouldn't be a big deal. He'd even leave a 5% tip because he was generous like that. Especially when it wasn't his money.

Passing the credit card machine back to the duty manager - who suddenly looked surprisingly pissed off for an American working in customer service - Tom asked Karen if she would drive them back to the hotel so they could meet up with Stuart and Bhavna. The group of them went outside and said goodbye to Dave and Sadie before getting in Karen's car for the short ride downtown.

"I'll see you both in the morning," Karen shouted as Tom and Martin got out of her car.

"Goodnight! Hopefully we can meet up again soon," said Tom.

"See y'all later," said Wendy as they pulled away.

"You like her, don't you?" said Martin.

"Yeah," said Tom as they walked into the hotel and headed to the bar to find the others.

"Hey guys!" shouted Stuart.

"Hi Stuart. How did it go this evening?" Tom asked as Martin went to the bar.

"It all went really well. I've sent you and Katrina an email and copied in Keith and Lisa. There isn't anything wrong at this end. Everything is fine apart from the software that Johnny Pervert landed them with."

"All of the systems and access permissions are totally correct and there is no unusual activity on any account in this office," added Bhavna. "We cannot find any evidence of a data breach or anything that would cause somebody to raise both of their eyebrows."

"Would you raise both eyebrows or just one?" asked Tom, trying to beat Bhavna at her pedantic game.

"It probably depends on how surprised you are," said Stuart. "You could theoretically raise one eyebrow in surprise and then - if things suddenly got more surprising - raise the other one."

"I guess," said Tom, too tired to argue but relieved that Karen hadn't been implicated in anything.

Martin returned with some drinks and then he and Tom started what was becoming a regular late night ritual of discussing what they'd found out about the data breach and updating the others on the progress of the murder investigation - although there wasn't that much to say on the latter topic tonight and there was soon going to be even less to report.

***

"Hey Pete!" said Wendy, answering her phone just as she and Karen got home. "Is everything okay?"

"Hi Wendy. Yes, I'm fine thanks. Where are you?"

"I'm at Karen's house."

"Is it just the two of you?"

"Yes. And the girls of course!"

"The girls?"

"Her stupid cats!" shouted Karen at the phone. "And one of them is a boy cat."

"I need to talk to both of you so could you put me on speaker?"

"Sure Pete," said Wendy, setting the phone on the kitchen table.

"Ladies, the case of the John Doe in Piedmont Park has unfortunately now been classified as a low priority one due to a series of high-profile homicides earlier today. We simply don't have the resources to tackle this at the moment so I've been assigned to the more pressing case. I'll keep this one open and will keep having a look at it when I can but I thought it only fair to tell you that the department wants us to focus all our efforts elsewhere for the time being."

"So the investigation is over?" asked Karen.

"Officially, yes. Unofficially I will still look at it in my spare time but we have so little to go on. It looks like a domestic homicide but we don't even have an ID for the victim so we're at a dead end. I'm sorry."

"Thanks for letting us know Pete. I'll talk to you soon," said Wendy.

"Goodnight," said Schroedinger and ended the call.

"That's a bummer," said Karen.

"Maybe we should investigate it ourselves," suggested Wendy.

"What the hell do you know about investigating a crime?"

"I watch a lot of cop shows on TV. I always know who the killer is before you do."

"That's just TV though. And most of those shows were re-runs from the 80s so how do I know you ain't seen them all before anyway?"

"You're just mad because I'm smarter at these things than you are."

"Maybe I spend all my brain energy at work - do you know that word? It's something most people do. You should try it someday."

"I did try it," said Wendy. "But I didn't like it and it's more fun living here with you and the girls."

"They ain't all girls!" said Karen.

"Well they should be. I'm going to ask Sadie where she had her operation done and see if they do cats as well as people."

"Can you even get a transgender cat?" asked Karen.

"I'll find out. But first me and my girls have got a murder to solve," said Wendy and headed upstairs to bed.

PART THREE

Chapter 27

Brighton, UK

It was a bright Wednesday morning in Brighton as Katrina walked along the beach towards the offices of Classic Country Clothing Ltd. During the summer she usually parked her car about a mile away from the city centre under the famous Victorian arches in Madeira Drive so she could enjoy the walk along the seafront. Her grandfather had once been a driver on the Volk's Electric Railway that ran from Brighton Marina to the city centre and whenever she saw the distinctive brown and yellow carriages trundling along it brought back fond memories of him.

The walk took 20 minutes or so each morning and gave her time to prepare herself for the day ahead. She enjoyed her job and the people she worked with but, as with any job, some days were more challenging than others and the last week had certainly been challenging. It had also been quiet. The absence of two team members in any company would be noticeable but with Tom and Martin both gone it seemed to have sucked all the energy out of the group. There was no good-natured banter (usually aimed at Colin), no embarrassing stories (often at Martin's expense) and no slightly inappropriate comments (always from Tom).

As Katrina reached the building in the heart of The Lanes - Brighton's lively centre that was full of boutique shops, restaurants and bars - she wondered if she missed having Tom around. He was less politically correct than most people, well everyone to be honest, but he did liven the place up and since he now had Martin as a foil, the interplay between them had certainly brought a new dynamic to the team. It had also earned him a few more visits to HR.

"Good morning team!" Katrina smiled as she reached her desk.

"Hi Katrina," said Sue. "Colin called just now to say he'll be a bit late."

"Okay. Did he give a reason?"

"He said his car had been stolen."

"Oh no! He's only had it a week or two hasn't he?"

"Yes. He was at the garage filling up with petrol and someone drove off with it while he was paying for his fuel and his bacon roll."

"That's terrible," said Katrina, visibly shocked.

"He tried to run out and chase after them but the cashier stopped him because he hadn't paid yet. They thought it was a pre-planned robbery and called the police."

"What did they do?"

"They detained him and confiscated his bacon roll," said Sue.

"So that's another one of my team in the police station," Katrina sighed, wishing that she could drive an electric train backwards and forwards along Brighton Beach all day instead of having to deal with all of this drama.

"They let him go and he's on his way in," Sue added.

"Please tell me you don't have any plans to get arrested today Sue," said Katrina as she turned her laptop on and waited for the screen to come on.

"Well, I was thinking of hanging around the train station later on to see if I can earn a bit of spare money," laughed Sue.

"Don't even joke about that," warned Katrina. "I need at least one person I can rely on."

Katrina's laptop had now come on and she immediately opened her emails. As she did so, she could see the IT director walking towards the team.

"Morning Keith," she said.

"Hi Katrina. Can we borrow you for a few minutes in HR? It's about the email from Stuart."

"Sure. I'll be right up."

"Thanks. Good morning Sue."

"Hello Keith. Are you having a good day so far?"

"We're making good progress but we've still got a way to go."

Katrina followed Keith out of the main door and up the stairs to HR. They walked through the sparsely populated office and headed over to where Lisa was talking to Debbie. As they walked through the office Katrina wondered if the reason for the relatively empty office was Tom's absence. If he wasn't walking around the building upsetting people then they clearly wouldn't need as many HR staff to deal with the fallout. If he ever left or (more likely) got fired, they could make most of the HR team redundant.

"Good morning," said Lisa as they approached. "Can we talk about the email from Stuart and have a quick update on where we are with the Atlanta situation?"

"Sure," said Keith as they all went into Lisa's office.

"Firstly, the good news seems to be that nobody in Atlanta appears to be involved in the data breach. I know we thought it might be the previous IT director they had who recommended the whole system but apart from that questionable choice they seem to be entirely innocent over there."

"Agreed," said Keith. "I've had a few updates from Bhavna as well. I asked her to watch Tom and Karen to see if there was anything going on. Katrina says they get on well and I wanted to be sure he didn't have a blind spot in that area."

"Good idea," said Katrina. "Bhavna was a good choice. Did she see anything?"

"Nothing at all. She noted that Tom and Martin have been out with Karen and some friends of hers a couple of times but during the working day it's been totally professional and he's even annoyed her a couple of times with some of his questions."

"That doesn't sound like Tom," said Lisa with mock surprise, drawing a laugh from Katrina.

"To add to that, he was the one who suggested Stuart and Bhavna check all their computers so clearly he either had his own suspicions or was at least covering all the bases."

"How can they check everyone else's computers?" asked Lisa.

"Everything each user does is stored in personal folders and saved in a central place. They have a program that effectively sweeps all these folders and can check what programs are installed, where they send or receive emails and what websites they browse. Apart from a few social media and online shopping visits everyone was clear."

"That's good," said Lisa. "So where are we now?"

"We've deleted all of the data collected in error and the next step is to reprogramme the system so it only collects the data we need," said Karen.

"Which means Debbie from Dallas will soon be able to use our app without any of her personal data being compromised?" Lisa asked.

"I think Debbie from Dallas may be busy doing other things, but yes," said Keith with a chuckle.

"I probably should have said Bonnie from Boston," said a red-faced Lisa, realising what she'd said.

"Stuart and Bhavna will begin the work today but it will take a couple of days," said Katrina, not understanding what the other two had found so funny and trying to bring the focus back to the task in hand.

"Do you think they could be finished by the end of the week?" Lisa asked.

"It's possible. They've actually covered a lot of ground so far."

"That's good to know; we really need to clear this up quickly to avoid it becoming public. The last thing we need is a scandal when we're trying to break into a new market. What about the data breach?"

"Well, we're still working with a third-party security firm and I'm hoping for a report from them in the next day or so. They seem to think there is a security vulnerability in our system," Keith advised.

"In what way?" asked Lisa.

"It's basically a back door into our system. Sometimes systems are designed with these to let the programmers access them once they've been installed. If you build and install a system for a customer who promptly locks themselves out, the developers can access it remotely and get them back up and running again."

"So it's a good thing?"

"Not always. It's like hiding a spare door key under a plant pot. It allows you to get into your house if you lock yourself out but it also allows a criminal to get in if they find it."

"So that's what happened here?"

"Broadly speaking, yes. We don't yet know how it got there. It could have been there since the system was upgraded; in which case we've been the victim of a random cyber-attack. The other possibility is that it was a more recent addition; in this case, it would be a targeted attack."

"Which one do we think it is?" asked Lisa, unsure of which of the two answers she would prefer to hear.

"We don't know yet. The security firm should hopefully give us some answers tomorrow."

"We have fixed it though," Katrina added.

"We've shut the back door?" Lisa asked.

"Yes; we've locked it too so it doesn't happen again," said Keith, who always enjoyed explaining technical things in an everyday way so non-technical people could understand them.

"Thanks Keith. Please let me know when you hear from the security guys. Katrina, I need you to let me know when the work in Atlanta is nearing completion. We may as well bring the guys home rather than pay for them to stay another week in a fancy hotel."

"I will," Katrina acknowledged. "Although from what I hear from Tom the word 'fancy' wasn't the first word that sprang to mind when they got to the hotel."

"Really? What was the word they would have used?"

"Shit hole."

"Technically that's two words," said Keith. "But I know the company is famously parsimonious when it comes to travel expenses. Did we fly them over in economy class or did we make them go in the hold with the luggage?"

"I didn't know that was an option or I might have put one of them down there - if only to give the flight attendants some peace," said Lisa. "Thanks very much for the update. Let me know more when you have any more information."

"Thanks Lisa," said Katrina as she and Keith got up and made their way out of her office and across the open-plan HR department which led to the stairs.

***

Keith reached his office on the ground floor and found his assistant Sanjay waiting for him by the door with a very excited look on his face. Sanjay was in charge of dealing with the external security firm so Keith was hoping this was good news.

"Hello Sanjay. What can I do for you?" Keith asked.

"We have found more details of the security vulnerability and it is quite new," Sanjay babbled, almost incoherently.

"That's interesting," said Keith. "Go on, but...slow down."

"After lots and lots of searching," Sanjay took a breath to calm himself "the security firm found some unusual changes. These were made at the time of the last security update but were not part of the update itself. It seems that the vulnerability appeared at the same time as the update."

214

"Are they saying that the back door arrived with the security update?"

"Not with it, but at the same time."

"We installed an update and it opened a back door?"

"Not exactly," Sanjay continued, his voice getting higher as he got more excited. "The new vulnerability was added just after the security update finished. It was added separately by another source."

"Where did it come from?"

"They don't know. All we know is that after the update some malicious code was also added to provide access to anyone who knew it was there. It was added at the end of February from this building."

"Who would have had the capability to do this?"

"Only senior members of the IT department and the directors."

"None of the directors have the right level of IT knowledge," said Keith. "Most of them can't even work their phones properly so that means the focus falls on our department but I can't believe anyone here would have done something like that. How many people have that level of access?"

"Not many," said Sanjay. "You, me, John, Linda and Oleg."

"Well it wasn't me," said Keith.

"Nor me," said Sanjay.

"I can't believe it would be one of the others either."

"There is one further possibility," said Sanjay quietly.

"Who?" asked Keith, mentally scanning the list of people in his department. "I can't think of anyone else in IT."

"At the end of February we lost a director who had significant IT experience."

"Roy White?"

"Yes. Although the staff called him Racist Roy."

"So did the directors," said Keith. "Would he have had the access needed for this?"

"Certainly. He would have kept his IT access permissions from his time running the department and as a director he could authorise any system changes."

215

"Okay Sanjay. Talk to the security company again and see if they can confirm this came from the computer Roy used. I think you might be onto something."

"I'll get on it right away," said Sanjay and went back to his desk.

Keith went into his office and called Lisa to let her know what the current thinking was. They couldn't be sure yet but it looked as if they might have identified the culprit and if that proved to be the case then Keith would be a very relieved man. It wasn't that he thought his staff weren't vindictive enough to do something like this - because they certainly were - but if it had been one of them they would certainly have been fired and it might have cost him his job too.

***

"What happened to you this morning?" asked Katrina with a slight smile as Colin bustled his way into the office and sat down.

"Someone stole my car while I was filling up with petrol. What a cheek!" Colin replied, flustered and suddenly looking around for something he'd lost.

"What's the matter?"

"I haven't got my laptop."

"Where is it?"

"In the car."

"Don't worry, I'll ask Keith to get you a spare one."

"Thanks."

"So you were paying for your fuel and someone just ran up, jumped in your car and drove off?"

"That's about it."

"Why did you leave your keys in the ignition?"

"I always do. It's a small local garage close to home and they all know me and always give me extra bacon in my bacon roll. I'm normally the only one in there at that time."

"Will the insurance company pay out?" asked Sue.

"They said they probably wouldn't because they think it's my fault."

"Leaving the keys to your new car in the ignition while you walked off to get a bacon roll is somehow your fault? I'm shocked," said Katrina, making a jazz hands gesture.

"Now you put it like that I can see their position," Colin admitted. "If they don't recover it, I'll have to get a new car. Although the police think it might be easy to find because it's bright yellow."

"Good point," said Sue. "Nobody in their right mind would want a bright yellow car."

"Hey!" said a hurt-looking Colin.

"I mean thieves, not normal people."

"I'll just wait to hear from them and see what they say before I go and buy another one. Diane will be pleased though."

"Why would your wife be pleased you had your car stolen?" asked Katrina.

"She didn't like the colour."

"Do you think she could be the criminal mastermind behind the theft? She may well have paid a couple of ne'er do wells to steal it so you'd have to buy a new one."

"I hadn't thought of that," Colin admitted. "Although she did say something on Saturday about wishing someone would steal it."

"Well, there you are then; case solved," said Sue. "It's not just Tom and Martin that have had the chance to play amateur detectives. What are you going to do now?"

"I'll just keep buying yellow cars. She's got a very short attention span so she'll eventually get bored and stop stealing them," said Colin.

Chapter 28

Atlanta, USA

After a good night's sleep, Tom, Martin, Stuart and Bhavna had decided to mix up their morning routine and had forsaken the buffet option to order a hearty but strange American breakfast from the menu. This had involved eggs, bacon, shredded potato, pancakes, some fluffy scones that were called biscuits, gravy that looked like porridge and some strawberries - all of which were piled on the same plate. After this 'interesting experience' as Stuart had called it, they took a taxi and arrived at work relatively enthusiastic about the day ahead.

The team had been entrusted with reviewing what customer data was being captured, deleting anything unnecessary (or illegal) and ensuring that the software didn't capture it again. So far, Martin had identified how the data capture process worked and Tom had obtained authorisation from the directors back in the UK to remove the data that wasn't needed. Stuart and Bhavna had done this and were now working on reprogramming the software so the problem didn't happen again.

Everything was going according to plan so that was good news. Or was it? As the four of them settled at their desks Tom began to wonder if they were working too quickly. At this rate they would be finished by the end of the week and would be called home early; he was hoping to spend at least another weekend here with Karen and the others. He thought about his life in Brighton where the only real excitement he had was trying not to get caught whenever he let his neighbour's dog take a shit in the park and it didn't compare well against the few days he'd had here. There was another reason why he wanted to stay longer and that reason was just walking through the office door.

"Good morning y'all. How are we all doing today? Happy Wednesday!"

"Hi Karen," said Tom with a big smile.

"Hi Tom. Do you and Martin want to come and get some coffee with me in the kitchen?"

Tom and Martin got up and followed her across the office. When they reached the kitchen, Karen told them about Wendy's conversation with Detective Schroedinger the previous night and how the police department no longer saw the case as a priority.

"Now Wendy and her damned cats think they're going to solve the case themselves," said Karen, starting to laugh.

"I'm not sure how helpful the cats will be," said Tom.

"They've got a better chance of solving it than Wendy has," said Karen, laughing harder now.

"Probably," Tom agreed. "It would be good to know what happened to that guy though. I wonder if we're next on the murderer's hitlist. We did see their car speeding off."

"I'm sure you're safe."

"It's probably best to not go back to the park for a while just in case we get our heads beaten in with a spatula or something," said Martin.

"Why a spatula?" Tom asked.

"The murderer might have run out of ladles."

Tom's phone rang and he excused himself - it was Katrina with her daily request for an update, except this time she had an update for Tom.

"Hi Tom, I hope it's still going well over there," Katrina began. "We have some big news over here to share with you."

"Hi Katrina. What's up?"

"Keith and Sanjay have been working with the security company and they think they've found the source of the data breach. Some malicious code was installed at the time of the last security patch and it opened a back door."

"Shit."

"Exactly."

"Do they know who did it? A back door suggests it wasn't a random cyber-criminal from Russia or China."

"They have a theory and are 99% sure of it now. The external security consultants are here now checking one of the computers upstairs."

"Whose computer are they checking?" Tom asked, partly excited but also slightly worried that things were moving even faster than he'd feared and they'd soon be asked to go back.

"They haven't confirmed it yet but I saw them going into the office at the back of the Logistics department."

"Wasn't that Racist Roy's old office?" Tom asked.

"I'm not allowed to tell you at the moment, but it was the office right at the back that overlooked the car park."

"Roy's office overlooked the car park. He used to take great pleasure showing me his allocated parking space knowing that I had to pay to rent a space on somebody's drive."

"As I said before, I can't tell you exactly who it was but we'll know for certain by the end of the day."

"Cool. Will he be arrested?"

"Whoever did this has committed a crime so, yes, I'd expect the police to be involved at some point. How are you doing over there?"

"Well, we know there's no involvement from anyone here so it's just a case of reprogramming the software so it doesn't happen again and then Karen and I will test it."

"It sounds like you might be finished earlier than we thought."

"I'll let you know how it goes."

"Ok thanks. I'll email you once we've confirmed who caused the data breach."

"Thanks Katrina."

"You don't sound very thrilled."

"Sorry, it's just that I'm really enjoying what we're doing over here and the people are great so the thought of having to come back doesn't fill me with excitement."

"If you complete the work early you'll have the satisfaction of a job well done and there might be a promotion coming up here soon."

"I know," said Tom, not feeling any more excited.

"What if I told you Colin had his car stolen while he was buying a bacon roll? Would that cheer you up?"

"It totally would!"

"Well it happened this morning," said Katrina and explained the conversation she'd had with Sue and Colin earlier that day. It certainly did cheer Tom up and once the call finished he went straight over to tell the rest of the team. Tom knew how much Martin enjoyed hearing car stories so watching the discomfort on his face as he started with 'I have a funny story about a car' would be even better, although now he'd admitted to what happened with his first car it wouldn't be quite as humiliating. That was a shame.

Just as the working day in the UK was coming to an end, Tom received an email from Keith confirming the investigation into the data breach. Roy White had indeed been the culprit and the external security consultants were producing a file that would be passed to the company's legal team and also to Sussex Police. The email left Tom in no doubt that the company would prosecute Roy to the fullest extent. There was also a non-disclosure agreement for Tom to digitally sign and return to confirm he would not pass this information on to anyone else.

Tom replied to the email to confirm his acceptance and then saw an email from Katrina advising that Colin's car had been found. It had been abandoned and set on fire on the nudist beach in Brighton and the local fire brigade were now on the scene - although from what Katrina had said, the beach had been quite busy so the firefighters had stayed on the scene long after the fire had been extinguished.

"I bet the firefighters are loving their job right now." Tom said to Martin as he told him what had happened to Colin's car.

"Have you ever been on the nudist beach?"

"No. Have you?"

"We went once before the kids came along. Irma wanted to see what all the fuss was about."

"What was it like?" said Tom, imagining Irma lying naked on the beach and trying not to think of Martin lying next to her.

"It was full of old men and a bit disappointing really. If it's the same today, the firemen won't be happy. The female firemen might be though."

"I think they're all just called firefighters. I don't think you can have female firemen."

"I bet my dumbass sister Wendy could," said Karen, who had caught the end of the conversation on her way to the kitchen. "She's got a boy cat that she calls a girl. There's something not quite right with her."

"I think she's great," said Martin.

"Me too," Tom agreed. "Are you guys free tonight Karen?"

"Sure. I'll check with Wendy but we can meet up and do something. Do you guys like burgers?"

"Definitely," said Tom and Martin together.

"Well there's a place in Midtown that's really cool so we could go there."

"What about Wendy?" Tom asked. "Isn't she a vegan?"

Yeah, but she recommended it. They do those impossible burgers - you know the ones without any meat in them but are supposed to taste like real food?"

"I've heard of them," said Martin. "Do they do normal burgers too?"

"Hell yeah. They've got a bar in there too so we can stay as long as we want."

"Brilliant. What about the other two?" Tom said, pointing to Stuart and Bhavna who were over the other side of the office talking to the guy who maintained all the computer equipment in the Atlanta office.

"Can't you make them work late again?" Karen suggested. "Bhavna's a right pain in the ass and I don't think I could cope with her and Wendy together."

"I'll see what I can do," said Tom.

"Thanks," said Karen as she left and headed off to the kitchen.

"Can we finish a bit earlier today?" asked Martin. "I need to call Irma and she wants me to send her some of the photos I've taken so far."

"Sure. We'll make a move soon and chill out at the hotel for a bit."

"We'll probably have to ask the others if they want to come out with us."

"Maybe we could sneak out somehow," said Tom, trying to think of a way to avoid Stuart and Bhavna that evening. "You could pull the fire alarm and in the confusion everyone will run out of the front door while we sneak out the back."

"There's probably just one fire exit that you all have to go out of."

"I haven't seen any fire exits in our hotel, have you?"

"No. I haven't seen any fire alarms either," said Martin.

"That's good then."

"Well, it's not really. If there was a real fire, we might all die."

"You've been making some good points since you've been over here," Tom said as Stuart and Bhavna came back to their desks.

***

Wendy was sitting in Karen's house talking to her cats when her phone rang. She hated talking to strangers so she never answered any unknown numbers but this time it was from a local number she knew well and took a chance that it would be the person she thought it was.

"Hi," said Wendy, hoping it was who she thought it was but terrified in case it wasn't.

"Hey Wendy. The guys are thinking of going out tonight. Would you be interested in a burger at that place in Midtown you took me a while back?"

"Hey sis! Sure. That will save us cooking."

"What the hell do you mean by 'us'?! Usually it's me cooking while you just stand around talking to your damned cats and get in my way."

"In that case you won't have me getting in your way so we all win," Wendy replied cheerfully.

"What? Never mind," said Karen. "Do you want to message Dave and Sadie and tell them what we're doing? They'll probably want to come too."

"No problem sis!" See you soon."

Karen ended the call and stared at her computer screen for a few seconds. She needed to find a way of getting Wendy out of the house. There was nothing inherently wrong with her sister but her constant upbeat cheerfulness irritated her. Why are the dumb people always the happy ones? As she mulled this over, she saw the UK team make their way out of the building. Tom waved to her and smiled and she realised she was going to miss him when he went back home.

The taxi ride back to the hotel was spent deciding on what they were all doing that evening. Tom and Martin let Stuart and Bhavna go first and it turned out that Stuart was going to see a baseball game. He loved sport and was taking the opportunity to go and see his first live American sporting event. He admitted that he didn't know the rules but was just going for the spectacle and the hot dogs. One down, one to go.

Martin asked Bhavna what her plans were but she confessed to not having any so Tom had to invite her out with the rest of the group. Bhavna hesitated for a few seconds before deciding that she'd rather stay in the hotel and continue the work she was doing. She admitted that her preference was to complete everything as soon as possible and go home so she was happy to work in the evenings. That's got rid of both of them, Tom thought as they got out of the taxi so he arranged to meet Martin in the bar before going off to join Karen and the others.

***

An hour after arriving at the hotel, Tom walked into the bar and saw Martin sitting at a table playing with his camera and laptop. He went and ordered a couple of beers and sat down where his friend had a perplexed look on his face. Something technical was clearly bothering him.

"How's it going Martin?"

"Not bad mate. I'm just loading up these pictures to the laptop so I can email them to Irma."

"Cool," said Tom as their drinks arrived.

"Cheers mate," said Martin. "Some of these pictures aren't quite as good as I'd hoped."

"Lens cap?" asked Tom, taking his first sip of what was supposed to be one of the most popular lite beers in America but in reality tasted like fizzy urine - only without any of the flavour.

"There are a few of those, yeah. Why didn't anyone tell me?" asked Martin wearily.

"We don't really know much about cameras," said Tom.

"Nor do I," laughed Martin. "I was hoping that buying an expensive model would make it easier but some of the pictures aren't that great. It's like my photography skills have deteriorated since I got here."

"Let's have a look," said Tom, moving his chair next to Martin so he could see his laptop screen.

"These ones are very blue," said Martin.

"You took them in the aquarium so that's understandable. Can't you manipulate them with some editing software when you get home?"

"Yeah, I think so. The ones I took at the Coca-Cola museum and in the park are okay though."

"That's a good one," said Tom, pointing at the screen.

"The one where you've got your arm round Karen?" Martin laughed. "I know why you like that."

"I meant the composition. You did a good job there. Can you email it to me?"

224

"No worries mate. These ones of the park and the lake at sunset are quite good. The colours really come through."

"I'm glad you've got some good ones amongst all the close-up shots of the inside of the lens cap," said Tom as Martin continued scrolling through them.

"I'm pleased with most of them," said Martin, just as he scrolled to another dark photo.

"And we're back," said Tom with a laugh. "Another lens cap!"

"Yeah," Martin laughed, realising that arguing was futile.

"You've got quite a collection of those. You should probably give them their own exhibition called 'Lens Caps Through the Years' and charge people to come and see it."

"Hold on," said Martin. "That one's not a lens cap, it's just a blurry image with some light parts."

"It looks like it's sideways on as well," Tom added. "How much had you been drinking when you took that?!"

"I don't remember taking it to be honest."

"What's the next picture of?"

"There aren't any more; that's the last one. I haven't used the camera since Sunday night."

"Turn the picture round the right way," Tom said, beginning to wonder what this mystery picture was that Martin couldn't remember taking.

"It looks like..." Martin began.

"The back of a car."

"Is that a number plate? Zoom in a bit."

Martin zoomed in on the image and lightened it as much as he could on the company laptop's rudimentary picture editing software. They both stared at the picture for a few seconds then looked at one another.

"If this was the last picture you took, it means it must have been taken at Piedmont Park. Look, you can see one of those ornamental lamp posts," Tom said, pointing at the screen.

"So, this was taken as we were almost run over?"

"Yes."

"That blurry mass must be you," said Martin. "It looks like you're running towards me."

"I was trying to save your life, as usual," said Tom. "That must be the car that almost knocked us both over the wall. "Yes. Zoom in a bit more on the back of the car."

"It's still a bit blurry."

"But you can see some numbers...it looks like 303. Can you send that to me and I'll send it to Karen? Maybe Wendy can give it to that detective."

Martin saved the image and emailed it to Tom's personal email and then continued looking through the rest of his photos for decent ones to send to Irma. She wasn't a big fan of lens cap pictures so he deleted all of those and then sent her three emails with four pictures on each one, making sure they were all scenery shots and didn't include any of the women they'd befriended.

Tom received the picture of the car and immediately sent it to Karen with a message for her to ask Wendy to send it to Schroedinger. He then ordered another beer and looked up at the big screen TV behind the   bar where the baseball game was being shown. He thought about Stuart being in the stadium and wondered if the broad-caster had a 'Beard Cam' which would show a close-up of Stuart in the same way they did with 'Kiss Cam' when they zoomed in on happy couples and forced them to kiss on live TV. That would be an interesting twist he thought as he returned to Martin - alt-hough there was that one time when a guy was reluctant to kiss the girl he was with because he was worried his other girlfriend might be watching the game on TV.

Chapter 29

Atlanta, USA

Tom and Martin arrived at the restaurant suggested by Karen and found everyone else waiting outside, talking over each other and getting very animated. Martin's photo had clearly had an effect and Karen came over to them as they got out of their Uber.

"Hey y'all! You made it," she said, giving Tom an unexpected hug.

"Hi Karen. I guess you got the photo I sent?"

"We sure did and Wendy sent it to Detective Schroedinger."

"Hi guys," said Wendy as they approached the rest of the group. "Pete was very interested in that photo and he's going to get his techy people to enhance the image and see if they can match it to a vehicle."

"We should go inside in case the murderer takes us out in a drive thru shooting," said Martin.

"It's called a drive-by," said Dave, trying to be helpful. He didn't have a lot of cash with him so the more people that survived the evening the less chance there was of him having to pay.

"What's the difference between that and a drive thru?"

"A drive thru is where you get food."

"What happens if you do a drive-by at a drive-thru?" Tom asked. "What would that be called?"

"Just go inside before one of the customers on these outdoor tables comes inside and does a drive-by on your ass," said Karen, noticing a familiar-looking young goth woman sitting with some friends looked like she was about to break down in tears. Or kill someone.

"Good idea," said Tom. "I don't mind getting shot after I've eaten but not before."

"I like your shirt," said Karen as they were shown to a table. What does 'LUFC' stand for?"

"It's my football team, Leeds United. You call it soccer here."

"Are they good?"

"I think they're excellent and they have a lot of mad fans. They just don't win as much as they should."

"They're like the Pittsburgh Steelers NFL team," said Martin, sitting next to Tom. "They take a lot of fans to their away games and make a lot of noise. I've seen them play my local team a few times and it's deafening."

"We can't help it if we're a bunch of passionate individuals," said Tom.

"You're a bunch of noisy bastards."

"Are you both going to fight like a couple of racoons in an empty trash can all night?" said Karen, interrupting them before they came to blows.

"We're okay," said Tom.

"That's good," said Karen. "Don't make me whip your ass."

Tom looked at Karen and she looked straight back at him. They both knew what the other was thinking and were trying to remain calm. The server came over with the menus and the tension subsided again. As she took the menu, Karen moved her chair closer to Tom's and rested her knee against his leg. He looked at her and smiled, hoping they'd get a chance to go out without the others one evening.

***

Half a mile away from Peachtree Street Northeast where burger menus were being scanned, Detective Schroedinger was working late and was scanning the photo he had received from Wendy. He'd called in a favour from one of the department's technical guys and together they sat in Schroedinger's office as Pat the technical guy worked some magic on his laptop.

"There you are, Pete. It looks like a real old licence plate - probably from the 1960s. The last 3 digits are 303 and there can't be that many classic automobiles around to check that against."

"That ties in with the witness account of the vehicle being a vintage car. He was British so he couldn't identify a make or model so all we had was an old dark car. This helps a lot."

Schroedinger turned to his desktop monitor and clicked on the shortcut to the software that was linked to the Department of Motor Vehicles database. He entered the last three digits of the licence plate along with the state of Georgia and waited for the database to run the search. It would normally take a few minutes so he turned back to Pat but was interrupted by a sound from his monitor.

"That was quick," Pat said. "Did you get a hit?"

"We've got two possible vehicles - both owned by women. We have a dark blue 1964 Hudson Hornet owned by Mary Normanson who lives close to Piedmont Park and a dark red 1963 Buick wildcat convertible owned by Pastoress June Lawrence. She lives down in Riverdale."

"Who's your money on?" asked Pat, seeing a frown on Schroedinger's face.

"Mary Normanson lives close to where the body was found and the car fits the description given by the witness..." Schroedinger had noticed something and his voice trailed off.

"So?"

"She's 74 years old."

"That might rule her out," said Pat. "What about the other woman?"

"She's 61 years old and a preacher. That's not the normal profile of a murderer; also, why would she drive all the way to the middle of Atlanta to dump a body when there are a lot of much better places nearer to where she lives?"

"People do crazy things when they're under pressure."

"I know, but the witness said the car definitely looked like a dark blue or black and this photo matches with that, even though it's dark."

"I agree. Looking at this picture it looks more like a Hornet than a Buick and it looks more black or dark blue than red. Maybe Mary Normanson loaned her car to someone else? Or maybe it was stolen?"

"It's not been reported as stolen but a family member may have borrowed it. I'll go and talk to each of them tomorrow but I'm not convinced that either of these two sound like murderers. Can you find me some pictures of the rear of each of those two makes of car and print off two copies of each? I'll see if the witnesses recognise either one of them."

Wendy's phone buzzed and she saw a message from Pete asking where she was and if the British guys were with her. She messaged him back and told him where they all were and was surprised when he said he'd be there in a few minutes.

"Hey everyone," Wendy said during a gap in the middle of a particularly raucous and animated conversation about unsuitable ex-partners. "Pete is coming down to see us shortly; he's got something he wants to show Tom and Martin."

"Cool," said Tom. "As long as it's not the inside of a jail cell."

"Why would he throw your ass in jail?" asked Karen.

"He's done a few questionable things in the past," said Martin. "I could easily write a list for the detective if that helps?"

"How long ago were these 'questionable things'?" asked Karen.

"A few years ago, mainly; when we used to go on holiday together."

"Well the statute of limitations has probably passed now," Karen laughed. "You're going to need some more recent shit if you want to get him arrested. And local to Atlanta too."

"Maybe we'll see you there," said Sadie to Tom. "Some of the police stations are nicer than others so make sure you get taken to a good one."

"Yeah," agreed Dave. "Although we haven't been arrested since we met up."

"That's good," said Wendy.

"Maybe," Sadie replied. "Police station coffee is better than the stuff Dave makes so it would be nice to have a decent cup sometimes."

"Good evening," said the now familiar official voice from behind Wendy and Sadie.

"Good evening Detective," said Karen. "Would you like to join us?"

"Thank you, Karen, but I'm here on official business," said Schroedinger, reaching into his pocket and fishing out four sheets of paper and turning to address Tom and Martin.

"I understand that you were the only witnesses to the car that left Piedmont Park last Sunday evening?"

"Yes, we were," said Tom.

"Please can you each look at these two pictures independently and let me know if either of them looks like the car that you saw. Please don't confer with one another."

"No problem," said Tom, taking his two sheets and watching Schroedinger pass two similar sheets to Martin.

"If either of the car shapes are more recognisable than the other please give me that picture back."

Tom studied the two pictures - one of them was a photograph of a dark blue car with a slightly smooth rear end that sloped downwards while the other was a dark red car with a squarer rear profile.

"I'm not sure," said Tom, handing one of the sheets back to Detective Schroedinger. "But I would say it was this more likely to be this one."

"I'm going to say this one; it looks more like the picture I took and it did seem to have a sloping back," said Martin and handed the picture of the dark blue Hudson Hornet to the detective, whose face immediately betrayed his frustration.

"Thank you both very much. We have a couple of leads that we are chasing down and I'm hoping we might be able to solve this case if one of them pans out."

"Cool."

"Just one more thing before I go," said Schroedinger. "I'm looking at your shirt; are you a Leeds United supporter?"

"Yes I am. Since I was a kid."

"My father was in the US Air Force and was stationed in the UK in the early 1970s before he got married. He said they were the best soccer team in England at the time so he followed them."

"That's awesome, Detective."

"He passed away five years ago so I follow them on and off in his memory. I've not been to the UK but maybe I'll make it over to a match one day to see what all the fuss is about. Have a good evening everyone. Wendy, can I talk to you outside?"

"Sure thing, Pete."

"Goodnight everyone. Enjoy the rest of your evening."

Wendy and Schroedinger left the restaurant and went outside leaving the others wondering if this was good news or bad. Whatever it was, Wendy had always said that Schroedinger was not a big talker so it probably wouldn't take long.

"What car did you think we saw?" asked Martin.

"The red one," said Tom.

"I said the blue one," said Martin to much laughter around the table.

"You two fools didn't witness shit," said Karen. "I'm surprised one of you didn't say you saw my damned car!"

"He's bound to believe Tom," said Dave. "They're besties now."

"No we're not," Tom protested. "We support the same team, that's all."

"Maybe he'll fly over to the UK and they can go to games together," said Sadie. "Is he going to stay with you? That would protect you against home invasions if you had a detective living with you."

"No! He's not my best friend, he's not coming over to the UK and he's certainly not staying in my house," said Tom, wondering why they all suddenly thought he was in a bromance with Detective Schroedinger.

"I'm with Tom on this one," said Martin. "There's only one person from Atlanta he'd want staying with him for a few days and it isn't Schroedinger."

"Who's that then?" said Sadie, as all eyes focused to the person on Tom's right.

"Oh, shut the hell up everyone," said Karen. "Do you see that skeleton sitting on that motorbike up there?" They all looked up and saw a decorative skeleton riding a motorbike above their heads. "Don't make me beat y'all to death with one of his bones. Because I will if you don't stop cackling like a bunch of sexually frustrated hens."

"Nobody said anything about being sexually frustrated," said Sadie. "You mentioned that."

"Somebody reach up and get me one of those bones up there. I need to whoop all your asses."

Wendy walked back into the restaurant and heard her sister's laugh long before she could see her and the rest of the group.

"Hey Wendy, come and save me from these fools."

"What are they doing?"

"Never mind. Is everything okay?"

"Pete asked me out. He wants to see me this weekend."

"Go Wendy!" said Sadie and Dave together amidst cheers from the others at the table.

"Pete's off this weekend so he wants to take me away for a couple of days to see how we get on together again."

"Do you think he'll talk?" Karen asked.

"I hope not. I'm in the middle of a dry spell so I hope he just gets on with it," Wendy laughed.

"Go Wendy!" said Sadie again. "It'll be awesome."

"Seeing him work this case has changed my mind about him. He's got a serious job so he's got to be serious. I think I misjudged him before so I'm going to give him another chance."

"I'm sure you'll have a great time," said Sadie. "We should get away for a night or two, Dave."

"I don't have much money at the moment but I hear they're building a swanky new police station in Augusta. We could go up there when they're done and I could start a fight and get us both arrested so we can try it out."

"I'm in if the coffee's good," said Sadie.

Chapter 30

Atlanta USA

Detective Schroedinger woke up at the usual time but not to the usual Atlanta weather. After a long period of clear skies and hot sun this Thursday morning was dull and overcast. His first task was always to check his phone for any calls, texts or emails that related to his active investigations but there was nothing there this morning other than a text from Wendy with a single heart. He looked at the timestamp - just after midnight; she'd probably sent it at the end of the evening after a few whiskeys.

As a tee-totaller, Schroedinger didn't understand the attraction of alcohol and as a police officer he had seen the effects of it on people's behaviour first-hand and the impact it subsequently had on other people's lives. He began to question whether asking Wendy out had been such a good idea after all. He was aware he needed more of a buzz in his life but wondered if Wendy would provide too much of a buzz. Also, did she really take life seriously enough for him? Or did he take life too seriously for her?

The case of the body in Piedmont Park seemed to be nearing its conclusion and once it was solved, he would have no need to see her again on a professional level. This could work both ways; once it was solved, the only way he could see Wendy would be on a personal level. If the weekend went well, they could move forward towards a relationship but if it didn't go well then at least they wouldn't see one another again. And if he could solve the case before tomorrow night it would make things less complicated if the weekend didn't go well.

Schroedinger got ready for work and sat at his kitchen table drinking coffee and watching the TV news. It was an established routine and the doom and gloom on the news always prepared him for the doom and gloom he would face during the day. His first task would be to see Mary Normanson and then he'd either visit the preacher in Riverdale or send a local uniformed officer to see her. He got up from his table, turned off the TV, put his empty cup in the sink and headed out to visit his first suspect - although he still wasn't convinced that either of these two people would prove to be the murderer.

The drive to Mary's house took less than 20 minutes and he was soon knocking on her front door. As he waited for the occupant to answer, Schroedinger cast his eye around the property; it was a two-storey house with a wide front porch where a table and two chairs had been set up. Potted plants formed a guard of honour on either side of the six steps he'd just walked up to reach the porch that he was now sheltering under as the rain began to fall. There was a driveway to the left with a garage at the end where the car would presumably be kept but before he could investigate further, the door opened and a bright, cheerful old lady stood in front of him.

"Good morning, young man. How may I help you?"

"Good morning ma'am," said Schroedinger, showing her his badge and police ID. "Are you Mrs. Mary Normanson?"

"Why certainly," said Mary. "Won't you come in and have some tea?"

"Thank you, ma'am. I'd like that very much," said Schroedinger, following her into the house and towards the kitchen at the rear.

"Please take a seat, Detective," Mary said as she turned the kettle on. "I don't get many visitors these days so it's always nice to have some company. What can I do for you?"

"We're investigating an incident involving a classic automobile and are checking on anyone who might own such a car."

"Oh, this is so exciting!" said Mary as she poured them both some tea. "Would you like milk and sugar, Detective?"

"Just milk please," said Schroedinger. "Do you own such a vehicle?"

"Yes, I do. Well, I say I do but the car was always my late husband's. He passed away last year and I need to change the ownership papers. Is this what this is about? I really should have done it sooner but I've been so busy."

"What car do you have Mrs. Normanson?"

"It's a Hudson Hornet. That door behind you leads to the garage; please feel free to have a look for yourself while I fetch you some cookies."

Schroedinger got up and went through the door Mary had indicated and pulled the light switch cord inside the garage. In front of him was a dark blue Hudson Hornet. He went to the rear of the car, looked at the licence plate and saw the last three digits were 303. This was certainly not how he'd expected this visit to go.

"Thank you Mrs. Normanson," he said as he turned off the light, closed the door and returned to the kitchen where his tea was waiting. Something was bothering him.

"Is everything alright Detective?"

"Yes, everything's fine, thank you. Did you say your husband passed away last year?"

"My poor Walter passed last October. He was 81 years of age but had Alzheimer's for the last few years of his life. It was so very sad because he was such a lovely man."

"Do you have any pictures of the two of you together?" Schroedinger asked.

"Of course, Detective! If you'd care to follow me into the sitting room there are plenty of them."

As they went to the sitting room, Schroedinger couldn't help but notice how sprightly Mary was for somebody who was clearly in her mid 70s. She was certainly not frail and moved with the agility of someone much younger. She also had a very clean house; in his experience, many older people had cluttered houses full of ornaments and photos collected over the many years of their existence. A lot of them weren't always that clean either. It was as if the occupants had decided that with relatively little time left on this earth they would dispense with cleaning their houses and focus on enjoying themselves instead. Perhaps her sprightliness meant she had more energy to clean her house than most people.

"There you are, Detective," said Mary, gesturing to an array of framed photographs on various shelves around the room but picking the nearest one up and handing it to him. "This is the most recent one. That was taken last year on the fourth of July at a family party. It's hard to believe that just three months later he was gone."

"Can I ask how your husband died?"

"He had a heart attack, Detective. It was his second in two years. He was as strong as an ox in his younger days but a few years into his retirement his body started to give up."

"I'm very sorry for your loss Mrs. Normanson."

"Thank you, Detective. What does Walter have to do with your investigation?"

"I'm not sure at the moment," said Schroedinger, lost in thought as he moved from one framed photograph to the next.

Schroedinger studied each of the pictures in turn. The facial features were the same as those of his John Doe back at the morgue and the smaller than average head confirmed his identity.

"I'm sorry to ask this, but did your late husband suffer from microcephaly?"

"I'm not sure Detective. He always knew his head was smaller than most people's but insisted that it wasn't microcephaly. He'd been examined by various doctors when he was younger but they said it was just nature giving him a small head. He made up for it by having a big heart."

"That's more important isn't it?" said Schroedinger, suddenly thinking of Wendy. She had such a big heart too and it was only now he was in the presence of Mary who was quite clearly missing her late husband that he finally appreciated it.

"A heart full of love is much nicer than a head full of brains," said Mary.

"Can I ask one more thing Mrs. Normanson?"

"Of course, Detective."

"Your husband died in October last year - is that correct?"

"Yes, he did, October 25th to be precise. I had him cremated on November 1st - the day after Halloween. Walter always loved Halloween and it was such a shame that he missed it. I wanted to cremate him on October 31st but the crematorium was going to be closed that day so they did it the next day instead."

"And which service did you use for that?" Schroedinger asked.

"I can't remember the name but they were right by the golf course. Walter loved golf so it seemed fitting. I wish I could remember their name."

"Don't worry, Mrs. Normanson. I know the one you mean. I won't take up any more of your time today. Thank you for the tea."

"Oh, it was my pleasure Detective."

"I must compliment you on your home, Mrs. Normanson. It's exceptionally clean; it's almost like being at home," Schroedinger said with a slight chuckle.

"I don't like dirt or dust of any kind. Walter always used to tease me and said I had a phobia of dirt and I should be more relaxed."

"I know there are a number of phobia workshops across the city, Mrs. Normanson. A friend of mine goes to one to help her deal with various issues she has."

"That sounds interesting, Detective. I might just look those up - although they'd have to be during the day because I really don't like driving too far at night these days."

"I'm sure you'll find one that meets during daylight hours. There was one in the north of the city that met on Tuesdays and Fridays but there was an incident there recently so it may not be on anymore."

"What happened?" asked Mary.

"One member of the group offered to kill another member."

"Oh my, that's not really the type of place I would like to go. I have a phobia of being killed, Detective. Although I guess a lot of other people have that too."

"I'm sure they do," said Schroedinger, turning to head out of the sitting room.

As he made his way towards the door, Schroedinger noticed a shelf that he hadn't seen on his way in. It was full of trophies and photos of what looked like Mary Normanson in a leotard.

"Are these trophies all yours Mrs. Normanson?" Schroedinger asked. "They're very impressive."

"Thank you, Detective. I'm very proud of them."

"How did you win them all?"

"I was a wrestling champion when I was younger. It was a long time ago and it wasn't fully legal back in those days so I hope you won't arrest me? I enjoyed it but had to give it up when I got married to Walter because he didn't like the idea of me cavorting around in a leotard in front of other men."

"Don't worry," said Schroedinger with another chuckle. "I'm not here to arrest you for it; I think the statute of limitations has passed on that anyway."

"Thank goodness," said Mary.

"These trophies look quite new."

"Oh, they are. I won these quite recently."

"You returned to wrestling?"

"Yes, I did, Detective. I've always kept myself fit and would have continued in my career if I hadn't have got married. My Walter was a lovely man; he was kind, generous and was always so very thoughtful. He gave me three wonderful children but didn't want me to carry on with my wrestling career so I stopped out of respect for him,"

"But you started back up again recently?"

"Yes, I did. When he started suffering from Alzheimer's disease, he didn't know whether I was in the house or not so I would tell him I was going to the grocery store but joined a senior citizens wrestling group instead."

"I see," said Schroedinger, not seeing at all.

"I won the Atlanta Seniors Wrestling Championship four years straight and the Georgia State Championship three times. I would have won last year as well but the tournament started the day after Walter died and it didn't seem right to leave his body here while I was competing."

"That's very noble of you."

"I know, Detective. That slutty bitch from Kirkwood won."

"Excuse me?" said Schroedinger, shocked at Mary's sudden descent into vulgar language.

"Mary-Beth Crowder. She flirts with the officials and wears revealing leotards to distract them from their jobs. I beat her in the final last year and the year before but she kept coming back for more."

"Will you enter next year's tournament?"

"I sure will. I'm going to grind her face into the dirt," said Mary, clearly animated.

Schroedinger was taken aback at this sudden turn in Mary's character. A sweet, kind old lady had now shown signs of becoming a raging demon. Clearly wrestling brought out that side of her and whoever the woman in Kirkwood was he felt sorry for her.

"Well thank you again, Mrs. Normanson. I'll be in touch if I need any more information from you."

"You're very welcome, Detective," Mary replied as she opened the front door for him. "Please come back any time."

Schroedinger got in his car and drove along the street for a minute or so before pulling over. He had planned to visit the other suspect in Riverdale but suddenly Mary Normanson seemed a lot more likely to have committed the crime. She looked strong enough to move a body and clearly had a fire inside her that could become a temper under the right provocation. Mary Normanson had now gone from being a person of interest to his main suspect. There was just one small problem - Mary's husband had been cremated in October but they'd found his body just last week, totally intact and with no signs of having been anywhere near a furnace.

The next stop that morning would be the crematorium but if that proved to be a dead end, he'd ask a uniformed officer to visit the pastoress in Riverdale. The rain began to ease slightly as he pulled away from the side of the road and headed north, wondering if he was really making any progress or was just telling himself he was.

Chapter 31

Atlanta, USA

It was close to lunchtime and Tom had yet not received his daily call from Katrina so clearly there was something happening back in the UK. The last he'd heard was that the police were involved and Racist Roy appeared to be the man they had their sights on. In the absence of any clear direction and not looking to rush through the work and finish early in case they were brought home he decided to hold a meeting. That would drag things out a bit.

He called the rest of the UK team together for an update and asked them each for individual progress reports. Stuart and Bhavna had come to the end of their reprogramming work and were now effectively finished so they could potentially go home. Martin had also finished his work but Tom wanted him to help test the changes the other two had made. Looking down at the list of their individual tasks he realised that aside from testing the system now only captured and stored relevant customer data there was nothing else left to do.

Tom planned to check the data capture part with Karen but he would also need Martin to check the data was stored correctly. This last task wasn't particularly difficult, but it was very boring and Martin enjoyed boring tasks. Or was it Stuart? Tom knew it was one of them but it didn't really matter who it was because Martin was getting it. This would all be done tomorrow so they would hopefully be able to stay here for the weekend at least before they had to fly home.

The four of them agreed to take an early lunch break and then spend the rest of the afternoon writing individual reports on what they had done. These would ultimately be combined and presented to the directors when they got back to the UK. Assuming the other three didn't mess it up, this would set Tom up to get that promotion Katrina had mentioned. As the others returned to their desks Tom called Katrina to update her on their progress before she left for the day.

"Hi Tom, how's your day going?" Katrina said, through a lot of wind noise.

"Hi Katrina, we're good thanks. Have I caught you at a bad time?"

"No, I'm just walking back to the car. It's been an intense day today and there have been a few more developments. Give me a moment to get to the car and I'll explain. Could you get the others and put me on speakerphone?"

"Sure thing Katrina."

Tom called the others over and they headed towards an empty room where the call would not disturb the rest of the office. Just as they were about to go in Karen shouted over to them.

"Hey guys! I wouldn't go in there if I were you - that's the House of Jizz!" she half-shouted and half- laughed. "Try the room in the corner instead. There won't be as much jizz in that one."

"What do you mean 'won't be as much'?" Tom asked but she and the rest of the office had already started laughing - although most of her co-workers were upset that she'd warned them.

"Hello Tom?" said Katrina over the phone. "Is everyone there?"

"Yes Katrina, we're just going into the room now."

"Thanks."

"Right, we're all here now. Martin, Stuart and Bhavna are with me."

"Hi guys - we've got some good news that you'll all find interesting."

"Good afternoon from us and good evening to you," said Bhavna.

"Hi Bhavna. Anyway, our security consultants have traced the source of the data breach. It seems that our old friend Roy White put a back door in the system at the time of the last security update. It looks like he did this on the day he resigned so he could steal the data once he'd left the business - although it was only the data from the American company that was extracted."

"So he was anti-American as well as anti-everyone else?" asked Stuart.

"It would appear so but the police have arrested him today. I'm sorry I've not been around but I've been up with Keith and Lisa in the legal department putting a report together."

"Have they nabbed him?" Tom asked. "Did he 'come quietly' or did he run and force them to chase after him and shoot him?"

"I think you've spent too much time in America," said Katrina.

"The police are questioning him but it seems that he was part of an online forum and met up with some bad people. From what little we've been told, he wasn't happy that traditional British clothing was being sold overseas. He was against it when the idea was first suggested and after being in Atlanta around such a diverse group of people it triggered him and he snapped."

"That's terrible," said Bhavna. "I had always heard that he was a very unpleasant man but this is truly awful.

"You're right Bhavna," said Katrina. "The external security consultants have fixed the breach, removed the back door and secured our data. I understand that you and Stuart have finished the reprogramming work over there?"

"Yes we have. Everything is complete and all that is needed now is for Tom, Martin and Karen to test it."

"How long do you think that will take, Tom?"

"Probably the best part of a day."

"That's excellent news," said Katrina, although Tom didn't think it was excellent for him.

"Does that mean we get to come home early?" asked Martin.

"I have some good news for you all in that area. Tarquin and Lisa are so impressed with the way you've all worked together, put the hours in and sorted the problem out quickly that they've given you all next week off as additional paid leave. I'd like to add my congratulations to you all as well because you've done an amazing job. Well done everyone!"

"Thanks Katrina!" Tom said, closely followed by the other three. "When do we fly back?"

"This is the part you might like. The cost of booking new flights for Saturday is about the same as the refund we'd get from the hotel for that week so you've got the choice of flying back on Saturday and having the week off at home or staying in Atlanta and having a free week there before coming home on your original flight next weekend. Just remember you won't be able to claim any expenses for meals or taxis for that week though."

"That sounds awesome," Tom said. "When do you need to know?"

"By 9am UK time tomorrow so we can re-book flights and cancel hotel rooms for those that want to come home."

"I will definitely be coming home," said Bhavna,

"Me too," Stuart added.

"I'll be coming home as well," said Martin. "One of the boys isn't feeling too good according to Irma so she'll need the help."

"Are you all sure?" asked Katrina.

"Yes," said a chorus of three voices.

"I'll let you know later if that's okay?" said Tom.

"No problem, Tom. Email me later so I can tell Lisa and Debbie tomorrow morning."

They ended the call and left the room they'd borrowed. Tom went over to see Karen on the way back to his desk and told her what Katrina had told them. In return, she showed him an email she'd just received from Lisa advising that she was also being given a week's paid leave next week for her part in resolving the crisis.

"Hell, I didn't do shit," Karen laughed. "I mean, you didn't do much but I did even less. It was those three over there who did most of the work."

"Yes, but we supervised it," said Tom.

"You didn't supervise anything!" she said, still laughing.

"I made sure nothing else went wrong."

"You broke our damned coffee machine on your first morning!"

"I fixed it again."

"No you didn't. You watched Stuart fix it."

"But I told him to fix it and I supervised him," said Tom, knowing this would be an argument he wasn't going to win.

"Well, whatever. But I still don't think you did enough to get yourself a free week off. What are you going to do when you get back home?"

"Er..." Tom hesitated, unsure if he was making the right choice. "I was thinking of staying here for the week."

"You bet your ass you're staying here," said Karen. "I'm sure as hell not going to put up with my dumbass sister and her stupid cats for a whole damned week. I need to get out of the house as much as possible and wherever I go, you're coming with me."

"Really?"

"Sure! If I go out alone, she'll want to come with me but if I take you along, she'll get the message and stay home."

"That sounds good," Tom said. "Shall we order some pizzas for lunch?"

"That's the most sensible thing you've said all week. In fact, that's the only sensible thing you've said all week," Karen said as her laugh erupted across the office.

***

While some people in Atlanta were ordering pizzas, Detective Schroedinger was heading towards the crematorium. His visit to Mary Normanson had convinced him that she would be strong enough to dispose of a body - maybe she was even capable of murder - but everything was circumstantial at the moment. The car, the proximity of her house to the park and her physical prowess all pointed towards her - or possibly a family member who had access to her car - but if her husband had been cremated several months ago how, he still wasn't sure how she could have killed him last week.

Schroedinger reached the crematorium and called one of the uniformed officers who was on duty today. He may as well send him down to visit the pastoress in Riverdale while he was following the Mary Normanson line of enquiry. Satisfied that both angles were being covered he stepped out of his car and headed towards the main building where a portly, middle-aged, bald-headed man with a long, unkempt beard was painting the frame of the front door. The rain had stopped and he was painting at a speed that suggested he thought it was about to start again soon.

"Good afternoon, sir. How may we help you today?"

"Good afternoon. I'm Detective Schroedinger from Atlanta PD."

"Good to meet you Detective. We haven't had anyone from the police around here since the snowstorm of 2014. An officer came to check we were okay but it was so icy he fell over more times than a one-legged man in a butt-kicking contest. He was madder than a wet hen when we started laughing at him."

"Would you happen to be the proprietor?"

"Yes sir. I'm Dwayne P. Cleverley the sixth and I'm proud to be at your service."

"The sixth?"

Yes sir. This crematorium has been in my family for six generations. Well, not this exact one, you understand. When my great, great, great granddaddy first went into business in Tennessee in 1914 it was a lot more low-key than it is now."

"How so?"

"Well, truth be told, they just dug a big ole pit, threw people in it and set fire to them. Things have changed quite a bit since the old days but I guess the principle is still the same," Dwayne continued. "The business has been passed down from father to son or daughter ever since. Apart from Granddaddy Clyde of course."

"What happened to him?" Schroedinger asked.

"Well, the story differs depending on which member of the family you talk to, however most folks around these parts say that Clyde was murdered by someone else in the family and thrown in the furnace so the other party could take over the business; but of course, there is always another version."

"What's the other version?"

"Clyde was one dumb son-of-a-bitch but had always fancied himself as one of those inventor types," said Dwayne. "You could usually find him down in his barn making stupid stuff and testing it out on himself; the family say that when his daddy died and he inherited the business the first thing he did was test the furnace and it burned him to a crisp."

"Were the police involved?"

"Yes sir, they were, but they knew his cornbread wasn't done in the middle so they decided it was death by misadventure and the business passed down to my daddy. Now, he was not a cheerful man, my father, but I remember on the day he took ownership he was as happy as a tornado in a trailer park. I took over the business two years ago when he retired. Anyhoo, Detective, I'm sure you didn't come here for the history of my family. What can I do for you?"

"I'm investigating a case and need to check one of your services from November last year."

"Sure thing Detective. What is it you need?"

"I'm investigating a homicide but the victim appears to be somebody that was cremated several months ago."

"Do you have a body?"

"Yes we do."

"Would you like us to cremate it for you? If you've got it in the trunk of your car we can do it right now. I'll just call my assistant Erica to switch old Betsy on."

"No," Schroedinger replied. "Is it possible that your furnace would not have been operational on any given day?"

"There's no chance of that Detective. Every cremation we do is videotaped and the ashes are given to the deceased's relatives. We also have a mighty fine selection of high-quality urns at remarkably affordable prices. They make us a lot of money because folks don't usually want to take their grandma home in a grocery bag."

"Does the furnace work every time?"

"Yes siree, Bob. Old Betsy is the most reliable furnace in the whole state of Georgia."

"You mentioned you have video footage of your services?"

"Yes, we make two copies from the CCTV feeds. One copy of the tape goes to the relatives - this is included in the price and is our unique selling point that helps us stand out from our competitors. We keep the other copy but only for three months because we recycle the tapes to help the environment. If it was November it's likely to have been recorded over in February but we can go and take a look real quick if you'd like. If you'd care to follow me into the office, I'll show you our system - just be sure to watch the paintwork around this door."

The two men went inside, walked across a small entrance hall and through a battered door into a large, mahogany-panelled office which contained two large wooden desks and a row of six assorted precarious-looking chairs. Death was a lucrative business but Mr. Cleverley had clearly not spent any money on his office or its furnishings. A young woman with long, light brown hair was sitting at a computer looking bored but perked up when the two men walked through the door.

"This is my assistant, Erica."

"Hello," said Erica with all the enthusiasm of somebody who sat at a computer all day.

"Good morning, miss," said Schroedinger.

"This is a proper bona fide police detective Erica. He's looking for details of one of the services we did back in November. Have you got the keys to the main cupboard?"

"They're here on my desk," said Erica and went back to looking at her computer screen.

"Thank you kindly, young lady," said Dwayne, picking up the keys.

"You're welcome," said Erica, who hadn't actually done anything at all.

"See here, Detective," Dwayne gestured for Schroedinger to join him at a floor-to-ceiling cupboard he'd just opened that was full of boxes and files.

"Have you found something?"

"No sir, I have not. This shelf here has all the tapes on and they are numbered from one through ninety and from A through D. We do a maximum of four services each day. Today we are on day 43 so we'll be using tape 43A first, then 43B and so on. We'll be using tapes 44A through D tomorrow so this one should have last been used at the end of January."

Dwayne took out the VHS tape with 44A written on it and put it in what looked like a 30 year-old VCR and pressed play. He directed Schroedinger's gaze to a big TV on one of the walls and he could clearly see the date stamp from the camera was from the end of January. Dwayne used a ridiculously simple system with very antiquated technology but it seemed to work so Schroedinger couldn't fault it, although the video was not of the highest quality.

"Is this the same video that you would give to the relatives?"

"Yes sir. Usually the person who organises and pays for the service."

"The picture is not of the best quality is it?"

"No sir, but that's just how they like it. Most of the people we get in here are happy to have a record of them being here but they don't want anybody else to be able to iden-tify them. With these videos, they can spot themselves because they remember where they sat but nobody else can recognise them because the video is just too poor. It's a security measure."

"I see," said Schroedinger. Do you keep any other records?"

"We do, but this is privileged and personal information you understand. You would probably need to get some kind of court order to access it. I'm not trying to be difficult, Detective but our clients pay for discretion. My lawyers would be right up my ass if they knew I gave client details out without the proper authorisation."

"I totally understand Mr. Cleverley."

"You see, Detective, we cater for the poorer and less noble elements of society and some of them pay cash because they don't have bank accounts. I don't mind telling you that back in the day some of my predecessors weren't too fussed about how the body came here or even how it went from being a live body to a dead one."

"I think I get what you're saying," said Schroedinger.

"My great granddaddy often got woken up in the middle of the night with an urgent cremation request because folks round here knew they could rely on him."

247

"To dispose of a dead body quickly?"

"Yes sir. I once heard that some of the bodies they brought in would still be warm. Many of them still had bullet holes with blood leaking out of them too."

Schroedinger stared at Dwayne P. Cleverley dumbfounded. The man was clearly as dumb as a rock and was admitting to a family history of body disposal for criminals. This was certainly something that somebody should look into but for now he just wanted to solve the current case and go away for the weekend. He was beginning to see why some people poured themselves a large drink when they got home each night after work.

"These days everything's legit, Detective," said Dwayne with a broad smile. "We even pay most of our taxes."

"I'm glad to hear it," said Schroedinger. "I guess I'll need a warrant to see the records I need."

"I'm sorry I can't be of more help at the moment Detective. There is a book of condolences you can look at though. It's not classified and most of my clients choose not to sign it but you're welcome to have a look."

"Does it go back to November?" Schroedinger asked, not sure what it would tell him even if it did.

"Yes sir, it surely does," said Dwayne, reaching back into the cupboard and pulling out a large white box. "Here you go, Detective. This one covers October and the first week of November and this one covers the rest of November."

"Thanks," said Schroedinger, taking the first book and thumbing through its pages.

"Not everyone signs the book I'm afraid, but some do. We often get asked to send them copies of the completed pages as a souvenir so they can remember who was at the service and who wrote what about their loved ones. Given the type of people we get in here, sometimes the comments can be 'less than complimentary' said Dwayne, letting out a big, hearty laugh. "In some cases, they're quite defamatory and the other family members get upset. It's not unknown for us to see the same set of mourners again within a couple of weeks because one of the original guests has taken exception to another's comment about their daddy or their uncle."

"I'm sure," said Schroedinger, distracted by what he was reading. He'd found the service for Walter Henry Normanson and he'd also found a number of messages of condolences, although only one two of these were of interest to him:

"My darling Walter, I will miss you always. Rest in peace until we are together again. Your loving wife, Mary."

This confirmed he was looking at the right service, but beneath this was another message:

"May you rest in peace, dear brother. I wasn't here for you much in life but I'm here for you today. Sleep well, Norman."

Detective Schroedinger read the messages once more. Walter had a long-lost brother who had come to his funeral in November, but how did he find himself dead in April? As some of the fog had begun to clear from this mind, more fog had just rolled in.

"Do you mind if I make a copy of this page?"

"No problem," said Dwayne. "Let me do that for you."

Dwayne took the book over to a photocopier that looked as if it was bought at around the same time as his VCR and took two copies.

"One for luck," he said, passing the copies to Schroedinger.

"Thank you for your help today, Mr. Cleverley."

"Anytime, Detective," Dwayne said as they headed to the door. "And remember, if you have any bodies you need to dispose of 'off the record' I'd be prepared to offer you a 5% police discount."

"Goodbye Mr. Cleverley. We have our own team that handles all of our unidentified victims."

"I know, but that's just the official ones. If you ever find yourself up a creek without a paddle because you've interrogated a suspect a bit too vigorously, we'll be here for you, come rain or shine."

"I'll bear it in mind," said Schroedinger as he reached his car, got in and drove away as quickly as he could without looking back.

Chapter 32

Atlanta, USA

Schroedinger drove back to the police station armed with the most promising lead he'd yet had on this case. Assuming there were no complications from the visit to the other potential suspect, he could now apply for a warrant for the forensics team to search Mary Normanson's house for evidence that she'd killed her brother-in-law Norman. His phone rang and he pressed the button automatically to take the call on his vehicle's speakerphone system.

"Hey Detective, it's Officer Hampton. You asked me to check out a house in Riverdale?"

"Good afternoon, officer. Do you have anything for me?"

"Unfortunately not, Detective. I went to visit the property but it was unoccupied. I spoke to a neighbour and she told me that the owner - Pastoress June Lawrence - has been in hospital for a couple of weeks."

"What happened?" asked Schroedinger.

"Well, the neighbour said she was doing some work on her roof and was at the top of a ladder when her two dogs got out of the back yard and ran round the front to see where their owner was. These are big dogs, Detective, I saw them. They were Great Danes like the one in that cartoon with the meddling kids."

"Please get on with what you found, officer."

"Sorry, Detective. Anyway, the neighbour saw the whole thing happen; the dogs ran around the corner and crashed right into the ladder and knocked Miss Lawrence off."

"That must have been awful."

"She fell down 12 feet onto a concrete driveway and broke her hip."

"So where is Pastoress Lawrence now?"

"She's in a private hospital and her neighbour is looking after the dogs."

"Did you have a look around the property?"

"I did, Detective. The garage had a small window in it and I could see what looked like an old car under a tarpaulin. The thing is, the car was up on bricks and the wheels were piled up in the corner of the garage. If I had to guess, I'd say that car hadn't been driven for a long time; there was a lot of junk stored on it and around it and the tarpaulin was covered in dust like it hadn't been moved in ages."

"Thank you, Officer Hampton. You'll send me a full report with the neighbour's name, won't you?"

"Of course, Detective. It'll be with you by the end of the day."

Schroedinger ended the call and pulled the car over to review what he had learned today. He always thought best when he was sitting alone in his car without any distractions and he now felt as if he was on the cusp of solving this crime. He checked the three core pillars to establishing guilt - means, motive and opportunity - and found he had two out of three. Apparently that wasn't bad when it came to relationships, but when it came to murder, he needed all three.

He had the means; the suspect's wrestling experience clearly gave her the strength and agility to manoeuvre a body around, despite being in her mid-70s. He also had the opportunity; the deceased was clearly Mary Normanson's husband's long-lost brother who had come to town for his funeral. Given the physical likenesses between them and a similar age range, it was likely they were twins, or at least born within a year or two of one another. Schroedinger didn't like to guess but if he did, his money would be on them being twins.

The only hurdle that remained was a motive. Why would Mary Normanson murder her late husband's brother? There didn't appear to be any foul play in her husband's death - he'd check that when he got back to his office - and he could find no reason why she would wait six months to kill his brother if it was premeditated. Did he call round for dinner one day, complain about her cooking and she threw a sandwich grill at him? After first having hit him 20 times with a ladle?

Schroedinger started his car again and drove back to the police station. He'd check the death certificate for Walter Normanson and apply for a warrant before going home and hopefully they'd both come through tomorrow. He needed some light relief so he started to think about his upcoming weekend away with Wendy. Was he doing the right thing? Would things be any different this time? She was a lively and fun woman and even though they'd only seen each other for a couple of months she had started to get on his nerves as they spent more time together. Did opposites attract or did they lead to irreconcilable differences?

As he pulled into his designated parking space at Atlanta PD, Schroedinger thought about Mary Normanson and the happiness she had clearly shared over the years with her husband. He wondered if he would ever have that and, if he did, who it would be with. Wendy had been fun for a while but to be with her long term would require him to show far more tolerance of her wild side than he had shown before. On the other hand, while she might be a total airhead, she had a kind heart and would never hurt anyone. She certainly wouldn't smash anyone's head in with a sandwich grill.

***

It was the end of the day at Classic Country Clothing (UK) Inc. and everyone was about to leave the office and head their separate ways. The UK team had decided to stay on a bit later to finish some critical updates so Tom and Karen could test them tomorrow morning.

"Are you guys going to stay here and fix this shit for us once and for all tonight?" Karen asked as she was about to leave.

"Yes, if that's alright," said Tom. "It'll take a couple of hours and then we'll be done. Stuart and Bhavna will be doing most of the work."

"Now why doesn't that surprise me? You really are great at avoiding work aren't you?"

"He's the best," said Martin. "He's got awards and certificates for it at home."

"I bet he has," laughed Karen.

"We won't need Stuart or Bhavna tomorrow so they're going to stay in the city. It will just be us two."

"It will be nice to have a day off after the late evenings Stuart and I have had," said Bhavna.

"Where are you two off to?"

"I think we'll go to the aquarium and then the zoo," said Stuart. "We would have done that last Sunday if we hadn't got food poisoning."

"Our flights are at lunchtime on Saturday so tomorrow will be our final day here; thank you for letting us have the time off."

"No worries at all. You both deserve it," said Tom as sincerely as he could, knowing that he'd asked them all to work late and sacrifice their Thursday evening so he and Martin didn't have to deal with Bhavna on Friday.

"I'll see you guys in the morning then," said Karen, picking up her jacket as Delores did the same in the seat next to her. "Hey, Delores."

"Yes?"

"Can I ask you something about your jacket?"

"Sure Karen, it's lovely isn't it?"

"No, it isn't. That is the ugliest jacket I have ever seen. Where did you get it from?"

"I'm sorry you feel like that, Karen," said Delores, looking hurt. "I got it from an online shopping website. It links buyers with suppliers in China to keep costs low and you can buy anything you want on there."

"Did you actually order that specific jacket?" asked Karen, not surprised that Delores had said it was cheap.

"Well, no, as a matter of fact I didn't order this exact thing," Delores admitted.

"What exactly did you order?"

"I ordered a multi-coloured Jack-in-the-Box toy for my son for his birthday."

"And they sent you a jacket instead of a Jack-in-the-Box?"

"Yes."

"Do you even like the jacket?"

"Not really, but if it annoys you I'm going to keep wearing it."

"Me and my big mouth," Karen sighed. "Have you used these people before?"

"A few times."

"Are they always that bad?"

"It can be a gamble," said Delores. "I once bought a rug for my living room that was meant to cover the whole floor but the sizing was a bit out."

"How big was it?"

"About the size of a facecloth."

"Oh man! Anything else?"

"Well, I ordered some Coke socks for my brother as a joke gift for Christmas."

"Why the hell didn't you buy them downtown?"

"It was cheaper online. Also, he prefers Pepsi so I got them to send the parcel to him directly so he wouldn't know they were from me."

"Did he like them?"

"I don't know. I haven't seen him since he got arrested."

"He got arrested?!"

"There must have been a misunderstanding in China because they sent him some normal socks filled with cocaine. The package was stopped as it went through customs and the DEA went round and arrested him for buying drugs off the internet."

"Didn't you step in to clear his name?"

"He's now doing 20 years in a federal prison," Delores said. "I'm worried that if I come forward they might send me away too."

Karen stared at Delores but said nothing more. She made a mental note not to set up a 'Secret Santa' event at Christmas and then picked up her things and said goodnight to everyone. Going home to Wendy would be a breeze after this.

***

Detective Schroedinger had spent the remainder of his afternoon gathering information on Walter Normanson's death and trying to establish if he had a brother anywhere in any of the national databases. He'd also applied for a search warrant that covered Mary Normanson's house, garage, land and any motor vehicles in her possession and was wondering if tomorrow he'd be arresting his first ever septuagenarian.

Walter Normanson's death certificate recorded 'Congestive Heart Failure' with no other notes or observations so it appeared that his widow's statement had been true. There was no luck in obtaining a birth certificate for either him or his brother, however, although this was unsurprising given his age and the lack of adequate records maintained during World War 2 when they were likely to have been born.

With nothing more he could reasonably do tonight, Schroedinger made his way home. He'd call Wendy when he got in and check she was still available for their weekend away. His plan was to drive her to Nashville. A weekend of live music and dancing would impress her, even though he knew she'd get drunk and he'd have to carry her back to their hotel each night.

Tom was busy sending emails to Katrina, Lisa and Keith in the UK to confirm he would be staying on in Atlanta and updating them with the progress they had made. The others had sent him their reports so he'd also combined them with his and was all set for the final testing tomorrow. He'd actually worked quite hard today and was both surprised and disappointed with himself.

Tomorrow would be another full day but at least Miss Pedantic and Mr. Beard wouldn't be with them - especially as he was sure Stuart's beard had grown since they'd been in Atlanta and now looked big enough to house a family of cats. Maybe Stuart could re-house Wendy's 'girls' and help Karen reclaim her house again.

The taxi arrived and took them back to their hotel. Tom and Martin went straight to the bar and ordered some fried chicken and two beers each while Stuart and Bhavna went back to their rooms, promising to join them after they'd showered.

"Is there something going on between those two?" asked Martin as two servers brought over their cutlery and condiments. One of them looked familiar.

"Good evening y'all, my name is Annie and this is Becci. She's new and will be training with me tonight. She's going to be helping us out in the final few weeks before we close down because everyone else is leaving."

"Good evening," said Tom. "You look very familiar, Becci. I haven't seen many goth waitresses in Atlanta."

"Or anywhere," Martin added.

"Oh, hello," said Becci. "Will there just be the two of you this evening?"

"I think so. There are two upstairs who may join us later on but for the moment it's just us."

"That's good. I think I might be able to cope with two of you," Becci said as she and Annie moved on to serve another table.

"What did she mean by that?" Martin asked.

"She was the one from the bar by the park. Every time she came over, we were laughing about something and she didn't join in. I thought the culture over here was that the waitresses joined in as much as they could so they got a bigger tip. She didn't even smile, let alone laugh."

"She's a goth."

"Fair point."

"Hey guys!" said Stuart as he walked across the bar with Bhavna.

"That was a quick one," said Tom.

"A quick what?" Bhavna asked. "How do you know what we were up to? Stuart, did you tell them?"

"I meant a quick shower. You said you were going for a shower."

"Yes of course," said Bhavna, looking embarrassed. "Are we going to sit around and gossip all day or can we order some food?"

"We've just ordered but you might be able to add it onto the bill if you go to the bar."

"I will do that," Bhavna said and walked quickly over to the bar with her head down.

Stuart sat down, gave Tom and Martin a quick wink and then began telling them what he had accomplished during the day. Everything had been completed and just needed testing tomorrow and he admitted that he couldn't wait to go home.

"What do you think of it here?" Tom asked him and Bhavna as she returned to the table and sat down next to Tom and opposite Stuart.

"We haven't really seen much of the place to be fair. We got food poisoning and spent the whole day in bed on Sunday and haven't been far from the hotel or the office since then."

"Tomorrow will be good," Bhavna added. "I am excited to be able to visit the aquarium and the zoo. Maybe we can also visit some other places as well if we have time."

"Well I hope the food is okay tonight; you don't want to spend the whole day in bed together again tomorrow do you?"

"Certainly not," said Bhavna.

"Stuart?" Tom asked.

"Sorry, I was just checking my phone. Did you say something about us spending the day in bed together again?"

Becci brought their food over and once again caught the tail end of a conversation she had no interest in hearing.

"Enjoy your meals everyone. How long are you in Atlanta for?"

"Three of us are leaving on Saturday morning but Tom is staying for another week," said Bhavna, pointing at Tom.

"That's so great," said Becci. "Will you be staying at this hotel?"

"I think so," said Tom.

"And will you be seeing your American friends at all?"

"I hope so. I won't be working so we'll probably hang out together a fair bit."

"And will you be bringing them to this hotel?"

"Probably not. They all live in Midtown and Cumberland so we'll spend our time up there."

"Thank fuck for that," said Becci. "Enjoy your food."

"I like her," said Tom. "She's different from most people here."

"You like everyone," Martin said. "Just don't let Karen hear you say that."

"What do you mean?"

"We all know about you and Karen. Glances here and there, always sitting next to each other, endless messages when you're not in the same room."

"We're just friends and have to work closely together," Tom replied sheepishly.

"It looks like you two are having a holiday romance," laughed Bhavna.

"I'm not the only one though, am I?"

"I recommend that we all eat our food before it gets cold," said a red-faced Bhavna, looking down at her plate and beginning to eat furiously.

The rest of the meal was eaten in relative silence. As soon as Bhavna finished, she made her excuses and went upstairs. Most business trips followed a familiar and predictable pattern - colleagues who don't know each other get thrown together for a few days, unfamiliarity turns into familiarity, friendships and bonds are formed and then being in close proximity with people who aren't family or close friends begins to suffocate everyone and arguments and disagreements rear their heads until everybody hates each other and wants to go home.

Tom and Martin had been lucky on this trip because they already had a lifelong friendship but the strain was clearly beginning to tell on Bhavna. Stuart was faring slightly better but even he had lost some of his deadpan humour as the week had gone on. Either that or the sex with Bhavna wasn't very good.

Stuart signalled that he'd be heading upstairs for an early night as well - to obvious comments from Tom and Martin - and he soon left them to their evening in the bar to talk about work, old times and why Becci the goth waitress had only smiled when she knew they weren't going to be bothering her again.

Chapter 33

Atlanta, USA

Breakfast on Friday morning was a more subdued affair than it had been since they'd arrived in Atlanta. Stuart and Bhavna's romantic liaisons had been discovered - or at least guessed - and they were both quieter than usual (and less annoying in Bhavna's case). Martin was worried about one of his boys and Tom was just keen to get the day over with and have a free week off in Atlanta. His mind had already left the project they were working on and was thinking about how he'd be spending the time and if he'd really get to see Karen as often as she'd hinted.

"We'd better make a move soon," said Martin, bringing Tom back from wherever his mind had gone off to.

"Okay, let's do it. You two have a great day and we'll see you tonight probably."

"Thanks. We're off to the zoo first and then the aquarium," said Stuart.

"I would like to visit the Botanical Gardens as well," Bhavna added.

"It looks like we're visiting the Botanical Gardens too," Stuart said with a sigh.

"Well, have fun you two!" said Tom as he and Martin left the breakfast table and went outside to call a taxi.

"I don't see it with those two," Martin said once they were safely outside the hotel. "He seems really miserable doing what she says all the time."

"Maybe he likes a dominant woman?"

"That might be it."

"Or maybe he's just practicing his 'miserable face' for married life."

"It's not all bad," Martin said.

"Isn't it?"

"At least I can have regular sex."

"When was the last time you actually had sex though - regular or otherwise?" Tom asked.

"Nine months before Ben was born," said Martin glumly.

* * *

Detective Schroedinger arrived at his office to find the search warrant for Mary Normanson's property had arrived so he called together a small team of forensic officers as well as two uniformed officers and they made their way along 10th Street to the southern end of Piedmont Park. Their convoy of three vehicles turned right half way along that road and after a short way down the next road, turned into the street where Mary Normanson lived.

After giving them all a quick recap of the case, Schroedinger led the team to the house and knocked on Mary's front door.

"Why, hello Detective. How are you today? I see you've brought some friends. Won't you all come in?" said Mary with a big smile that knocked Schroedinger off his stride for a moment.

"Good morning, Mrs. Normanson," he said. "I'm afraid I have a warrant here for a search of your property."

"Don't be afraid, officer."

"Oh, right," said Schroedinger, beginning to wonder if this had been a complete mistake.

"What can I do for you all? I'm afraid I don't have enough mugs to offer you all some tea."

"That's perfectly fine Mrs. Normanson. We're investigating the murder of a man who looked very similar to your late husband and have reason to believe that you may know something about it."

"Oh my!" said Mary. "Shall we go through and sit down? It's been quite chilly this morning so I've lit the fire. I do love a real fire for the cooler days, don't you Detective?"

Schroedinger went into the sitting room and sat in the chair by the window. Mary sat opposite him while the three forensic investigators split up to search the kitchen, the garage and the upstairs of the house. The two uniformed officers stood by the sitting room door with their hands on their gun holsters in case this sweet old lady in her mid-70s tried anything.

"We are in the process of identifying the deceased but we believe him to be a man by the name of Norman Normanson, although he doesn't appear on any of our national databases. Have you heard of him?"

"Now that you mention it, Detective, yes I have. That would be Walter's twin brother. Did you know they hadn't seen one another for more than 70 years?"

"Please go on, Mrs. Normanson," said Schroedinger.

"Walter told me that when he was very young, his parents separated and they each took one of the two boys. Walter stayed with their mother and grew up in Kentucky while Norman was taken to Brazil with their father."

"You said that they hadn't seen each other for 70 years. Are you saying that once the family split up the two brothers didn't meet up again?"

"That's right, Detective. They sent the occasional letter and email to one another but Walter wouldn't fly anywhere and Norman always said he didn't have enough money to come here. He said he planned to visit us one day but you know how these things are Detective. We all plan to do things one day but never get round to doing them."

"Was Norman Normanson at your husband's funeral?"

"Oh no, Detective. I'm sure I would have recognised him if he'd have been there."

Schroedinger paused; Mary Normanson had suddenly stopped being the kind, sweet old lady and had just lied to him. He took the photocopied sheet of the book of condolences out of his jacket pocket and showed it to Mary.

"This is a copy of the condolences book at the crematorium that you and Norman Normanson both signed. It looks like you were there together."

"Can I see that please, Detective? My eyesight isn't as good as it once was."

Schroedinger passed the sheet of paper to Mary; she took it from him, studied it for a couple of seconds and then threw it on the fire.

"Silly me," she said as one of the officers drew their weapon.

"Don't worry," said Schroedinger, calming the officer. "I have a second copy here."

Mary looked upset and her discomfort increased as the lead forensics investigator came in from the kitchen.

"Detective, we have blood splatters under the refrigerator and the oven. We also have blood in the trunk of the car in the garage. We also have a selection of heavy kitchen utensils made from what looks like the same metal as the fragments found in the victim's skull."

"Mrs. Normanson," Schroedinger began. "I'm arresting you for the murder of Norman Normanson. Officer, please read Mrs. Normanson her rights and take her into custody."

Schroedinger got up and walked towards the door while the two uniformed officers moved forward to arrest Mary. She started to get up from her chair but suddenly rolled across the floor and grabbed the poker on the other side of the fireplace. Before the officers could react, she was back on her feet and had swung the poker at them, narrowly missing both of their heads. She was ready for a second swing when Schroedinger raised his gun and pointed it straight at her.

"MRS NORMANSON!" he shouted as she turned to look at him. "Please do not make me discharge my weapon."

"He was a horrible man and fully deserved it," said Mary. "How could twin brothers be so very different?"

"Would you like to confess?" Schroedinger asked, lowering his weapon.

"I'm sorry Detective."

Mary put the poker on the chair and offered her wrists to the officers. She was soon in handcuffs and being taken to the patrol car. Schroedinger watched from the front door as they walked down her front path. Before they reached the car, a neighbour appeared from the house next door.

"Hi Mary! How's your Friday going?" she said with a wave.

"Hello Dorothy," said Mary. "To be truthful, I've had better Fridays. Forgive me for not waving but I'm in handcuffs."

"I'm sorry to hear that. Why are you being arrested?"

"Well you know that Norman who was staying here for a while?"

"The man who looked like your Walter?"

"Yes," said Mary. "He died quite suddenly last week and the police think I killed him."

"Oh my word! That's terrible. Why on earth would they think you killed him?"

"Because I did. Have a nice day Dorothy."

The officers put Mary in the back of the patrol car and drove her to the station, leaving a shocked Dorothy standing with her mouth open. Schroedinger went back inside Mary's house and spoke to the forensic investigators again. The whole house was just as clean as it had been when he'd last visited, although she had clearly missed some areas underneath the major appliances when she'd scrubbed the kitchen after the murder.

After finishing his discussion with the forensics team and leaving the uniformed officers to secure the property, Schroedinger left the house and headed to the police station. He'd solved the crime and would hopefully get a full confession from Mary Normanson before he went away for his weekend with Wendy. It had been an unusual week so far, but a good one.

***

Tom and Karen were busy testing the reprogramming work that Stuart and Bhavna had done and Martin was making sure that everything was now correct from a data storage perspective. A lot less data would now be collected and anything stored would be encrypted so that it was no longer accessible by a three-year child with a pretend smartphone.

"The fact that we got into it so easily means anybody else could have done too," Martin sighed as he inspected the new, secure version they had implemented.

"I'm surprised nobody did," said Tom. "I think we just got lucky because the company isn't that well-known yet. We're probably still flying under the radar when it comes to brand awareness."

"Maybe if we let this leak it would create more brand awareness," Martin suggested. "We'd be on the news."

"I don't think that's the type of publicity they want, but I will check with Lisa when I get back."

"Are you definitely staying on?"

"Yes. It'll be nice to chill out here in the hot sun, eat some more fried chicken, try some Georgia peach cobbler, get some fresh country air and enjoy some of that Southern hospitality. I might even buy myself a checked shirt and a baseball cap."

"And wear it backwards?"

"Of course! I'll start a brand-new trend when I get back to Brighton."

"You'll have the fashion police after you," Martin laughed.

"Probably, but it's better than the normal police," said Tom. "Have you finished what you need to do here?"

"Yes, you and Karen can finish the rest of the testing now."

"Okay; you may as well take the afternoon off rather than sit here."

"Thanks. I think I'll go to the College Football Hall of Fame. I'd like to find out why Americans love college football so much. Some games attract 90,000 fans and it's basically school kids."

"That's more than our professional teams get watching them," said Tom.

"I know," said Martin, wasting no time in packing up. "I'll let you know what I find out later."

"Okay. I think Karen and the others will be coming out with us tonight. I'll let you know."

"See you later," said Martin and made his way out of the American premises of Classic Country Clothing (UK) Inc. for the final time.

***

Interview room number two was small, dark and cramped but it was the only room available that afternoon so Schroedinger, a young female officer and Mary Normanson crammed into it and sat around a small table, their legs practically touching.

"Couldn't you find a smaller room for us Detective?" Mary asked.

"It is a bit cozy, but it's all we have."

"I understand Detective. Now what would you like to know?"

"You have the right to an attorney - would you like to call one?"

"Goodness no! They're such a waste of money. If I get a good one, I'll go free which, you know as well as I do, wouldn't be fair. On the other hand, if I get a bad one, I'll be sent to prison where I'll have a bed, my own room and three meals each day. Which is what will happen if I don't appoint one anyway so please carry on."

"Thank you Mrs. Normanson. I understand your logic and wish all our suspects were as cooperative as you. As you know, we record all of these interviews using audio and video so why don't you start by telling us exactly what happened with Norman Normanson?"

"Certainly, Detective," said Mary and gave her statement:

"Walter and I were married for 52 blissful years and we were very happy. We had three beautiful children and our life was wonderful until he got Alzheimer's. He deteriorated over the time he had it and then the poor man had his second heart attack last October.

Walter had been in contact with his brother Norman on his comphuter so I sent him an email with the bad news. He surprised me by saying he would come over to the funeral and he arrived in Atlanta two days before we put Walter into the furnace. The man at the crematorium was so very friendly but he wasn't very bright. I hate to say it but if he threw himself at the ground I think he'd miss more times than he hit. Anyway, where was I? I get confused sometimes, Detective.

Oh yes! Norman had booked into a cheap hotel for five nights and I assumed he would go back to Brazil but he said that he'd like to stay a bit longer before going back home. He told me he had a return ticket that allowed him to stay 30 days and because he was my dear late husband's brother, I invited him to stay with me. He stayed in the spare room you understand. I don't want you thinking I'm a hussy, Detective. Maybe in my younger days before I met Walter you could say that I enjoyed myself but certainly not now - although there was that one time afterwards, but that can be our little secret can't it?

I've lost track again haven't I? Well, Norman moved in and at first it was fine. He re-minded me so much of Walter that it was almost like he had come back to me. It gets very lonely as a widow and I didn't have the heart to continue with my wrestling - not after I'd lost my title to that shameless harlot from Kirkwood. When I've finished this statement I'll tell you what she was offering the male judges if they gave her the title. She was even going to take her teeth out, Detective!

Anyway, once Norman had settled in, I started to pretend he was Walter; it was so nice to see him sitting in his favourite chair again. It was the chair you sat in this morning, Detective - the one by the fireplace and the poker that I tried to kill your two officers with. Please tell them I'm very sorry for any inconvenience I may have caused them.

Now, Norman was very lazy and sat in the chair all day watching television just like Walter did but he was mean and expected me to do everything for him and would only leave his chair when he went for his daily walk around Piedmont Park. My Walter would always help around the house where he could - until he got Alzheimer's disease - but Norman just sat and watched television all day and night or went out to the park. It soon became infuriating and then he told me his flight ticket had expired so he'd have to stay for good.

Do you know what else he did Detective? Well, he didn't do it but he tried to. Yes, that! After a few weeks he started trying to get into my bed at night. Every single night, Detective. Not just once a month like normal people. And it wasn't very impressive at all. I've seen my fair share in those videos on the internet since my poor Walter passed away and I have to say that Norman would have needed a fluffer and then a wooden splint.

Last Sunday evening, I was doing the dishes and he tried it on again. In the kitchen this time, Detective. Is a girl not safe anywhere in her own house? I was so mad that I grabbed the nearest implement I could find and stabbed him with it. Unfortunately, it was a ladle so it wouldn't make a hole in him so I hit him over his tiny little head with it. He started to scream but I kept hitting him and managed to hold one of his arms behind his back so I could hit him again. I knew my wrestling experience would come in useful one day, Detective.

After what seemed like a very long time, he finally fell to the floor so I thought I would drive his body somewhere very far away and just leave it. I finished doing the dishes first because I don't like to go out and leave the house in a mess and then I went to move him. That was when he grabbed my ankle. A lot of men liked my ankles when I was a young woman, Detective and I was very popular at high school - although I think they would possibly use the word slutty nowadays. My dance card was always full and some-times I would have more than one dance partner in the same evening.

Anyway, when Norman grabbed my ankle it gave me such a start that I panicked and I hit him with a sandwich grill. He made me buy it for him from one of those television shopping channels but I never used it myself so it didn't think it would matter if I broke it. It was the only time he went into the kitchen, Detective, to make himself a grilled sandwich and it came to symbolise everything I didn't like about the man. It was quite fitting that I hit him with it - I certainly wouldn't have used my favourite teapot on him. When I hit him with the sandwich grill, he finally died so it was clearly every bit as sturdy and well-constructed as the shopping channel had advertised. Do you think I should write them a product review Detective? I know how much people rely on them before they buy things these days.

I've gone off at a tangent again haven't I? Well, I loaded Norman into the trunk of my car and was going to drive him to a quarry but the only one I know of is a long way out of town and it was now dark. I really don't like driving in the dark Detective. If Norman had had the common courtesy to die more quickly I could have got there and back before it got dark but he had to be his usual stubborn self so I took him round to Piedmont Park. He always enjoyed it there - just like he enjoyed his sandwich grill - so I thought it was fitting to lay him to rest by the lake. Also, I wanted to get home to watch my favourite show on television so I couldn't go too far from home.

That's my statement Detective. I hope I've covered everything, apart from nearly run-ning down two young men in the park on the way home. My night vision is terrible and I didn't see them until I was nearly on top of them. Please apologise to them for me if they ever come forward. I'm so glad I didn't kill them or your two officers this morning or I'd be a serial killer. How many people do you need to kill to be classified as a serial killer Detective?"

When Mary had finished her statement, she was shown to a holding cell and Schroedinger went to retrieve and view the video they'd taken of her confession. He couldn't help but feel sorry for her. She'd had a great life and a happy marriage until her husband had got Alzheimer's and started to decline. He'd then died and she'd allowed his brother to move in as some kind of replacement husband. Being subjected to unwanted attention in her own home wouldn't have been pleasant and she'd finally snapped and killed him.

Schroedinger could suddenly see the appeal of a loving partner to share his life with - especially his final years. Mary was such a sweet woman and was clearly lonely after her husband died which made Schroedinger wonder if he could really live on his own for the rest of his life. Maybe Wendy wasn't such a bad choice after all. His taciturn personality probably annoyed her just as much as her vacuous personality annoyed him.

He heard the door to the holding cells open and watched as Mary Normanson was escorted through. He could see certain judges on the circuit treating her with clemency and potentially letting her off, although she seemed to want to be sent away so she could enjoy the company of others - even if they were mostly hardened criminals. Maybe the best thing the courts could do would be to put her in a secure nursing home - preferably one with no horny octogenarians in it.

Chapter 34

Atlanta, USA

Tom and Karen had finished their day's testing and the job was now complete. Everything was now done and the Classic Country Clothing (UK) Inc. smartphone app no longer collected details of people's browsing habits. The data it did collect was reasonable and could be used to tailor offers to its customers more accurately and was stored securely so no third parties could access it.

Tom had received an email from Katrina confirming that Racist Roy and his equally unpleasant bunch of associates were in custody and he now had a week off in Atlanta. Life suddenly appeared perfect and while he wasn't sure what he'd be doing each day, Karen had offered to show him around the city and the surrounding areas. As he closed his laptop for the last time in Atlanta, he couldn't help but feel pleased with his week's work.

Not only had he been specially selected to fly to Atlanta to lead a team of people to fix a serious problem, he'd done it without doing a great deal of work himself, made some great new friends and been a crucial witness to a grisly murder that - while it may not have shocked the city of Atlanta to its very core - had at least been featured on the nightly news, just after a story about a man with a dancing pet raccoon.

"Hey Tom," said Karen as she approached his desk. "Instead of you getting a taxi back to the hotel, why don't you come back with me and we'll go down later with Wendy?"

"That sounds good. I'm not sure where all the others are at the moment so I'll message them."

"There's a new restaurant and bar opened close to the Skyview so we could try that. They specialise in fried chicken and it's meant to be awesome."

"I'm in. I'll let the others know."

"Okay, come on. Let's get out of here," said Karen as they walked towards the door.

Tom got in Karen's car and started to message Martin and the others to let them know the plan for the evening. He was immediately startled by the speed at which she sped out of the car park towards the main road and decided the messages could wait until she'd slowed down, although when that would be wasn't yet clear. Karen turned onto the I-75 and it seemed as if she was trying to push her accelerator pedal through the floor of her car.

"Are you trying to kill me?" Tom asked, half-jokingly, but with a small amount of terror.

"I'm just driving us home," laughed Karen.

"It does look a bit like you're trying to kill me though."

"Could you prove that in a court of law?"

"No."

"Well, there you are then."

"I was hoping for more of a denial than that. I don't feel very reassured."

"Friday nights can be busy up here so we've got to get ahead of the traffic."

"You just want to get me back to your house. don't you?" said Tom with a cheeky grin.

"Oh, I bet you wish that were true," laughed Karen as she squeezed her car between two large trucks.

Tom held onto his laptop and closed his eyes as she weaved through the traffic. Over-taking cars on both sides had always seemed a good idea to him but seeing it in practice was like being in a giant slalom race with other vehicles that were ten times bigger than the one he was in. As Karen moved expertly (or luckily) through the traffic, Tom wasn't quite as keen on the idea now and was relieved when they finally reached their exit and found themselves on quieter roads. Karen's speed didn't reduce significantly on the smaller roads but at least there weren't as many other vehicles to crash into.

A few minutes later they turned into a quiet suburban road and Karen pulled the car to the side of the road and stopped. They both got out and headed towards her front door when a familiar figure opened it for them.

"Hi sis! Have you brought your boyfriend back?!"

"Oh man, see the shit I have to put up with?" Karen said to Tom as they both greeted Wendy.

"The others have all been doing different things today so Karen suggested I come up here and then we all go downtown together later."

"That'll be great! I've had a call from Pete. He wants to meet us later on because he's solved the case of the body in the park. He's so clever!"

269

"That's not clever, dumbass. That's just doing his damned job," said Karen. "Maybe you should try getting a job - now that would be clever."

"I'm thinking of auditioning for one of those reality TV shows, you know the ones where they put a bunch of different people together and see how well they get on. They are making a new one here called 'Zombie Farm' and they need 12 people to live on a farm that's threatened by zombies. Each week one of them gets voted off the show and the winner gets a million dollars."

"Do the losers get thrown to the zombies?" Tom asked.

"They haven't said. I'm not sure I'd like that - especially if they use real zombies. It would be okay if they were actors though."

"You'll have to excuse Wendy; there's a tree growing in the backyard that's got more sense than her."

"I love trees!" said Wendy. "Apart from the green parts, obviously."

"When we were kids, she climbed up the stupid tree, fell out of it, banged her head on every branch on the way down and then climbed back up it just so she could fall out of it again. Just agree with her and your life will be a whole lot simpler."

"Don't be mean, sis. I helped solve a murder."

"How exactly did you help?"

"I told Pete to keep going when he was about to give up. I was the fire beneath his wings."

"I bet he appreciated you burning his wings," laughed Karen. "Now get your ass ready and both of you start messaging people to meet at Skyview at seven o'clock while I have a shower."

***

Martin stood alone with his camera in Centennial Park taking pictures of the fountains, the Ferris wheel and the College Football Hall of Fame that he'd visited earlier. He'd explored the American obsession with college football and read up on the rivalries between different schools but was still not entirely sure he understood why three times as many people would watch a college game than watched his favourite professional Premier League football team. Even the professional NFL games didn't draw the same crowds as some of the amateur college ones.

As he continued his early evening walk around downtown Atlanta, he received a message from Tom suggesting they met at the Ferris wheel at 7pm. He messaged back to tell him he'd be there but he'd just met Stuart and Bhavna who were going into the aquarium and wouldn't make it. He knew Tom would be happy and now they were assuming the other two were getting together late at night, he saw them both in a whole new light.

Martin continued taking pictures for a while and then went over to the Ferris wheel to wait for the others. He bought himself a bottle of water from the kiosk and then sat at one of the tables, thinking about all that had happened this week. He'd enjoyed his time in Atlanta but would be happy to get back to Irma and the boys. He was a family man at heart and while there were a few disadvantages, he was more than content with his life.

"Hey Martin!" said Dave as he and Sadie approached where he was sitting.

"Hi guys. How are you doing?"

"We're good thanks," Sadie replied for both of them. "This is your last night then?"

"Yeah, three of us are going home tomorrow. Tom's staying for a week though."

"I wonder why," said Sadie, grinning and squeezing Dave's arm.

"He probably wants to bone Karen," said Dave.

"Well duh!" said Sadie. "I think we all know that."

"So why..." Dave began but was interrupted by the arrival of Tom, Karen and Wendy.

"Hi y'all," said Karen. "I'm glad you could all make it. There's this great new place around the corner that supposedly does the best fried chicken in Atlanta. Shall we get going?"

The group made their way to the restaurant and were shown to a table in the corner and handed menus, while the waiter proudly pointed out their vegan selection.

"That's very kind of you," said Wendy. "I'm a vegan but my girls love chicken," said Wendy.

"Well miss, we'd be happy to serve them if they came in."

"You wouldn't want to serve these 'girls' because they're her damned cats - and one of them is a boy," Karen told the waiter.

"Can I get you some drinks?" the waiter asked Tom and Martin, who seemed to be a bit more sensible than the others.

"Just a round of beers please," said Tom.

"Coming right up sir," said the waiter, thinking he'd focus on this customer all night if he wanted to get any sense at all from this table.

"Pete said he'll be coming in later to tell us about the case. He's solved it and they have a sweet little old lady in custody," Wendy told them all as soon as the waiter had left.

"That can't be right?!" said Dave. "How did she kill a tall man and drag him to the park?"

"Apparently she was a wrestling champion," said Wendy. "Pete says she murdered him with a sandwich grill and drove his body to the park because it was too far to drive him somewhere remote."

"If she hadn't chosen the park, we wouldn't have found the body and I wouldn't have seen Pete again," said Wendy with a broad smile. "So everybody wins!"

"Apart from the man with the tiny bashed-in head," said Dave.

"Yes, I guess so," said Wendy. "But he was dead anyway so he probably doesn't mind that his murder brought Pete and I back together."

"Well why don't you ask him when you die - assuming you both end up in the same place?"

The waiter returned to the table with their drinks and began to wonder what was wrong with these people. He had just taken a second job at a bar near Piedmont Park because a waitress had suddenly quit over some weird customers. Surely not? He placed their beers on the table and returned to the bar as quickly as he could, passing a stern-looking man who appeared to be heading towards that table. Perhaps he was a mafia hitman who'd take them all out.

"Pete!" said an excited voice from behind him as he picked up the next round of drinks to take to an adjacent table. It didn't sound like the stern-looking man was a mafia hitman if they were on first name terms with him. That was a pity.

"Good evening everyone," said Detective Schroedinger as he pulled up a spare chair and joined their table.

"Good evening Detective," said Karen. "Are you here to update us on the case? I hear you've solved it and Wendy is very impressed."

"Thank you, Wendy," Schroedinger said with a slight smile.

"You're the best Pete!"

"Let me begin by saying thank you to you all for discovering the body. I'm sure it would have been found eventually but time is always of the essence in these cases. Luckily the perpetrator wasn't a flight risk and lived close to the park but, in many cases, they can be out of the country before we even know a crime has been committed."

"I told you we helped them solve it Karen," said Wendy, looking at her sister indignantly.

"It appears that the victim was called Norman Henry Normanson but we haven't yet been able to confirm this. Unfortunately, I can't share too many more details with you because the case has to go to trial, but the accused is a woman in her 70s who was being sexually harassed by Mr. Normanson who was her late husband's twin brother."

"Wow! You wouldn't have thought he still had it in him at his age," said Tom.

"Apparently he came here for the funeral of her husband and persuaded her to let him move in with her. There's no record of him in the system because he'd been living in Brazil since he was a young boy. We're still working to corroborate the details of the confession we received from our suspect."

"Don't you have a birth certificate or any childhood pictures?" Dave asked.

"Unfortunately not. It looks like he was born during World War Two and records were pretty sketchy back then."

"There are a lot of pictures of me in the system," said Dave.

"I'm sure there are," said Schroedinger with a sigh.

"I even saw one of those e-fit pictures they made of me once. I don't always get arrested when I get drunk; sometimes I get away so the bartenders have to give a description of me to the police sketch artist."

"What was the picture like?" asked Sadie. "Did it capture your awesome rugged jawline and your manly good looks?"

"Not really. They took a composite from different bartenders and I looked like an escapee from the CDC research and testing lab."

Schroedinger stood up and said goodnight to them all, telling Wendy he'd pick her up tomorrow morning at ten o'clock for their weekend away and told her they'd be going to Nashville. She got up and gave him a hug - partly out of excitement and partly to embarrass him - and then watched him leave the restaurant shaking his head.

"Pete's going on a communication skills course next week," Wendy said as she sat back down at the table. "I think it will be really good for him - and also for me. But mainly for me."

"Does he still talk in grunts and words of one syllable?" asked Karen.

"Yes, although I get around that by talking more so it works out."

"I've got to go on a course at work in a couple of weeks. It's called 'Respect your Colleagues' or something like that," said Tom.

"Is it just you or the whole company?" asked Karen. "I haven't heard about it."

"It's just me, a bunch of losers from the Sales department and some idiot from Accounting."

"I'm surprised they don't make you stay in there permanently," laughed Karen. "You don't like anyone there!"

"I told you not to tell anyone," said Tom. "Anyway, I like Martin and Katrina is alright too."

"Well I'm sure you'll come out of it a better human being," said Karen.

"He won't," said Martin. "This is the third one he's been on since I started. He just comes out of them thinking everyone else in the company is more stupid than they were before he went in."

"That's true," said Tom, drowned out by the mocking laughter coming at him from the rest of the table.

***

On the northern edge of Centennial Park, Stuart and Bhavna were leaving the aquarium and were headed back towards the part of downtown where both the hotel and the restaurant where their colleagues and four random Americans were having their meal. The zoo, the Botanical Gardens and the aquarium had all been fun but their day hadn't ended yet.

"Should we go and call in on Tom and the others?" Stuart asked.

"I would prefer not to," said Bhavna. "He is just about acceptable in small doses but I think I may have overdosed this week."

"I know what you mean. I keep catching him looking at my beard; I think he might have a weird fetish for men with beards."

"You do not need to add the gender Stuart. Women do not have beards."

"My grandmother did."

"Well, that was in the olden days. Things are very different today and you should know this."

"Why are you so bossy, Bhavna?"

"I beg your pardon Stuart?!"

"You spend the whole time correcting people and telling them what to do. It's annoying and upsetting," Stuart explained, suddenly noticing a complete lack of people nearby that could call the police if Bhavna tried to kill him.

"You were quite happy to do what I told you last night."

"That's outside work...people take on different personalities."

"Are you saying that you enjoy 'Mistress B' but you don't enjoy bossy Bhavna?"

"Yes," said Stuart as they reached their hotel.

"Well, in that case Stuart, Mistress B will not be visiting you tonight."

"Okay," said Stuart and went off towards the bar.

"Unless you text her a grovelling apology," said Bhavna as she headed to her room.

Stuart sat at the bar and focused on the TV while the barman brought him a beer. It had been a risk talking to Bhavna like that but he'd got away with it and - as he took his first sip from the bottle in front of him - he texted her an apology and wondered what sort of an evening he would be enjoying with her this time.

Tom and Martin's selfishness in wanting to spend time with Karen and her friends had worked to his advantage and what had started out as an annoying colleague on the flight over here had suddenly turned into a weird relationship. As they were recovering from their food poisoning, they had bonded and had shared some unusual evenings together. He wasn't sure what would happen when they got back home but for now, things were very interesting.

A message on his phone came through with just one word - 'Now!' - so he hastily finished his beer and went upstairs. Somewhere, under several acres of beard hair, was a smile as wide as the Chattahoochee River.

Chapter 35

Atlanta, USA

All across the city of Atlanta and the state of Georgia people were waking up to a hot and humid Saturday morning. In a small house with three bedrooms, two sisters and four cats, coffee was brewing against a background of the younger sister hurriedly packing her bags for a weekend away.

"Pete will be here soon! It's your fault I'm not ready!"

"How in the name of Jack Shit is it my fault, Wendy?"

"You shouldn't have let me drink so much last night," said Wendy. "I can't remember much of what happened."

"Do you remember dancing on the table?" Karen asked.

"Yes, I remember that."

"And do you remember falling off of the table?"

"No, but I do have a bruise on my arm. Maybe that's where it came from?"

"Well, you landed partly on your head. I was hoping it might have knocked some sense into you but it looks like you're still a dumbass," said Karen, pouring them both some coffee.

"My head hurts too. I thought that was just the alcohol."

"Well, drink this and maybe you'll feel better."

"Thanks sis!" said Wendy, taking the black coffee and hoping it would help sober her up before Schroedinger arrived.

As she sat and sipped the hot black liquid, Wendy's phone buzzed with three messages and she looked down, expecting them to be from Schroedinger. It wasn't, so she read them aloud to Karen:

"Hi Wendy! Dave and I got arrested last night on the way back from the bar. It was our first arrest together and it was so romantic! We walked home and I saw some of my old friends sitting in the parking lot of a strip club so I went to say 'hi' and offered to bring them some comfort behind a dumpster. Just as soon as I'd got started, the police arrived and we all got arrested! 1/3"

"Dave was very gentlemanly and tried to attack the officers but he was so drunk he managed to punch the dumpster instead of the cops! It was a hoot! We got put in the same patrol car and he got taken to the hospital to look at his hand - he's broken a small bone but he'll be okay. 2/3"

"We've just been let out and are going for some coffee. That was the only downside to the whole night - the coffee in this station isn't very nice. Have a great weekend away with the Detective! I did mention his name while Dave was fighting with the officers but it didn't really help. Love you all! 3/3"

"The only downside was bad coffee?!" Karen asked when Wendy had finished reading Sadie's messages.

"She always says that some police stations have better coffee than others. It's a shame they got taken to one of the bad ones."

"How about they don't try to smash shit up and then they won't get arrested and can drink coffee at home like normal people?"

"You're so boring, sis! Let them have their fun," said Wendy.

"Says the woman just about to go away with the most boring man in Georgia."

"He's very talkative when he's working. It's just when he's off duty he's a bit quiet. Maybe we'll solve another murder together while we're away - that would liven him up a bit."

"When will you two lovebirds be back?" Karen asked.

"Monday night, I think. Pete needs to be back at work on Tuesday to finish his report on the case of the old lady and that man with the small head."

"Do I get three days of peace and quiet? Hallelujah!" said Karen, looking up at the ceiling.

"Yes you do - I know it will be quiet but you'll have the girls here to keep you company."

"Ain't that just peachy," Karen sighed as the doorbell rang and Wendy ran to answer it.

"Hi Pete!" she shouted before she'd even opened the door.

"Good morning."

"Good morning, Detective. Can I offer you some coffee?"

"Thanks, but we need to be going as soon as possible. It's a four-hour drive."

"Can't we take a patrol car and put your lights on all the way?!" Wendy asked, ramming the last few things into her bag.

"No," said Schroedinger.

"When are you going on that communication course, Detective?"

"On Wednesday," said Schroedinger.

"Pete is great at work but he struggles a bit in real life, don't you Pete?"

"Sometimes," said Schroedinger. "Are you ready?"

"I sure am!" said Wendy, going over to give Karen a hug. "You'll look after the girls for me won't you sis?"

"We will," said Karen.

"Thanks," said Wendy and then paused. "What do you mean 'we'?"

"Stop asking so many stupid questions and go!" said Karen. "If you accidentally leave her in Nashville I promise I won't file a missing person's report. We'll just immediately consider it a cold case," she added with her booming laugh.

"I'll bring Wendy home safely, Karen. Have a good weekend."

"Bye sis!" said Wendy, giving Karen another hug. "Bye girls!"

Karen closed the front door on the chaos that was Wendy. Hopefully they'd keep driving and just elope and get married so some sanity would be restored to Karen's world again - although she wouldn't wish that on Detective Schroedinger. He was doing her a huge favour just taking Wendy off her hands for the weekend and for that he would always be her favourite police officer.

Looking around her house now that Wendy was gone, it did seem suddenly quiet. The cats needed to be fed so she planned to do that first and then tidy the house before getting ready to go out. This week had been interesting - it had probably been the most interesting week of her entire life - but it had also been fun. The nights out with the UK team had been great, although if she'd designed this week for herself, she probably wouldn't have included finding a dead body in a park.

As Karen fed Wendy's cats, she thought that Norman Henry Normanson may have planned the week differently too.

***

In downtown Atlanta, Tom had woken up, showered and got ready for the first day of his free week in Atlanta. He went along the hotel corridor and knocked on Martin's door. After a few seconds, Martin opened the door and they went down to the next floor to find Stuart and Bhavna. They knocked on Stuart's door but there was no reply so they checked on Bhavna but again, no reply.

"Surely they haven't got food poisoning again?" said Tom. "I mean, you could understand it once, but it would be a bit careless of them to get it twice."

"I'm not sure they'd have any choice, to be fair."

"Maybe."

"It won't be a good flight if they have got it," said Martin. "I hope I'm not sitting next to them."

"That's very public-spirited of you."

"I'm just saying."

"Let's go down for breakfast and catch up with them later," said Tom turning away from Bhavna's door, unaware of Stuart standing on the other side of it waiting for them to leave so he could go back to his room undetected.

"What are you going to do while you're here?" Martin asked as they reached the stairs and a half-naked Stuart quietly sneaked from Bhavna's room across the corridor to his own room.

"I don't know yet. I'll probably just hang out with the others. Karen was talking about going to Stone Mountain one day for hiking. They've got a cable car ride there too."

"But you don't like heights."

"I'll close my eyes."

"But you don't like the dark either."

"I might have to give it a miss then."

Tom and Martin went into the restaurant and were greeted by a young goth waitress who asked them if they were ordering from the menu or going to the buffet. To Becci's relief, they both selected the buffet so she showed them to a table and left them to it. As she walked away, she noticed that they seemed to be talking about normal things; maybe they just turned weird in the evenings.

"Are you looking forward to getting back with Irma and the boys?" Tom asked Martin when they returned to their table with their food.

"Yes and no. It's been great over here with no responsibilities each evening but I'm not sure I could do it long-term. I like being married and being a family man."

"I can understand that," said Tom. "It's all very well being single and independent but sometimes it must be nice to come home to a loving family."

"I wouldn't go that far but it is nice to be part of something."

"I think I'd like half a wife," said Tom, as Becci came to refill their coffee.

"Which half? The top half would be good because you'd have someone to talk to."

"I'd get the boobs as well," Tom added as Becci stared at him and overfilled his coffee cup.

"Well, obviously."

"I meant having a part-time wife. Maybe one week on and one week off."

"I think that's called having your cake and eating it," said Becci, unable to resist the urge to put these fools straight.

"You're right," Tom agreed. "But if you brought me some cake now, I'd eat it."

"Do you want some cake?" Becci asked.

"Not really. But if I had it, I'd eat it," said Tom. "There's no point in having cake and not eating it."

"I'd like some cake if you have any," said Martin.

"But don't eat it when it arrives," said Tom, earning a death stare from Becci.

"When are you leaving?" Becci asked them both.

"I'm going today but he'll be here for another week, won't you?" said Martin, then looking at Tom.

"Er….yeah," said Tom looking down at his overflowing coffee cup.

"Lucky me," said Becci as she walked away in despair, just as Stuart and Bhavna joined them.

"Morning guys," said Tom. "We're almost finished here."

"No worries, we'll see you when we check out," said Stuart as he and Bhavna went and sat at a clean table.

"I'm sure there's something going on between those two," said Martin as he and Tom got up from their table and left the restaurant.

"There definitely is. Didn't you see Stuart sneak out of Bhavna's room this morning as we turned to go down the stairs?"

"No?!"

"Yes. He must have crept out just after we knocked on her door because I saw him carrying his clothes across the hallway out of the corner of my eye."

"Are you sure it was Stuart?"

"You can't really miss his beard."

"True."

***

The clock on the wall behind the hotel reception desk struck eleven as Stuart and Martin were checking out. The lift doors opened behind them and Bhavna came out with her case and walked over to join them.

"Have you ordered the taxi like I told you too Stuart?" she said as she gave her key to the young man behind the desk.

"Yes," said Stuart. "It'll be here in ten minutes."

"Thank you. Life is much more fun when people do what you ask."

"I'm beginning to realise that," said Stuart with a grin.

"Hello mate," said Martin, as the doors of the other lift opened and he saw Tom come out of it and approach the reception desk. "Why have you got your case with you?"

"Are you checking out?" asked Stuart.

"Yes I am," said Tom.

"I thought you weren't coming back with us today?" said Bhavna, confused for once.

"Hi y'all! It's a hot day out there! I hope you have a good flight!" said Karen, walking through the lobby and standing next to Tom. "You'd better not be as annoying as my dumbass sister or you can stay your ass here," she said as her laugh erupted across the lobby.

"Are you...?"

"Yes he is. He's offered to keep me company while Wendy is away with Detective Schroedinger."

"I'm a gentleman like that," said Tom with a smile.

"I hope you're good with cats...Wendy left four of them for me to look after," laughed Karen.

"I'll try my best," said Tom, knowing that he wouldn't actually try at all.

"I'm sure we all know what your best looks like and it ain't that good," said Karen, laughing again as the taxi pulled up and others began to gather their bags.

"Have a safe flight," Tom said to them all as they said their goodbyes. "I'll see you all next Monday."

"That's if I haven't killed you first," said Karen, squeezing Tom's hand as they stood and watched Martin, Stuart and Bhavna leave the hotel and begin their journey back to the UK.

Chapter 36

Atlanta, USA

As Tom and Karen left the hotel and the taxi took the rest of the UK team to the airport, Wendy and Schroedinger had reached the halfway point in their own journey and were passing through Chattanooga. Across Atlanta, Sadie and Dave had found an independent coffee shop opposite the police station they'd just been released from which served the quality of coffee their refined palates desired and Mary Normanson was looking forward to spending the rest of her life in prison.

She was hoping to make some new friends there and maybe join a gang. That would be exciting! She started to imagine fashioning shivs out of bars of soap, trading narcotics with the others and digging an escape tunnel with her bare hands. Life was certainly looking up for her at the moment.

The loss of her dear Walter - first to Alzheimer's and then to death - had shown her how lonely life could be on her own and Norman hadn't proved to be much of a replacement for his brother, despite looking the part. He was far too physically-minded and at her age she didn't appreciate being constantly mauled. She'd enjoyed it when she was younger, of course, and had quite the reputation amongst the boys in Atlanta - as well as in most of the surrounding towns - but not now. She was glad she had got to meet Walter's brother but was equally glad she'd killed him.

That nice Detective, however, that would have been a different matter. It was such a pity that he hadn't been the one to put the handcuffs on her - she certainly would have enjoyed that she thought as she lay on the bed in the cell at the police station.

Mary closed her eyes and reminisced about her life in Georgia. She saw Walter's smiling face in her mind - or was it Norman's? It must have been Walter's because Norman had only smiled when he'd walked into her room naked. She thought about all the things she'd done down by the banks of the Chattahoochee River as a young woman and then she looked back at meeting Walter for the first time. She remembered how they had begun courting, his proposal and their subsequent wedding that had upset most of the young men in Atlanta.

Mary's thoughts moved forward to them having three wonderful children together and the things they had done as a family before reminiscing on her two wrestling careers and all of the trophies she'd won.

Mary thought she'd lived a good life on balance. There was one small blemish with a neighbour when Walter was at work one day in 1969 and she hadn't paid a speeding ticket that she'd got in 1978 but aside from that she'd been a good person - as long as you didn't count the murder.

She felt so tired - it must have been all of the excitement this week - so she let herself drift slowly off to sleep and felt content and blessed as her eyes closed. In her mind, she was back down on the banks of the Chattahoochee River; the sun was shining and the birds were singing on a beautiful spring morning. Her beloved Walter was walking towards her and was reaching out to take her hands. Mary had missed Walter terribly since he'd developed Alzheimer's but here he was once more - smiling, happy and with all of his faculties fully restored. She walked towards him, they embraced tenderly and Mary left the physical world behind her.

Chapter 37

Atlanta, USA

Karen was driving Tom out of the city and was telling him of all the things they'd be doing in the coming days. While she loved her sister dearly, she couldn't face spending all day and all evening with her once Schroedinger brought her back from Nashville so she was planning to go hiking, visit the various attractions in the city that locals rarely go to. This would limit the time they would have in the house listening to Wendy's latest fads and phobias and would also let her appreciate her city from a different perspective.

"We'll go to Stone Mountain tomorrow - it's far too hot today - then I'll take you to the Atlanta Botanical Gardens, the Atlanta History Center, the Martin Luther King Center and the zoo if you like that type of thing?"

"It all sounds cool," said Tom. "I'm just happy to be able to stay here while the others go back."

"A couple of them are weird, aren't they?"

"Stuart and Bhavna?"

"Yeah,"

"There's something going on between those two. As we came down this morning, I saw Stuart sneak out of Bhavna's room with half of his clothes in his hand."

"Oh man! That's awesome. They seemed so much up their own butts I didn't think they'd have time for anything else."

"Well they had time for each other last night."

"Good for them. That woman really needed to get laid," Karen laughed as she left the I-85 that went through the city and joined the I-75 headed north.

"Your driving hasn't improved much since yesterday," said Tom.

"Are you sure you don't want to walk?"

"I could get a taxi."

"Good luck with that. Did you know I once tried out for a rideshare company?"

"Which one?" Tom asked.

"Both of the major ones and an unlicensed one that was run by an ex-con from his garage."

"What happened?"

"I got rejected for being 'overly aggressive' behind the wheel," Karen laughed. "Can you imagine that?! And think very carefully before you answer."

"Well, in that case....I'm shocked," said Tom diplomatically.

"You ain't shocked at all!" Karen laughed. "I wasn't expecting to get the major ones but I thought that a creepy guy running a shady business and not paying any taxes wouldn't have had such high standards."

"Us creepy guys can have high standards too."

"Well, don't be expecting too much this week," said Karen as she turned into her street and pulled up outside her house.

"I'm sure spending the week with you will be awesome."

"You might wish you were back at that shitty hotel by Monday," Karen said as they got out of the car. "Do you want some coffee?"

"Yes please," said Tom as he took his case out of the car and followed Karen to her front door.

"The mailman's been," Karen said, taking a large envelope from her mailbox. "I sent off some DNA to get myself tested and find out what my roots are."

"I love these mailboxes you have at the end of your path. We can't have those in the UK."

"Why not?"

"People would steal each other's mail."

"We don't have that problem here. I'd be more worried about drunk drivers."

"Why is that?" asked Tom, struggling to see the connection.

"If you forget to get your mail until the evening there's a chance a drunk driver might come down the street and run you down. It happened to Dave. He was telling Wendy about it last night."

"That's awesome!" said Tom. "Dave's a legend."

"He's pretty cool for a redneck," Karen admitted. "Only Dave could get hit by a car checking the mail."

"I wonder if I could be part redneck? I might do one of those DNA tests when I get home."

"Don't waste your money," said Karen. "It'll just tell you that you're a dick and we already know that."

"That's not fair," said Tom, watching Karen walk away from him and go into the kitchen.

"It doesn't matter if it's fair or not - it's true," she shouted from the kitchen.

"You might be right there."

Tom sat down on the sofa and looked around the room while he waited for Karen to return with the coffee she'd promised. Yesterday's visit hadn't allowed him much time to check the place out but it was definitely Karen's house - chaotic, busy and loud. The decor was vibrant and colourful like its owner and he was glad to be out of the hotel. He'd complained so much about the hotel on Friday afternoon while he and Karen were doing their final system testing in the office that she'd given in and offered to let him stay with her this week. She'd also told him she knew that was exactly what he wanted her to do.

Karen returned with the coffee and sat down next to Tom, picked up the envelope with her DNA test results in and opened it.

"What does it say?" asked Tom.

"It's got this pie chart here, look," said Karen, showing Tom the contents of the pack.

"It says I'm 40% African, 38% Native American, 12% French, 6% Italian and 4% Chinese. How the fuck am I part Chinese?!"

"Do you like Chinese food?" Tom asked, rather unhelpfully.

"Hell yeah, but it shouldn't affect my DNA."

"I wouldn't have thought so, otherwise your DNA would change every time you ate chow mein."

"Maybe if I ate more pizza I'd become more Italian?"

"It would be interesting to find out," Tom agreed, laughing along with Karen.

"I never knew I had all these different nationalities inside me."

"Have you got any English in you?"

Karen paused and looked at Tom.

"Really?" she said and then let her laugh fill the room. "Is that the best you've got?"

"Yes," said Tom meekly, looking at Karen's changing expression.

"You're gonna regret that; get your ass upstairs!"

Tom ran up the stairs and the events of the last few days flashed through his mind. It had been a good week so far and looked as if it was about to get even better and as Karen pushed him onto her bed he couldn't help thinking that - on balance - the month of April had been far kinder to him than it had been to Norman Henry Normanson.

Epilogue - Two Months Later

Brighton, UK

It was a warm, bright and sunny Monday morning and Tom had been back in his familiar routine for several weeks. The week he'd spent in Atlanta with Karen had been every bit as good as he'd hoped and they'd had a great time together. He'd got the promotion that Katrina had hinted at and even HR seemed pleased to see him - although they hadn't called him up quite as often as they previously had.

Tom parked his car on the driveway he'd always rented and began his walk down the hill towards the clock tower in the centre of Brighton. He then turned left into North Street and ultimately took a right turn into Ship Street. As he walked past the old post office and headed towards the head office of Classic Country Clothing Ltd., he turned to the person walking alongside him and couldn't help but smile.

"Are you nervous?"

"Hell no! Why would I be nervous?" his companion asked as they walked through the main door.

"It's your first day at HQ."

"If you think I'm worried about some hoity-toity Brits looking down on me for drinking my tea the wrong way then you're a bigger dumbass than my sister. Hell, you'd be a bigger dumbass than her four cats too," Karen laughed as they approached the reception desk to sign her in.

"Hi Bert," said Tom as they approached the desk. This is Karen from our Atlanta office. She's over here for a couple of weeks of IT training."

"Hello Mister Tom, sir," said Bert. "Very good, sir. Would you mind signing in please, Miss?"

"No problem," said Karen. "Good morning to you Bert. Y'all have a great day now."

"Thank you, Miss," said Bert. "Although there's only one of me here."

"Don't worry Bert, it's an American South thing," Tom clarified.

"Okay Mister Tom," Bert said and then turned to Karen. "Well, Miss, I'll be fixing to get you an ID badge today from that office over yonder and if the creek doesn't rise, you'll have that doohickey by lunchtime and be happier than a dead pig in the sunshine."

"Woah Bert! You're my man!" said Karen offering him a high five. Unfortunately, Bert wasn't quite ready so Karen accidentally slapped him in the face.

"Are you okay Bert?" said Tom, trying not to laugh too much.

"Yes thank you, Mister Tom."

"Where did you learn all those phrases Bert?" Karen asked.

"My wife LeeAnn is from Louisiana. We met at Live Aid in 1985 and it was love at first sight," said Bert proudly. "We got married the very next month and she's been with me ever since. I'm retiring in a few months and she wants to move back home."

"Are you looking forward to that?" Tom asked.

"Not really. I'd rather stay here where we have friends and family but she wants to move back home to Baton Rouge."

"What will you do?" asked Karen.

"We've decided to compromise," said Bert with a smile.

"That sounds very sensible," said Tom.

"She thought so too," Bert agreed. "So we're moving to Baton Rouge."

***

Katrina and some of the other members of Tom's old team had settled into their desks as Tom and Karen walked into the office. After his promotion, Tom was now at Katrina's level and had his own team who sat behind her, although they only trusted him with one person at the moment. Hopefully he would soon have an empire of underlings to do his bidding and he could take over the world - or at least take some more time off while they did all his work.

"Hey y'all! I'm Karen. It's great to meet you."

"It's lovely to meet you too!" said Katrina, extending her hand. "This is Sue and that's Colin."

"It's great to meet you guys!" said Karen.

"Hi Karen! It's good to see you again," said Martin, turning round from his new desk on Tom's team. "How are the others?"

"Well, my dumbass sister Wendy is thinking of moving in with Schroedinger this week so hopefully she'll be taking her damned cats with her and I'll get my house back soon."

"What about Sadie and Dave?"

"They're still living together in Dave's parents' basement. Neither of them got arrested last week so I think they're balancing each other out. Either that or they're planning a heist."

"Dave was cool," said Tom.

"Yeah, well he had an accident at his new job a couple of weeks back so now he's in the middle of a personal injury lawsuit. He should find out if he's won sometime this week."

"What happened?"

"He got a job at Atlanta Zoo and some of the animals attacked him," said Karen.

"But he had a phobia of animals didn't he?" Tom asked.

"He sure did, so they gave him a job in the gift shop."

"That seems safe enough," Martin said. "How did he injure himself?"

"The maintenance men were fixing some fences outside and a few of the flamingos got out and made their way towards the gift shop. Dave saw them come through the door, panicked and fell into a display of cuddly giraffes. He's suing them for mental trauma."

"The cuddly giraffes?"

"The zoo."

"Will he win?"

"I don't know," said Karen. "But if he does, y'all might want to prepare yourselves for him and Sadie to come over here because he really wants to see England."

"What exactly do they want you to do over here?" asked Sue, bringing the subject back to work.

"Well after the problems we had with the database back in April, the company said it would be more cost-effective to transfer the knowledge you've got here to me so y'all don't have to come over and help us wipe our own butts if it ever happens again."

"That sounds like we won't get to go to Atlanta again," said Martin.

"You told us you didn't like the hotel anyway," said Sue.

"No, it wasn't very nice," said Martin.

"And you broke your camera when that old lady nearly hit you with her car," said Colin.

"Well, yeah, that wasn't very good either."

"And you didn't want to be away from Irma and the boys," Tom added.

"I suppose not," Martin said with a sigh before turning to Karen. "Have they given you a better hotel here than the one they gave us in Atlanta?"

"It depends what you mean by the word 'hotel'" said Karen, glancing at Tom.

"Where did they put you?" Katrina asked.

"Well..."

"You're staying with Tom aren't you?" said Martin.

"It was the gentlemanly thing to do," said Tom modestly. "I've got plenty of room."

"You live in a one-bedroomed house."

"I know," said Tom.

"Well I think it's very generous of Tom to give up his bed for Karen," said Colin. "I've slept on the sofa a few times and it's not very comfortable," he added as the rest of the team looked at him and burst into laughter.

"Shall we go and make some coffee?" said Tom.

"Please," said Karen.

As the two of them walked towards the kitchen, out of the corner of his eye Tom could see Sue, Colin and Katrina each passing some money over to Martin. Finally, something had gone right for the dopey bastard - although it had taken a lot of messages to convince Martin to select the right option on that particular sweepstake.

At the end of the day, Tom didn't care about the rest of them; everything he wanted was standing next to him in the kitchen trying to operate the coffee machine.

"Are you going to help me work this thing or do you just want to stand there and look at my butt all day?"

293

"Can't I do both?"

"Just make the damned coffee," said Karen.

"Yes ma'am!" said Tom with a grin as he said a silent thanks to Racist Roy and Johnny Pervert for making all of this happen.

Printed in Great Britain
by Amazon

58581039R00172